P9-DEL-126

Dear Reader,

I love New York City. The people are damn serious
about the way they live life. They work hard and
play hard and needless to say, it got me thinking.
Were the people of New York City just as hard-core
back in 1830 as they are now? You better believe
they were. And those poor bastards didn't have our
modern conveniences, either. Back in 1830, people
were trying to pave dirt streets with gold, even though
they had nothing but sweat. So what happens when
an American-Irish woman named Georgia with only
coal clutched in each hand meets a British aristocrat
who only ever had gold? You get a story known as
the Prince and the Pauperette. But why stop there?
After all, there is so much more to a story than poor
vs. rich. I wanted to get down and dirty and twisted,
digging into the real facets of life back in 1830, while
giving you a good laugh and a good cry. As a writer, I
get to play god (bwahahaha) and the idea of a person
starting over against their will has always fascinated
me. So I took away the hero's memory and made
him crawl back to the basics in life. Basics he forgot
to appreciate. Basics he never thought he'd be able to
return to. And he does it all while touching the life of
one very special woman who makes him realize true
love is not only real but priceless. I hope you enjoy
my historical version of the Prince and the Pauper.

Much love,

Delilah Marvelle

**Also available from Delilah Marvelle
and HQN Books**

The Scandal series

Prelude to a Scandal
Once Upon a Scandal
The Perfect Scandal

Coming Soon

Forever a Lady

DELILAH MARVELLE

Forever
and a Day

HQN™

Recycling programs
for this product may
not exist in your area.

ISBN-13: 978-0-373-77636-8

FOREVER AND A DAY

www.Harlequin.com

Printed in U.S.A.

Acknowledgments

Thank you to my former editor Tracy Martin. I'm going to miss you, Tracy, but hey, there are people out there who need you far more than I do. May all of your dreams come true.

Thank you to the entire Harlequin and HQN team. Marketing: Without you, no one would know about me. Scary. Art Department: Can I marry you for giving me such glorious covers? Keep it coming. Tara Parsons: Girl, you work *way* too many hours but boy am I ever glad you do. Thank you. Emily Ohanjanians (my new editor!): I'm looking forward to getting my butt kicked in. Bring it.

Thank you to Donald Maass, my agent and writing mentor, who brings clarity into my writing and my career every time.

Thank you to Jessa Slade, author extraordinaire, who not only gives me incredible feedback but calls me out on every demon that shouldn't be there. Thank you to Maire Creegan, who is about to rip up the historical romance genre Brontë style, and who also knows how to rip up my historical romance Brontë style. London, baby. London.

Thank you to the New York City Library for not giving me weird looks as I tirelessly researched and asked endless, stupid questions both in person and via email. You and all of your amazing resources and archives gave this New York City series depth. Thank you.

To my husband, Marc.
You gave up your dream for mine.
That is why this book is for you.
I love you, Fire Boy. Engine 28 is waiting.

Part 1

CHAPTER ONE

*To endeavor to forget anyone is a certain
way of thinking of nothing else.*
　　　　　—Jean de La Bruyère, *Les Caractères* (1688)

*6th of July, 1830, early afternoon
New York City*

GEORGIA EMILY MILTON rarely cared to notice any of the
well-to-do men strutting about Broadway as it was a
long-standing rule of hers to never yearn for anything
she couldn't have and/or didn't need. But as she bustled
down the crowded, respectable stretch of Broadway,
heading back toward the not-so-respectable trenches of
Little Water, an astonishingly tall, well-groomed gentleman strode toward her at a leisurely pace, making
her not only slow but inwardly wish she had been born
a lady.

Weaving past others to ensure a better view, she
caught staggered glimpses of an impressive, muscled
frame garbed in a gray morning coat, well-fitted trousers and an embroidered waistcoat with double-row
buttons. Gloved hands strategically angled his dove-
gray top hat forward and down to better shade his eyes

against the bright sun gleaming across the surrounding stretch of shop windows.

His hat alone had to be worth two months of her wages.

As he smoothly rounded several people and strode toward her side of the pavement, his smoldering gray eyes caught and held hers from beneath the rim of his hat. The pulsing intensity of that raw, heated gaze bashed the breath out of her.

Tightening his jaw, he aligned himself directly in her path, the expanse between them lessening with each frantic beat of her heart. That black-leather-booted stride slowed when he finally came upon her. He formally— albeit a bit too gravely—inclined his dark head toward her, publicly acknowledging *her* in a way *his* sort never did during the day.

He behaved as if he didn't see a rag in calico skirts, which had washed itself over from Orange Street, but an elegant young lady strolling alongside her mother with a lace parasol in hand. For making her feel so uncommonly attractive, Georgia considered blowing him a kiss. Fortunately, she knew how to keep herself out of trouble.

Glancing away, she set her chin as any respectable woman would, and sashayed past his towering frame, purposefully letting her own arm brush against his, only to stumble against the dragging skirts of a washerwoman who had rudely darted before her. Of all the—

His large hand jumped out and grabbed hold of her corseted waist, balancing her upright with a swift jerk. Georgia froze as her reticule swung against her wrist, hitting the sleeved coat of his solid forearm that held her in place.

Her heart slid off into oblivion upon realizing her bum now dug against a solid, male thigh. *His* solid, male thigh.

His head dipped toward her from behind, his muscles tensing as he pressed her backside more possessively against his front side. His arm tightened around her waist. "Are you all right, madam?"

His voice was husky and refined, laced with a regal British accent that made the Irish girl in her inwardly put up both fists.

"That I am, sir. Thank you." Trying to shake off the intimacy of that hold, Georgia tried to politely ease away.

He released her, his hand skimming from her waist toward the expanse of her back, making the skin beneath her clothing zing.

Her eyes widened as that same hand curved its way back up her side, intent on outlining the rest of her body.

Though she tried to peddle away, he tightened his hold on her upper arm and drew her back firmly toward himself. "Madam."

Sucking in a breath, she jerked away and shoved him back hard, causing him to stumble. "Don't you be gropin' me!"

"Your bonnet." He held up both of his hands in a quick truce and gestured toward it. "One of the ribbons came loose. That is all."

"Oh." Her cheeks bloomed with heat as she reached up and patted around the curve of her bonnet trying to find it. How utterly humiliating. "I'm ever so sorry, sir. I didn't mean to actually—"

"No worries. Allow me." Setting a large hand against the small of her back, he guided her with forceful nudges over to the shop window beyond, removing them from the pathway of hustling pedestrians.

Realizing that he intended to affix the ribbon himself, she glanced up wide-eyed. "There's really no need for you to—"

"Yes, there is. You will lose the ribbon otherwise. Now, please. Hold still." He angled her toward himself and leaned in close, lifting the discolored, frayed ribbon dangling off the side of her bonnet.

Georgia awkwardly lingered before him as he wove the length of the ribbon back into place. Although she wanted to dash away, knowing that her bonnet was an atrocity not worth touching, sometimes a girl needed to gaze up at the stars that so willingly sought to shine. Even if those stars were far beyond the reach of a penniless girl's imagination.

As his fingers skimmed her bonnet and tucked the ribbon, she resisted reaching up and grazing her hand adoringly against that smooth, shaven face. What, oh, what would it be like to belong to a man such as this?

Glimpsing a single black band fitted around the shifting gray coat of his bulking upper biceps, she glanced back up at him, her heart squeezing. He was in mourning.

"'Tis almost affixed," he offered conversationally, his eyes scanning her bonnet. He leaned in closer. "I'm using one of the other pins to keep it in place."

"Thank you," she murmured, lowering her gaze.

His coat smelled like mulled spice and cedar. It was divinely warm and inviting, even on a summer's day. The double row of buttons on his embroidered waistcoat shifted against the expanse of his broad chest as he finished maneuvering the last of her ribbon into place. She could tell by the reflective metal gleam of those buttons that they weren't painted brass made to emulate silver, but were, in fact, *real* silver. Only an elite group of men in New York could afford silver buttons. It was an elite group she knew she'd never be able to touch, not even with an outstretched toe.

"There we are." Meeting her gaze, he drew his gloved hands away and offered in a low baritone, "And how are you today, madam?"

Blinking up at him, she noted the way his eyes and his brow had softened, lending to a boyish vulnerability that didn't match his imposing height of more than six feet. She tried to quell the anxious tingle knotting her stomach. Despite the full bustle on Broadway, this glorious man sought to share in a bit of conversation with *her*. "I'm very well, sir. Thank you."

She refrained from asking how he was out of respect for the band around his arm, and instead offered a flirtatious smile, gesturing toward the pleated rim of her bonnet. "Rather impressive. Have you considered takin' up haberdashery?"

He slowly grinned, the edges of those handsome gray eyes and that firm full mouth crinkling, brightening his overly serious appearance. "No. I haven't."

Of course he hadn't. He had silver buttons. He probably owned every haberdashery in town. Or in the town from whence he came.

He shifted toward her, his large frame blocking whatever view she had of the street. "Are you from around these parts?"

She refrained from snorting. "You're overly kind, to be sure, but given that my bonnet can't even hold a ribbon, most certainly not. Only gold-feathered peacocks can afford these parts, sir. I'm merely passin' through."

"Gold-feathered peacocks?" He smirked and set his hands behind his back, broadening his impressive shoulders. "Is that what you like to call those of wealth?"

She scrunched her nose playfully. "Nah, not really. I'm bein' polite, seein' that you're one of them, and I've roughed you up well enough."

A gruff laugh escaped his lips. "Rest assured, I am quite used to it," he remarked, still intimately holding her gaze. "I've already endured more than my share of elbowing from the public given that I'm *British*. Too many Americans still remember the burning of Washington, but I swear to you I didn't do it."

Georgia burst into laughter, smitten with his marvelously wry humor. "Ah, now, can you readily blame them? You Brits are nothin' but gadflies cloaked in a fancy accent."

He paused and leaned in, heatedly searching her face without any further attempt to mask his unabashed interest. "Might I cease being polite for one brief moment and ask whether you would like to join me for coffee over at my hotel? It's been quite some time since I have allowed myself a moment of leisure. Honor me."

The wistful intensity lingering within that taut face was so galvanizing, it sent a tremor through her body. Though tempted to glimpse how the other half lived over the rim of a porcelain cup, she knew better than to involve herself with a man who wore silver buttons. It would never last beyond the toss of her skirts and a single night.

She eyed the people weaving past. "I don't mean to be rude, sir, given that you've been nothin' but kind, but I really ought to go. I've a long day ahead of me." She gestured toward the pavement as if that explained everything.

His hopeful expression melted to disappointment. "I understand and will detain you no more." He inclined his head, touching the tips of his gloved fingers to the satin rim of his hat. "I bid you a very good day, madam."

By all that was blue, his manners were as divine as the rest of him. "And a very good day to you, as well, sir. I appreciate the unexpected service you rendered my bonnet."

His mouth quirked. "It was an honor to be of service. Good day." Stepping back, he eased his large frame around a passing couple. Glancing back at her one last time, he smiled and disappeared into the surrounding wall of bodies.

Georgia eased out a wistful breath knowing she had just glimpsed life as it might have been had she been born a genteel lady of high society. Ah, money. If only it could also buy a woman true love and happiness, she would be the first to dash into the local bank and point a pistol at every clerk, demanding tens and twenties.

Swiveling toward the opposite direction, Georgia resumed her steady march home, which was still a good forty-minute walk. Why couldn't such refined gentlemen exist in her part of town? It wasn't in the least bit fair that her only selection of men smacked the bottoms of passing women and whistled through crooked, unchalked teeth. Not for long, though. She was only six dollars short of moving west and couldn't *wait* to climb into that stagecoach and leave her piss of a life behind.

A towering, broad frame suddenly appeared beside her and veered in, startling her. "Madam."

Her eyes widened. Upon her soul, it was her Brit. Slowing her step, she offered a quick, "Yes?"

He swung toward her, trotting backward in an effort to face her before jumping into her path and coming to an abrupt halt.

Georgia squeaked and skid to prevent herself from dashing herself against him.

He leaned toward her. "I can only apologize for being so uncommonly bold, but I must have your name."

She glanced up in astonishment. "And what do you intend to do with my name, sir?"

He lifted a dark brow. "Perhaps you and I can discuss that over coffee? Couldn't you make time for one small cup? Just one? My nickel."

What was he thinking? Did she really look the sort? "I appreciate the offer, sir, but I don't drink coffee. Or men. I'm swearin' off both until I move west."

His eyes darkened. "I am not asking you to drink me."

Despite the warmth of the day, another shiver of awareness grazed the length of her body, knowing full well what the man meant. "Not yet you aren't, but you're invitin' me to join you for coffee *at your hotel*. I may be third-generation Irish, but that doesn't make me stupid."

He lowered his chin. "Coffee was merely a suggestion."

"Oh, I know full well what you're suggestin', and I *suggest* you leave off. Do I look desperate for a toss *or* coffee?"

A smile ruffled his lips. "Have mercy upon a smitten man. What is your name?"

It was times like these that she hated her life. Such an attractive man graced with wealth and status would only ever view her as a one-night commodity. Although she knew better than to want more for herself, given that she was nothing but a Five Points widow, her dear Raymond had taught her she had a right to want the universe, and by God, she was going to get it.

There was only one way to go about protecting what little honor she had. She'd give him the name of the best prostitute in the ward. That way, everyone would benefit from her cleverness should he decide to hunt the name down. "The name is Mrs. Elizabeth Heyer, sir. Emphasis on the *Mrs.* Sorry I can't join you. My husband wouldn't be pleased." She quickly rounded him. "Now if you'll excuse me—"

He stepped before her, blocking her from moving any farther. "I ask that you provide your *real* name."

"I just did."

He shook his head from side to side, never once breaking their gaze. "It took a few breaths too long for you to answer and you didn't even look at me when you said it. Why? Do I unnerve you?"

She glared up at him. "If you haven't noticed, I'm tryin' to take my leave."

"If you were married, you would have mentioned it earlier." He leveled her with a reprimanding stare. "Do you mean to say that you are the sort of woman who enjoys bantering with men whilst her husband isn't about? Shame on you if that is true, and shame on you if it isn't. Either way, the lady appears to be a liar."

Curse him for honing in on the details.

He leaned in. "Don't deny that you are blatantly flirting with me in the same manner I am blatantly flirting with you."

Her eyes widened. She stepped back. "If I were flirtin', you'd know it, because I'd be draggin' you straight home instead of takin' up coffee. I'm not one to play games, sir. I either do somethin' or I don't."

"Then do something." His jaw tightened, his expression stilling. "I'm not married. An afternoon of conversation is all I ask." He met her gaze. "For now."

The smooth but predatory way he said it caused her to instinctively step back. Regardless of the fact that she was no longer married, it was obvious the sanctity of matrimony meant nothing to him. "And what shall I tell my husband, sir, should he ask how I spent my afternoon?"

His eyes clung to hers as if methodically gauging

her reaction. "If you are indeed married, I will not only desist, but run. I am not interested in creating a mess for you *or* myself. I was merely looking to get to know a woman who genuinely piqued my interest. Is that wrong?"

Georgia could feel her palms growing moist. Tempted though she was to experience one spine-tingling adventure of ripping off all the clothes of a most provocative stranger, she knew it wouldn't end well if Matthew and the boys were to ever find out. They'd probably hunt him down and kill him. After they robbed him of everything he was worth, that is. It'd be a mess either way.

She glanced around, ensuring she didn't see anyone she recognized. "Unlike you, sir, I'm lookin' to marry. Not dance. A woman of little means, such as myself, needs a dependable relationship better known as forever and a day. Not your version of a day and a night. I think that about says it all. Good day." Without meeting his gaze, she swept past.

He wordlessly angled away, allowing her passage.

Georgia quickened her step and scolded herself for having encouraged him in the first place. Fifteen decades on the rosary praying for her Jezebel soul ought to readmit her into heaven. Although fifteen decades wouldn't even begin to include Matthew's sins from this week alone that she had yet to pray for. That man required a set of his own damn beads. Not that he believed in God or anything else for that matter. All he believed in was money, money, money.

She paused on the pavement and instinctively tightened her hold on her reticule, allowing others to weave past. For some reason, she had this niggling feeling that she was being followed by the Brit she thought she'd left behind.

Pinching her lips together, she swiveled on her heel and froze upon glimpsing him four strides away, despite her having already forged well over a block. Her reticule slid from her calico-sleeved elbow down to her wrist, mirroring her disbelief that the man was following her like a dog she'd unknowingly fed scraps to. "Are you following me?"

Gray eyes heatedly captured hers as he came to a halt. "Instead of coffee, how about you and I go for a walk and get to know each other that way?" He smiled, ceremoniously announcing that he was capable of being respectable and that it was now up to her to decide as to how they should proceed.

Georgia dragged in a much-needed breath, her heart frantically pounding. Did he actually think she was going to change her mind based off that smoldering need blazing in those gunmetal eyes? She didn't even have time for a tryst. Not with all the laundry she had yet to do.

A quick movement shadowed the corner of her eye as a youth darted in and yanked back her wrist with the violent tug of her own reticule. The glint of a blade whizzed past.

Her eyes widened as she jerked around, realizing that the strings on her reticule had been slit by a passing thief. *"Ey!"* Georgia pounced for it, trying to reclaim what was hers, but the lanky youth skid out of reach, shoving past people, and dashed out of sight.

Her heart popped realizing she'd just been robbed by a ten-year-old. Hiking up her skirts above her ankle boots, she sprinted after the damn whoreson, shoving herself through those around her. "You'd best run!" she shouted after the boy, trying to keep up. "Because I'm about to shuck you like an oyster!"

"I'll anchor him," the Brit called out from behind.

His broad frame sped past her, and dodged left, then right, then left again, disappearing into the bustle of Broadway.

Having lost sight of him *and* the boy, Georgia paused to frantically ask others if they had seen a youth being chased by a gent in a dove-gray hat. She was repeatedly pointed onward and downward. So onward and downward she went.

Dragging in breaths, she tried to keep up with the pace of her own booted feet as the jogging facade of Broadway shops tapered into pristine Italian row houses. If she didn't get that damn reticule back, she'd have to dig money out of her box to make the rent. Again.

Shouts and a gathering crowd of men on the upcoming dirt road made her jerk to a halt and snap her gaze toward a pluming dust that was settling. An overturned dove-gray top hat lay oddly displaced outside the crowd in the middle of the street.

She sucked in a breath, scanning the men who were yelling at women to stand back. What—?

The driver of an omnibus, who had already brought

his horses to a full halt, untied the calling rope from his ankled boot, hopped down from his box seat and hurried into the crowd as passengers within the omni craned and gaped through the small windows.

"Oh, God." Her stomach clenched as she scrambled forward.

The Brit had been struck by the omni and was lying motionless there on the street corner of Howard and Broadway.

LIGHT EDGED IN THROUGH the waving darkness and pulsed against his eyelids. Slowly opening his eyes, he squinted against the glaring brightness of the sun that pierced through a cloudless sky. Taking in several jagged breaths, he drifted, unable to lift his head from the dirt-pounded street that dug into his shaven cheek and throbbing temple.

Several booted feet and countless hovering faces blocked his skewed view of painted placards posted on buildings and a blue sky that rose beyond a street he did not recognize. Shouts boomed all around him and the dust-ridden, heat-laced air made it difficult for him to breathe.

A bearded man with a cap slung low against his brow leaned over him. "Good to see you stayed below the clouds, sir. Are you able to get up?"

Why were there so many people gathered around him? What was going on? He rolled onto his back, wincing against the searing, razorlike sensations coiling throughout the length of his body. He staggered to sit up, only to sway and stumble back against the dirt road beneath him. The scuffed imprint of a booted foot that had been pressed deeply into the dirt beside him drew his gaze.

One day it happened that, going to my boat, I saw the print of a man's naked foot on the shore, very evident on the sand, as the toes, heels and every part of it.

He winced, pushing the odd, misplaced voice out of his head. His vision blurred as the acrid taste of blood coated his mouth and tongue. Something trickled down the side of his face, its wet warmth dribbling toward his earlobe. He swiped the moisture away with a trembling hand and glanced toward it. The fingertips of his brown leather glove were smeared with blood.

"Hoist him up," a female voice insisted from within the blur of surrounding faces. There was a pause. "Oh, saints preserve us." She sounded more panicked. "We need to get him over to the hospital."

He swallowed and glanced up toward that lilting female voice that appeared concerned for him. Was he in some strange part of Ireland? Despite trying to find that voice, there only seemed to be an endless blur of male faces floating around him.

Hands slid beneath his morning coat and trouser-clad thighs. A group of men jerked him upward with a unified grunt.

Pain whizzed straight up to his clenched teeth and skull. He gasped, twisting against their pinching grasps. "Gentlemen," he seethed out between ragged breaths. "Whilst your concern is appreciated, I hardly think a full procession is necessary."

"Such posh manners for one who is dying," one of

the men carrying him hooted playfully. "One can only wonder what'll come out of his mouth when he's dead."

A quick hand reached out and knocked the cap off the man's head. "Less tongue, more muscle. Move!"

"Ey!" the man yelled back, stumbling against him and all the others carrying him. "Keep them mammet little hands to yourself, woman. I was only having a bit of fun."

"You think it *fun* watchin' a man bleed? Keep movin' him, you lout. Lest I make *you* bleed." The freckled face of a young woman with the brightest set of green eyes he'd ever seen suddenly peered in from between all of the broad shoulders carrying him. Her rusty arched brows came together as she trotted alongside him, trying to hold his gaze through moving limbs. A loose, soft-looking strand of strawberry-red hair swayed against the wind, having tumbled out of her frayed blue bonnet.

"Where are you stayin'?" She shoved the loose strand of hair back into her bonnet with a bare hand, trying to keep up with the men carrying him. "Close? Far?"

Gritting his teeth, he tried to focus, but couldn't.

"Are you from around here?" she insisted, still bustling alongside him. "Or are you visitin' from abroad? You mentioned a hotel. Which hotel are you stayin' at?"

"Hotel?" he echoed up at her, his throat tightening. "When did I mention a hotel?"

She squinted down at him, searching his face. "Never you mind that. We need to contact your family. Give me a name and address, and after we deliver you to the hospital, I'll run myself over to them at once."

Family? He blinked, glancing up at the swaying, hazy blue sky above as he was guided up toward a hackney. Countless names and faces flipped through his mind's eye like the pages of an endless book whipping past. There were so many names. Strada. Ludovicus. Casparus. Bruyère. Horace. Sloane. Lovelace. Shakespeare. Fielding. Pilkington. La Croix. They couldn't all be related to him. Or…could they?

I was called Robinson Kreutznaer, which not being easily pronounced in the English tongue, we are commonly known by the name of Crusoe.

Wait. Crusoe. Yes. It was a name he remembered very well. Robinson Crusoe of York. Was that not him? It had to be, and yet he couldn't remember if it was or it wasn't. Oh, God. What was happening to him? Why couldn't he remember what was what?

He winced, realizing that he was now being tucked against the leather seat of an enclosed hackney. The firm hands that had been pushing him to sit upright against the seat left his body one by one as all the men turned away and jumped down and out of the hackney, leaving him alone against the seat.

Everything swayed as he slumped against the weight of his heavy limbs. He panicked, unable to control his own body, and fought to remain upright by using his gloved hands against the sides of the hackney.

The woman with the green eyes shoved her way past the others and frantically climbed up into the hackney, slamming the door behind her. "I'm takin' you in myself. I'll not leave your side. I promise."

The vehicle rolled forward as she landed beside him on the seat with a bounce. She leaned toward him. "Come." Her arms slid around him as she dragged him gently toward herself. She guided his shoulder and head down onto her lap, scooting across the seat to better accommodate his size.

He collapsed against the warmth of her lap, thankful he didn't have to hold himself up anymore. Wrapping a trembling hand around her knee, he buried it into the folds of her gown, taking comfort that he wasn't alone. The scent of lye and soap drifted up from the softness of her gown, which grazed his cheek and throbbing temple. He could die here and know eternal peace.

Her hand rubbed his shoulder. "I want you to talk. That way, I'll know you're doin' all right. So go on. Talk."

He swallowed, wanting to thank her for her compassion and for giving him a breath of hope even though he sensed there was none. Was death nothing more than a long sleep? His hand slowly and heavily slid inch by inch from her knee as he felt his entire world tip.

"Sir?" She leaned down toward him and shook him. *"Sir?"*

A snowy, rippling haze overtook the last of his vision, and though he fought to stay awake in those heavenly arms, everything faded and he along with it.

CHAPTER TWO

The height of cleverness is to be able to conceal it.
—François de La Rochefoucauld,
Maximes Morales (1678)

Nine days later, early evening
New York Hospital

GEORGIA LET OUT AN EXASPERATED breath and adjusted her bonnet, setting both ankled boots up onto the wicker chair opposite the one she'd been sitting in for the past ten minutes. She leaned forward and shook the bundled length of her brown calico gown to allow cooler air to relieve the heat of the room that would not dissipate.

Falling back into the wicker chair again, she glanced impatiently toward the surgeon who appeared to be far more invested in his desk than in her. "How much longer, sir? I've yet to cross back into town before they cease all rides and I really have no desire to walk over fifteen blocks in the dark."

Dr. Carter casually reached out and gripped the porcelain cup beside him. Lifting the rim to his mustached lip, he took a long swallow of murky coffee, before setting it back onto the saucer beside him with a *clink*. He leaned over the sizable ledger on his desk and scribed something. "His condition remains the same, Miss Milton. As such, you may go."

She glared at him. "'Tis *Mrs. Milton* 'til another man comes along to change it, and I didn't pay a whole twelve and a half cents for the omni to hear *that*. Last week you claimed he was fully recovered. I expected him to be gone by now. Why is he still here?"

The tip of his quill kept scratching against the parchment. "Because, *Mrs.* Milton, I am still conflicted as to how I should proceed." Wrinkling his brow, he paused and reached toward the inkwell with a poised quill. "His mental state isn't what it should be. I haven't disclosed his condition to anyone outside a trusted few out of fear he could be tossed into an asylum."

Her lips parted. "An asylum? Why would anyone—"

"Since he regained consciousness nine days ago, Mrs. Milton, he has been unable to provide me with a name or any details pertaining to his life. I even had to reacquaint him with the most basic of care, including how he was to shave and knot his own cravat."

She dropped her legs from the chair and sat up, her heart pounding. "Dearest God. What do you plan to do? What *can* you do?"

He shrugged. "I intend to dismiss him within the week. He doesn't belong here any more than he does in an asylum."

Her eyes widened. "And what of his family, sir? We have to find a way to contact them before you let him wander off. What if he should disappear and they never hear from him again?"

He stared at her, edging back his hand from over the

inkwell. "If he hasn't the means to remember them, I haven't the means to find them. Do you understand? There is nothing more that I can *physically* do for him."

"There is plenty more you can *physically* do for him!"

"Such as?" His tone was of pained tolerance.

"You can contact the British Consulate about whether or not they're missin' a citizen."

"I have already done that. No one is missing."

Damn. "Well…isn't there a way to bring in an artist and acquire a sketch of his face?"

"That has already been done. I mandate profile sketches of all my patients. It allows for extended funding from the government."

"Good. We'll be able to make use of it and submit his sketch to every newspaper and hotel across town. Someone is bound to know who he is, given he appears to be of the upper circles. Though I recommend no reward. That would only attract imposters."

Dr. Carter tossed his quill aside and leaned into the desk, scrunching his gray pin-striped waistcoat and his overcoat in the process. "This is a hospital, Mrs. Milton. Not an investigative branch of the United States government. You clearly have no understanding as to how these things work."

How typical that she'd be treated like some stupid, scampering rat darting through the legs of society. She managed to refrain from jumping up and smacking him for it. "Last I knew, sir, and correct me if I'm wrong, but the New York Hospital is funded by a contributin' branch of the United States government. As such, *you* have an obligation to oversee the well-bein' of every citizen that passes through these doors, be that citizen a Brit or not. Have the laws somehow changed? Is that what you're tellin' me?"

He sighed. "The funding I receive from the government is very limited. It doesn't provide for these sorts of things."

She rolled her eyes. "Everythin' involvin' our government is very limited. They only give the people just enough to prevent revolution whilst robbin' every last one of us blind. In my opinion, these politicians ought to be boiled in their own whiskey. They don't give a spit about anythin' but their own agenda."

A tap resounded against the door of the small office.

"Yes?" he called out, lifting his chin toward its direction. "What is it?"

The door swung open and a balding man hurried in, bare hands adjusting a blood-spattered, yellowing apron that had been carelessly tied across his waistcoat and trousers. "Bed sixteen is shaving, despite orders that he remain in bed. He insists on yet *another* bath and intends to depart within the hour. What am I to do?"

Dr. Carter blew out a breath. "There is nothing we can do. If he insists on departing, I cannot physically hold him. Send him into my office. I'll ensure he pays the bill and will direct him to one of the local boardinghouses."

"Yes, Dr. Carter." The man jogged back out.

Bed sixteen? That was the Brit's bed. Georgia's wicker chair screeched against the floorboards as she jumped onto booted feet. "You intend on lettin' him walk out into the night despite his condition? And plan on layin' him with a bill, too?" She pointed at him, wishing she had it in her to grab his head and pound it into his own desk. "A thug is what you are. A bedeviled, government-funded thug who ought to be—"

"Mrs. Milton, please. I haven't the time for this."

"You'd best make the time, Dr. Carter, as it only involves the poor man's *life*. Directin' him to a local boardin'house is like tellin' a fox to take up residence with the hounds. At the very least, you ought to turn him over to the state."

He rubbed his temple. "Mrs. Milton." He dropped his hand to his side and sat back against his leather chair. "The man is far too old to become a ward of *any* state." He swept a grudging hand toward the open window beside him that mirrored a quiet, moonless night. "Given his size and level of intelligence, I doubt he'll run into any trouble."

The bastard didn't even care that the minute that Brit put his polished boots on the wrong street, he'd be dead. She marched toward him, halting before his desk. "Whilst I know the world is full of woes we can't mend, we sure as hell ought to try. I want you to board him."

He blinked. "What? Here?"

"No, you dunce. In your home. What better way to care for your patient than givin' him a room next to your own?"

Dr. Carter threw back his head and puffed out a breath. After staring up at the ceiling for a long moment, he leveled his head and confided in a very impersonal tone, "I cannot take him home with me. My wife would throw a fit if I commenced bringing home all of my patients."

"Better your wife than me."

He pointed at her. "I'm asking you to leave before I have you tossed on your goddamn nose. I've had enough of this." He swept a finger to the door. "Get out."

It was obvious this man wasn't taking her seriously. Setting both hands atop his piled ledgers, she leaned across the desk toward him and lowered her voice a whole octave to better deliver her threat. "Before you go about tossin' me out on my *nose,* Dr. Carter, I want you to think about whether or not your life means anythin' to you."

He rose to his feet, towering above her. The broad planes of his aging face tightened as he leaned toward her across the desk. "Are you threatening me?" he rasped, placing both of his hands parallel to her own.

"Nah. 'Tis just a question like…between friends, don't you see." Georgia narrowed her gaze to match his. "But supposin' the Forty Thieves, who provide me with whatever protection I require, were to hear of my distress? What then? I'd be thinkin' it'd be in your best interest to help this man along. Because if you don't, I'd reckon that the quality of your life will diminish to the point that the Holy Virgin wouldn't even be able to help you."

His eyes held hers, his rigid brow flickering with renewed uncertainty. "I am a servant of the state. No rabble has power or say over me."

Georgia continued to stare him down. "Toss me on

my nose and count all of the men who will show up at your door. I dare you. Go on. Toss me."

Dr. Carter edged back and away, slowly removing his hands from the desk. Swiping a trembling hand across his face, he sat and shifted in his seat, refusing to look at her. "Might I ask why you are so intent on assisting him? Is he a customer who never fully disclosed his name and owes you money? Is that what this is about?"

Georgia lowered her chin, her pulse roaring in her ears. "How dare you? I sell hot corn on the hour of every summer and scrub clothes for priests in three wards, barely makin' *half* of what you eat in an effort to stay respectable." She snapped a finger toward the open door. "I don't know who the hell that man is any more than you do! Cursed that I am, I feel guilt for what happened to him. *He was hit runnin' after my reticule.* I may not be fobbin' high society, sir, but how does showin' an ounce of concern for a man make me a whore?"

Dr. Carter fell back against the chair and sighed. "I simply wanted to know what I was attaching my name to."

"Well, now you know. I do laundry. Not men."

He cleared his throat. "Thank you for *more* than clarifying that."

"I still don't understand a spit of any of this. How does a man forget his own name and life?"

Running the tips of his fingers against his mustache, he eyed her. "I've actually read about a condition similar to his known as 'memory loss' in one of my medical journals. It involved a soldier who was rendered blank after a severe blow to the head during the war. I myself never thought it medically possible, but it's obvious this man's memory is for the most part gone. I wanted you to be aware of that given your concern."

She swallowed, bringing her shaky hands together. This was her fault. She should have never looked at him that day. Perhaps things might have been different. Perhaps he'd still have had a mind. "Don't you know anythin' about him? Anythin' at all?"

"A few things, yes. 'Tis obvious by the clothing he arrived in, his speech and mannerisms, as well as the money that was found on his person, that he appears to be of British affluence."

She huffed out a breath. "I already knew that. His buttons were made out of silver, sir. Not even bankers can afford silver buttons."

"Then you know about as much about the man as I do, Mrs. Milton." He held up a hand, shifting in his seat. "Threats aside, I will agree that assisting him is the right thing to do, but my time is very limited, so I am going to ask for your assistance, in turn. I work as many as twelve hours a day and my wife and six children barely see me. What little time I do have, I spend with them and hope to God you'll not impose on what I consider to be incredibly precious."

Georgia blinked, her throat tightening. Now she felt like a bloke of the worst sort, having bullied a family man. "I didn't mean to toss threats, but I learned a long time ago that generosity and compassion have to be threatened out of people."

He held her gaze for a long moment. "You are far more impressive in nature than you let on."

She set her chin. "The frayed gown has a tendency to mislead people into thinkin' I'm as equally frayed. Now let's get on with this. What will you have me do? I'll see to it if it means helpin' him. That's all I really care about."

He sighed. "Find a means to board him until he is claimed."

She lifted a brow. He wanted *her* to board him? Impossible. There was only one bed in her low closet and it belonged to her. Even if she did manage to get past sharing it with a man she didn't know, he'd only end up leeching resources she barely had. "Bein' a respectable widow, sir, I've neither the money nor the means."

Dr. Carter leaned over and yanked open one of the drawers on the desk, scooping up a stringed, small leather satchel. "I retrieved everything from his pockets when he first arrived to prevent anything from being stolen. The patients here aren't particularly trustworthy." He tapped it. "Inside, you'll find a fob and a pocketbook containing one hundred and thirty-two dollars. It should be more than enough to oversee all of his expenses. I'll even waive the hospital fee if you promise to board him for however long it takes to locate his family."

Georgia gawked at the lopsided satchel. "One hundred and thirty-two dollars? Away with you. Who wanders about the city with *that* much money in one pocket?"

He smirked. "A pirate, I suppose." He paused and

shifted awkwardly in his seat. "I should probably disclose that he claims to be a Salé pirate."

She gasped. "Whatever do you mean he *claims* to be?"

He cleared his throat. "If you intend to board him, which I hope you will, I highly recommend you not exasperate his situation. He isn't in the least bit dangerous, but riling him into questioning his own sanity will only result in pointless paranoia. If he says he is a Salé pirate, he is. Do you understand?"

Heaven preserve her soul. What was she getting herself into? Whilst, yes, she wanted to help, and the man seemed infinitely divine on the street, she didn't know who this Brit was or what he was capable of. What if he'd already been deranged prior to being clipped by the omni and his so-called "memory loss" was, in fact, who he really was?

"Abide by calling him Robinson Crusoe," he continued. "He prefers it."

She blinked. "I thought you had said he didn't know his name."

"He doesn't. He thinks Robinson Crusoe *is* his name."

She squinted, not understanding his point. "Beggin' your pardon, but Robinson Crusoe sounds like a very legitimate name to me."

He blinked rapidly. "You obviously haven't read the book."

Now he really wasn't making any sense. "What book?"

Dr. Carter leaned toward her, awkwardly refusing to meet her gaze. "Mrs. Milton."

"Yes?"

"Robinson Crusoe is the name of a character from a book. 'Tis a story decades old and well-known amongst boys and men alike. The main character is a sailor whose ship is overtaken by Salé pirates who force him into becoming a slave. He manages to escape, only to be shipwrecked on an island frequented by cannibals. So you see...our Salé slave and pirate thinks he is this character. He thinks he is Robinson Crusoe."

Her eyed widened. "That doesn't sound like memory loss to me. He sounds...deranged."

"I know. Believe me, I know. But he isn't." He shifted toward her. "In trying to understand his most unusual condition, I presented him a map of the world and asked him where we were and where he lived. Imagine my astonishment when he points to France and mentions rue des Francs-Bourgeois in Paris. 'Tis a street I know very well, given my wife's parents had lived on that same street prior to the Revolution that pushed them out. 'Tis still an impressive area frequented by those of affluence and one Robinson Crusoe would have never frequented. I have written to his address to inquire, but without a name or house number, it may lead nowhere.

"So you see, he may not remember *who* he is, but he still remembers factual things outside of this Crusoe. Factual things that must pertain to his own life. I have therefore concluded that his condition isn't one of full-blown fantasy but an inability to decipher between fact and fiction. That doesn't make him deranged. It only makes him…unreliable. Something to keep in mind whilst you board him." He plucked up a piece of stationery from his cluttered desk, along with an ink-slathered quill. "I will require your name and address before you depart with him."

She angled toward him. "Don't you think that a man who claims to have met cannibals is a walkin' liability I ought to avoid? Regardless of if he knows life outside of this—this *Crusoe?* What if he should eat me and all of my neighbors in honor of his cannibal friends? What then, sir?"

Dr. Carter burst into laughter and caught himself against the desk, eyeing her. "He won't—" He laughed again, shaking his head. "No. He won't. Not this man."

She set her hands on her hips. "I'm bein' quite serious and I wish to Joseph you'd be, too. I've seen far too much to question what is or isn't rational. Men are never rational, sir. They only pretend to be and I'm rather worried I may end up swimmin' in my own blood."

His features sagged. "I cannot predict what he will or will not do, but the man is genuinely compassionate and protective of others. Throughout his entire stay, he's done nothing but lecture us on our inability to tend to patients and is always getting out of bed to assist others in the hall, despite having orders that he rest. If that assurance isn't enough, I suggest you let him walk out into the world, Mrs. Milton. For he is neither your responsibility nor mine. So what will you have me do? The choice is yours."

Oh, now, that just wasn't fair. She sighed. "I'll find a means to board him," she grouched, waving toward the parchment. "The name is Mrs. Georgia Emily Milton and the tenement is 28 Orange Street. Orange. Like the bastard who destroyed Ireland."

Dr. Carter paused, leaned over the parchment and sloppily scribed her name and address. "Thank you."

This was going to be a mess. She'd probably have to hover over this Brit like a hen over a cracked egg. But then again, if there was anyone who understood cracked, it most certainly was her. "About how long will I have to board him? Exactly?"

"That I cannot say. It could be a few days or several months, depending on how long it takes for someone to recognize him."

She refrained from groaning. Though she hated submitting to guilt, for it was a pesky emotion that always got her into trouble, she owed the man this much, given it was *her* reticule that had sent him under an omni.

Dr. Carter set aside the quill, swiped up the satchel and held it out. "I will leave this in your care and will be in touch. Make the money last. We don't know how long it will be before anyone claims him."

"Don't you worry. I'll ensure both he and *it* lasts." She reached out and tugged the small, weighty satchel from his hand. Why did she have this eerie feeling that she was taking on a man who was about to do far more than ruin her month?

CHAPTER THREE

She Ventures, and He Wins.
— A Comedy Written by a Young Lady (1696)

A MAN OBNOXIOUSLY CLEARED his throat from behind
Georgia where she still lingered before Dr. Carter's
desk. "I realize the hour is anything but convenient,
Dr. Carter, but I'm asking to depart all the same before
I lead a revolt in the hall. None of the goddamn linens
in our beds have been tended to in over three days. For
those men who have fluids pouring out from more than
the usual places, I find it vile and disturbing. You and
your minions ought to be hanged for your wretched dis-
regard for humanity. *Hanged.*"

The harsh British voice startled Georgia into turning
to the man. She instinctively pressed the small satchel
in her hand against her hip, her eyes jumping from a
broad chest up to a taut, masculine face. The man didn't
sound quite as mindless as Dr. Carter had led her to believe.

The Brit, who lingered all but a stride away, glanced
down at her and paused. His black hair had been
brushed back from his forehead with tonic, giving him
the appearance of the distinguished gentleman she had
met on the street, but that sizable scab and the large yel-

lowing bruise marring the right side of his cheekbone
and square jaw made him look like one of the boys.
Dried blood from the day of the accident still spattered
parts of his knotted cravat and full sections of his outer
gray coat near the width of his broad shoulder.

Merciful God. They had never even washed his
clothes. The rest of him appeared to be well scrubbed,
though she sensed it was not anything the hospital had
bothered with, but something he had insisted on.

Shifting toward her, he searched her face and drew
in a ragged breath. "I know you."

She smiled awkwardly. "Aye. That you do."

He half nodded. "Yes." His shaven face flushed.
"Forgive me. I didn't realize anyone would be coming."
Stepping toward her, he reached out and swept up her
hand, making her almost drop the satchel that was still
pressed in the other one.

Her heart flipped at the base of her throat as he bent
over to softly kiss her bare hand.

No one but her Raymond had ever kissed her hand
like that. It was the signature of a gentleman who could
see beyond the rags. Georgia swallowed against the
tightness of her throat and tried to tug her hand loose
only to find that the man wouldn't let go. "Might I...
have my hand back? Or do you plan on keepin' it?"

He glanced up and tightened his hold, that large hand
taking complete command of hers.

It was obvious he planned on keeping it.

With a solid twist, she tugged her hand out of his, a
rising heat overtaking her cheeks. "I realize things are
a bit muddled for you, Brit, but when I ask for some-

thin' back, you give it back. Be it a hand or anythin' else. Agreed?"

He edged closer, his pensive expression gauging her. "I apologize for being unable to remember the details pertaining to our relationship, but are you my wife?"

Her lips parted. Oh, the poor man's mind had been completely bashed. He didn't remember her at all, and given his cheeky behavior on the street that day, he probably *did* have a wife, damn bastard.

Dr. Carter cleared his throat from behind. "Mrs. Crusoe, I recommend you heed my earlier advice of not riling him into a form of paranoia. 'Tis best."

Mrs. Crusoe? Georgia swung toward the man and pointed at him. "Oh, no. Oh, no, no. There isn't goin' to be any of that."

"Mrs. Crusoe." Dr. Carter's voice dropped to a low warning. "I hold you responsible for his health and his delicate state of mind for as long as he is in your care. I will say no more."

Oh, this couldn't be right. How could feeding into a man's delusions be responsible? It wasn't! She swiveled back, intent on settling this *before* she took him home. "Never you mind him, Brit. You and I most certainly aren't married. In truth, I barely consider us friends."

"You barely consider us friends?" His mouth tightened as he continued to stare. "That isn't at all what I remember."

She quirked a brow. "And what exactly do you remember?"

He shifted his scabbed jaw and glanced toward

Dr. Carter before recapturing her gaze. "'Tis hardly respectable to say, given that we are not married."

Her eyes widened. "I beg your pardon?"

He smoothed his blood-spattered cravat against his throat and set his chin, avoiding her gaze. "Whilst I am pleased that you are here, for I was beginning to wonder if anyone would come, given my inability to remember names, I ask that we save this conversation for another time. Would you be so kind as to return me to my flat? I'm exhausted."

She paused. "Your flat? You mean you know where it is?"

His brow wrinkled. "Yes and no. I thought it was located on rue des Francs-Bourgeois, but Dr. Carter informed me that we are not in Paris, but in New York. So I suppose the answer is no. I don't know where my flat is." He shrugged. "Not that it matters. You know where I live, don't you?"

She tapped her own temple. "If I knew where you lived, Brit, I'd be droppin' you off right now and thankin' the good Lord for havin' saved me from a guilt I've no right to feel."

He eyed her. "I sense there is an animosity between us."

"You'd be sensin' right, given what you wanted out of me before you earned that knock to your head."

"I see." He blew out a pained breath and muttered, "I suppose that leaves me to find myself a hotel, as I am not one to perpetuate arguments I cannot even remember." He paused and glanced down at himself, patting his coat pockets. "Did I not have a pocketbook? How am I to pay for anything?"

Dr. Carter gathered several ledgers from his desk, organizing them. "Your pocketbook is already accounted for, Mr. Crusoe. How are you feeling?"

"Aside from these damnable headaches, I feel remarkably well. Better."

"Good. 'Tis my hope that the headaches will fade in time. Try to rest." Dr. Carter rounded the desk with a stack of ledgers in hand. "Now if you'll both excuse me, I intend to retire early tonight and call upon an acquaintance of mine who happens to be the owner of the *New-York Evening Post*. Perhaps we can get this story into tomorrow's paper, seeing it has yet to print. Given its popularity, I'm certain other newspapers will follow suit. We'll commence there and hope for the best." He inclined his head and strode out of the office.

Georgia swiveled toward the Brit, who quietly observed her with marked curiosity. His gaze drifted down the full length of her and paused on her boots, which peered out from beneath her ankle-high skirts.

"The leather on your boots is almost white," he commented. "You should buy yourself a new pair."

He was like a child. "How very observant. If only I could afford a new pair." Stepping toward him, Georgia grabbed up his gloved hand and pressed his satchel into it. "This is yours, Brit. It has all of your money in it, so I suggest you keep it safe 'til we get across town."

He hesitated, shifting the satchel in his hand before slipping it into the inner pocket of his gray coat. "Why do you keep calling me Brit?"

"Because that's what you are. A Brit."

"I would rather you call me Robinson. I don't like the way you say Brit."

"Not to disappoint you, *Brit,* but I usually call people whatever I want. 'Tis my born right as a United States citizen. I may not be able to vote, but no man is goin' to tell me I can't use my tongue." Georgia paused and pointed to his sleeved coat, noting that the band was missing from his arm. "You had a mournin' band. Did you lose it? Or did you strip it?"

He glanced down at his arm. "I was wearing a… mourning band?"

"That you were. Right there on your arm."

He glanced up, searching her face, his features taut and panicked. "Who died?"

Georgia's stomach dropped all the way down to her toes as she met his gaze. There was an aching vulnerability lingering within those handsome gray eyes that seemed to depend on her for everything. It made her want to give the man everything.

She softened her tone. "I don't know who died. All I know is that you were wearin' one when I last saw you."

He dug his gloved fingertips into the biceps of his right arm and winced. "Why can I not remember?"

"Try not to worry. Rememberin' is overrated, anyway. Trust me. I wish there was a way *I* could forget half my life." She drifted closer, sighed and leaned toward him to get a better look at what needed to be stripped before they crossed into the other side of town. She fingered the sturdy material on the seam of his morning coat. The fine fabric had to be worth ten dollars without the stitching. "Heavens, you're a walkin' merchant cart waitin' to be robbed. We'll have to alter your appearance 'til we're able to get rid of these clothes."

He stiffened, lowering his gaze to her probing fingers. "And what is wrong with my appearance *or* my clothes?"

"Everythin'." She sniffed, the heat of his muscled body wafting the subtle fragrance of tonic and penny shaving cream. "I hate to say it, but you even smell wrong."

He blinked rapidly. "Are you suggesting that I bathe? Because I just did. Fifteen minutes ago."

"Nah, I'm suggestin' quite the opposite. I only bathe and scrub once every two days and even that's considered a bit much in the eyes of where I live. But then again, I'm a woman and you're not. In my ward, if a man starts playin' with too much soap and tonic, he's likely to get a reputation for wearin' pink garters."

"I don't wear pink garters."

"I didn't say you did. But that won't keep the boys from sayin' it. And you sure as hell don't want a byname with the word *pink* in it. Now let's get rid of some of these fineries, shall we?" She tapped at his cravat. "Off with it."

He paused, his gaze trailing down to her lips. "Does this mean there is no further need for a hotel?"

Georgia nervously smoothed her hands against the sides of her calico skirts, sensing he was still confused as to who she was. Wetting her lips, she chose her words carefully, hoping not to send him into a panic. "I can only apologize for Dr. Carter. He means well, but it isn't right makin' you think I'm someone I'm not."

His brows flickered. "I don't understand."

"I'm not your wife or your mistress or whoever you think I am. The name is Georgia. You know, like the state. You can call me that, if you want, but I prefer Mrs. Milton until we get to know each other more." She gestured toward his throat. "Now remove your cravat."

He stared her down. "If I ever decide to undress for you, Mrs. Milton, it won't be upon your command but mine."

She glared at him. "Oh, now, don't you get cheeky with me, Brit. I'm not askin' you to undress for my sake. I'm askin' you to undress for *yours*. We can't have you prancin' about in silk over on Orange Street. You'll get dirked. Now take it off."

He stepped back. "Absolutely not. What would your husband say, *Mrs.* Milton?"

Her lips thinned. Perhaps it was best he thought Raymond was alive. It would keep him from thinking she was up for a toss. "The man would say, for the good of your own breath, you'd best take off the cravat."

"Oh, no, he wouldn't. He would say, 'If you take anything off in the presence of my wife, you will cease to breathe.'"

She let out an exasperated laugh. "As amusin' as I find you and this, all omnis cease runnin' in an hour. Do you want to walk fifteen blocks in the dark? I don't. Now take off the cravat. Even with it bein' spattered with blood, it makes you look too much like a gentleman."

"I should probably point out that I consider myself to *be* a gentleman."

She quirked a brow, challenging him. "Really?"

"Really."

"I thought you were a Salé pirate. Isn't that what you told Dr. Carter?"

He shifted his jaw and glanced away. "I cannot trust what I do or do not remember."

"Which is why you'll have to trust me over yourself, dear sir, because I'm not the one sufferin' from memory loss."

He muttered something and scrubbed a hand through his hair. He winced, letting his hand fall back to his side. "Remind me not to touch my head."

Georgia softened her tone, hoping a motherly approach would get him to cooperate. "We really ought to remove that silk from around your throat. Won't you take it off? For me? Please?"

Stepping closer, she reached up and forcefully unraveled his silk cravat, trying to figure out how the damn thing was supposed to come off. The fabric kept sliding against her fingers like cool water. Their gazes locked and she paused, trying to steady her breathing.

He jerked outside of her tugging hands and shifted his broad shoulders, stepping back. "I'm not at all comfortable with you touching me. You are, after all, a *very* attractive woman and I would hate for this to progress beyond anything either of us would be able to control."

She set her hands on her hips. What a cad. "If I were lookin' to progress things, *Robinson,* I'd be goin' straight for the trousers. Rest assured, a man's throat never once made me moan and I highly doubt yours will, either."

He stared at her, his expression strained. "Refrain from talking to me in such crass tones."

"I wouldn't have to talk *at all* if you were cooperatin'. Now cease bein' so damn stupid. I'm here to help." She stepped back toward him, reached up and forcefully finished yanking his cravat off. She tossed it, letting it cascade to the floor.

His gloved hand jumped up to cover his exposed throat, his shaven face flushing. "I really don't understand why—"

"Silk just isn't somethin' men in my parts wear. Men there are poor. Some of them are *very* poor. There's no need to give them a reason to hate or rob you. You bein' an uppity Brit is goin' to be bad enough. Men will probably fist you based on your accent alone."

"Oh, and you plan on taking me there?" He lifted a brow. "Shall I thank you for your overall lack of concern for me now? Or later? After I get fisted?"

She rolled her eyes. "You needn't worry. I'll see to it you fall under the protection of the boys."

"The boys?" He lowered his chin. "You intend on placing me under the care of your children? I assure you, madam, my mind isn't *that* far gone."

She gurgled out a laugh. He was so bizarrely adorable. "Nah, it isn't like that at all. Though sometimes I do wonder." She glanced toward the open doorway and lowered her voice. "They're men who act like boys, so I call them boys, see? They're known for havin' a black reputation, and believe me, they live up to it, but I know how to yank their collars. I'm just makin' sure nothin' happens to you prior to my yankin' those collars."

"And who are these men to you?" He eyed her. "Are you involved with any of them?"

"Not in *that* way, no. They're more like flea-ridden dogs I can't get rid of." She scanned his clothes again and sighed. "I'll have Matthew loan you some of his clothes. You're about his size. Give or take a few stones."

He squinted. "Matthew? Who is that? Your husband?"

"No. My son."

His lips parted. "You have a son *my* size? You don't appear to be a breath over twenty."

She grinned, tilting her face up toward him. "Thank you for that, but I'm well over twenty. I'm *two* and twenty."

He scanned her face. "That still doesn't make you old enough to have a son my size. He isn't really your son, is he?"

"Not by birth, no."

"So whose boy is he?" He leaned in, trailing his gaze to her lips. "And why are you taking care of him?"

She stepped back. "Don't look at my lips."

He stepped toward her. "I will keep looking at them until you tell me everything I want to know."

She scrambled back, sensing that he wanted to do far more than look at them. "He's Raymond's boy. All right? Not mine. Raymond's."

"And who is Raymond?"

She glared at him. "I'm not about to tell my life story

to a man who doesn't even know his own. Now give me your hand." She pointed. "We can't have you wearin' those gloves."

He set both gloved hands behind his back and eyed her expectantly. "I don't intend to cooperate until you tell me who Raymond is."

"The man is dead," she bit out. "All right? Now cease actin' like a bogey and give me your hand." She forcefully grabbed his arm and jerked it out from behind his back, tugging it up toward her. Digging her fingers beneath the cuff of his linen shirt, she peeled the fitted leather glove from his large hand and tossed it toward the desk.

Without any resistance, he quietly watched her strip the glove from his other hand. His large and remarkably smooth hand tightened possessively around her own.

She paused, entranced by the heat of his hand penetrating her skin. Her body seemed to drift, while her mind remained anchored and fully aware of him and that hand. There was something very different about his touch. Whilst incredibly firm and strong, it was also… soft. Slowly turning his large palm upward, she ran the tips of her calloused fingers against the smoothest masculine palm she'd ever encountered. It was as if he had never touched *anything* with those hands.

Georgia glanced up. "You most certainly aren't a pirate."

"And how do you know? I could be."

She lifted his hand and tilted it palm upward for him to better see. "Look at your hands."

He hesitated and lowered his gaze to the hand she held up.

She traced her fingers toward the length of his long fingertips and back toward his large smooth palm. "They're untouched. See? If you were a pirate, you would have handled ropes and crates, which would have covered your hands in calluses. Given their softness, 'tis obvious your only trade is money." She snorted. "That would explain why you couldn't remember how to shave or knot a cravat. You had servants doin' it for you."

His mouth tightened as he tilted his hand against hers, intently observing it. "They are smooth, aren't they?" He sounded disappointed.

She gently shook his hand, not wanting him to feel shame in what he was. "I'm sorry. I didn't mean to make you feel bad. 'Tis a blessin', not a curse, I assure you. 'Tis also the truest mark of wealth there is."

He glanced up. "So I am a man of wealth?"

"With hands like these and silver buttons to match, you most certainly are." She lowered her voice in warning, squeezing his hand. "Whatever you do, though, Brit, don't tell anyone, and *don't* parade that money in your satchel. You can't be trustin' anyone but me from here on out. You hear?"

His fingers curled and tightened around her hand, squeezing his warmth against her own. "And who are you to me?" A huskiness lingered in his uncertain tone as he searched her face. "Why do you care?"

He reminded her so much of herself when she was younger, unwilling to trust but having no other choice but to trust. Although her only family, her dear da, had disappeared many years ago for reasons she would never know, she'd see to it that this man's family didn't suffer in the way she had. Someone out there loved him and missed him, and she would ensure he was returned back into their arms where he belonged.

"Consider me a friend who understands what it's like to be dependent on the love and generosity of others." She slid her hand from his and pointed to that double row of silver buttons. "Those will have to come off, too."

He glanced down at his waistcoat, his brows coming together. "What? The buttons?"

"Yes, the buttons. They're silver, aren't they?"

"I suppose they are. What of it?"

"It means you're likely to be robbed of them."

He fingered one of the buttons. "But they're attached to my waistcoat."

"Not for long they aren't. Let me show you how it's done over on my street." She yanked her full skirt up to the knee, exposing the leather holster attached to her thigh, and slid a small blade out before letting her skirts drop again.

He stepped back, his eyes jumping toward the blade. "What are you doing?"

"Trust me." She grabbed his waist and dragged him back over toward herself. "I only want the buttons."

He grabbed hold of her wrist, twisting the blade hard and off to the side, away from himself. "All I ask is that you keep it pointed *away* from me."

"Oh, cease your brayin'." She jerked her wrist from his grasp, ignoring the sting. Firmly holding the top silver button away from the embroidered fabric of his waistcoat, she slashed the threads beneath it, catching the button with her other hand.

He searched her face, the resistance in his body waning as the edge of his full mouth quirked. "I like you."

"Oh, do you, now?" she tossed up at him. "Let's just see how long that lasts. Very few men like a woman with a quick tongue."

Holding her gaze, his large hands curved around her waist, causing her to stiffen. He leaned in close, despite the blade in her hand pointing toward him, and asked softly and adoringly, "*Mrs.* Milton, are you really married? Or are you pretending to be? Because I find you endearing. Tongue, mind and all." He paused and added, "I also find you to be incredibly attractive. Incredibly."

The man had apparently lost the last of his mind *and* his ability to censor his own thoughts. She lowered her gaze, the heat of those lingering hands making her stomach tingle. "I'm not married anymore," she admitted, her throat tightening at the thought of Raymond. "I was, when I was younger, but he died."

"Ah." His hands drifted away from her hips. "Did you love him?"

She edged back and half nodded. "Yes. Very much."

"I'm sorry for your loss."

She half nodded again. "Thank you."

He was quiet for a long moment. "Were you and he ever in Paris? Is that where I may know you from?"

She glanced up at him. Her and Raymond in Paris? Oh, now she'd heard it all. Raymond hated the French about as much as he hated the mayor and his politics. Whilst she? She only knew about Paris from Raymond. About all the gardens the Parisians had, the rows of palaces that once belonged to kings, the way they cobbled their streets and even had churches that were almost as old as God himself. "Raymond had been in Paris on business in his younger years when he still had money. As for me, I've never once lived a breath outside of New York. I was born here, and though I'm tryin' to move west, I'll most likely die here and be buried with a wooden marker that'll rot away and make everyone forget I was born a redhead."

He averted his gaze. "You are far too young to be speaking in such gray tones."

"Where I live, gray is about the only color one sees. But one gets used to it, especially if it's all they know." She focused once again on his waistcoat. "Now hold still."

She leaned in, working the blade against the threads behind each button. She quickly detached all the buttons, catching them in her palm one by one, until his waistcoat hung open, exposing the whitest and brightest linen shirt she'd ever glimpsed. It was as if it had been snatched right off the tailor's bench.

She released him, shoving all six buttons into the stitched pocket just beneath her left arm. "There."

Gathering her calico skirts back up, she slid the blade securely back into the holster and let her skirts drop. She paused, sensing he was staring. Having been surrounded by men since she was nine, shortly after the death of her mum, she'd lost all sense of modesty around those who were used to seeing limbs being bared and rarely stared. But this man made her aware of just how important modesty was. It kept a girl out of trouble when it counted most.

She awkwardly glanced toward him. "You didn't have to look."

"I couldn't very well help it." His jaw tightened as he met her gaze. "Do you lift your skirts for all the boys?"

She pursed her lips, attempting not to be entirely insulted. "Only the ones I intend to gut. So I suggest you mind your tongue."

"Don't you worry. I intend to mind my tongue *and* my eyes." He glanced away, jerking his now-open waistcoat against his linen shirt and abdomen. "I must say, the prodigal destruction of a perfectly good waistcoat brings this man to tears."

She paused. "The *prodi-what?*"

"Prodigal," he provided.

"And what is that supposed to mean?"

"Wasteful. *Prodigal* means wasteful."

"Oh, does it, now? Well, I never heard of the word."

"And whose fault is that? Not mine, to be sure. Buy yourself a dictionary, my dear."

She glared at him for being so rude. "If I could afford one, I would. Though I really wouldn't be surprised if you just made that word up in some pathetic attempt to impress me."

He raked a gaze down the length of her and smirked. "I can think of a dozen other ways to go about impressing you, Mrs. Milton, and making up words doesn't readily come to mind."

She squinted. "You mean it really is a word?"

"Yes, of course it is a word."

"Huh." She eyed him. "I'm confused."

"About what? The word?"

"No." She waved toward him. "How is it you remember *prodi-whatever* but can't remember much else?"

He paused. "That I don't know." He shrugged, averting his gaze. "I just remember words, that is all. I see them. I hear them. I cannot readily explain *why,* but I do. And as I said, the *prodigal* destruction of a perfectly good waistcoat brings this man to tears."

She lowered her chin. "Before your tears flood this room and the city, I ought to point out that a silver button can be pawned for as much as seventy-five cents apiece over at the local junk dealer. Over four dollars was dangling off your chest for the world to see. Never give anyone a reason to fleece you, I say, or they will." Stepping back, she eyed his appearance again. "You still aren't rough enough. You shouldn't have shaved."

She bit her lip and glanced around, wondering what she could do without altogether ripping the seams of his outfit apart. She supposed she could soil it, but with what?

She paused. Coffee. How fitting.

Glancing toward Dr. Carter's desk, she plucked up the porcelain cup of coffee he'd left on the desk and dipped her finger into it to ensure it wasn't hot. It wasn't. "I don't think Dr. Carter will mind. Hold still. Here's a toast to what should have been." Turning back to him, she flung the entire contents of the dark, gritty liquid onto the front of his linen shirt and open waistcoat.

He sucked in a breath and jumped back, his hands popping up into the air. He frantically swiped at his wet, stained clothing and glared at her, his dark hair falling from its neat, brushed state. "Damn you thrice into the pits of hell, woman." He gestured rigidly toward himself, his face taut and his eyes ablaze. "Why did you think it necessary to ruin a perfectly fine linen shirt?"

He was certainly prim for a man who thought he was a pirate. He couldn't even swear right. "We're improvisin', is all. No one's linen shirts look *that* snowy white where I live."

He gave her a withering look. "Forgive me for having a clean shirt. Shall I rip the seams a bit for you?"

She heaved out a breath. "If you can't survive bein' stripped by a woman and havin' coffee thrown at you, you most certainly won't survive where I'm takin' you. You're over six feet tall. Act like every inch counts, will you? Be a man."

He released his shirt and stalked toward her, veering in tauntingly close. "'Tis damn well hard to be a man around you. Damn. Well. Hard."

She rolled her eyes and huffed on her way out of the office.

Men. They were all so self-righteous no matter what their upbringing or how hard you hit them on the head.

CHAPTER FOUR

Of old there was nothing, nor sand, nor sea, nor cool waves. No earth, no heaven above. Only the yawning chasm.

—Saemundar Edda, Codex Regius
(early fourteenth century)

ROBINSON INTENTLY WATCHED the shadows of wood buildings as they bobbed and rolled by through the small dirt-streaked window at his elbow, waiting to recognize just one thing. And yet he didn't. Not the buildings. Not the streets. Not the omni he rode in. Not even the night itself. It was as if he were looking out upon a chasm that meant nothing to him. How much longer would he have to live feeling as if he were seeing everything for the first time?

He tightened his jaw and glanced toward the young woman sitting beside him on the bench. Georgia. Like the state. Who the hell named their daughter after a state? It would be like naming one's daughter after *Paris*. It bespoke of too much grandeur with very little to show.

Her sloppily gathered strawberry locks quivered within her frayed, beribboned bonnet with each strong sway of the omni that sent her shoulder bumping into his shoulder. Despite the sways that forced their bodies to touch, she indifferently stared out across the narrow space toward the bench opposite their own, which had long been emptied of passengers.

Something about her was so achingly familiar, but for some reason, it didn't match any of the erotic images she evoked in his head. He could vividly see pale, freckled limbs and cascading long red hair similar to hers splayed out against linen, but there simply wasn't a face associated with it. Who was the naked woman in his head if it wasn't this Georgia? Was it a wife he couldn't remember? Or a…mistress?

God help him either way.

He dragged in a breath. "What do you know about me?" he eventually inquired above the clattering of the wood wheels.

Georgia shifted toward him. Her seductive eyes met his through the dim light of the lantern that swayed above the closed omni door, shifting shadows. "I know as much about you as you know about yourself."

"Are you certain I never mentioned having a wife?"

"You told me you had no wife."

"Oh." Had he lied to her? No. He wasn't that sort of man. Or rather, he could *sense* he wasn't that sort of man. He shifted closer to her on the bench, his thigh bumping hers. "And how do we know each other again?"

"We met on Broadway. You affixed one of the ribbons on my bonnet when it came loose and it led to a bit of conversation."

"Ah. And was I at least courteous and respectable toward you during our initial interaction?"

She eyed him. "Courteous, you most certainly were. Respectable? Mmm. No. Not really. Not given the way you insisted I join you for coffee. You wouldn't leave me alone."

He cleared his throat. "There isn't anything wrong with a gentleman insisting on mere coffee, is there?"

"If the coffee is at his hotel, I'd say there is."

He lowered his chin. "I propositioned you?"

"Right there on the street." She waggled her brows and nudged him. "You practically *poured* coffee down my throat."

What breed of a bastard ambushed a woman on the street and tried to drag her over to his hotel under the pretense of coffee? If he ever did remember being that sort of man, he'd up and fist himself. "I can only apologize for my behavior."

"Apology much appreciated and accepted."

Scanning her full lips, Robinson tried to conjure a memory of what might have been. He would have remembered making love to a mouth like that, wouldn't he? But then again, he really couldn't remember making love to any mouth. It was alarming to know all about what went on between a man and a woman and yet not remember *doing* any of it aside from some random flash of nakedness belonging to God knows whom. "So what happened between us? Did you and I ever…?"

Her brows rose. "What sort of woman do you take me for? I said no and sent you on your way, is what. You were the one followin' me like a dog."

He leaned toward her. "If nothing happened between us, and you know as much about me as I know about myself, why are you taking me home with you? Aren't you at all worried I might be deranged or how this might affect your reputation? I don't quite understand your reasoning."

She clasped her bare hands, bringing them to the lap of her calico gown. "Don't complicate this, Brit. I'm only doin' this because I've got guilt as deep as the Hudson and you've got money to see us both through. I also wasn't about to let you aimlessly wander the city in your condition."

He shrugged. "I would have managed."

"Yes. The way you *managed* that day on the street and ended up where you are now, completely oblivious to yourself and the world."

Robinson lapsed into agitated silence, trying to recapture what he *could* remember. He remembered the hospital and all of the brass beds that lined the hall. He remembered the oatmeallike plaster ceiling that peeled in sections above his bed. He remembered the endless conversations he'd shared with Dr. Carter, who had patiently assisted him in doing things he already knew how to do but oddly couldn't remember doing. Like how to shave, tie a cravat and read from a book of poems by Robert Burns. "Dr. Carter mentioned an omni being responsible for my condition, but refused to share any details pertaining to the incident. What happened?"

"'Twas sad," she admitted quietly. "Some pignut slit the strings on my reticule and you chased him in an effort to retrieve it. That's when the omni swiped you."

It was so odd to hear about himself doing things he didn't remember doing. "Rather heroic of me."

"Actually, here in New York, we call that stupid. A reticule isn't worth one's life. For pity's sake, you tried to dash past a movin' omni, and, well…those maggots drive like a priest on the way to confession. They never stop. In one short breath—" She leaned in and smacked her hands together. *"Bam!"*

He lowered his chin. "Bam. I see. And that is when I awoke in the hospital, yes?"

"No. You were conscious thereafter, though not for very long. I knew somethin' wasn't right. You could hardly move or talk. I stayed with you the whole while after I delivered you into Dr. Carter's care. I even tried visitin' your bed when you regained consciousness, but Dr. Carter wouldn't let me, seein' you and most of the men in the hall were half-naked. So I just called on Dr. Carter's office when I could to ensure you were doin' well."

He searched her face. "What made you repeatedly inquire about me?"

"Hospitals aren't known for their care, Brit, as much as their morgues. I was worried."

"Yes, the care most certainly was lacking. Some patients slept in their own vomit and were rarely cleaned. I assisted them and others whenever I could. Aside from the stench, I couldn't bear watching grown men choking on what little was left of their pride."

She observed him. "How much did Dr. Carter tell you about your condition? Did he talk to you about it at all?"

He shrugged. "Somewhat. He seems to think that when I was flung to the ground, it jarred my brain and affected my ability to recall events."

"Did he mention that Robinson Crusoe isn't really your name?"

He glanced at her, his throat tightening. "No. That he did not."

She shook her head. "I don't understand his so-called medical advice. How are you supposed to assimilate if you aren't given the means to decipher what is and isn't real?"

He set his trembling hands on his knees. Why would Dr. Carter have maliciously allowed him to believe otherwise? "How does he know it isn't my name? It could be. I sense that it is."

"Not accordin' to him. He claims that some of the events you speak of, includin' the name itself, all came out of the pages of a book about a shipwrecked sailor."

September 30, 1659. I, unhappy Robinson Crusoe, having suffered shipwreck, was driven on this desolate island, which I named the Desolate Island of Despair, the rest being swallowed up in the tempestuous sea.

Pushing out an uneasy breath, he tried to force away those misplaced words that never seemed to stop. "What year is it? I never did ask Dr. Carter."

She eyed him. "July of 1830."

Oh, God. He pressed his fingers against his temple, wishing he could shove reality back into it. When would this damnable haze lift? "I cannot be this Robinson. Not given that the year in my head is September of 1659. What in blazes is wrong with me? Why do I have some—some…*book* burned in my head but nothing else? It doesn't make any sense."

She grabbed his hand and shook it. "Try not to rile yourself over it. Give it time. I've no doubt your family will settle you back into your way of life when they come."

He gently clasped his other hand over her small one, basking in its unexpected warmth and comfort. "What if I don't have a family? What will become of me then?"

"Oh, hush. Everyone always has *someone* in their life. Be it family or not." She slipped her hand from his, patting his forearm before setting it back onto her lap. "More than enough time has passed to ensure people are lookin' for you. And if they're lookin', you'd best believe they'll see the newspapers when it goes to print. They'll come for you. I know they will."

Robinson nodded, hoping she was right, because he didn't want to live like this anymore. He felt like a ghost without a gravestone to refer to. "I appreciate you taking me in."

"There's no need to thank me. I'm only puttin' a roof over your head and feedin' you. Anyone can do that for a nickel and a dime."

Money. She would need money, and given her worn boots and frayed bonnet it didn't appear as if she had very much of it to begin with. He pressed a hand against the satchel weighing his inner coat pocket. "I'm willing to give you half of everything I have in return for your generosity."

"I'm not about to take half." She lowered her gaze to his shoulder and leaned in. "But if you'd be willin' to

give me six dollars," she bargained, "I'll see to it that all
of your food and rent is paid for out of my own pocket.
I know six is a lot to ask for, but it would help me fill
the last of my box. I earn more than enough from laundry to cover basic expenses, give or take a quarter. We
won't be eatin' mutton or chops, but porridge, oysters,
yams and the likes I can easily fit on the menu."

Sensing that she wasn't accustomed to asking for
anything, he gently offered, "If you require more than
six dollars, so that we may eat better *and* fill your box,
I should hope you will ask for it."

She smiled, her features brightening. She leaned
back against the wooden bench. "You're beautifully
kind, Robinson, but six dollars is all this woman needs
to buy herself a new life."

He blinked. "You intend to *buy* yourself a new life?
For six dollars? Is that even possible?"

"Of course it's possible." She lowered her voice. "I'm
movin' out west, you see. To Ohio. I've a good friend
who used to be a neighbor of mine—Agnes Meehan,
who moved out that way with her father shortly after my
husband died. She wrote me sayin' there's cheap land to
be had, and if I could find my way out there with fifty
dollars, I could invest in half an acre and work my way
toward a better life. So I've been savin' for that half
acre ever since, and six dollars is about the last of what
I need. That'll put me at sixty. Five for the stagecoach,
five for food and the rest for the land."

She faced the bench opposite them again, staring
out before herself with a dreamy smile still touching
her lips. "I intend to farm that half acre and set a one-

room cabin on it. It won't be much, barely a few logs slapped together on a scrap of land, but it'll be more than enough for me. And just beyond that pile of logs, I'll plant a row of apple trees that'll blossom every spring and bear barrels of fruit. Apples, flowers and freshly overturned earth will scent the air durin' the day, and at night I'll stand outside on *my* land, lookin' up at starry skies, listenin' to the wind."

She released a breathy sigh and half nodded. "I'll be self-made. Not man-made. Though I do plan on marryin' again. The thought of livin' alone depresses me."

Robinson intently observed her, the clatter of the wheels overtaking all sound. God, did he admire the wistful dreaminess in that lilting voice. It made him want everything she had just described, right down to the whistling wind and the apple trees. It held a peaceful and divine purpose found by honest, hard work cradled within a dream and a promise that *something* could be his. Compared to this void writhing within him, telling him that he owned nothing, not a family or a home or a woman of his own, it was paradise in its truest form.

She glanced out the window. "Time sure does flit. The next stop is already ours. Pardon my reach." She leaned forward, setting her bare hand on his thigh to balance herself and reached across him to pull on the rope attached to the driver's leg. "Sometimes these damn drivers claim not to feel the rope. So I make sure they do."

She set her chin and yanked the rope several more times, the faint scent of crisp soap and lye drifting toward him as she swayed against each solid tug.

A familiar shiver of awareness raced through him. That scent. It was so hauntingly familiar. It whispered to him that if he buried himself within that fragrance, he would forever know compassion, comfort and peace.

He instinctively slid his hand to her back, grazing the small hooks on her gown, and pressed her warmth against the side of his body, desperately wanting to touch her. "Georgia?"

She stiffened and glanced up at him, her hand falling away from the rope and drifting down to his thigh. Her lips parted as her shadowed green eyes searched his face. "What is it? Is something wrong? You not feelin' well?"

Art thou afraid to be the same in thine own act and valour as thou art in desire?

Were those *his* words responding to his heart in *this* moment? He didn't know, but something chanted that if he didn't attempt to make this woman his, he'd be missing out on the greatest opportunity he'd ever known as a man.

He drew her closer toward himself, his hands rounding her slim shoulders, and whispered, "I want to kiss you. Can I?"

She let out a shaky breath, the warmth of that mouth grazing against his own. "I'm not very good at kissin'."

Cradling her against the curve of his arm, he pressed her softness against his tensing body. "At least you remember what it's like."

She tilted her lips upward toward his own and smirked. "You're just tryin' to make me feel sorry for you."

"Do you?"

"Oddly, yes. I do feel sorry for you."

"Good." He lowered his lips to hers. Closing his eyes, he savored the warmth of her soft mouth lingering against his own and better molded his lips against that delicate mouth.

Her moist lips parted. Though he wanted to slide his tongue deep into that mouth and ravage it, he didn't know if that was something he was supposed to do, so he lingered, hoping she would take the lead. He could barely breathe.

Her hot velvet tongue instantly slid against his own, grazing his teeth. He bit back his own need to groan, as an ache overwhelmed his entire body. He slowly gave in to circling his tongue against hers, sensing the tongue was more than permissible.

She tasted like spiced…whiskey?

She grabbed hold of the lapels on his coat and dragged him down, down onto her, shifting her entire body beneath his own, until they were both practically hanging off the bench. He tightened his hold on her shoulders and waist and dug his booted heels into the floor of the omni to keep them both from falling.

Pressing herself more savagely against him, she pushed her tongue deeper into his mouth, responding to his tongue so fiercely his heart pounded in disbelief. Entranced by the unexpected passion pouring out of her, he reveled in the way that wet tongue moved so erotically against his own. If *this* were the one and only kiss he were to ever remember as a man, he would honor it with never-ending, glorying pride.

May the lightning of heaven consume me, if I adore thee not to distraction!

Crushing one hand against her bonnet, he slid his other hand down the smooth fabric of her gown, curving it to her firm, corseted waist. He dug the tips of his fingers into the fabric separating them, feeling as if he were racing against his own mind and breath, trying to remain grounded in this incredible reality. He trailed his hand back up toward her breasts, rounding his hand around its softness and weight. His cock swelled from the touch, and the need to rip his clothes apart, in an effort to show her just how divine she was, consumed the last of him. He kissed her harder, frantically digging and grinding his erection into her thigh.

Georgia tightened her lips in an effort to force out his tongue, digging her fingers into his biceps.

Reluctantly breaking their kiss, he dragged her back upright and repositioned her sidesaddle onto his lap. He cradled her for a long moment, her uneven breaths matching his own. It was the first time in nine days he felt like he finally belonged to someone and he swore to himself that he would never let this or her go, lest he be swallowed back into nothingness.

The omni around them swayed to a halt as the driver called out their stop. She shifted to move, but he fiercely held her in place. Reaching up, he trailed the tips of his fingers down past the faded ribbon of her bonnet toward the soft slope of her curving throat. "Take me out west with you," he insisted in a barely composed tone. "I want everything you spoke of. Right down to the wind and the apple trees. I will give you every last nickel in my pocket if you promise to take me with you."

Her eyes widened. She shoved his hand away and scrambled outside of his grasp and off his lap. Stumbling forward and onto her feet, she caught herself against the narrow pathway between the two benches leading to the rear door of the omni. "Whatever do you mean you want my land and my apple trees? We barely know each other. Even worse, you don't even know your name."

He sat up. "You will need someone to build your cabin, till the land and chop timber. I can do that for you. I can."

She gawked at him, then shook her head and frantically arranged her skirts. "No. Don't you be stickin' your hands into my head and playin' with my dreams like that. They're my dreams. You hear? Not yours. *Mine*."

He swallowed, his chest tightening. "I need help, Georgia. I need help if I'm going to rebuild a sense of reality. And I think you're the one to help me do it."

"Stop it," she tossed at him in a harsh tone. "I'm not takin' you with me and I most certainly can't help you in the way you think I can."

"I know you can. I felt it before and after we touched."

She glared at him. "I know what you felt, Brit, and it wasn't *that*. I've got plans and I'm sorry to say this, because I like you, I really do, but my plans don't involve a man who doesn't know his up from his down.

A woman such as myself, who has very little to begin with, needs a grain of security. And you aren't it."

He scrambled to his feet. "But that kiss—"

"I shouldn't have allowed for it. All right? I shouldn't have taken advantage of you. You're not in your right mind and it was wrong of me. Now just...just get off the damn omni before it takes off and we're forced to walk half the night." Throwing open the door, she hurried down the small stairs leading out of the omni and disappeared into the night, leaving him to feel again he belonged to no one and nothing.

CHAPTER FIVE

At Christmas I no more desire a rose
than wish a snow in May's newfangled shows.
  —William Shakespeare, *A Pleasant Conceited*
     Comedie Called, Loues labors loft (1598)

ROBINSON JUMPED OUT AFTER Georgia, his boots thudding against the shadowed dirt road, and slammed the rear door of the omni. The boxed carriage reared forward, its large wheels kicking up dust that bit into his watering eyes. An overwhelming stench of festering sewage penetrated his nostrils.

"Bleed me," he growled, burying the lower half of his face into the crook of his arm in an attempt to block the assaulting stink.

He swung toward Georgia, who was already crossing the wide, dimly lit street. She dodged an oncoming huckster and a peddler cart, disappearing from sight.

He lowered his arm, his heart pounding knowing that his only connection to reality was abandoning him. "Georgia!" He jogged after her, the acrid air crawling down his throat. He swallowed, mentally willing away the sensation of nausea that threatened to heave out his innards. "Do you intend to loathe me for wanting to share in your dream of going west? That hardly seems fair."

Her shadow reappeared on the pavement just outside the dull, yellowing light of a gas lamppost. She paused and glanced back at him, dropping the folds of her skirts. "Your family is waitin' for you, Brit. Try to remember that. Someone is out there sheddin' tears for you, worryin' themselves into a grave whilst you foolishly talk of chasin' a dream that isn't even yours to chase."

Why did he feel as if she was wrong? Why did he feel as if there was no one waiting for him? Not a mother. Not a wife. No one. "'Tis very difficult for me to care about people I can't even remember, be they shedding tears for me or not."

Though he couldn't see her face against the wavering shadows, he could *see* the softening of her rigid stance. She blew out a breath. "I suppose I understand." She waved him over. "Come. We shouldn't linger. Trouble brews in the dark around these parts."

Drawing in the sharpness of the dank evening air, he crossed the dirt road toward her, the lone gas lamp flickering as it unevenly lit the mired path before him.

He scanned the stretching width of the dank street. Cramped wooden buildings loomed in the surrounding darkness, murky-yellow lamps lighting broken windows stuffed with rags and heaven knows what else. Silhouettes of men and women lurked on the streets and hovered in doorways. Others casually lounged on the curb of the pavement in small groups, chuckling and having muted conversations as if respectably sitting around a table to dine.

An old man holding a dented tankard staggered past on an angle, bellowing in an off-key tone, "The devil and me, together we pee, yessiree, the devil and me."

Robinson swallowed against the knot lodged in his throat. Is this where she lived? All of this felt wrong. She didn't belong here amongst these grimy shadows and broken windows stuffed with rags. No wonder she dreamed of apple trees and open fields.

A headache pinched his skull, making him squint in an attempt to fight against his sudden discomfort. He quickened his stride until he paused before her and a doorstep leading into a large two-story building.

Something snorted and darted past his legs, making him jump aside in heart-pounding astonishment. A round, furless creature wobbled down the pavement and into the inky shadows of the night.

He pointed at it. "What the hell was that?"

"A pig," she remarked, lowering her gaze and moving around him. "They're always wanderin' the street lookin' for food. Much like everyone else 'round these parts."

He eyed her. "A pig? In the city?"

She set her chin. "I hate to disappoint you, Brit, but in this ward, pigs are considered highly respectable citizens."

Sensing she was still irked with him, he edged toward her. "If I had known that I would upset you like this, I would have never kissed you. Know that."

She crossed her arms over her chest. "It wasn't your

fault. I willingly gave in to it. I just…I don't want this turnin' into a mess, is all. I've got plans for a better life and I don't want those plans to fall aside, see? I'm not gettin' any younger and the Five Points is agin' me fast."

He dragged in a breath and let it out. It chafed knowing that he was nothing but an inconvenience to her, especially after that kiss. Did she kiss all men like that? "I have no intention to impose upon your plans," he managed.

"Good. It means we'll get along." She gestured toward the doorstep leading into a small building whose sparse windows were lit by warm light peering out from behind lopsided curtains. "Follow me and mind the step."

He lingered as she withdrew a key from a stitched pocket within her gown and opened the entrance door. Waving him into the blurring abyss of a narrow stairwell, she closed the main entrance door behind them.

Grabbing his hand firmly, she guided him into the darkness. "Don't let go."

"I won't." He tightened his hold, fingering her small, callus-roughened hand. It was odd to feel as though he was under *her* protection and mercy.

She gently shook his hand. "Use your other hand to balance yourself against the wall as we go up. There are sixteen stairs. The first always trips everyone up, even me. So mind it."

He bit back a smile, touched by her mothering. After a few blind pats, he found the wall she was referring to and lifted his booted foot, placing it on the first step.

He caught the edge and carefully slid into place. "You do this every night?"

"I have to sleep sometime, don't I?"

"Are there no lamps to make use of?"

"There are, but they're usually dashed out by nine-thirty. We've had too many fires down the street." She tightened her fingers around his hand and tugged him upward. "Can't you go any faster? Raymond was three and fifty the day his heart stopped and he managed to run these stairs up and down in the dark as if he were twenty."

It wasn't much of a compliment having *that* pointed out. Robinson released her hand and hurried up the remaining stairs, boldly taking two at a time in the darkness. Angling past her warmth, he jumped onto the landing with an impressive thud. "*There.* Did Raymond ever skip stairs in the darkness the way I just did?"

"Never mock a dead man who doesn't deserve it." Her hand caught his arm. She tugged him toward the end of what appeared to be a blackened corridor. "There are two floors and four tenements on each floor. Most of the people livin' here are men. Don't know how that came to be, but don't think the worst of me. It's just how it is. Unlike them, I'm fortunate enough to afford my own tenement. Raymond knew the landlord, so I only pay three dollars a month for what could easily be six."

She released his hand and patted his arm. "Stay where you are." There was a *chink* of a key being pushed into a lock and then a *click* and the door creaked open.

Her heels echoed against the floorboards and he

could hear the flint being struck. A glass oil lamp sput-
tered to life, brilliantly illuminating not only her pale
face but a small yellow-wallpapered kitchen one could
easily cross in but three strides. The heavy scent of
starch, lye and soap drifted toward him.

"You'll get used to the smell," she offered conversationally. "It's better than the one outside, to be sure. I
do all of my work in the front room as opposed to the
yard outside, see. That way nothin' gets stolen."

She set the glass lamp onto a wooden table set across
from a brick hearth bearing a cauldron. She loosened
the tie beneath her chin, the blue ribbons cascading in
a flutter to her slim shoulders. She stripped the oval
bonnet from her head with a sigh and glanced down,
neatly retying the ribbon into a perfect bow. Bustling
toward the wall, she leaned over a coal bin and hung
her bonnet gently from a nail positioned next to another
nail that held a faded wooden rosary.

Her thick bundled hair appeared almost brown in the
dim light, with only hints of bright red as she turned
back to the chair and swept up a plaid apron. She affixed it around her waist with three quick movements.

His eyes dropped from her slim shoulders to her
aproned waist. It was like being her husband and peering into a very intimate routine. He rather liked it. It
made him feel as if he were walking into his own home
and into the arms of a woman who was his.

Remembering the way her hot, wet tongue had eagerly moved against his own, he gripped the wood trim
harder to force out any thoughts of wanting her in that

way again. It was obvious she didn't want more of it. Not from him, anyway.

She glanced up and turned toward him. "Are you goin' to stand there and let the world know I'm home? Shut the door."

He cleared his throat and stepped into the small room, shutting the door with a thud. He paused, noting three metal bolts. He gestured toward them. "Do you want me to bolt all three?"

"That's what they're there for, Brit. To keep the world out. Unless your boxing skills are better than mine."

She had a reply for everything. He affixed all of the metal latches into place and turned back toward her. Sensing she was still annoyed with him, he held up both hands in truce. Meeting her gaze, he set them behind his back, locking a hand over a wrist against his spine. "I won't grab for you."

She smiled, pulled out one of the two chairs from beside the small table and gestured toward it. "Sit. I'm over it."

If only he was.

He strode toward the chair, pressing his hands tightly against his back, and sat, causing the chair to creak in protest. It wobbled beneath him. Carefully sliding back into it out of fear he'd break it, he slipped his hands out from behind his back and set them on his knees. He shifted, eyeing the small kitchen, and leaned forward to scan the two other adjoining rooms that light didn't spread into.

She gestured toward one of the small rooms he was looking at. "That there is the closet."

"The closet?"

"Where I sleep."

"Don't you mean the bedchamber?"

She dropped a hand to her side. "Is that what you Brits call it?" She tsked. "You boyos certainly like to make everythin' sound so much fancier than it really is. It's a closet with a straw bed and a trunk. Nothin' more."

He lowered his gaze down to his boots, sensing she didn't particularly like the British. "Where do you want me to sleep?"

She sighed. "You can sleep with me on the bed. There's room and I don't mind."

He glanced up. She was really looking to make him suffer. "I hardly think it wise we share a bed."

"There was no bed on that omni, Robinson, and yet neither of us could keep our hands to ourselves. Between these three small rooms, our bodies are goin' to be rubbin' up against each other quite a bit, so you'd best get used to it."

He feigned a laugh. "I might not physically survive you or this. I'm still a bit astounded by that kiss you gave me. It was remarkable enough for me to want more."

"I'll agree that it was, but you really need to try to keep everythin' buttoned up in those trousers from here on out. If the urge is particularly strong, just ask for some privacy and make use of your hand. All right?"

He shifted his jaw, feeling his body temperature rising. It was like she was a man, not a woman. "I ask that you not talk like that to me, Georgia. I find it unsettling and vulgar coming from your mouth."

She clicked her tongue at him. "I'm a nun compared to all the other women around me, but I'll do my best not to offend." She drifted past him toward the cupboard and pointed toward a corked bottle. "I've got whiskey, if you want it. Came straight from the barrel down the street. 'Tis the best in the ward at a dime a gallon and has enough smoke and bite to make it worth your while."

He let out a low whistle. "In England we call that death."

A giggle escaped her. She turned toward him, tilting her head to one side to better observe him. "Do you remember anythin' about England?"

He paused. "No. Not really."

"Ah, you're better off, I say. You're cursed enough. Now. How about you drink up a good tin of whiskey? It'll help you sleep."

He shook his head. "No. I would rather not. My mind is muddled enough without—"

A resounding thud hit the adjoining wall, sending a tremor throughout the room.

He rose to his feet. "What was that?"

She winced and waved toward the main wall opposite them. "Never you mind John Andrew Malloy over there. He feels the need to entertain the masses every now and then. Just ignore it."

"You mean he's hosting a formal gathering? At this hour?"

She pursed her lips as if he were a complete dolt. "Not quite."

Steady, rhythmic thuds grew more and more pronounced as muffled moans filtered through the wall. "That's it, Georgia. Come on. Let me hear it."

A woman cried out, mingling with those thrusting grunts.

His brows rose as his face and skin prickled with astounded heat. He glanced over at Georgia and gestured toward the wall. "By God. Did he just…say your name? Or did I imagine that?"

She turned and quickly headed over to the cupboard and commenced arranging and rearranging all of her plates, even though they were already arranged.

Apparently, he hadn't imagined it at all.

Rapid, feverish thumps rattled the plates Georgia tried to reorganize. "Take it, Georgia. Take every last—"

A woman gasped against a massive thud that vibrated the floor beneath Robinson's boots. "Now, now, not so hard, John! I'm not running a charity here."

Georgia cringed and swung away, slapping a hand over her mouth.

Robinson's throat tightened as the need to protect her honor descended upon him like a massive wave crashing to the shore. She didn't like it. And neither did he.

Stalking over to the wall, he banged his fist against the plaster, causing it to tremor beneath each hit. *"John Andrew Malloy!"* he boomed, leaning toward the wall and pounding it again. "Unless you want a fist to find its way through this wall and into your skull, I demand you desist using the name of a woman you aren't even with!"

She choked on a laugh, dropping her hand to her side, and swung toward him. "Shush! He'll hear you."

He stepped away from the wall and adjusted his coat in riled agitation. "I hope to God he does. That is vile. You shouldn't have to listen to that. And neither should I."

She groaned and yanked her apron up over her face and head, burying herself in it. "If John comes over here, I'll up and die."

"If John comes over here, *he* is going to up and die."

An anguished moan and one last "Georgia" ripped through the air. Everything soon lulled itself back into silence.

Georgia quietly lingered before the doorless cupboard, her head still buried in her apron. "I'm *never* comin' out knowin' you heard that." She suffocated a giggle. "Not ever, ever, ever."

At least she had a sense of humor about it. "You have to come out sometime."

"No, I don't."

Knowing she was being silly, he edged toward the bolted door and, despite hearing nothing, said in a taunting voice, "I hear footsteps."

She whipped her apron down from her face and gawked at him in exasperation. *"You do not."*

"No. But I got you out, did I not?" He leaned against the bolted door and crossed his arms over his chest, trying to appear indifferent even though he was thoroughly agitated to know some man was yelling out her name in the throes of passion. "How often does he do that to you? And why?"

She rolled her eyes, her smooth cheeks flushing. "He has a bit of a fancy for me."

"*A bit?* He was saying your name."

"Oh, all right, more than a fancy." She glanced toward the wall and lowered her voice, pointing at him. "This doesn't leave the room."

Now, this he had to hear. "I won't say a word."

She heaved out a breath and waved toward the wall. "John Andrew and this redhead from over on Anthony Street started seein' each other about a month ago. I thought it was movin' toward matrimony and was actually quite happy for him. Then I ran into the woman one mornin' whilst gettin' my yams, and she thanked me for the business I was givin' her. I told her I most certainly didn't know what she was talkin' about, and that's when she laughed and told me all about how John Andrew Malloy pays her fifty cents to ride her up the hole he *shouldn't,* all whilst callin' her *Georgia*." She snorted. "I about fainted. But better her than me, I say."

Robinson drew in a ragged breath and let it out. He was going to slaughter this John Andrew Malloy.

A door slammed in the distance beyond, making them both pause. Steady footfalls headed toward them from next door, followed by a knock that vibrated the bolted door he was still leaning against.

"Ey, Georgia!" a man called from the other side. "Open up."

Her eyes widened as she slammed down a reprimanding foot. "Drat you and that mouth, Robinson!"

She hurried toward him, shaking her head, and waved him away with both hands. "Step aside before he chews my door to bits."

"I intend to chew *him* to bits. Pardon me." He whipped toward the door, his chest tightening as he undid the bolts. He was going to scatter the bastard's innards across the entire length of the corridor.

"No." Georgia shoved him away from the door and swung a finger toward the shadowed wall where the lamp didn't reach. "Step into the shadows and put your back against the wall. I don't want him seein' your face."

He squinted at her. "Are you defending this man?"

"No. I'm defendin' *you*." She lowered her voice to a whisper. "John happens to be one of the boys. And the rule around here is not to stir the pot before you've had a chance to put anythin' in it. You don't want him spreadin' rumors and havin' people hunt you down. He's known for it. Now get in the shadows."

He threw up both hands in exasperation and fell against the wall behind him with a thud.

"Don't say a word until I get rid of him." She pointed at him one last time as if that were going to keep him in place, then unbolted the door and swung it open.

His brows rose a fraction at what came into view in the dim light just outside his shadowy hiding spot.

A tall, shirtless youth who looked barely old enough to shave casually leaned against the doorway outside, his smooth, muscled chest and face glistening from the sheen of sex-induced sweat. Wool trousers were crookedly affixed on those narrow hips and his two large feet were as bare as the day he was born. He edged in toward Georgia, long strands of blond hair falling into his eyes. "I've had a long day, Georgia. Don't make it longer by telling me what I can and can't do in me own low closet."

"You're touched in the head, John. *Touched.*" She tapped her forehead with a finger. "I couldn't care less about what you do in your low closet. I just don't want to hear it. You're bein' overly stupid and loud."

The edge of John's mouth lifted. "Just imagine how overly stupid and loud it'd be if it were happening in *your* low closet?"

Georgia set her hands on her hips. "You'd only snap at the first thrust, John. There's barely enough of you as it is."

Robinson bit back an exasperated laugh and shifted against the wall. She certainly knew how to serve up a good tongue.

John paused. "Is that Matthew? Was he the one up and banging on the wall like Fecky the Ninth?" He pushed past Georgia, striding into the room, and jerked to a halt, scanning Robinson. His eyes widened as his sweat-sleeked face flushed all the more. He glanced back over at Georgia. "Who's this prick? And what's he doing in your room?"

Robinson narrowed his gaze and pushed away from the wall, ready to fist the runt back out into the corridor where he belonged.

"Back against the wall, Robinson," Georgia warned, pointing at him. "And don't say a word."

Gritting his teeth, Robinson fell back against the

wall, but held the youth's gaze, challenging him to come at him.

John swiped his hair out of his eyes and leaned toward her, his bare chest rising and falling more steadily. "Christ, Georgia. You can't be trusting men you don't know. Get rid of him. Before I do."

"Don't be playin' all high and mighty, John, whilst you're playin' with your whores loud enough for the whole buildin' to hear." Georgia grabbed the youth by the arm, directing him to the open door. "I've been behind on the rent by a whole dollar forty-five since my reticule was swiped and I'm boardin' him to make up for it, is all. So you needn't be jerkin' your chin at me. I know what I'm doin'." She tried shoving him into the corridor.

John yanked his arm away from her and spun back. "You're doing more than boarding him." He swiped a hand over his face. "You're fecking him for extra money to move west, aren't you?"

She gasped. "I'm *not* feckin' him!"

"Like hell you aren't."

Robinson shook his head from side to side. "Have a little more respect for the woman," he called out from up against the wall he was still sentenced to. "And while you're at it, sir, put on a shirt lest you blind us all with your lack of refinement."

John's eyes widened. "Smite me. He's a fobbing Brit. Sir and all!" Shoving past Georgia, John veered toward him and said through clenched teeth, "You'd best leave lest I bloody you up well enough for your whore of a mother in England to feel it."

Robinson pushed away from the wall, straightening to his full height of six feet four inches, towering well above the boy by a whole head and a half. "I'd like to see you try, little John."

"Get out!" Lunging, John snapped out a clenched fist up toward his face.

Robinson vaulted aside as John's white-knuckled fist smashed into the wall behind him, denting the plaster with a muffled thud that resounded within the room.

"John!" Georgia grabbed John by the waist and dragged him back toward her. "Enough. *Enough!*"

Robinson held out a strained hand in warning, even though what he *really* wanted to do was smash the boy's skull into pieces.

John swatted away Georgia's hands from around his waist and veered back toward him, his lean chest rising and falling against impassioned breaths. "No one makes a whore out of Georgia. No one. Especially not some prick of a Brit."

Holding the youth's gaze, Robinson removed his coat and tossed it toward the chair, readying himself for whatever was about to happen. "The only one making a whore out of Georgia right now is you, John. I suggest you leave. Before she has to witness something she oughtn't."

Georgia grabbed the youth by the arm with both hands and yanked him back, using her own body to maneuver his. "As you can see, John, despite him bein' a Brit, he's a gent who knows how to control his own two fists. Unlike you." Turning him back toward the door, she shoved him out into the corridor. "Now get back to your girl."

"She's not me girl," he tossed back, turning back toward her. "I'm only fecking her to keep meself sane, because living next to you on the hour is like living next to the Garden of Eden. Snakes and all!"

"Don't you worry, this *Eve* is movin' the entire garden west and soon. Good night…*Adam*." Slamming the door, she bolted all three locks.

"Georgia!" The door rattled. "Georgia, please don't do this. I've got two dollars and thirty-four cents saved up. 'Tis yours if you need it and I sure as hell won't ask for spit, in turn. Just don't…don't feck him."

Georgia hit the door with a hard, fast fist, rattling the door. "Is that all you think I'm good for? A bloody feck? Off with you, you knacker, before I tell Matthew to slice you up like custard pie and serve you to the locals!"

There was a mutter as footfalls faded. A door slammed.

"What a vile little maggot," Robinson drawled. "Is *feck* what I think it is?"

Georgia turned and glared at him. "If that were Matthew or any other man, you would have been dead by now. Don't think that because you stand well over six feet that you can talk back to these men. This isn't Broadway where people settle things with a bit of conversation. People here settle for blood. I want you to remember that the next time you mouth off."

He shifted his jaw. "He was disrespecting you and he was disrespecting me."

"Get used to it. It's called life. Sometimes, you've

got to swallow your pride to ensure you don't die." She snatched up the lamp from off the table and disappeared into the adjoining room, momentarily leaving him in shadows.

Robinson swiped an exhausted hand across his face and winced as his fingers scraped against his scab. Seething out a breath, he leaned against the wall. "How old was that bastard, anyway? He looked rather young to be carrying on the way he did."

"He's one and twenty," she called out from within the low closet. She unfolded yellowing linen and spread it onto the straw mattress, smoothing it out. "Not nearly as young as you think. I was eighteen when I became a wife."

He stared at her. "You were rather young."

"Young? Don't be silly. Most girls marry younger to avoid fallin' into the hands of a brothel, and unlike them, I actually married for love. And a fine love it was." She half nodded and turned away, her voice fading as she breathed out, "Even if it didn't last."

Leaning over, she quietly arranged and rearranged the linen on the bed as if not at all pleased with the way it was laying. He sensed she was actually doing it to avoid any further discussion pertaining to her marriage.

He trailed a hand against the uneven plastered wall as he made his way toward her. "So John is one of the boys?"

"That he is. He can read and write now because of them."

"Little good reading and writing has done him. He appears to be deranged."

She glanced back toward him, straightening. "He serves his purpose, pays out his quota from his own weekly earnin's and works on command durin' political campaigns. That's all the boys want and need. And though John sure as hell doesn't show it, for fear other men would snicker, he has a rather soft heart and is always helpin' others. He was initiated into the group barely a year ago, after one of our boys was stabbed to death over at the docks." She huffed out a breath. "What a mess that was."

His brows rose. "So you mean when one of them dies, they up and replace him with another? Don't you find that infinitely disturbing?"

"'Tis no different than a gent's club over on Broadway losin' a member and needin' a new one. I'll have you know there's actually a sizable waitin' list. Half the ward is forever complainin' to Matthew and Coleman that they ought to make the group accommodate more men. Those two thievin' banshees, however, consider any number beyond forty not only financially unmanageable, but unlucky."

"And why is that?"

"Because they're known as the *Forty* Thieves. Not the fifty-six or the eighty-two thieves."

A sensation of odd familiarity trickled through him. He blinked, wondering why he already knew something about these men.

Let us now leave Ali Baba to enjoy the commencement of his good fortune and return to the forty thieves.

Wait.

Wasn't that a story?

One he knew and had read in youth?

In a certain town of Persia lived two brothers, one of whom was named Cassim, the other Ali Baba. As their father, at his death, left them but little property, which they divided equally between them, it might have been expected that their fortunes would be the same; chance, however, ordered it otherwise.

By God. It was indeed a story. Just as *Robinson Crusoe* had been. What the hell was wrong with him? "The Forty Thieves? As in…Ali Baba and the forty thieves?"

Her face brightened. "Yes. Do you know of it?"

"Oddly enough, I do. 'Tis known as *The Arabian Nights' Entertainments*. I must have read it. Because I know of it. The moment you mentioned the Forty Thieves, almost the entire story placed itself into my head."

She paused. "It did?"

He nodded. "This sort of thing happened to me at the hospital, too."

She searched his face for a long moment. "*Robinson Crusoe* is a book. So is *The Arabian Nights' Entertainments*. How very…odd. You appear to remember books. If you can remember some of the books you've read, I imagine you'd be able to remember other things, too. Don't you think?"

He paused. "I suppose."

"Dr. Carter mentioned you were confusin' fiction for fact, which may mean that everythin' you know about yourself isn't necessarily missin'. It may be buried, is all."

"Buried?" he drawled. "Where?"

She shrugged. "I don't know. Isn't it odd you keep rememberin' things that weren't there before? I recommend you spend a bit more time diggin' around in that head of yours. You might be able to remember somethin' of worth."

He leaned forward. "I have been digging, Georgia. Believe me, I have been digging for nine whole days, trying to make sense of it, but the shovel isn't large enough and the dirt is piled rather high. I have *no* understanding as to why my mind can't remember certain things."

He drifted closer toward the doorway, blocking the entrance of the small room she was in. "Let us set aside this talk. It only agitates me. I do, however, want to know more about these men who call themselves the Forty Thieves. Are they dangerous? Do they quarter people and deliver them into a cave full of treasure after a bit of 'Open, sesame'?"

She gave him a withered look. "There's all sorts of black talk about who and what they are, and the boys merrily feed off it, but they're not murderers, Brit. They're rebels of a low status lookin' to lead a better life by providin' one another the sort of things our government has failed to provide, given they're nothin' but Irish and Negro men. When Matthew and Raymond first came to Orange Street, they were set about creatin' a group to shake a fist at the government and reorganize the chaos on the street. Though Raymond died before the group was fully established, Matthew and the boys have been shakin' their fists in his honor ever since.

They're all daft, if you ask me. Matthew thinks he can change the world, though he can barely feed himself."

Rebels of low status rising against corrupted power? He didn't know why, but they sounded like his sort of people. The sort who wanted to rise above what little they had been given. "Men who seek to change the world for the better ought to be admired, Georgia, not mocked."

"Oh, I'm not mockin' him or the others. I'm only mockin' the way they go about it. Matthew forever steals in order to maintain the expense it brings and it's leechin' his morals dry. He's what I call a saint without a name or a halo."

"I'd like to meet this Matthew of yours. I'm rather intrigued by his agenda."

Georgia captured his gaze. "*Intrigued?* What in the name of Beelzebub do you think this is? A penny and a show?" She made her way toward him, shaking her head. "You've *no* understandin' of what it's like to have your knuckles bleed in the name of poverty. You've never had your face spit at and called *black* even though your skin is *white*. Men in this ward, Brit, be they Negro, Jew, Italian or Irish, join in on thievin', not because they want to, but because the world doesn't give them a chance to earn a sliver of their dignity. And just because you don't remember your pretty way of life over on Broadway, it doesn't mean you're suddenly one of us. You'd best remember that every time you get to talkin' about bein' *intrigued*."

Robinson leaned against the frame of the doorway and leveled her with a firm gaze. "Maybe my life wasn't quite as pretty as you think. Maybe I don't remember a goddamn thing about my life, Georgia, because there is absolutely *nothing* of worth to remember."

She blinked rapidly. "Don't say such things lest they come true."

He glared at her, tensing. "Does it matter what I say when you appear to be so intent on insulting me and a life I cannot even remember?"

She lowered her gaze, fingering the edge of her apron. "I'm sorry. I don't mean to be harsh, but Matthew and the boys are as Irish and Negro as they come, and I wanted to warn you of it before you go associatin' with them. They'll gladly take your money and the boots off your feet. That's just how they are. And despite what you think, I'm not one of them." She dropped her hand away from her apron and lifted her gaze to his. "I'm sorry I insulted you."

Touched by her candor, he nodded. "I am genuinely touched, madam, that you care enough to apologize. Thank you."

She half smiled. "There you go with that 'madam' again." She wagged a playful finger. "You'd best not be usin' that around women."

"Oh?" he chided gently. "And why is that?"

"Because every woman in the area will maul you for a chance to hear it. They're used to associatin' with knights of the broom, hoe and shovel, not a gentleman with an impressive face and body to match."

His lips trembled as he fought off a grin. "You find my face and body impressive?"

"Oh, now, don't let it go to your head. 'Tis a warnin'

to ensure you live into old age, is all. Men around here are monstrously territorial when it comes to their women. The wrong look at the wrong woman and you're dead. Try to remember that."

He lifted a brow and thumbed toward the wall. "That would explain John Andrew Malloy over there. Were you and he ever…?"

She glanced off to the side and sighed. "It didn't last. He wasn't lookin' to go west and I wasn't lookin' to be chained to a life full of babes here at the tenement. So I ended it before it got too serious and the poor sop hasn't recovered since."

Jealousy hit hard as he realized she had probably done far more than kiss the man, given the bastard's need to ride whores. The acrid sensation of grudging envy eerily whispered of something he knew all too well. "Did it ever go beyond a kiss?"

She glared at him. "I don't see how it's any of your business."

"Considering I dodged a fist for you, I would say it is. How did you become involved with him and all of these men, anyway? Who are they to you?"

She untied the apron from around her waist and smacked it onto the bed. "Raymond was one of the original founders, when they were still meetin' over on Centre Street. By marryin' Raymond, I married into their way of life, and when he died, I was left with Matthew and Coleman and a group of men who *still* think I'm some queen bee in need of coddlin'. Bastards. I can't wait to be rid of them."

Robinson slowly crossed his arms over his chest and

glanced down at the wood floor beneath his booted feet, feeling himself momentarily drift. That name. Coleman. Where did he know it from? "Who is Coleman?"

"He's a dark, dark soul, that one. After Raymond died, both he and Matthew split all rights to the group and it's been like that since."

Mr. Coleman, your own papers are enough to condemn you.

He glanced up, both brows popping up. "How utterly bizarre. Edward Coleman is the name of an English Catholic courtier who had been hanged, drawn and quartered for treason in 1678. Though, obviously, given the year, it cannot be the same Coleman."

Her eyes jumped up to study his face. "You remember the oddest of things. If only you could remember somethin' we could actually use. You know, like your full name and address? Even the name of your dog would be more helpful than you tossin' out the name of some *Catholic* who's been dead since 1678."

He couldn't help wondering if the only reason she wanted him to remember was so she could collect her money and be rid of him. "I only hope you aren't disillusioning yourself into thinking that my six dollars is going to buy you anything but disappointment."

She squinted at him. "Don't you be talkin' down at me when all but earlier you were wantin' my land and my apple trees."

He set his chin, annoyance digging into him. "'Twas a momentary lapse in judgment I don't intend to replicate."

"Pff. You're only irked because you know I'm right.

Now get into bed, already." Turning toward a cracked mirror on the wall behind her, she slid out pins from her hair. In a single sweep, that heavy mass of pretty, thick hair cascaded past her slim shoulders, swaying against her waist and backside.

He edged back, resisting his own stupid urge to frantically peel away everything and get into bed with her. "I probably shouldn't sleep with you, Georgia."

She lowered her chin. "There's no need to overthink this, Robinson. Beds are used for sleep, too, you know."

He shook his head. "No. If I get into bed with you, sleep will be the last thing on my mind. That I know. Isn't there another place for me to sleep?"

She sighed. "If you want to break your back and share the floor with the roaches, by all means. I don't care. I was tryin' to be hospitable, is all."

Roaches. Oh, that was not good. He knew what those were from his stay at the hospital and could already hear the sound of their wiry feet darting toward him. "I'll sleep in a chair."

She smirked. "We'll see how long that lasts, *Mr. Silver Buttons*. There's a basin full of fresh water on the sideboard there in the front room if you need to wash up. I've got extra chalk and a brush for your teeth, too. As for the privy, it's in the back of the buildin'. Now, good night, Brit."

"Good night," he called as he settled into his chair for a long night. He shifted against the rickety chair, paused and shifted again, unable to get comfortable. This was clearly going to be the beginning of hell.

CHAPTER SIX

*'Tis the common wonder of all men, how among so
many millions of faces, there should be none alike.*
— Thomas Browne, *Religio Medici* (1642)

ODD.

Georgia's eyes fluttered open, thinking she'd heard
her name in the distance. She scrambled up in bed,
dragging the rough linen with her, and blinked, only
to find everything was at a lull. Bright summer light
peered in through the open doorway from the narrow
windows of the front room beyond. Was it morning already?

The entrance door outside the low closet suddenly
jumped against its hinges, making her jump along with
it.

"Georgia Emily!" Matthew bellowed from the other
side. "Open the door. *Now!*"

Robinson's large frame stumbled out of the chair he'd
been sleeping in, his chest heaving from the unexpected
assault on the silence. Glancing toward her through the
open door of the low closet, he paused. "You."

"Yes, me," she assured him, pushing aside the linen.
"You do remember me, I hope."

"All too well." Reaching down toward the chair, he

grabbed up his coat and jerked it up and onto his arms and broad shoulders, covering his shirt and buttonless waistcoat. He glanced toward her, clearing his throat and smoothing his scattered black hair away from his face.

A thundering crack echoed within the room as the door jumped against the bolts again. *"Georgia!"* Matthew boomed from the other side. "Open the door!"

Robinson thumbed toward the door. "I hope to God you aren't letting him in. He doesn't sound friendly."

She stifled a laugh and pulled her homespun nightdress down over her exposed legs, scooting out of bed. "He's not all that bad." She hurried out of the small room.

The door jumped again against all three bolts. *"Georgia!"*

"I heard you the first time!" she belted out, squeezing past Robinson.

Robinson leaned back and snapped up both hands so as not to touch her. "You should get dressed," he gruffly offered, glancing away. "I can see your chemise and corset through that flimsy nightdress of yours."

"'Tis only Matthew. Raymond's boy. I could walk around naked and that man still wouldn't look. Not that I would walk around naked. I'm just sayin'."

Robinson pressed himself farther against the wall and looked up at the ceiling. "Can you pass?"

She purposefully leaned in closer knowing their close proximity was flustering him. It was all too charming. "This may be your only chance of seein' all the goods, Brit. Revel in it." She caught the tip of her tongue with her teeth and playfully poked him in the chest. "Stay where you are and *don't* mouth off, lest we have a repeat of yesterday." Scurrying over to the door in bare feet, she unbolted the latches and cracked it open.

A booted foot shot out, giving her a jolt.

Georgia jumped back as the door flew open and slammed against the wall, shaking her pots in the cupboard. "Was that necessary given that I was already openin' the door?"

Matthew loomed in the doorway, meeting her gaze with a single penetrating coal-black eye. The faded brown leather patch that covered his blind eye had been crookedly affixed against his sun-tinted chestnut hair as if he'd barely remembered to put it on. His frayed linen shirt was still unlaced and he hadn't even bothered to tuck it into his wool trousers.

Georgia held out a hand. "You're overreacting. You know John is still sore about me not takin' him back, so I wouldn't believe a word of anythin' he says."

Matthew lowered his stubbled chin. "If this British *fop* of yours didn't stay the night, then he has nothing to worry about, does he?" He shoved past her and strode into the room. Glancing toward Robinson, he slowly shook his head. "But he *did* stay the night. So he's dead."

Reaching beneath his shirt, Matthew withdrew a pistol from the leather holster sitting on his hips and coolly leveled the pistol at Robinson's head. He cocked it. "Step outside, Brit. I don't want to get blood all over the walls."

"Matthew!" She jumped between him and Robinson, her pulse roaring, and pressed her body protectively against Robinson's frame, widening her stance. "Do you remember the man who was hospitalized for tryin' to reclaim my reticule? The one I told you about? Well, this be him. I'm boardin' him. He promised me six dollars if I'd take him in for the month and you *know* I need the money if I'm ever to move west."

Matthew didn't bother to lower his pistol. Instead, he offered her a blunt, wry stare and angled the muzzle menacingly down at her. "Six dollars for rent? When he can easily board himself down the street for three cents a day? Are you bloody yanking my cacks, Georgia? Hell, for six dollars, *I'd* feck him and take him in."

She narrowed her gaze, not in the least amused. "Whether I'm feckin' him or not is neither your business nor John's." She reached out and pushed the pistol away from her face in disgust. "Look at you. Pointin' a pistol at me like some Quaker on opium out to shoot himself a few Irish. Your father would spit upon your behavior if he saw this. I may be younger than you, Matthew, but I'm still legally your mother and I'm not afraid to take a crop to your head. So leave off. You hear? Leave off and never touch this man or point anythin' at him again, or by Joseph, I'll feck him in front of *you* and *John* and all of Five Points just to shut everyone up!"

Silence pulsed within the room.

Robinson's large hand pressed against the small of her back and curved possessively around the waist of her nightdress, making her heart pound. He dragged her back against the muscled heat of his body, as if he'd been riled by raw pride.

She drew in a shaky breath and let it out, trying not to focus on the fact that her entire backside was now draped against Robinson's entire front side. She reached back and gently pinched his muscled thigh through the smooth fabric of his trousers for being bold enough to actually grope her in front of Matthew's still-pointed pistol.

Matthew sighed and lowered the gun. "What's his name?"

"Robinson Crusoe," she obliged.

Matthew arched a brow. "His name is *Robinson Crusoe?*" He snorted dismissively. "Lest you forget, *Mum,* I grew up with personal tutors and read the damn book in its entirety at an age when you were barely crawling. What's his *real* name?"

She sighed. "He doesn't know his name, Matthew, and hasn't been able to remember much of anythin' since he awoke in the hospital. Dr. Carter is tryin' to locate his family, and I'm givin' him a place to stay and watchin' over him."

Matthew squinted at her with his visible eye, the patch shifting against his cheekbone. "The devil, you say. He can't remember his own born name?"

"No, he can't," she insisted. "Dr. Carter calls it 'memory loss.'"

"Memory *loss?* What the hell is that?"

"I don't know! He just can't remember things."

Matthew squinted at her again. "Can he at least talk? Or did he *conveniently* forget that, too?"

"I can talk, Mr. Milton," Robinson interjected in a chiding tone. "And despite your doubts pertaining to my condition, I assure you, 'tis *extremely* inconvenient being in my own head. I suggest you put the pistol away."

Matthew popped up the pistol and pointed it at Robinson's head on an angle. "I don't do *soft* merely because a man asks me to. Georgia might not have a reputation to uphold, but *I* do."

Georgia jumped forward at the insult, snapping up a rigid fist. "You're about to get cropped!"

Robinson swept out a quick hand, forcing her back and away from Matthew with the length of his muscled arm. "Mr. Milton. Georgia mentioned that you may be in need of funds. I would be more than willing to provide a monetary contribution to bring an end to this hostility."

Georgia lowered her fist and glanced up at Robinson, who intently stared Matthew down, clearly not intimidated by the pistol pointed at his head.

Bravo. It would appear Robinson was far savvier than she'd thought. Matthew, after all, was a walking almshouse willing to set aside *everything* in the name of money.

Matthew lowered his pistol. "Consider me a friend the moment your generosity touches this hand, *Mr. Crusoe.*" Uncocking the pistol with a swift movement, he tucked it back into the leather holster on his hip, burying it beneath his untucked shirt. Matthew swiped his palm against the thigh of his trousers, reached out and shook Robinson's hand. "I've never willingly shook a Brit's paw before, but I'm a man of business first and foremost and providing for my boys *is* my business."

Matthew adjusted his faded leather patch the way he always did when excited about something and casually inquired, "Exactly how much money are we talking here? I need clothes, boots, food, maps, parchments, ink, wax, quills and books. And that's just the short list. Whilst Coleman teaches our men how to better fight, I teach them how to read and write so they can fully understand their rights as is scribed in the United States Constitution. Because my motto is what my father's was—muscle is of little worth if there is no thought behind it. That is how and why Ali Baba dismantled all forty thieves and that is why we call ourselves such."

Robinson let out a whistle. "*That* is not at all what I expected from a group of gallivanting thieves."

Matthew inclined his head. "We only steal when we have to. Which, sadly, is most of the time, given the expense of maintaining and educating forty men." Gesturing toward the wall, Matthew shook his head. "John over there is *still* at the level of reading that would shame a bogtrotter and can't write legibly for shite. I told him just this morn, when he pranced over huffing about you and Georgia, that until he's at a respectable level of education, *no* woman will respect him. Especially Georgia here, who was mentored by my own father. I was barely twenty when I first met her. She was naught more than a scrap he took in after finding her asleep in his coal bin, looking like the dirty angel she still is. At the time, she didn't even know what the hell a quill was for. Now look at her. She outreads me, outwrites me, outwits me and even finds the men around these parts to be so damn stupid, she's heading out west."

Robinson paused and glanced over at her, capturing her gaze. His gray eyes simmered with genuine admiration. "I find her to be utterly remarkable," he admitted huskily.

Her pulse skipped.

Averting his gaze to Matthew, Robinson casually remarked, "Thievery and pistols aside, Mr. Milton, I admire that you seek to educate these men. Without an education, they can't think for themselves, let alone rise above circumstance."

Matthew reached out and thumped him on the back. "I can see why John was all nettles about you. You're a good-looking book and it made him feel like the stale hoecake that he is."

Robinson smirked. "You flatter me. That boy would make *any* man look good."

"Right you are in that, Brit. Right you are in that." Pausing, Matthew held up a bargaining hand between them. "So how about we come to a mutual agreement? For however long you're in these parts, I'll see to it you fall under *my* protection. What does that mean? It means that by the end of this day, every man in this ward, right down to the sweeper, will know that if they touch you, they touch me. And I don't like men touching me. So I most certainly won't like men touching you. Sounds dirty? Believe me, it is."

Pointing at Robinson's face and then sweeping a forefinger over to where Georgia lingered, Matthew tossed out, "Now, whatever the hell *this* is that is going on between the two of you, I don't want to know. But despite my letting the two of you play, don't think that you can dirk this girl's heart, Mr. Crusoe. Because if you do, I'll not only gouge out both of your eyes with my own thumbs, but I'll hand you over to the boys for a *very* long night that will only end when the last drop of your blood streams its way into the gutter. Do you understand?"

Robinson held up both hands. "Blind. Blood. Dead. I understand. There won't be any dirking of her heart. I wasn't planning on it."

Matthew smirked. "He's a smart one, this one."

Georgia crossed her arms. "Certainly smarter than you."

Matthew grudgingly angled back toward Robinson. "Seeing Georgia is getting a full six for putting a roof over your head, I'm asking for an even six myself that will assure you live. Anything less than six would be insulting considering what I'm offering."

Robinson reached into the inner pocket of his coat. "After I give Georgia her due six, I'll give you half of everything I have left. Will that do?"

Georgia gasped and grabbed hold of Robinson's coat from behind, frantically jerking on it. "Don't you be up and givin' him half! You haven't even counted it!"

Robinson glanced back at her from over his broad shoulder and said in an unusually cool tone, "It's only money, Georgia. Now let go of my coat."

She released him and huffed out a breath. "Robinson—"

"Enough." He glared at her and pulled out the leather satchel. "I'm not as mindless as I appear."

Saint Peter save them all. She anxiously rounded him and grabbed hold of Matthew's forearm, shaking it. "Matthew. You shouldn't take half. 'Tis all he has and I've no idea when his family will come."

Matthew held up a hand. "He's the one offering."

"Yes, I know, but he's not in his right mind." She shook her head and glared at Robinson. "Don't give him a penny over six. He's a thief who deserves to be hanged, not coddled."

Robinson ignored her, loosening the string on the leather satchel. He turned toward the table and dumped its contents. A brass fob clattered onto the whitened wood, along with a leather pocketbook. He shook the satchel again, forcing out a folded wad of large paper notes that fluttered out, landing primly atop the pock-etbook.

Seeing all that money on her table was like seeing a mythical creature in the flesh.

Matthew let out a low whistle and veered toward the table.

Robinson spread out all the money with a single sweep of his large hand, pushing aside the fob and the empty pocketbook toward the satchel he'd tossed onto the table.

Leaning against the table, Matthew angled himself toward the pile. "Is this all you have?"

Georgia reached out and punched his arm. "*What?* This isn't enough?"

Robinson lifted the fob and dangled it, letting it sway

from side to side on its chain. "'Tis all I have. Not that I can even remember how any of this came to be in my pocket." Using his other hand, he draped it over his palm, letting the chain unravel over his hand and sway. He fingered the glass front of the watch.

Matthew leaned in with an ear to it. "Do you have a key to wind it?"

"No." Robinson's brows came together as he separated the glass and the watch itself from the gold casing. He brought it closer. "'Tis numbered *365* and reads... *Thomas Hawkins, London*." He glanced up. "London. That must be where I'm from."

Matthew jabbed him. "You think?" Leaning in to better scrutinize the watch, Matthew paused and then reached out, digging the tip of his nail into the metal. He glanced up at Robinson, eyes widening. "Shite. This here isn't painted brass. 'Tis gold. Who the blazes are you? A wealthy merchant of some sort?"

Robinson lowered his gaze to the watch. "If I knew who I was, Mr. Milton, I wouldn't be here handing out dollar bills."

Matthew patted him on the shoulder. "Ah, no worries. I rather like you being here handing out bills. We'll have to get to know each other more, is all. I'm always looking for friends in the upper circles."

Georgia's eyes widened. "Don't you be talkin' to him like that. He's not some politician whose mores you can easily buy with a word and a vote. Get out. Take your damn money and leave, Matthew. Go. *Now*."

"I'm only trying to help, Georgia," Matthew chided as he leaned toward Robinson and gestured to the watch. "Men usually etch their names on the back of a watch to keep them from being pawned. Perhaps yours is on the back. Have you looked?"

Georgia scrambled toward them. "I don't know why I didn't think of that. Is there anythin' etched on it?"

Robinson turned the fob over in his hand, facing its smooth gold back upward. "No." He paused, staring down at it. "I feel like I'm holding the key to a door that refuses to open." Tossing the fob down with a clatter, Robinson glanced back at her, his features tightening. "Did you know how much money I had in the satchel before you gave it to me? Is that why you were panicking about my giving Matthew half?"

She nervously eyed him. "Dr. Carter told me the amount, but I swear to you I never opened it or touched it. I gave it to you the moment you entered the office."

Robinson's brows flickered. "So why did you only ask for six dollars? Knowing I had more to give?"

It was as if the man was astounded to find that she wasn't a thief. "To ask for more than what I need is greed. Somethin' Matthew prides himself on, not I."

Robinson paused and glanced toward the pile again. "Mr. Milton. I cannot give you half."

Matthew shrugged. "All I need is six."

"Good." Robinson fished out several of the notes from the pile, counting them out, one by one, and then folded them together. Turning toward her, he held out the grouped banknotes between bare fingers. "Four and forty dollars to oversee your journey and your land. Take it."

Stunned, Georgia gawked up at him. She hadn't

known such extraordinary generosity and kindness from a man since Raymond gathered her up out of his coal bin and showed her a world of words, patience and respect she never thought possible.

She swallowed and shook her head. "I only need six."

Robinson's eyes softened. "You will need the extra money."

She shook her head again. "I can't take it, Robinson. It's too much."

Matthew snatched the notes from Robinson's hand, stalked over and shoved the money into her hand. Grabbing her hard by the shoulders, he propelled her toward Robinson. "Thank the man, instead of playing all high and mighty. You'll need it given your lofty plans of wanting to play farmer."

Crumbling the bills in her trembling hand, Georgia awkwardly glanced up at Robinson, who still lingered before her expectantly. Bless the man for being her ticket west.

She smiled. "I'm only takin' this, Robinson, because I most likely will need it. Thank you. It means so much to me knowin' that you care."

He inclined his head. "I care more than you think." Turning away, he counted out the rest of the money and divided it again. Gathering up half, he folded them and held it out toward Matthew. "Four and forty, down to the dollar. I have decided to split everything three ways. I think it only fair."

Matthew hesitated. "Are you certain you want to hand over that much?"

Robinson waved it at him. "Take it."

Matthew plucked up the money and stuffed it into his own trouser pocket. "Thank you. I, uh…" He cleared his throat, appearing unusually awkward. "You'll not regret investing so generously in me or the ward."

Robinson crossed his arms over his chest. "I hope not."

Matthew's brows came together. He hesitated, patting his pocket. He glanced over at Georgia and then back over at Robinson. "These notes *are* yours, aren't they?"

"They were in my pocket." Robinson swung toward the banknotes on the table and riffled through all the notes, laying them out. "They appear to be fairly crisp and were all issued by the same bank. So the likelihood is that, yes, they are indeed mine."

Matthew hit his shoulder. "You may not know this, but banks keep records of everything that goes in and out of their vaults. If I take these here notes over to the bank that issued them, they might be able to trace their origin, which could give us a name. Maybe even your name."

Robinson glanced toward him. "You would do that for me?"

"Of course. Consider it an extra thank-you for your unexpected generosity toward me and Georgia." Matthew swiveled back toward her and smacked his hands together. "Four and forty in my pocket and I didn't have to use a pistol or a fist. I like him."

She rolled her eyes. "Could you drop off some clothes for him later today? He's only got what he's wearin'."

"Will do, luv. Will do." Matthew strode toward the door, stepped out and enthusiastically slammed the door behind himself, his footfalls disappearing with a pounding dash down the stairs.

Georgia met Robinson's gaze and slowly shook her head from side to side. "Givin' Matthew such a profane amount of money is only encouragin' him to be an even bigger leech than he already is. You do realize that, don't you?"

Robinson turned away and gathered his money, neatly tucking everything back into the leather pocketbook. "Better to pay a leech in coin than in blood." Still keeping his broad back to her, he dragged over the fob and set it onto the leather pocketbook and asked in a grudging tone, "Why do you hate me?"

Georgia blinked in astonishment. Tightening her hold on the banknotes in her palm, she wandered over to where he stood, lingering behind him. "I don't hate you." She leaned toward him and touched his arm with her other hand. "Why would you say such a thing?"

His muscles hardened beneath her fingers as he fully turned toward her, his body grazing her. He purposefully pressed himself closer, as if to physically intimidate her, and lowered his gaze to hers. "Because your tone isn't always as warm as I wish it to be. Do you even like me?"

He was so endearingly forward and real. It made her soul want to melt like butter in a pan. She softened her tone. "I do like you, Robinson."

He eyed her. "You do?"

"Of course I do."

He held her gaze. "Do you like me enough to kiss me again?"

She bit back a smile. "I like you well enough to kiss you on the cheek. Will that do?"

"No. I want you to kiss me on the mouth."

"I'll kiss you on the cheek and then we can decide if there's room for more. Take it or leave it."

He hesitated, then leaned down toward her, offering his good cheek. "Fine."

Lifting herself on her bare toes, she grabbed hold of his linen shirt to balance herself and touched her lips to the warmth of his cheek, the stubbled, unshaven hairs rasping against her own skin. She kissed that cheek softly, only to kiss it again and again, finding herself slowly giving in to wanting so much more of him and that tender warmth. Sliding her hands up to his solid shoulders, she kissed his cheek again.

His hand quickly encircled her waist, his broad chest rising and falling more notably against her own as he dragged the heat of his moist lips across her entire cheek, guiding them down toward her lips.

Georgia half closed her eyes and leaned heavily against him, unable to breathe against the feel of his tensing muscles. She fought the urge to seize that mouth that lingered so close to her own. She also fought from raking her own fingers down toward the flap of his trousers, dragging up her skirts and riding him there against the table just to know what it would feel like. She doubted he'd resist, but as lost as he was in that head of his, the last thing she wanted to do was take advantage of him.

"Do it," he murmured against her skin. His tongue darted out and erotically traced her lips with its wet warmth.

Her stomach flipped, realizing he was in tune with her thoughts. She released his shirt and scrambled away and out of his hold. "We shouldn't."

He leaned heavily against the table, causing it to creak and sway beneath his weight, and gripped the edges, turning his knuckles white. The thick line of his erection was visible against the flap of his trousers. "Why not? Am I not attractive enough?"

Only a man who had knocked out every last thought from his head would require an explanation as to *why* they shouldn't bend to lust. She quickly held up the folded banknotes. "I ought to put this away."

He leveled her with a heated stare. "You didn't answer my question. Do you not find me attractive?"

"We're gettin' too involved, Robinson. All right? It isn't that I don't find you attractive—I do, believe me—it's just that we don't even know who you are and I'm rather worried this won't end well for either of us." She turned away and hurried into the front room.

Though she could have easily stripped him and let what boiled between them explode, she knew nothing good would come of it. Men of wealth didn't marry penniless girls from the Five Points. They only ever fecked them. That much she knew, even if *he* didn't. And though she had no qualms of submitting to this bubbling desire coiling within her, for she was no prim virgin, she sensed far more than her body was going to get fecked. Her dream of owning land and being a self-made woman would be ruined. What if she ended up pregnant?

Hurrying over to the patched wool curtains, she pulled each across the set of three windows facing the street, dulling the bright morning light spilling into the room.

Robinson strode into the front room and crossed his arms over his chest, leaning against the farthest wall. "What are you doing?"

"Ensurin' no one sees where I keep my money." She wandered over to the wall she had tacked from ceiling to floor with posters and handbills Raymond had gathered throughout the years from political rallies. She never cared for male politics but the posters and handbills had proven useful, for they hid all the holes in the walls.

She paused before a slogan poster that read *True Democrats Meet Here.* She glanced back at Robinson and intoned, "Open, sesame."

Turning back, she untacked the bottom of the poster from the wall. She leaned in. Reaching into the jagged four-inch hole in the plaster of the wall, between protruding thin wood lattices, she patted her way down and to the right until her fingers grazed her box.

Grasping it, she carefully angled it so as not to let the contents spill and pulled the carved wooden box up and out of the wall. She brushed off the dust from the posy-engraved box. Lifting the lid, she tucked in the last of what she would need atop those pennies, dimes, nickels, quarters and folded banknotes.

She pressed the lid back onto it, smoothing her hand

over it with genuine pride, knowing she had at long last achieved what she never thought possible. She had a full ninety-eight dollars and ninety-six cents thanks to Robinson, when she'd needed only sixty to head west and claim her half acre.

She smiled, fingering the box to ensure it was real. "My father gave this box to me. 'Twas like he knew I'd be fillin' it with a dream he'd never be able to be a part of."

A large hand touched her lower back, making her jump. She glanced back at Robinson from over her shoulder, realizing he'd been standing behind her all along.

He pushed away her long, unbound hair over her shoulder, causing her skin to frill from the graze of his fingertips. His eyes trailed down toward the box in her hands. "What happened to your father?" he inquired in a soft voice that made her want to turn and rest her head against his shoulder.

Shifting toward him, she lowered her eyes to the box, pressing its smoothed edge against her stomach. Her throat tightened. She rarely spoke about her father anymore. "I'll never know."

Robinson slid his arm around her and pulled her closer against his muscled warmth. "Forgive me. You needn't feel obliged to tell me anything about him."

"No. I want to. I feel like I'm honorin' him when I do." She leaned against him. "Da worked over at the docks paintin' ships and haulin' crates since I was old enough to remember. He never missed a day of work. Not even when he was sick. A day's wage meant more to him than his health, no matter how much I nagged him about it. On that fifth of June, he pinched my cheek the way he did every morn before leavin' to work, and insisted that after I sold all of my matches, that I stay away from the boys and make turnip soup for the both of us. So I went about my day and, by the end of it, made soup, filled his bowl for supper and set a spoon beside it at exactly a quarter to five the way I always did."

Fingering the box still in her hands, she swallowed. "I sat there waitin' two hours. It was so unlike him. He was always punctual in everythin' he did." She swallowed again. "So I went over to the docks lookin' for him. All the men were still there, includin' the foreman. They claimed he'd never even showed up for work that mornin'. 'Twas the first in thirteen years. I panicked and took it straight to the watch, knowin' somethin' wasn't right. They were useless and only called me in to identify bodies that never belonged to him. Bein' a mere fifteen with barely eighty-two cents in a jar, I took to sellin' as many bundled matches as I could, prayin' on my rosary he'd come back." Tears rimmed her eyes, remembering those nights spent cradling her father's clothes unable to breathe or think.

Robinson rubbed her back soothingly, his large hand gently gliding up and down. "So what…happened?"

She let out a shaky breath, nestling her cheek against his chest. "He never did come back and his body was never found. That's when the landlord started pesterin' me for the rent. I asked him for a means to find work, seein' I didn't have the money." She shook her head in disgust. "He only unbuttoned his trousers and asked if I was a virgin. I bloody took off without even gatherin' my clothes, knowin' how it would end."

She drew in another breath, remembering that soundless night she'd spent in a coal bin tucked out of sight, expecting someone to crawl out of the darkness and rape and kill her. "Da, damn him, always taught me to believe in the best. Even when there was no best. I tried to honor him through all of it by keepin' my chin up. I really did. I was fortunate Raymond took me in. Very fortunate."

Tears blinded her. She choked back a sob and buried her face against Robinson's chest, hot tears trailing down her cheeks. "Sometimes…I still imagine that Da had actually gone out west himself to start life anew and maybe I'll find him when I get out there. 'Tis better than imaginin' him sliced up in some ditch outside the city without the dignity of bein' buried by his own daughter."

"Oh, Georgia," Robinson whispered brokenly.

She sniffed, freed a hand from the box and poked his chest. "And that's why we've got to get you back to your family. Whether you remember them or not, they're sufferin' all the same. And you don't want that for them. They deserve to have you back. I know I'd want you back if you were mine."

Robinson's hands trailed up her back, curving around her shoulders, and found their way up and into her unbound hair. Cradling her moist cheeks with his palms, his thumbs brushed away the tears still rimming her eyes. He tilted her face upward toward him.

Through blurred vision, she saw her own pain reflected in that rugged face, as if he himself had endured everything she had just shared. It made her cry even more, for it was the first time in years since anyone, aside from her dear Raymond, had so genuinely acknowledged her pain. Though she always tried to be as hard as steel to the world, sometimes a girl couldn't give that tough upper lip and pretend it didn't hurt. Especially when it *did* hurt.

Robinson kissed her forehead several times, easing her back into a sense of calm. "I vow to you, Georgia," he murmured, "you will never find yourself in a coal bin or at the hands of vile men seeking to rip away your honor. Not whilst I breathe."

She closed her eyes, pushing out the last of the tears, and swallowed his words whole. The last wretched pinch of the past faded as he continued to graze kisses against her forehead.

She tightened her hold on the box nestled between them and slid her arm around his waist, not wanting to let go.

After delivering one last lingering kiss to her forehead, Robinson released her and stepped back, allowing her arm to slip from his waist.

Georgia lingered with her eyes still closed and made a haunting wish upon her soul. It was a dark and incredibly selfish wish that sought to take back everything that was ever taken from her. She wished that this remarkable man was as alone in the world as she was and that he would never remember who he was or what had once been. That way, she could be his equal, without him or his circle judging her, and they could move west and take on that half acre of land together. Oh, wouldn't that be something.

CHAPTER SEVEN

*If you have great talents, industry will improve
them. If you have but moderate abilities,
industry will supply their deficiency.*
—Joshua Reynolds, Discourse to Students of the
Royal Academy (11 December 1769)

ROBINSON AT LONG LAST understood how this red-haired
rose had grown its thorn. That thorn had sprouted out
of misfortune and self-sustained pride, trying to pierce
anything that dared touch its delicate petals. Though
he didn't want to release the softness of that pale, tear-
streaked face, he knew it was best to step away, lest he
kiss more than her lips.

Gently releasing her face, he stepped outside of her
embrace, even though he still desperately wanted to
cradle away the pain she had endured at the hands of
despicable fate. With each passing breath, he was beginning to realize that he had nothing to offer this woman
aside from mere words and physical touch. This incredible woman deserved a man in full possession of his
wits, who knew where he stood in the world.

She lingered before him, her long, unbound hair
splayed in waves across her slim shoulders. The scoop
of her nightdress revealed the pale curve of her neck

and hinted at the dip of those small breasts that were hidden beneath that plain nightdress. Her eyes were still dreamily closed, hands still clutching her box.

He took another step back, digging his palms into his hips in an effort to keep himself from stepping back toward her. With but a few tears, the woman had made him realize just how utterly helpless he was in his damn condition.

When she at long last awoke from her reverie, her green eyes met his. Though they were still tear-glossed, there was an unexpected new vivid heat and softness radiating from them.

He swallowed and didn't know what he was supposed to say or do in response to what he was seeing in those eyes. All he knew was that something intimate had been unleashed between them and nothing would ever be the same.

She quickly turned back to the wall and lifted the poster, pushing the box back down into the hole from whence it came. Carefully, she tacked the poster back into place, then turned back to him and set her chin, resuming that seizing-the-world-by-the-throat facade. "Well, enough with the tears and the gossip. I've got hours of laundry and I've yet to knot my hair and dress."

He paused. "Do you require assistance?" He held up both hands. "These are yours to do with as you please." He lifted a brow. "Within reason, or we might not get anything done."

She smirked and angled a hip toward him. "Whilst

I appreciate the offer, I highly doubt you'd be able to stomach *my* work."

He lowered his hands and tauntingly stared. "Give me the chance to prove you wrong."

She paused. "You're really lookin' to help?"

"I wouldn't have offered otherwise, Georgia."

"All right. Can you bring up water from the pump just down the street? The washbasin is already full. I'll just need ten buckets for the rinsin' basin."

"Done."

She grinned and pointed at him. "You're glorious."

He set a hand on his chest and offered a half bow. "I try. I'll set to work. Where can I find the pump?"

She pointed toward the curtain-drawn windows, swinging her hand right. "When you leave the tenement, turn right. The pump will be three blocks down, set within an enclosed alley on your right. Whatever you do, don't leave Orange Street. Matthew's jurisdiction changes from street to street, so you're better off not wanderin'."

"Yes, madam. Might I ask where the pail is?"

She gestured toward a dented tin pail tucked beside two massive basins that sat on unevenly nailed wooden stands. Eight wool sacks, which were all filled to tipping with male clothing, were piled against the wall.

He cringed at seeing those sacks. He didn't know much about laundry but that looked like a tremendous amount of work.

He strode toward the pail. "Once I bring all the water, I'll assist you with everything else." Leaning over, he swiped it up by the bent handle.

"Thank you. The day will be warm with the sun out the way it is." She pointed. "You ought to remove your coat and waistcoat. And while you're at it, drape it over the washin' basin. I'll launder both given the hospital never did."

"I appreciate that. Thank you." Robinson set the pail down again and stripped his coat and buttonless waistcoat, draping both across the large basin. Rolling each long linen sleeve up to his elbow, he slowly turned back toward the pail.

Robinson paused and heatedly watched Georgia sashay out of the front room and into the kitchen. Her hands casually gathered up and bundled her long hair, knotting it into place. Narrow but shapely hips swayed and shifted beneath her frayed nightdress as she disappeared into the closet beyond and took to folding the rumpled linen on the straw bed. All the while she hummed a melodious ditty as if life were glorious now that he was fetching her ten pails of water.

His jaw and every single last muscle in his body tightened as he continued to watch her with a yearning that almost choked him. How he wanted to replace that flash of a stranger's nakedness still lingering in his head with *her*. All he'd need do was stride over to that closet, grab her, shove up that nightdress and pound his lust into her and make it real.

He swallowed and glanced away, lest he actually do it. It appeared he was done for. Because he not only wanted to pound his very body and soul into her, he wanted to see that woman every single goddamn morning for the rest of his life.

He blew out a breath and snatched up the empty pail. Angling into the kitchen, he reached out and opened the entrance door.

"You should eat somethin' along the way," Georgia called out from the closet, pulling out a gown from an open trunk. "I've no doubt you're hungry. There's a jar with my food allowance in the cupboard beneath my bonnet and rosary. Two nickels ought to be more than enough. Have at it. Nobody will be able to give you change for full dollars here."

Robinson grinned at the thought of food and swiveled back toward the cupboard. "I will most certainly have at it. I'm famished." Passing the closet, he glimpsed her stripping her nightdress, those ivory limbs catching the corner of his eye.

His grin vanished as he averted his gaze with the snap of his chin toward his shoulder. Jogging over to the glass jar, he dug a hand into it and fished out two nickels with a scraping *tink* from the pile of coins covering the bottom. He dropped the coins into his right trouser pocket and stalked back over to the door, keeping his gaze affixed straight ahead and chanting to himself not to stray from his set plan to leave.

"I suggest you buy a baked yam off Martha," she called out again. "It's on the way to the pump and will melt your tongue off. Just tell her I sent you and she'll only charge a penny."

"Will do." Jumping out, he slammed the door behind him and momentarily leaned against it, bringing the pail against his knees. He was going to have to talk to Georgia about setting more boundaries. He couldn't have her stripping in front of him like that. Not unless she wanted him between her thighs. He hissed out a breath and pushed away from the door.

Rounding to the narrow staircase that was lit by a dirty lone window pouring in skewed sunlight from above, he pounded his way down the oak stairs. He strode along the ashen passageway and out the entrance door that had been left open, illuminating a brightly lit dirt street filled with carts, horses, men, women and children hustling by. The stench that had assaulted him last night slammed against his nostrils again, taunting him to gag. He tightened his hold on the pail and swallowed back nausea, chanting to himself that if Georgia could survive breathing in this air, so could he.

Charging out of the tenement and into the open, wide street, he veered right and into the boisterous crowds of shouting voices. He trailed past rows and rows of cracked, dirty windows and small, narrow doors leading into grocer and junk shops and other tenements. Most of the doors he passed appeared to have been smeared with greening black sludge that had been swiped off either people's boots, their asses or a horse's ass, or…all of the above. He decided it was best to stay closer to the street itself as opposed to those doors and windows.

The heat of the sun pierced through the blue sky, pulsing against the side of his shoulder, as it penetrated the linen of his shirt and his skin beneath. Each booted step he took made him realize he was going to be mopping up his own sweat within minutes.

He wrinkled his nose and dodged an incredibly large

pile of rotting cabbage and hay that had been mashed into horse dung. It was obvious where all the smells were coming from.

Robinson eventually paused on the corner of a looming intersection where two wide streets crossed. Carts and horses pushed through throngs of dust and sweat-covered people who were shouting out their wares and their business. He glanced over toward a lonely-looking cart set against one of the buildings beside him.

A short, dark-skinned woman with razzed, curly black hair that had all been tucked into a small straw bonnet leaned against a wooden cart whose crooked sign had been scrawled with the unevenly painted words *Baked Yams*.

He'd found his first destination: breakfast. Thank God.

Walking over to her cart, the sweet sugary scent of whatever she was selling momentarily pushed out the stench of the street and made him realize he was not only hungry but damn well starving. He leaned toward the woman, who had yet to notice him. "Martha, I presume? Good morning. Georgia said I should visit if I wanted my tongue melted off. So here I am."

She grinned, her teeth shockingly white against her dark skin. Leaning toward him, she scanned the length of him from boot to face. "You's a good-looking white boy."

He eyed her, feeling his own face blooming with heat at the unexpected compliment. He cleared his throat. "Uh, thank you."

"Oooh, and shy, too! Not many of those 'round here."

Martha chuckled and bustled around the cart toward him, wiping her hands on her apron. Waving toward the small pile of odd-shaped, melted-looking brown tubes, she said, "Pick yourself a fat one."

He visually probed the pile and pointed to the largest one hidden against the tin platter set atop the cart. "That one there looks friendly enough."

Grabbing up a fork, she stabbed the one he had pointed out and swept it upright, holding the yam out toward him. "A penny. Seeing you know Georgia."

He grinned and took the fork from her. Setting down his pail, he dug into his pocket and pulled out a nickel. He held it out and carefully detached the warm yam from the prongs.

She plucked the coin from his fingers, stabbing the fork back into one of the yams in her cart, and pulled away the collar of her gown, revealing a hidden leather satchel tied around her neck. She dropped the nickel into it and then dug into another satchel hidden beneath her apron. Pulling out a handful of pennies, she handed him back four and winked. "Be sure to come on back now."

He stuffed the pennies into his pocket and swiped up the pail. Leaning toward her, he smiled. "If these yams are any good, madam, you will be seeing me on the hour."

She laughed, reached out and smacked his backside hard.

He jumped in astonishment and dodged past the cart before she took it into her head to do it again. When he had set enough of a distance between him and backside-smacking Martha, he slowed and hesitantly brought the odd-looking food into his mouth. He bit into its mushy softness, the sweet warmth coating his tongue like sugar and molasses. He groaned in amazement, almost falling over to the wall beside him. It was the best thing he'd eaten since waking up in the hospital. When he was done getting all of Georgia's water, he was *definitely* going back for more and didn't care how many times his backside got smacked for it.

A scrawny girl with dirty bare feet and unkempt blond hair, wearing a lopsided sooty gown, darted in front of him. She held up an unraveling wicker basket filled with bundled matches. "A cent a piece, suh," she pleaded, craning her thin neck all the way back to stare up at him.

He shoved the remaining yam into his mouth and chewed it, slowly shaking his head from side to side as those big blue eyes begged in a way no words could. He held up a finger and lowered himself to a knee. Swallowing the last of the yam, he smiled. "A cent a piece, you say?"

She nodded, pressing her lips together.

So much for the rest of his breakfast. Digging into his pocket, he scooped out all he had and presented it with an open palm. "If you can count how much I have in this here hand, the sale is yours."

She eyed him and quickly leaned toward his open palm, her thin brows coming together. With a tiny dirt-encrusted finger she pointed to each and every coin and mouthed the amount to herself. Upon finishing, she glanced up and announced, "Nine cents."

He grinned, genuinely impressed. "Very good. You appear to be a woman of business. Now hold out your hand."

She popped out a bare, cupped hand, staring at it with intent. Trying to keep a straight face, he placed each coin into it, one by one by one, to add to the drama of her sale.

"There you are," he announced. "*Nine* cents."

Shoving it into the pocket of her stained apron, she commenced industriously plucking up bundles of matches for the amount he'd paid for.

"I only need one," he provided.

She glanced up, dropping all the bundles back into her basket. "You want your eight cents back, suh?"

He shook his head, still smiling. "No. I only need one bundle of matches, but you earned an extra *eight* cents for being so impressive with your counting."

She grinned, exposing two missing front teeth, and promptly held out his single bundle. "You speak all gentlemanly like."

He leaned down toward her, slipping the bundle from her bare fingers. "That is because I *am* a gentleman. It was a pleasure doing business with you, miss."

"And you, suh." She bobbed a curtsy and dodged around him, disappearing.

He straightened, swiping up his pail, and tucked the bundle of matches into his now-empty pocket. It was money well spent. He strode down the remaining stretch of the street until he reached a pump that was tucked in a side alley to his right, and paused.

A long line of white, black and mulatto women in

bonnets and aprons lingered patiently with their pails, waiting for an older black woman to finish filling the pail that was set below the spigot. Drawing closer, he realized that he was the only man with a pail.

The elderly black woman paused to swipe her brow with her heavily stained apron. She heaved out a breath and resumed pumping with trembling strokes. That quaking, thin arm and water-spattered wool gown bespoke of the several visits she'd already made.

Refusing to watch the woman suffer, he quickly strode past the long line of women, set his pail down beside the pump with a *clang* and rounded the old woman. "Allow me. Please."

She glanced up, releasing the wooden handle, and blinked up at him past loosened strands of white, frizzy curling hair falling out her lopsided bonnet. Her gaunt face was heavily scarred with indentations similar to that of a whip, making those large black eyes and the whites around them all the more haunting. Stale sweat and bitter mulled wine drifted off her skin. 'Twas obvious this poor weathered and scarred face had seen very little kindness in her life.

He smiled assuredly, sensing she didn't trust him, and reached out for the handle to demonstrate. "I only wish to assist you, madam."

She edged back, step by step, eyeing the pump until she had left him with enough room for him to take her place.

Grabbing hold of the handle with his right hand, he pulled it up and pushed down hard, past the resistance, spraying cold water out and into the rusty pail. In three more solid pumps, it was full. He reached down, lifted the heavy pail and held it out for her. "There you are."

She hurried toward him. Hefting the pail out of his hands and into her own, she paused and blurted, "Your motha done raised yah right, suh. Bless yah and bless her." She nodded in agreement with herself, turned and waddled away, heading back toward the street.

Robinson grinned, watching the old woman waddle away. His mother, whoever she was, did indeed raise him right if he was able to *still* remember how to be a gentleman. It gave him a heaping measure of hope that perhaps Georgia was right. Perhaps someone, maybe even this mother of his, *was* out there missing him.

Swinging back to sweep up his pail, he paused, his fingertips outstretched in midair. The long line of lingering women holding their empty pails had moved notably closer to him, some whispering to others from behind bare hands. Others even leaned over and stood up on their booted toes to get a better look at him past all the other bonnets.

They behaved as if they'd never seen a man before. "Good morning, ladies," he offered in an apologetic tone. "I'm not veering to the front of the line. I was just—"

"No worries. We're much obliged, to be sure. You must be new 'round these parts." A young brunette with plump breasts bustled toward him, kicking up her dragging plaid skirts, and set her pail beneath the spigot of the pump. She stepped back and away, smoothing her hands against her dusty skirts, and smiled as if he'd already offered to fill her bucket.

He hesitated. Not wanting to be rude given that she clearly thought he had offered, he turned back to the pump. Grabbing hold of the wooden handle, he asked, "Might I be of service to you, madam?"

She grinned, wringing her hands. "You'd be the first."

"Hopefully not the last." He glanced around the small alley filled with women. "Where are all the men in this town, anyway? They should all be out here saving your hands."

A wave of giggles erupted.

He blinked. Did they not think he was being serious? Though if all the men around these parts were anything like John and Matthew, it wasn't any wonder these poor women were out pumping their own water.

After he filled the pail, the young brunette hurried forward to lift it, momentarily lingering before him. Meeting his gaze with wistful large brown eyes, she offered, "I live just down the street at 31 with my mum. She's hoping I'll marry soon. I've been looking for a man, but findin' one worth keepin' is hard to come by in these parts." She paused and added, "I make the best ash-pones in town. You ought to come by sometime."

"Ah." He really had *no* idea what an ash-pone was, but clearly her invitation was supposed to be a thank-you, tossed in with a calling card, with a little bit of innuendo and possibly a marriage proposal. He inclined his head as politely as he knew how. "I am already spoken for by a beautiful lady I hope to make mine, but I appreciate the offer all the same. Have a good day."

As she departed, a pretty mulatto woman with stunning blue eyes hurried forward from the front of the line, setting her pail with a loud *clang* beneath the spigot. She set her chin, placing both caramel-colored hands on curvaceous hips. "And I thought there wasn't a damn gent left in this pig-infested ward. Amen for you, suh. Amen."

He laughed and grabbed hold of the handle again. It appeared Georgia was not going to be getting her water anytime soon. But then again…this could be a good thing. For maybe, just maybe, if he flexed his muscles long enough, Georgia would come hunting him down and he could take advantage of his popularity at the water pump by making her realize that he *could* be useful to a woman, after all, even if he were nameless.

CHAPTER EIGHT

*"You must sit down," says Love, "and taste my
meat."*
So I did sit and eat.

—George Herbert,
The Temple, "Love (III)" (1633)

THE SUN HAD ALREADY SHIFTED across the sky, casting
a change of light in the small front room that made
Georgia pause from scrubbing a bundled shirt. Dropping the shirt back into the soapy water, which had
long turned gray, she shook off water from her puckered hands and wiped them against her apron, turning
toward the empty kitchen and the quiet entrance door.

It was certainly taking Robinson an unusually long
time to bring back *one* pail of water. More than an hour
must have already passed. She hurried to the door, praying nothing had happened. Snatching her key off the
table, she opened the door and latched it shut with a tug
and a quick turn.

Tucking the key into her apron, she gathered her
calico skirts and descended the stairs, jogging through
the main entrance door and out into the street. She
paused and glanced down toward the direction of the
pump, squinting against the heat of the bright sun.

Through the bustling haze of dust, crowds, carts, horses and hucksters, she couldn't see a thing.

Gathering her skirts, she dodged people until she finally made it to Martha's yam cart. She skidded to a halt and grabbed hold of Martha's arm, drawing the old woman toward herself. "Martha. Did a tall, dark-haired gent with bruises and scrapes on his face buy anythin' from you this past hour? I sent him your way."

Martha's round face brightened. "That man sure as hell was tastier than anything I had to sell."

A breath escaped her. "Where did he go?"

Martha swept her roughened black hand down the street. "That way. Had a pail with him, too."

Georgia squeezed her arm. "Thank you, Martha."

She darted past the cart, gathering her skirts, and went back to dodging people on the pavement, praying that Robinson was still at the pump and that the line was merely longer than usual due to the blistery heat. Sweat pierced her face against the pulsing sun as she pushed her legs faster. Coming to the small alley, she jerked to a halt and scanned a long line of almost three dozen women.

She paused.

A man labored at the pump. Strands of his black hair fell in and out of his eyes with each downward thrust of a bulking muscled arm that stretched against the clinging wet linen of a snowy white shirt randomly stained with coffee.

It was Robinson. Apparently, he had just gotten to the pump. Thank goodness.

Robinson paused and then gestured rather grandly

toward the pail, offering it to some woman in a straw bonnet.

Georgia blinked as the woman leaned toward him and enthusiastically said something that made his mouth quirk, before she turned and teetered off with the weight of the bucket he had filled.

Another young woman in patched wool skirts scurried forward and set another empty pail beneath the pump. She stepped aside, lingering with pinched lips that bespoke of barely restrained anticipation.

Grabbing hold of the wood handle yet again, Robinson lifted and pushed it down with an anguished wince, forcing water out from the iron spigot and into the pail with a single gush.

Georgia snapped her gaze toward the long line of women dreamily watching him as if he were an unusually pretty gown on display in a shop window. Her lips parted in astonishment.

No wonder he hadn't come back!

Shaking her head, she moved past the line of women. Rounding her way toward the side of the pump, she crossed her arms over her breasts and watched in mingled amusement and adoration as Robinson's bulking arm flexed against his sprayed, water-dampened shirt. His linen shirt clung and outlined not only his impressive arms, but those broad shoulders and solid chest. Much like all the other women, she could have easily stood there watching him all day. Only she still had that darn laundry to do.

"Mr. Robinson Crusoe," she singsonged when he still hadn't noticed her. "Whatever are you doin'?"

He glanced up, midpump, his flushed, unshaven face reappearing. His brows rose as a slow, saucy grin overtook those rugged features. "Well, well, well. If it isn't Georgia come to hunt me down." He smugly went back to pumping, angling his chest and his arm in a way that showcased his muscles. He heatedly held her gaze with each thrusting pump. "Did you miss me? Tell me that you did and I'll ensure the next pail is yours."

She lowered her chin in disbelief. "Are you flirtin' with me? At the water pump in front of half the ward? Really?"

"Really." Still holding her gaze with unabashed heat, he willfully used the weight of his upper body in smooth, solid strokes to spray water out of the spigot and down into the open mouth of the pail. It was as evocative an image as if she were the pail and he the water. "Would you rather we take this elsewhere, Georgia? We can."

A ripple of awareness stroked its way to her stomach and *all* the way down to her booted toes. What on bloody earth had the water pump unleashed? Though she relished this new earthy and feral side of him, she was a little concerned. For if *this* version of Robinson decided to drag her into the low closet, she knew she wouldn't be able to say no.

Drawing in a ragged breath, she let it out and headed toward him. "I suggest you finish that there pail, fill the one you promised me and let's get back to doin' laundry before the sun sets, shall we?"

"Jealous?" he called back, forcing two more solid pumps of water into the pail.

"Only because I've been waitin' an hour for one pail of water," she called back.

When the woman who had been waiting bustled away, Robinson swiped up Georgia's pail, set it beneath the spigot and offered up one last show. He pulled the handle up and pushed it down in a single stroke. Gritting his teeth, he worked the pump faster, shifting against the handle.

When it was filled, Georgia swept in and grabbed the handle, lifting its pulling weight up and off the dirt. She smiled up at him. "Thank you, Robinson."

He lifted a brow. "Don't you think I deserve a kiss for that?"

"You are a flirt of the worst sort."

He grinned. "Be forewarned, this is only the beginning. I have decided to make you mine."

"Oh, have you, now?"

"Yes. I have." He released the wood pump handle, swiping his sleeve against it, and pointed to the pail. "Allow me." He grabbed its weight from her, transferring it into his right hand.

Together, they strode back toward the street.

Every female eye followed them out of the alley.

Georgia set her chin and smugly took hold of Robinson by his free, muscled arm, leading him toward the pavement in a manner a wife would lead her husband. Naughty though it was, there were very few times in her life she had gotten to brag about *anything,* and he most certainly was something to brag about, gent that he was.

As they both made their way down the street, she

tightened her hold on his arm and glanced up at him with a dreamy smile. To be sure, a finer gent she had never known since Raymond.

She blinked, her smile fading.

Though he eagerly leaned into her, his gaze was fixed forward, his dark brows knitted together as if he were counting steps. His unshaven jaw was unusually tight, causing a lone muscle to flicker just beneath his cheekbone. He looked as if he were in pain.

She released his tensing arm. "Are you all right?"

His features softened as he glanced down toward her, never once breaking their stride. "Of course I am. Why did you let go of my arm? I was rather enjoying that."

Reassured, she teased, "I think you were havin' far more fun back there."

He smiled awkwardly, adjusting his hand on the bucket. "It was as if they'd never seen a man before."

She laughed. "Not at the pump, they haven't. You weren't out there pumpin' water for those women the whole time you were gone, were you?"

"Not the *whole* time," he admitted gruffly. "I managed to swallow down a yam and spend nine cents on a bundle of matches before getting caught in a barrel of eyes and giggles."

"Nine cents for a bundle?" Georgia groaned and smacked his arm. "What? Were they spun of gold? They're only a penny apiece, you know."

"I know." He leaned toward her in between steps and said in an adoring voice, "You should have seen this little moppet. Eyes as big as cornflowers. A smile like powdered sugar, even with two teeth missing. I would have gladly given her more if I had it."

Bless his never-ending, generous heart. "That was very kind of you, Robinson, but you can't be givin' away money to everyone around here. You'll walk away naked and *still* not feed them all."

"Yes," he murmured, nodding. "I know."

Veering back into the shade of her tenement, Georgia gathered her skirts and hurried up the stairs to unbolt the door. "That was only the first pail, Brit," she called down as he mounted the stairs, coming up toward her. "You've got nine more to go, so I suggest you keep to pumpin' only for yourself or I'll never get the laundry done."

"Yes, madam."

Unbolting the door with the key, she pushed open the door and hurried back toward her basin of sitting laundry.

"Where do you want it?" he asked.

She grabbed up the heavy linen shirt soaking in the washing basin and bundled and twisted the fabric hard, squeezing out all the soapy water. She dumped it soundly into the empty rinsing basin and pointed. "Right there. Thank you."

"My pleasure." He dumped the large pail of water into the basin with a rushing splash. She paused as droplets of rust-colored water fell from the pail atop the freshly washed linen.

As he turned away and headed toward the door, he shifted the pail into his other hand. Flexing the hand he'd freed, he disappeared, leaving the door wide open.

Georgia paused and glanced back at the stained linen she had just laundered, noting that the rinsing water he'd dumped into the basin was its usual yellow tone. The droplets on the linen, however, were a rusty red.

Bloodred.

Oh, God. Those poor, untouched hands of his were probably rubbed raw after he'd foolishly pumped water for half the ward.

Quickly wiping her hands on her apron, she hurried out after him through the door he'd left open and called down the stairs after him, "Robinson? Robinson, will you come up here, please?"

He jerked to a halt on the bottom stair and turned back toward her. His dark brows rose as he jogged his way back up, the pail swinging from his movements. He thudded onto the landing before her. "What is it?" He smiled. "Are you worried I may never come back? Because I promise you this time I will."

She stepped toward him, took the pail out of his hand and set it aside. Meeting his gaze, she said softly, "You were pumpin' for quite some time. How are your hands?"

He fisted them and shrugged. "Fine."

She wagged her fingers. "Show me how perfectly fine they are. Only then will I let you go back to the pump."

Averting his gaze, he leaned over and swiped up the pail. "You need water."

"Not at this price." She grabbed his arm. "You're done."

"There is no need to coddle me, Georgia." He freed

his arm, turned and jogged down the stairs. "I'll be back."

She huffed out an exasperated breath. Damn him. He was only going to make it worse. Gathering her skirts, she rushed down the stairs and hurried after him. Before he could reach the entrance leading out into the street, she darted in front of him and slammed the oak door with a resounding *bang* so he couldn't leave.

She swiveled toward him, setting her hands on her hips. "You're done for the day. Now get upstairs."

He leaned down toward her. "Your mouth is much bigger than the rest of you. I think you have a tendency to forget that." Moving around her, he purposefully bumped her aside with his large frame, making her stumble.

"Robinson." She darted in front of him and shoved at his muscled weight. Grabbing hold of his exposed wrist, she tried to grab the pail. "Give it to me."

He yanked it up high into the air, breaking her grasp on his wrist with a swift tug, and stared her down with lethal calmness. "If you think that I will *ever* let you pump water in my stead, knowing what it's done to *my* hands, you are delusional, woman. *Delusional.* You are never touching this pail again. Now bite down on that tongue of yours for one long breath and get thee upstairs." Rounding her, he lowered the pail back down to his side and stalked toward the closed door.

Bless him for being the only man in the ward to have thought of saving a woman's hands. She jogged after him, grabbed hold of his arm and drew him back toward herself. "Robinson. My hands are used to the work. If you want, you can go back to the pump on the morrow, *after* we—"

He jerked his arm out from her grasp. "If I want to pump water for you, regardless of whether my hand is raw or not, you have no say." He shoved past her.

Jumping toward him, Georgia forcefully ripped the pail out of his left hand, and flung it aside with an echoing *clang* against the nearest wall. "You're done."

He narrowed his gaze as he rounded her to go get the pail.

"Oh, no, you don't." Gritting her teeth, she grabbed him hard by the linen of his shirt with both hands and used every ounce of her strength to shove him hard against the wall behind them. Tipping her full weight into that muscled mass, she made him stumble back against the wall with a solid thud.

His hands jumped up to steady her and keep her from altogether falling aside and onto the floor.

Georgia glared up at him, disregarding that she was draped against him like some wanton in need of a quick dollar. "I've been doin' this all my life," she rasped, tightening her hold on his linen shirt to balance herself. "Long before you and your gentlemanly ways ever came along, and as you can see, me and my hands are still here. There's no need for you to puss up your hands in some stupid effort to prove yourself to me. You want to prove yourself? Do so by havin' some respect for your hand, because that's all I want and that's all I need from you right now."

His eyes darkened. "Let me tell you what *I* want and what *I* need, and I can assure you, it doesn't involve water." He grabbed her hard by the waist and forcefully spun them around so fast, her heart popped.

He shoved *her* back against the wall, making her gasp.

Pinning her solidly into place with his body, he lowered his gaze and methodically watched his own hands trail up her waist and round up to her breasts, before sliding up to the curve of her throat. He sensually grazed her skin with his knuckles before sliding both hands into her knotted hair.

She could barely breathe against the feel of his hands.

Tightening his fingers against her hair, he tilted her face toward his. His chest rose and fell heavily against her own heaving bosom as he pressed her harder against the wall. "My hands matter not to me. *You* matter to me. Do you understand? *You*. If I wish to make my hands bleed to ensure that your life is a bit easier, allow me that. Or, by God, I will rip all of your clothes off in an effort to make you feel half of what is pounding through my veins here and now. Do you understand?"

She swallowed, her heavy breaths mingling with his in the quiet narrow corridor. Her world faded knowing that this incredible man desired not just her body, but her mind and her heart. Georgia Milton. From Orange Street.

The erotic tension in his muscled body that held her dominantly in place and the way those strong fingers dug into her hair made her want to rip *his* clothes off. "If you want to rip off all of my clothes—" she breathed out "—then do so. But you're not goin' back to that pump."

He lowered his chin. "You would let me rip off all of your clothes?"

She swallowed, unable to breathe or think or care about anything but physically embracing this raw, carnal passion pulsing between them. "You wouldn't have to. I would willingly take them off."

He held her gaze for a long, searing moment. "Are you telling me that you want this?" He pressed even closer to her, so that she could feel all of him. "Tell me you want me, Georgia. I need to hear you say it."

She felt herself growing wet in response to his unashamed grinding. She tilted her face up toward him despite the strong hold he had on her against the wall. "I want you."

His hold tightened, those fingers digging into her. "You are supposed to tell me to desist, Georgia. For God's sake, tell me to desist, before I ravage you here and now. Don't think I won't. 'Tis all I've been able to think about."

He was such a gentleman in the most inconvenient of times. "You haven't done anythin' yet. Do somethin', already."

He stared her down before lowering his mouth to hers, crushing it against her lips. Shifting his body against hers, he pressed his erection into her corseted stomach and demanded more of her mouth, never once pausing as he tilted his head to mold and remold himself against her. They kissed more and more ruthlessly, their tongues battling and their heated breaths mingling until they were both gasping against each other's lips. She felt herself physically unfolding to the point of trembling.

Blindly sliding her hands down his firm chest, she rounded his muscled thigh and rubbed it. It had been four long years since she'd known passion. She never thought she'd be able to cradle it again. Until now. Finding the rigid length pressing against the flap of his trousers, she achingly rubbed at the rounded tip of his hard cock, trying to feel him through the smooth wool.

His fingers tightened their savage hold, tugging on her hair, making her scalp burn. He broke their kiss. "Georgia." His breaths were ragged as he sensually moved against her stroking hand with the slow, even roll of his hips. "Not here. Upstairs. I want to lay you out and count every freckle."

She rubbed him through his trousers again. "Whilst counting the freckles would be fun, every man drags a woman off into bed. But you're not every man, Robinson, and I'm not every woman. Which is why we'll do it here and we'll do it now."

He captured her gaze, his hips pausing. "In public?"

She paused from stroking him. "Have you no sense of adventure, oh, Salé pirate of mine? This here be the high seas I speak of."

"It isn't the adventure or the high seas I'm worried about." He glanced toward the closed door leading out into the street and pressed into her. "What if someone walks in?"

"Then they do." She frantically unbuttoned his flap, shoved his undergarments aside and slid his warm, hard length out. A shaky breath of disbelief escaped her as she slid her fingers around that velvety hard length. She couldn't believe that she was touching him like this.

He searched her face and tightened his hold on her. "Georgia, you can't be bloody serious."

She paused and drawled up at him, "You're spoilin' the mood, you know. I kind of feel like Eve arguin' with a priest over what to do with an apple."

"You mind that tongue." He pressed her back against the wall and growled out, "You may be Eve, but I'm no priest." He fisted and jerked up her skirt, whipping it up past her thigh. Forcefully sliding his large, warm hand up between her thighs, he spread her with his fingers. "Something tells me I should start here. What do you think?"

She gasped as he used her own moisture to rapidly flick her. She could barely breathe as his finger rubbed faster and faster.

He intently held her gaze. "More?"

"Yes. More." Her chest tightened, her breaths coming in jagged takes as sensations rippled up her stomach and down past her thighs. She trembled and pushed her hips against that hand, desperately needing more. Gripping his arms in an effort to balance herself, she held his fierce gaze, feeling her moisture slowly slather his fingers as he flicked and rubbed, flicked and rubbed.

Georgia bit down on an anguished moan and felt herself being pushed toward that incredible edge of bliss.

Her body quaked at his heated movements. It was as if she was unleashing the man buried within. It made her feel incredibly powerful and feral knowing that she was penetrating that soul with her own passion.

"Do it," she whispered.

Releasing her wetness, he grabbed hold of her thighs with both hands. With a wince, he yanked her up and onto his hips, straddling her around his waist.

She paused. "Your hand."

"I'm not thinking about the hand." He shoved her skirts out of the way and draped them back, the tensing of his long, muscled arms holding her against the wall and himself. "I'm thinking about *this*."

The ache and burn within her exposed upper thighs increased as she tightened her straddle, widening herself to him.

Positioning the tip of his cock at her wetness with a quick hand, Robinson savagely thrust himself into her so hard, her back and body slammed against the plaster, vibrating the entire wall.

She gasped, her core threatening to ripple and burst against his rigid length as he slammed into her again and again and again, heightening each ripple to a throat-clenching crescendo.

He pounded into her, knocking the breath out of her with his large, muscled body. His wide chest rose and fell with each seething breath as he quickened each ram with the bang of his hips.

Although her back and shoulders pinched against each unrelenting thrust, sending her repeatedly into the plaster full force, it only seemed to erotically punctuate the pleasure raking through her overwhelmed senses.

Feeling herself edging and edging into her own climax, she clung to him, reveling in watching that rugged face flush against his impending pleasure. His upper lip beaded with perspiration as his square jaw tightened in desperate control.

She could feel his shoulders flexing, tensing and growing tighter beneath her hands as she frantically fisted his linen shirt, trying to remain coherent.

"Georgia…" he gritted out between each breath and thrust. He lowered his head and dug his chin into her hair, readjusting his hands on her waist. "For God's sake, *do it*. Do it, before I—"

She panted for breaths she could no longer take, racing to finish upon his command as an unrestrained moan burst through her lips, unleashing the rippling pleasure she'd been grasping for. She gave in to the trembling core between her thighs and the sensation of her body tightening in pleasure. She cried out and cried out again, bucking against him and grinding down on his length, unable to believe she was *still* climaxing.

When it ended, she rested her head limply back against the plaster, letting Robinson feverishly jerk in and out of her wetness.

She had never had it last so long. It was unreal. "Pull out when it's time," she rasped in between fading, heavy breaths.

Robinson slowed his thrusts to a mere in and out as he captured her gaze with lust-heavy eyes. Holding her more firmly against the wall, he dug rigid fingers beneath her thighs and masterfully stroked in and out, in and out, holding her gaze the whole time as if showing her who was in command. Suddenly, he slid himself out of her, dragging her body off his waist and thighs.

He settled her booted feet back onto the uneven wood floor, pushing down her skirts to fall back into place.

Pinning her against the wall, he stared at her mouth as his hand jerked between them. He tensed. "I want you to swallow me," he rasped. "Will you?" He closed his eyes.

Sensing that he was near release, Georgia dragged herself down his muscled body and took his rigid, velvety length as he had asked. Using her hands and mouth, she stroked him rapidly.

Seething out breaths, he stilled, his muscles tensing around her possessively as he grabbed her hair and trembled from his release, the warmth of his seed spurting into her mouth. He groaned and groaned again as she sucked and swallowed him until there was nothing left.

Releasing him, she slowly rose back onto her feet and somewhat shyly leaned against the wall, hoping that it had been just as incredibly marvelous for him as it had for her.

He grabbed her and collapsed against her; his muscled chest heaved beneath the linen of his shirt. He nuzzled his face into her hair. "Georgia," he breathed out. "Marry me. Marry me so we can be together always."

She drew in an astonished breath. Oh, dear God. She had seduced far more than his body. She had already seduced his soul. And it was wrong. It was so bloody wrong and not in the least bit fair to him or her.

Reaching down between them with trembling hands, and after pushing him back into place, she buttoned the flap. "I can't marry a man without a name. It wouldn't be legal."

"Then give me a name," he insisted against her hair. "I will take any name you give me."

"It still wouldn't be legal." Reaching up, Georgia cupped his face and kissed his nose and then his forehead and then the bruises still covering the right side of his jaw and cheekbone. "You and I must wait. We must wait until your family comes and decide then."

"And what if no one comes? What then?"

Then her dark wish would be hers to keep and kiss and hold. "I'll not make an orphan out of a man unless he truly is one."

He leaned away out of her grasp. "Why would you give yourself to me in so intimate a manner, only to take yourself back the moment I asked you to be mine? Do you think that because I have no name, I also have no heart?"

She swallowed back the anguish he was forcing her to feel and stepped toward him. "Oh, Robinson. Cease this. No one has more heart than you."

"And yet it isn't enough. Is it? You require a name, and a man with a past, over this mere heart." He shifted his jaw and stepped farther back, his gray eyes boring into her. In a low, harsh tone that was almost eerily not his own, he bit out, "How many men have you allowed to touch you in the way I just did? I want to know."

She stared. "I don't do this sort of thing on the hour, Robinson."

He leaned toward her and narrowed his gaze. "Is that

supposed to be your answer? Or perhaps there are far too many to count. Is that it?"

She stumbled back. There was a cutting razor edge that was slicing its way out of his naive soul. Was *this* who he really was? A man who had been bruised to the core by other women?

She narrowed her own gaze. "One. There's your damn number. *One.* And that one was my husband, mind you. Now I ask you, cease belittin' me, considerin' I'd venture to say, *Mr. Crusoe,* given your remarkable performance, your number's probably well above my mere one."

He glanced away, his flushed features softening as he lowered his gaze. After a long moment of silence, he closed his eyes, placing shaky fingers to his forehead, and choked out, "I didn't mean to... I..." He reopened his eyes and met her gaze, tears streaking them. "Forgive me, Georgia. Forgive me for suggesting that you..." He winced, rapidly blinking as if a headache was overtaking him. "I'm ruining this. I'm ruining everything. I'm...stupid."

She stepped toward him, her heart squeezing seeing his panic in having wronged her. "Shh. No, you aren't. I'm fine. I just don't want you talkin' to me like that. It isn't fair given that I only want what is best for you. Don't you understand that seizing you for myself whilst you have yet to belong to *yourself* isn't right?" She leaned toward him, wagging her fingers toward his hand. "No more pride, please. Show me."

He quietly held it out, unfurling it, palm up.

The entire width of his large palm, just below his

fingers, had been scraped clean of its skin, welted with crusting blood. "Oh, Robinson," she whispered, grasping it gently. "Don't suffer like that for me again."

He leaned toward her, his features twisting. "I suffer more knowing that I just accused you of—"

The entrance door banged open, making them jump away from each other in astonishment.

Matthew casually strode in with a wool sack draped over his broad coated shoulder and a folded newspaper in his bare hand. He jerked to a halt, scanning them. "Am I…interrupting something?"

Georgia's cheeks burned as she tried to remain indifferent. Thank *God* he hadn't walked in moments earlier. "No. I was merely…lookin' at his hand."

Matthew paused. "Whatever the hell is wrong with it?"

"He injured it."

"Did he?" Matthew dropped the sack onto the floor, slapping the folded newspaper into Georgia's hands, and strode toward Robinson. "Hand it up, Brit. I'm good with wounds."

Robinson edged toward the staircase, setting it behind his back. "A man has his pride, you know."

"Not whilst he's living in the Five Points." Matthew stepped toward him and forcefully grabbed his arm out from behind his back. Pulling it upward toward himself, he shook his head. "Damn. You scraped off half the skin. Hold it up."

Digging into his patched waistcoat pocket, Matthew retrieved a small bottle and uncorked it with his teeth in one solid pull. "Chant with me now," he said enthusiastically with the cork still wedged between his teeth. "Pain is ever so beautiful and divine. *Why?* Because it means you're still breathing. Now hold still."

Georgia bit her lip hard, her fingers crinkling the newspaper Matthew had given her to hold. She watched with a half squint as Matthew poured the entire contents of his whiskey onto the open wound.

"Christ." Robinson swung away, hissing out a breath through bared teeth as he repeatedly shook his hand against the effects of the liquid dripping off. "It burns worse than the damn wound itself."

"It always does." Recorking his empty bottle with the pop of his palm, Matthew tucked it back into his waistcoat. "So. I just got back from Wall Street. The clerk over at the bank informed me he'll have a name and address those notes were issued to in as little as eight days."

"Eight days?" Robinson met her gaze.

Georgia's heart dropped. Though he wanted her now, yes, the moment his family came and paraded him back to his lavish lifestyle, reintroducing him to who he really was, it would all come to an end.

Matthew grabbed the newspaper from her and snapped it open, smacking the back of his hand against the extended page. "Congratulations are in order, *Crusoe.* You are officially the latest in frenzied gossip to have hit this city. Even the damn clerk at the bank knew all about you, which is why he was exceptionally helpful. The *New-York Evening Post* is rather popular within business circles."

Georgia leaned over and grabbed the newspaper from Matthew. She held it up, scanning the framed words.

British Gentleman in Dire Need of Assistance

The article gave a small but accurate description of his appearance, right down to the clothes he had been wearing when he first appeared at the hospital, and asked anyone who recognized him to call upon Dr. William Carter at the New York Hospital for further information.

She lowered the paper, handing it off to Robinson. "Bless that bastard's beating heart. That was impressively quick. He must have high and mighty connections."

Robinson held up the paper.

Matthew strode back over to the wool sack he dropped earlier, swinging up the sack. "Here." He tossed it toward her. "I dug some clothes out of my trunk. Hopefully they'll fit."

Georgia caught the weight. "Thank you, Matthew."

Robinson glanced up from the paper he was still reading. "Yes. Thank you. I appreciate this."

"No worries. Oh, and Georgia—" Matthew sauntered backward toward the main entrance door and tapped at his neck with a bare finger. "You, uh, might want to clean up some of the blood he smeared all over your throat. You look a bit *too* ravaged." He smirked. "Did you have fun?"

Her eyes widened as she clutched the sack up higher

against her chest, wishing she could crawl into that sack and dump herself in the river. "Leave."

Matthew adjusted the faded leather patch against his cheekbone. "I'm not being an arse. I just want you smiling again, the way you used to." He paused. "Take him over to the dancing hole sometime. It'll be good for you." He pointed at her knowingly. "Just remember that I'm not playing uncle to some half-Brit babe around these parts. You'll have to move out west with that, because I have a reputation to uphold with the boys. I'm still Irish, mind you."

Georgia pressed her lips together, completely mortified, as Matthew turned and disappeared out into the street, leaving the door wide open. She glanced over at Robinson, dreading what the poor man must be thinking.

Robinson refolded the newspaper and wordlessly reached out to remove the sack from her hands. Without meeting her gaze, he turned toward the stairs.

She swallowed, watching him take one stair at a time as if he was waiting for her to say something.

Matthew, drat him, was right. Four sorry years had ticked by since she'd last danced in the arms of a man and it wasn't as if avoiding the dancing hole was going to bring Raymond back.

"'Tis Friday," she called up after him, hoping to break the awkward silence. "After I finish the laundry and we have ourselves a bit of supper, would you be up for dancin'? There's more to life here than blisters and blood, you know."

He glanced down at her, his features tightening. He

turned to fully face her, leaning his broad shoulder against the wall of the staircase. "Do you want me to go? Or are you asking me because Matthew insisted on it?"

She blinked up at him. "Well, I—"

"You are under no obligation to make me think I matter when I don't. I just…I need to know what is real and what belongs to me, given that I barely exist in my own head. I will confess that I am already attached to you, Georgia, and not solely in the physical sense. In truth, I don't think I would be able to walk away from you or this. Even if you told me."

Tears burned her eyes at his unexpected confession. He was truly a beautiful soul. "If you promise not to break my heart, Robinson, I promise not to break yours."

He pushed himself away from the wall, still intently holding her gaze. He adjusted the sack in his arms and said in a soft, low tone, "Your heart is safe with me." He paused and held up his hand, showing her the gash, which glistened from the whiskey Matthew had poured on it. "I should probably wrap this," he murmured, half nodding. "I'm sorry I didn't listen to you earlier. I was just…worried about your hands." He half nodded again and, with that, quietly turned and walked up the remaining stairs with his sack.

Georgia set a heavy hand on the wood banister and leaned against it, staring up after him as he disappeared through the open door of her tenement. It scared her knowing that her poor, poor heart could be broken again by allowing herself to love this nameless man. But maybe, just maybe, they would end up together and take each other and the west by storm.

CHAPTER NINE

Everyone complains of his memory,
but no one complains of his judgment.
> —François de La Rochefoucauld,
> *Maximes Morales* (1678)

LONG AFTER ROBINSON HAD finished helping Georgia gather up all of the laundered clothes from the rooftop, and they had eaten a surprisingly good meal of oysters and cabbage she'd prepared, Robinson donned Matthew's frayed linen shirt, along with a pair of patched wool trousers. Though the trousers were a bit snug against his backside, they were still comfortable enough for him to sit without ripping anything.

Georgia hurried toward him, draped in a plain blue cotton gown that brightened not only her face but those playful, pretty green eyes. She unpinned her lopsided, bundled hair. "Hand it over," she said, gesturing to the brush he held. "You're takin' much too long, *Miss* Robinson Crusoe."

It was like they had been married for years. He should be so blessed. "I'm almost done."

Dipping the brush bristles into the clean basin of water set on the sideboard, while ensuring he didn't get his bandaged hand wet, he leaned toward the small cracked mirror hanging on the wall. He brushed his black hair back with a few side sweeps and observed the scruffy, dark facial hair that was noticeably in need of tending. "I need to shave and bathe. I don't stink, do I?"

"I would have told you. Either way, tomorrow morn is bathin' day. I'll draw up a hip bath for the both of us."

He lowered the brush. "You mean we…get to bathe together? Naked?"

She rolled her eyes and snatched the brush out of his hand. "I meant we can share the water. A hip bath barely allows for one body, let alone two. Now get to waitin' on the landin' before we hit another wall and never leave. I'll be right out."

"Right." He awkwardly rounded her at the image she had conjured. Striding into the kitchen, he opened the door and quickly stepped out into the small corridor. Blowing out an exasperated breath, he fingered the linen on his bandaged hand, waiting for Georgia to finish tending to her appearance. He hadn't even been able to function around her, let alone think about anything but the way he had savagely taken her against that wall, banging his lust into her like some dog. Clearly, he was not a gentleman. Not at heart, anyway.

Echoing footfalls thudding up the stairs made him turn. His brows rose as John eventually came into view, his tall, lean frame garbed in a gray waistcoat, a faded black coat whitened at the seams from use and a yellowing, lopsided, droopy cravat that was in serious need of assistance. In his bare hand, he even held a single wilting daisy that swayed its white petals and yellow cap against his brisk movements.

Stepping up onto the landing beside him, John cleared his throat and announced coolly, "I'm here to see Georgia."

Despite that sorry, lopsided cravat, Robinson felt somewhat underdressed in comparison, what with only a frayed laced shirt and overly snug trousers. "She and I are going out," he managed, setting his shoulders.

John glanced away and asked, "Where to?"

"Dancing."

John snapped his gaze back to his face. "You mean she's taking you to the dancing hole?"

He eyed him. "Yes. Why?"

John rapidly blinked and lowered his gaze, fingering the flower in his hand. "She must really like you," he muttered. "She never goes. Not given its history."

Robinson shifted toward him, his brows coming together. "What history?"

John glanced up, leaned toward him and said in a quiet but harsh tone, "Whatever you do, Brit, don't feck with her heart. I may have stupidly disappointed her by not wanting to chase her dream of going west, but I never once fecked with her heart. Not even after she tore me asunder without giving me a chance to right things."

Robinson stared at him. Apparently, something very dark had happened to Georgia over at the dancing hole. Something she had yet to share with him. He flexed his hands, hating that he hadn't been around all this time to protect her from the world.

166 FOREVER AND A DAY

Georgia suddenly appeared in the doorway, her thick red hair bound in two youthful, pretty, long braids. "I'm ready." She paused with her iron key in hand and scanned John. "Why, John. You're standin' in a full coat and cravat. Who died?"

"No one. I felt like dressing up, is all." John held out the sagging daisy. "I hear you're going over to the dancing hole. It's been a while for me, too. Can I go with you?"

Robinson slowly shook his head. The bastard didn't even know how to go about trying. Georgia sighed, took the flower John offered and tucked it into her hair behind her ear. "I'm with Robinson and don't plan on dancin' with anyone but Robinson."

Biting back a grin, Robinson tried not to puff out his chest *too* much. If Georgia was already announcing to other men that she was his, he liked the way the night was headed.

John lowered his gaze and offered quietly, "I'm not tryin' to impose. I just hate the idea of sitting here by myself in the tenement tonight."

Oh, the bastard sure knew how to pump a woman's compassion.

Georgia sighed, turned away and bolted the door, slipping the key back into the small pocket beneath her arm. Whisking back toward them, she grabbed not only Robinson's arm but John's. "You can come along if you want. Just don't you be startin' any trouble." She tightened her hold, bringing them closer against herself. "I'd actually like the two of you to get to know each other outside of fists. You might find that you have a lot in common."

John stared dubiously at him from over Georgia's strawberry braids. Robinson returned the glare as they all walked in unison down the remaining stairs, bumping shoulders against the narrow space.

Striding out the entrance door, they made their way into the inky, humid night. Despite the late hour, crowds of men with coarse, unshaven faces, accompanied with coiffed women whose lips and cheeks were smeared with cheap rouge, filled the streets, appearing and disappearing into the shadows around them.

Georgia veered them to the left, still tightly holding on to their arms. "We really shouldn't walk in silence. It's awkward even for me. So. What should we talk about?"

"Let's talk about how I'll be getting each and every dance," John offered smugly. "Because Brits are about as deaf to music as they are to women and life itself."

Robinson refrained from reaching over and smacking him. "With that sort of attitude, you'll be dancing with the wall, or at best, a few chairs."

John leaned toward him from in front of Georgia. "You think you're funny, don't you? Well, you're not. You sound stupid, you feck."

Georgia shook both their arms. "Whilst I'm flattered to be the center of all this lovely attention, it isn't impressive listenin' to grown men bicker like women in a shop quarrelin' over who gets the last bonnet."

Both he and John fell into silence, because God only knew neither of them wanted to sound like women.

After directing them around a corner left, they all walked in silence through the darkness of narrow pathways and squat wood buildings lit by streetlamps and passing carts with flickering lanterns.

In the approaching distance, the loud cheers of a crowd and the rhythmic stamping of feet drifted toward them. A brightly lit entrance from a cellar with its large oak door held ajar by a barrel spilled fuzzy, yellow light across the pavement, fingering its way to the dirt road where men with cigars between their teeth lingered. The jolting strings of a violin and the quick, rattling shakes of a tambourine pierced the humid air.

Georgia released their arms. She glanced back at them and with a slow grin she lifted a foot, playfully tapping it. "I can already feel that fiddle makin' its way to my feet." Gathering her skirts, she disappeared down the small set of paved stairs.

Brushing past him with the turn of a hard shoulder, John tossed out, "I suggest you not make an idiot out of yourself. Dancing with a woman is an art." He disappeared down through the cellar entrance after Georgia.

"How hard can it be?" Robinson yelled back grudgingly, jumping down the stairs. He ducked against the low frame of the door and entered into a large open space that had been cleared of furnishings, save a few chairs set against the uneven walls, and rows of casks laden with tankards.

The entire timbered ceiling was covered with smudged lanterns, illuminating not only every nail, crack and splinter but all the flushed, glistening faces of men and women, both Negro and white, as they merrily whirled and danced in time to the loud stamping of feet and the violin and tambourine that tried to cut through the noise.

He glanced toward a row of people leaning against the wall on both sides of him. They clapped and stomped their feet, some pausing to openly scan him.

Georgia pushed her way past John, who was holding out a hand toward her. "Later, John. I'm dancin' the first few sets with Robinson."

With that, she grabbed hold of *his* arm and hurried them into the crowd, her braids swinging against her slim shoulders.

Robinson pointed back over at John and yelled out smugly over the music, "I see a lovely-looking wall over there! I suggest you go spark up a conversation. Who knows, you might get lucky!"

John narrowed his gaze and swung away, disappearing toward a table lined with bottles of whiskey. He tossed a quarter at a man and snatched up two bottles.

Following Georgia into the chaos of limbs and whirling skirts and clapping hands, she turned toward him and twirled once before lifting her skirts above her ankles and letting her booted feet merrily take flight to the music. She grinned, her braids hopping along with the rest of her. "I can't believe I'm actually doin' this. It's been years!"

"Has it? Well, at least you remember doing it. I don't even know what the hell I'm supposed to do." He awkwardly held a hand behind his back and tried to force his booted feet to find the rhythm in the melody that flitted like a million butterfly wings he couldn't make sense of. He stumbled against the worn leather boots of a bearded fellow beside him and winced, holding up a hand in apology to the man, who reached out and patted him on the back to assure him it was fine. The music only seemed to flit faster and faster and he felt as if he was about to snap his own legs in an effort to keep up.

Georgia grabbed hold of his waist and steered him closer toward herself. "Don't lift your knees so high!" she shouted, reaching down and tapping his closest knee down. "Otherwise, you're missin' beats and the steps that go with it!"

Robinson lessened the height of his knees, feeling like a court jester drunk out of striped trousers. He gargled out a laugh. "I simply cannot dance!" he shouted back, leaning toward her. "I'm about to fall over like an oversize bit of timber!"

She laughed. "You're doin' fine!" She leaned toward him and grabbed hold of his face, nuzzling her nose against his before letting go.

That amazing, loving little nuzzle made him want to not only dance but break out into a roaring song. No longer caring if he looked like the fool that he felt, he stomped and clapped and gave way to the music. With a grin, he watched Georgia spin left and then right and then left again, her quick-moving feet timed perfectly to the jovial music.

Her beautiful, flushed face and bright green eyes watched him in between every whirl and twirl, the radiating happiness that bubbled out of her, infecting him with a sense of freedom and happiness he wanted to seize and hold for the rest of his life.

Whatever history haunted this place, it appeared to be of no consequence, for he saw nothing but genuine happiness bursting through that smile and dance. Pride overwhelmed him knowing that *he* was here to share in that joy.

When the music eventually stopped and he with it, a loud cheer boomed around them, momentarily deafening him.

Georgia cupped the side of her mouth with a hand and jumped over and up, yelling past the bobbing heads, "Play us a lover's melody of old! I've brought myself a lover tonight, don't you know, and I want this to be a night to remember!" She veered back toward him and grabbed his arm, squeezing it tight. "I just announced to the world you're mine. Are you happy now?"

"You honor me." He grinned and glanced down at Georgia as men and women hooted and clapped.

The lanky Negro who'd been playing the violin jumped up onto his chair, adjusting his knit cap on his brow, and pointed the tip of his bow at Georgia with a saucy grin and a flirtatious wink. Quickly tucking the end of the instrument beneath his chin, he held up his bow, announcing he was about to begin and, with a graceful guiding hand that slid the bow across and back against the strings, commenced a beautifully sweet slow melody full of so much longing that it sought to melt the heart of every soul in the room.

Georgia turned toward him with a shy smile, reached up and primly set one hand on his shoulder. With the other, she carefully took his bandaged hand into hers, ensuring she wasn't touching the rawness beneath, and announced, "This is how a lady in your realm would dance to music. Am I right?"

He paused. "I honestly wouldn't know. But I like it."

He curved his other hand around her corseted waist and instinctively set it against the middle of her back. Drawing in a breath, he wordlessly whisked her away from the men and women crowding to their right and guided them to the left with a smooth, circling boxed step. He adjusted their step and held her rigidly against himself, pushing and guiding her body and feet with his arms. He instinctively took a forward balanced step, then a back balanced step, then a side balanced step, moving them left and right, before starting the steps all over again, across the planked floor.

It was the...*waltz*.

Yes. He knew it. Oddly, he knew it very well, and though the dance itself didn't match the music being played, it felt like the only step worthy of it. With each smooth step and elegant turn, he realized that he not only knew how to dance this waltz but that he could do it fluidly and exceptionally well.

Georgia's lips parted as she attempted to follow his sweeping movements. She glanced down at their feet and then up again, meeting his gaze. "What is this?"

"The waltz," he provided, whisking her past the other couples who had paused from their dancing to watch them. "Or at least I think that is what it's called."

"I like it."

"Do you?"

"Very much. It makes me feel all...*civilized*. Don't you feel civilized?"

He lowered his head toward her and drawled, "Yes. Because we certainly weren't earlier, up against that wall."

Finding they had more room on the floor, for others were moving back and away to watch, Robinson smiled and moved her forward with a step, then back, then side to side from left to right. Images of well-dressed crowds and dancing couples whisking forward and back on a gleaming wood floor lighted by crystal chandeliers and rows of mirrors flashed within his thoughts. He was there with them.

He kept dancing with Georgia, trying to hold that image, not clear on where it came from. Her uncertain steps slowly matched his own until she completely submitted to the repeated movements of their bodies swaying together. She quietly watched him the whole while, her flushed features searching his face.

When the violin ceased, he brought them to a sweeping halt and blew out a slow breath as a wave of applause filled the air. Georgia lingered in his arms and tightened her hold on his shoulder, still holding his gaze, even as the violin and the bugle commenced a new, rowdier tune bringing everyone stomping back onto the dance floor around them.

She mouthed something up at him, her brows and face softening, and though he couldn't hear it against the crowd and the music, he didn't need to hear her words. He could see the enchantment in those eyes. It was a heartrending form of enchantment that promised him love.

Only…something was unraveling. Something made

him feel as if that forever and a day he sought within Georgia's arms was about to be snatched away. Though he tried to push all thoughts of it away, he was beginning to wonder how it was possible to dance with a woman without remembering *how*. It whispered of dark possibilities he had refused to consider out of his desperate need to be near Georgia.

What if he had danced like this, so intimately, so lovingly, with the faceless woman who lingered in the back of his mind? What if he had lied to Georgia when he had first met her on the street just so he could crawl into her bed and then toss her? Perhaps the man who had emerged and had claimed her so savagely against that wall was, in fact, *him*. A man who sought to only… fuck women.

He swallowed and released her, stepping outside of her arms. He turned and quickly veered off the planked floor, a headache pinching his skull. His chest tightened as he frantically pushed his way past people, unable to breathe.

He hurried toward the entrance that led up and out to the street, the light and the darkness blurring into each other. Jumping out onto the landing of the pavement, he threw back his head and stood there, dragging in rancid breaths of air that only seemed to make everything blur all the more.

"Robinson?" Georgia hurried up the stairs and out toward him. She grabbed his arm. "What is it?"

He winced against the headache that continued to penetrate his skull, wishing desperately he could figure

out who he was and what he should do. "I'm overwhelmed, that is all. I need to rest."

She hesitated and whispered, "This is my fault."

"Don't apologize." He glanced away. "I didn't want
it to end. I'm just—"

"Hey, Brit," John hollered out. "Hey." John staggered
past Georgia with an almost empty whiskey bottle. He
gestured with the bottle. "You, uh, dropped something."

Robinson paused and patted his trousers, wondering
if the dollar he'd placed in his pocket was still there. It
was. "What did I drop?"

Robinson swiveled toward him just as John belted
out, *"This!"* and sent his other full fist swinging, pum-
meling it straight into Robinson's stomach.

Pain exploded up into his clenching chest, momentarily arresting his ability to breathe against the burning ripple that froze his stomach muscles. He stumbled,
his boots skidding against the pavement in an effort to
regain his stance and his breath.

"John!" Georgia shoved John hard and off to the
side, making the bottle slip out of his other hand. Glass
shattered as whiskey sprayed everywhere, resounding
like the crack of a pistol shot in the night.

Yanking out the flower from behind her ear, Georgia
whipped it at John and jumped forward, smacking his
face hard. "How could you? How could you ruin this
night for me knowin' I haven't been here in four goddamn years? Whiskey-slathered or not, what are you
tryin' to prove?"

John leaned toward Georgia and grabbed her by the

face. "I'm ready to…head west," John choked out, momentarily swaying. "I wasn't earlier, but I am now."

Gritting his teeth, Robinson jumped toward John and knocked that hand away from her and shoved him with a full violent thrust. "*Don't* touch her. Georgia, we should go before I lower myself to his level."

"Right you are in that." She grabbed Robinson's arm and stalked them past John. "We ought to get you into bed, anyway. Come."

"Yes, get him into your bed!" John called out mockingly after them, waving about a swiveling hand. "And while you're at it, Georgia…let the Brit feck you up the arse in the name of Ireland like the goddamn traitorous slut that you are."

Robinson twisted away from Georgia's grasp and stalked back toward John, his pulse roaring in his ears. "You and that piss-drunk mouth are dead."

Digging into his coat pocket, John unfolded a razor with a flick of two fingers. "*Bleed,* you son of a—" Angling forward, John stumbled and lunged toward Robinson with the outstretched blade.

Shit! Robinson skid aside just as the blade cut straight through the air of where he'd been. Knowing he had to stop that razor from lunging again, Robinson jumped back toward John and instinctively snatched hold of his outstretched wrist with both hands, rigidly freezing the blade and his arm so it wouldn't move. Gnashing his teeth, he used his weight and every ounce of his strength to twist John's wrist hard and off to the side until the tendons and the bone kept it from going any farther.

Despite John's grunting resistance, he eventually stumbled forward and against him, the razor slipping from his fingers. It clattered to the pavement at their booted feet.

Robinson shoved him back hard and scrambled toward the pavement, snatching up the razor before John could get to it. Refolding it with a flick into its handle, he turned and whipped the blade far out into the street, where it echoed into the shadows far beyond and disappeared from sight. He pushed out breath after breath, his pulse still roaring in disbelief that the bastard had almost sliced him.

John stumbled back, catching himself against the gas lamppost beside them.

Robinson swung toward him and narrowed his gaze. "If you go near Georgia ever again, I'll do more than fist you up. I'll *break* your arm and detach it from your shoulder and toss it down the street so that your little razor has itself a friend. Are we plain in this?"

John pushed himself away from the lamppost, jerking toward him. "You deserve to be sliced. *Sliced!*" he roared through his slurring. "Do you think I didn't see you…pounding and grunting into her? Do you think that I didn't place myself against a wall and restrain myself from…killing you *and* her with the cleaver I grabbed from the kitchen?"

Robinson pointed at John, his chest heaving in disbelief. "How we choose to love each other is none of your goddamn business. You are pathetic and vile!"

With gnashed teeth, John lunged at him again, flopping a fist toward his head.

Robinson darted aside, his heart pounding. Jumping back and forward, he threw out a raging fist, his bandaged knuckles connecting up and into that nose with full force. A sharp pop sounded in the night air as his arm jumped back. His hand writhed at the contact, causing him to push out a seething breath and stagger back. Wincing, he shook his bandaged hand out. Gash aside, had he never hit a man before?

John covered his nose with a quick hand, stumbling and wheeling forward. He gasped as blood slowly seeped through his clamped fingers, glistening in the low glow of light from the lamppost.

Georgia grabbed his arm. "Robinson, you've made your point. Now let's go."

He yanked his arm from hers. "I just have one last point to make, dearest." Rounding John fast, Robinson took advantage of his hunched position by grabbing hold of his shoulders and shoving John straight down toward the pavement in full force. "*That* is for watching us, you prick."

John stumbled to the ground, catching himself with his bloodied hands. Collapsing against the pavement, he rolled onto his back and choked up at him, "She deserves far more respect than you've been giving her... and you know it. You know it."

Robinson's chest knotted with regret. Though a vicious and dark part of him wanted to send a double fist crashing down into that sniveling face and into his gut, he knew John was right. Georgia did deserve far more than he'd been giving her. She deserved her field, she deserved her apple trees and, above all, she deserved a man who knew his own goddamn name.

Rounding John and the pavement, he gently took Georgia's hand and kissed it, wordlessly leading her down the street, their movements echoing in the darkness. Whoever the hell he really was, and whatever the hell his reasons for originally engaging her on the street had been, he only hoped he was worthy of Georgia.

ROBINSON SAT QUIETLY IN Georgia's dimly lit kitchen, fingering the scrap of linen she'd resoaked in whiskey and rewrapped around his hand. Though the wound no longer bled after the blow he'd delivered to John, it still stung. Christ help him if he really did have a wife. Or... children. Oh, God. What if he had children?

Georgia reappeared in the doorway of the low closet, her slim body outlined by the glow of the oil lamp she had lit beside her bed. "Robinson?"

He glanced up and drew in a breath, noting that she wasn't wearing a corset *or* a chemise beneath that thin linen nightdress. Through the wavering light filtering from her room, he could see the outline of breasts and nipples, slim thighs and sinewy limbs peering out through the sheer, plain cotton that swept down to the floor.

He met her gaze, trying to pretend he hadn't noticed her near-nudity, even though every muscle in his body roared with tension. "Yes?"

She leaned her braided hair against the frame of the door. "You were rather soft on John. Considerin'. I'm impressed."

"He was drunk," he muttered, lowering his gaze.

She sighed and tapped on the door. "Remove your clothes, save your undergarments, and get into bed. I'll not let you sleep in that chair another night. The bed is small, but there's more than enough room for the both of us."

He shook his head. "The chair is fine."

"Robinson—"

"No. The chair is more than fine."

She bit her bottom lip before dragging it loose to say, "You need better rest than what you've been gettin'."

"I'll be fine."

She leaned against the doorway, swinging out playfully toward him, those small breasts jiggling beneath the fabric of her nightdress. "We'll keep it respectable and only sleep. I promise."

He averted his gaze from those breasts he wanted to cup. The damned woman didn't even realize that everything about her made him want to toss the last of whatever gentlemanly ways he had.

Robinson removed his boots and let them thud against the floorboards. "I am not getting into that bed with you, Georgia."

Leaning far back against the chair, he crossed his arms, stretching the rough, yellowing linen of his shirt. "You and I should not touch again. Not until my mind is what it should be. My own."

She tsked, her nose crinkling. "You really need sleep."

He glared at her. "What if I'm married, Georgia? What if I have a house full of children and have yet to know it? What becomes of *this* or of *them?* By God. I have knowingly made a whore of not only *you* but *myself*."

Her grin faded. "Is that what's been weighin' on you?"

"What sort of man goes pounding a woman into a wall, only to then almost break a man's skull?"

She shook her braided head. Padding over to his chair, she leaned over and kissed his cheek soundly with soft, warm lips. The stinging scent of lye and starch still clung to her skin after their long day of laundry.

"Should you change your mind and wish to sleep on the straw mattress beside me," she murmured, nuzzling her nose against his cheek, "I'll not think any less of you. In my eyes, you will always be a gentleman worth knowin' and havin'."

Brushing her roughened fingers alongside the curve of his unshaven face, which caused his body and his jaw to tighten, she straightened and lingered. "Is there anythin' else botherin' you? Be honest."

He glanced up at her. After a long moment, he asked, "What happened to you at the dancing hole? Why is it John knows and I don't?"

She quietly stepped back, her features tightening. "I'd prefer to tell you another time. All right?"

"Do you not want me asking?"

"Nah. 'Tis all right to ask and I'm glad you did. I'm just not in the mood to cry." She lowered her gaze, fingering the waistline of her nightdress. "Set aside whatever guilt you feel about tonight and know that waltz made me forget for one beautiful moment that

I'd ever danced with any man but you. Somethin' I never thought possible after my Raymond. So thank you for that. I needed to know that I could move on and leave him behind. And tonight, I got my answer." She blinked rapidly, nodded and padded her way back into the closet. "Good night."

"Good night, Georgia." He swallowed, tilting his head back against the hard wood of the chair, and squeezed his eyes shut. Something kept chanting that time was ticking toward his departure, calling his mind out of the void and into a different reality.

Part 2

CHAPTER TEN

*Scarcely knowing where he was, or what to be-
lieve, for a few moments Verezzi stood bewildered, and unable to arrange the confusion of
ideas which floated in his brain...*
—Percy Bysshe Shelley,
Zastrozzi: A Romance (1810)

A RAPID POUNDING AGAINST the entrance door startled
Robinson into bolting up out of the chair and onto his
feet. He staggered, all of the muscles in his shoulders
and thighs tightly knotted and sore from sleeping in an
awkward position. He winced and then groaned, knowing he couldn't keep living like this. He'd be dead by
the end of the week.

Thunder boomed in the distance, making him pause
as the floor, as well as the windows, rattled. The rushing of rain whipped at the glass when the thunder silenced, wind pelting it hard on an angle. It was morning
already. Though not a very welcoming one given the
menacing weather.

"Georgia?" John yelled out from the other side, rattling the door. "*Georgia!* Where's Robinson? Get him
out here, will you? And hurry it up!"

He was going to bury that bastard in an unmarked

ditch outside of New York. Stalking toward the door, Robinson unbolted the locks one by one and swung the door open. *"What?"*

John's hardened blue eyes met his gaze. His swollen nose and bruised face were sleeked with rain, his unshaven square jaw dripping wet like the rest of him. Drenched, frayed clothing clung to his lean body, and his almost whitened leather boots trailed not only puddles of water but clumps of mud onto Georgia's doorstep.

Robinson stared him down. "I suggest you and the mud leave. Because I'm done with this. I'm done with you."

"I'm not here to put up fists," John muttered, shifting from boot and boot. "I'm sorry about the…razor. I was being stupid and had far more whiskey than I should have. Marshals were going door to door in the building looking for you. No one wanted to talk, thinking Georgia was in trouble, but as it turns out they're here to help you. So I…I told them which door you were at." He stepped back and thumbed toward the stairs behind him, where four large men in drenched uniforms were jogging up the stairs, their muddied boots echoing around them.

Robinson's breath hitched as all four men in full military regalia, with swords at their sides, filed onto the landing.

"This be the one," John announced in a low tone, gesturing toward Robinson.

One of the uniformed men formally inclined his head toward Robinson and gestured toward the stairwell behind them with a gloved hand. "His Grace will be most pleased to know you are safe and is anxiously waiting for you to join him downstairs."

Robinson stepped back. His Grace? He knew what that meant. It meant the man was a...*duke*. It meant that the man was of British nobility. Swallowing, he took another step back. How did he know that? "Who is this man to me?"

The mustached officer closest to him leaned in and offered, "The Duke of Wentworth is your father, my lord."

A displaced sensation of familiarity clamped down on him.

Imageless memories pierced his thoughts, bringing a rush of not only an estate but servants.

"My lord?" the officer inquired from somewhere before him. "Are you unwell? Do you require assistance down the stairs?"

Robinson refocused his thoughts. "No. I am quite well, thank you. I just..." He held up a shaky hand, feeling exhausted and overwhelmed. "I'm trying to remember things, that is all."

Another officer held out a sizable leather satchel that tinkered with what appeared to be coins. "This here is for Mrs. Milton. It bears gold coins amounting to an even hundred. His Grace asks that the moment these coins are delivered into her hands in honor of her generosity toward you, that you join him in the carriage outside."

Oh, God. This couldn't be happening. Everything was unraveling too fast for him to make sense of it all.

Robinson grabbed the weighty satchel. "Georgia?" He whipped back toward the direction of the closet just beyond the kitchen where she already stood in her calico gown, her hair neatly bundled and her feet bare. It appeared she had been awake for some time.

"My father is here," he whispered in disbelief, holding up the weighty satchel. "He wanted you to have this."

A lone tear spilled its way down her cheek. She nodded and swiped at it. "All that matters is that you've found what I had lost. 'Tis good to know you have a father. 'Tis more than good, actually. 'Tis absolutely marvelous."

He tossed the satchel toward the table with a thudding *chink* and stepped toward her, unfolding his arms. "Come here, Georgia. Come here, before I tell everyone to leave."

She let out a sob, hurried toward him and flung herself into his arms, pressing him tightly against herself. "I told you someone would come." She dug her entire face harder into his chest and tightened her hold. "I told you."

"That you did." He pressed the side of her soft cheek against his chest and held her for a long moment, praying this wouldn't be the last time he'd hold her. "It would seem I am bound to far more than wealth."

She leaned back and searched his face, still clinging to him. "What do you mean?"

He swallowed. "I am a lord, and my father, who is waiting downstairs, appears to be a duke."

She gasped, her eyes widening, and scrambled out

of his arms. A trembling hand drifted up to her mouth. She stared as if she no longer knew who he was.

The world faded as if he were being dragged into a reality he didn't want to be a part of. "Don't look at me like that. I'm still the same man."

"I knew you had money, but I never once thought you were some...aristo." She dropped her hand to her side. "Mother on high, had I known I most certainly wouldn't have—" She stepped toward him, looking panicked. "We can't have you lookin' like this. Your father is goin' to blame your wretched appearance on me."

He lowered his chin. "You do realize you just insulted my appearance?"

"Oh, hush up and stand still." Stuffing his linen shirt into his trousers, she smoothed it against his chest and shoulders, before readjusting his trousers on his hips with a firm tug. "There. Now—"

She turned, grabbed up his boots from beside the chair and set them before him with a thud. "Put your boots on. I'll go get a rag to polish them." She grabbed the other, small satchel from off the table, the one containing his fob, and shoved it into his hand. "Don't forget this. It has your money and your watch in it. Maybe now you'll be able to find the key that winds it." Turning, she jogged into the front room and disappeared.

Only Georgia would think of winding a watch at a time like this. He glanced back at her. "Georgia."

"Put on your boots," she called back, knowing he hadn't.

He heaved out a breath. Lowering his gaze to those

boots, he leaned over and yanked each boot on, dreading everything that awaited him. It would be like waking up in the hospital again. Not knowing who or what to expect. What if he didn't recognize his own father? What if he *never* recognized the man?

Georgia reappeared with not only a wet rag, but his waistcoat, coat and brush in hand. "Put them on. Apologize to your father about the buttons. Will he want them back? Should I go dig them out? I should, shouldn't I? They're silver."

He slipped into his embroidered waistcoat, which she had laundered and dried for him all but yesterday. "I don't think he'll want them. They are, after all, *my* buttons. Not his." He pulled on his coat, adjusting them both against his body and sighed. "Better?"

"Much. Lower your head for me." She turned him toward herself and reached up, brushing his hair back and out of his eyes with several quick strokes. She stepped back, smacking the brush against the palm of her hand and set her chin. "There. Much better. Now stand still."

Tossing aside the brush with a clatter, she kneeled before him on the wood floor and bent toward him, polishing his black leather boots with a rag as if she were now his servant.

His eyes widened. "Georgia, what—?" He leaned down and yanked her savagely back onto her feet, causing her to stumble. He shook her. "What the hell are you doing?"

She scrambled back, tightening her hold on the dirty,

wet rag she clutched, and awkwardly replied, "Now I won't get arrested for treatin' you like a hog."

He captured her gaze, his throat tightening. "You treated me like a damn king." In that breath and in that moment, he knew he could *never* live without her. Not even if he were married with fourteen children. Jesus, he was fucked. "I want you to meet him. I want you to come downstairs with me. Come."

Her brows pinched together as she stepped farther back and shook her head. "He doesn't want to meet me." She tossed aside the dirty rag and smoothed her hands against her gown. "I don't even own a gown worth bein' seen in." She edged back, her cheeks flushing. "I'm sorry I made you live like this. I really am."

He fought the need to grab her and shake her for saying such a thing. "Cease." He held out an impatient hand. "Now come. You're going with me."

"Don't do this to me, Robinson. Please don't." She pushed him toward the door, making him stumble against her weight. "What if you're married? I'll not be the cause of a broken marriage."

He leaned back toward her, clutching the small leather satchel hard. "What if I am unwed? What if I am free to love you? What then? Will you have me?"

Tears now streamed down her pale face, reddening those pretty green eyes. "A man such as you, belongin' to the duty of nobility and wealth, could never be free to love a woman like me. Don't you see that?"

His eyes widened. She didn't even sound like herself. "Are you being blinded by something as stupid as status and wealth? Do you really want the west? Or do you really want *me?* 'Tis as simple as that."

She swiped away her tears. "Stop it," she choked out. She swung away. "I haven't the right to impose what I want upon you."

His throat burned in an effort to keep himself from grabbing her and shaking the wits out of her. "People who love each other *will* impose upon each other. That is the price and burden of love. Unless, of course…you don't love me."

"This isn't about love, Robinson."

"Then what is it about?" Rancor sharpened his voice.

She shook her head again. "Regardless of whether you see it or not, I'll only be a woman you dragged out of the mud and I'll not do that to you or myself. I'll not hang our dignity like this. I just won't."

He leaned toward her and hit the satchel he was holding against his chest. "Our dignity? *Our dignity?* Dignity won't mean a goddamn thing if we're not together!"

A sob escaped her. "That's because you don't *know* what it's like to live without dignity. But I do, Robinson. I've been livin' without it since I took my first breath and I'll not do that to you. I'll not." She clamped a hand to her mouth and quickly veered out of sight, into the front room of her tenement.

"Georgia?" he echoed after her. "Come with me. Please."

Silence pulsed.

He swallowed, sensing that John and all four of the uniformed men were holding their breaths right along with him. It was degrading having his entire life fall apart before the eyes of men that he didn't even know. Robinson lingered in the doorway, staring straight into her kitchen at the hanging rosary there on the far wall, and silently willed whatever God there was to get her to bend to his command.

He waited and waited, swallowing back his disbelief. When she still didn't reappear, he reached out and slammed the door shut lest he grab her and force her into coming with him.

Through heaving breaths and a heavy-limbed haze, he lingered in the corridor as everyone silently awaited whatever was about to happen. It was pathetic. *He* was pathetic.

Robinson swung away from her closed door and tossed the satchel he was holding over to John, who was barely two feet away. "Take this with an apology for the fist I gave you."

John paused and snapped it back out toward him. "Nah, I was the one who—"

"Just keep Georgia out of trouble. That is all I ask." Robinson turned and shoved past everyone.

He pounded his way down the narrow stairs that led out toward the open entrance door. Thunder grumbled restlessly in the distance beyond the rushing rain as a strong, cool breeze forced its way in through the open door.

When he reached the bottom stair, he paused and then veered toward the uneven plastered wall, wistfully sliding the tips of his fingers against it, wishing he could recapture that breathtaking moment when Georgia had made him believe that he was the only man she would ever love.

He strode out of the tenement and onto the pavement, rain pelting his head, face and shoulders, soaking his morning coat within moments. A footman in a bright red uniform stood in the rain, his polished black boots encased in the mud road. He held the door open to a large black lacquered carriage.

Pausing a few steps away from the carriage, he allowed the cold rain to soak him and numb what little he felt. Georgia hadn't even fought half a breath for him. She, who wore a blade on her thigh and took on the world with fists and words to match, had set it all aside the moment it came to him. She obviously had never come to love him in the way he had come to love her.

An older gentleman's rugged face appeared, leaning far forward in the cushioned seat, a folded white handkerchief pressed against his nose and mouth. His silver tonic-sleeked hair glinted from the movement.

Dark brown eyes widened as the man scanned the length of him. Lowering the handkerchief with a black leather-gloved hand, the older gentleman rose from his seat, revealing full black attire from boot to shoulder, save his linen shirt and a white cravat. The man quickly leaned out of the door and waved toward the young footman still holding the door open. "Get him out of this rain, Gilmore!" he shouted, his pale features flushing. *"Now!"*

The footman rushed toward Robinson and grabbed hold of his arm, hurrying him at a jog toward the open door of the carriage and up the unfolded stairs. Robinson stumbled in and fell against the seat opposite the older man as the stairs were quickly folded back into place. The door was slammed shut, encasing Robinson in a world of gray velvet that smelled like mulled spice and cedar.

He paused, glancing at nothing in particular. He knew that smell. It belonged to his life. It belonged to the life of Viscount Roderick Gideon Tremayne. He sucked in a breath, bringing up a trembling hand to his temple. His name. He knew his name. It wasn't Robinson at all. It was…Roderick. He was Lord Roderick Gideon Tremayne. He swallowed and glanced at the man lingering before him. Why was it he had a name in his head but nothing else?

The duke scrambled out of his black morning coat and stumbled to his booted feet. Draping Roderick with his own coat, the duke leaned toward him and touched his face. "Yardley," he choked out, sitting beside him. "Assure me you were treated well."

"Yardley?" Roderick echoed, trying not to panic. "You mean my name isn't Tremayne? Who the hell is Tremayne?"

The man paused and blinked rapidly. "Tremayne is still you. 'Tis simply only one of your titles. As is Yardley."

A breath escaped him. "I see." At least a part of his mind belonged to him. "Call me Tremayne. Please. I don't know why, but I prefer it."

"Fine. Yes." The man grasped his wrist with gloved fingers, gently bringing his bandaged hand toward him—

self. "What happened? Dr. Carter didn't mention any injuries to your hand. Is it serious?"

"Hardly. I scraped some skin off, that is all." Roderick drew away his hand and set it back into his own lap. "Might we go? I don't care to linger."

The duke grabbed his arm, his fingers pinching the wet skin beneath his linen shirt. "Will you cease with this morbid nonchalance? You've been missing for twelve days. *Twelve!* I've had countless men scouring this city since your valet informed me you had never returned from your walk that afternoon. 'Twas only blessed chance the owner of the Adelphi had personally delivered yesterday's newspaper into my hands knowing that I was paying hordes of men, including the watch and all of its marshals, to hunt you down!"

Roderick awkwardly glanced toward him, trying to understand what type of relationship he had with his father. "Forgive me for the heartache I have brought you."

The man released his arm. "All that matters is that you are safe. We're leaving. Do you understand? Difficult though it may be for me to accept, given who he is and what he meant to your mother, we are done trying to convince Atwood to return with us to England. 'Tis his God-given right to stay behind and lead whatever life he chooses."

He sunk farther into his seat in utter confusion. "Atwood? Who is Atwood?"

The duke's eyes widened. He jerked toward him, searching his face. "You mean you really don't remember?"

"No. I don't."

The man paused, still searching his face. "But you remember why we left London? Yes?"

An eerie feeling clamped his gut. "No. I don't."

The duke hissed out a breath, momentarily closing his eyes, pinching his gloved fingers into his forehead. "Dr. Carter warned me of your condition, but I… How does a man lose all that he is in a single breath?" Re-opening his eyes, he dropped his hand to his side and shifted toward him, his features twisting. "You do remember me, though, yes? Given that you are acknowledging me?"

Roderick swallowed. "I'm sorry to say that I don't."

The duke leaned closer toward him, bringing with him the tangy scent of cigars, and lowered his voice. "Try harder, Tremayne. A son should *always* remember his father. Always."

Leaning back against the seat, Roderick whispered achingly, "Forgive me. It isn't by choice that I cannot remember."

His Grace rapidly blinked back tears. He glanced away and eventually said in a choked tone, "You look half-dead. I'll have the valet clean you up when we get to the hotel. We will be leaving on the next Red Star Line, which is in ten days' time. Fortunately, I didn't cancel those tickets."

Snatching up a cane from the seat before them with a trembling hand, the duke used the gold head to knock on the roof of the carriage before angling it against the seat.

The carriage rolled forward, causing Roderick to

sway against the sudden movement of the seat. He was leaving Georgia behind. She was going out west and he was going God knows where with a man he couldn't even remember.

Still in disbelief, he glanced toward the rain-sleeked glass window. A fleeting distorted image of Georgia rushing out of the tenement and into the rain in bare feet made him sit up.

She dashed toward the carriage, sliding against the mud, her head appearing well below the window as she jumped up in an effort to try to see him. *"Robinson!"* she shouted, her small bare hand popping up and hitting the glass of the carriage as it slowly rolled its way past faster and faster. She darted alongside the carriage to keep up, her lopsided, red bundled hair sagging against the downpour. "If you're not married or involved with any women, come back. If you'll have me, come back. I'll be here another week before headin' west!" A sob escaped her as she fell back and disappeared, letting the carriage roll away.

His breath caught in his throat as the clatter of the wheels and the rushing of rain muted all sound. She loved him. He knew everything between them had been real. He knew it had.

He jerked toward the man beside him. "Am I married or involved with any women?"

An astonished laugh escaped the duke's lips as he glanced away from the window and back toward him. "I… Well… You *had* a mistress you dragged over from Paris to distract you from obsessing over your brother's wife, but dismissed the woman when we left for New York. Is that what you wanted to know?"

He choked. "My brother's wife? I have a brother? And what do you mean I was obsessing over his wife? Do you mean to tell me I'm *involved* with his *wife?*"

The duke's features darkened. "You *had* a brother, Tremayne. And yes, you were involved with his wife. But that is all…done with."

Roderick threw back his head and raked his hands through his hair. That is why he was wearing a mourning band. The one Georgia had asked him about in Dr. Carter's office. The one he didn't even remember wearing. He'd been in mourning for his own brother. Dearest God. What sort of man beds his own brother's wife? He was an asshole and couldn't even remember being one! When would his life be his own and feel real? *When?*

He leveled his head and pushed out the breath he was holding. How he prayed Georgia would still love him, despite what he had once been, because he wasn't the man his father spoke of anymore. He wasn't. Nor would he be again.

Roderick flung the coat from himself and jumped toward the door. "Stop the carriage. Now."

"What for?"

"I'm engaged," he rasped. "Now stop this carriage."

The duke leaned toward him and grabbed his shoulders, shaking him twice. "Get ahold of yourself." Those brown eyes searched his face. "You are *not engaged.*"

"I am as of this moment. I wish to be formally engaged to Mrs. Georgia Emily Milton. The widow of

Raymond Milton and a woman I simply cannot and will not live without."

The duke's eyes widened. "The one I just handed gold to? The one Dr. Carter kept telling me was charming but next to bloody mad?"

"If she is mad, Your Grace, then the entire world is, too. She took me in and gave me a home and a mind when I had none and I am madly in love with her."

His Grace gasped, his aged face flushing. "You've only been gone for twelve days. Not twelve years."

"Time means nothing when two souls are perfectly matched. Now I am asking that you stop this carriage so that I may bring my fiancée home with me."

The duke's brown eyes intently held his gaze. "You may not remember who and what you are but that does not change who and what you once were and what you must continue to be. *You* are the sole heir to a dukedom. Do you understand? This woman has no place in your world and I will not permit you to degrade yourself and all that we represent."

Roderick swayed, fighting the nausea seizing him. "I will set aside everything to make her my wife. I will. Even you. Even my name. Let there be no doubt in that."

The duke narrowed his gaze and pointed at him rigidly with a black-gloved finger. "If you go against me in this, Yardley, I will strip you of everything, including your yearly annuity, and you will be left with nothing. Is that what you want?"

Roderick let out a shaky breath and forced more power into his voice. "I am not leaving her behind. I'm not."

The duke dropped his hand to his thigh and lowered his shaven chin against his knotted silk cravat. After a long moment, he confided, "When you marry, Tremayne, it will be a woman worthy of your name and your status. Not this. Not...*thi*s."

Roderick shifted toward him. "She *is* worthy. Upon all that I am, I swear to you, she is."

The duke stared at him. "You aren't even in your own damn mind anymore, boy." The duke waved toward the rain-slathered window revealing distorted dilapidated wood buildings. "I take it this is Park Lane to you now?"

Roderick shifted his jaw. "Do not mistake what she and I share. You know nothing of it."

The duke closed his eyes as if unable to look at him anymore and said in a barely contained voice, "Leave her here and don't complicate your life or mine. I will not say it again. I would sooner disown you than see you marry into a mess."

Roderick was more ready to fling himself into the arms of poverty and allow his hands to bleed every day on the hour knowing Georgia would be there to kiss it all away, but he *refused* to let Georgia live in the poverty that had quietly eaten away not only her pride, but the faith she had in herself as a woman and as a human being. He would change her life knowing that he was of status and of wealth and in time prove to this staunch man that Georgia deserved far more than dirt.

Roderick leaned toward him and said in a tone that he hoped was rational and persuasive, "I'll take her to London, then. As my mistress."

"Tremayne, for God's sake—"

"Are you informing me I am not permitted to take a wife *or* a mistress?"

The duke gaped. "You mean to actually drag this woman all the way to London?"

"Yes. Now pray convey, what is the amount of this yearly annuity you spoke of earlier? I must ensure she has everything. And I do mean everything. In this, I will not desist. I am not leaving without her. I'm not."

Those brown eyes hardened, no longer allowing for sympathy. "Your annuity is nine thousand a year, not including what you inherited from your brother. It should be more than enough, unless she plans to eat a barrel of gold on the hour."

Roderick stared him down. "There is no need for you to insult her. Now stop this carriage so that I may fetch her. Unless, of course, you prefer I altogether stay and abandon my duty to you and my name. Because I will. Do you think it matters if I live in a sty knowing my heart is feasting like a king? Better mud than death to what little remains of my mind and my heart."

The duke lowered his gaze, his gloved hand visibly trembling as he reached out and grabbed hold of his cane, yanking it up with a single sweep. "You and your heart will be the death of us both. Christ, do you ever remind me of myself in my younger years. 'Tis a curse, is what." He hit the roof twice with the gold head of that cane, causing the carriage to slow, and glanced toward him. "I am trusting your word in this, Tremayne. Respectable men take on mistresses all the time, but they *don't* bloody marry them. Is that understood?"

That will change. "Yes, Your Grace."

Roderick reached out and swung down on the latch, flinging open the carriage door. Without waiting for the carriage to come to a complete halt, he jumped out into the pelting, whipping rain, bracing himself against the still-moving road beneath him. He stumbled against the hard impact of the slippery mud beneath his boots, sliding against the thick mud.

Regaining his balance, he turned around and squinted against the rain-hazed street. In the distance, he could see Georgia had already turned and was walking in the opposite direction. As the rain came down harder, she gathered up her soaked skirts and sprinted away, kicking up a trail of mud and water.

"Georgia!" Hundreds of icelike droplets poured down so rapidly he could hardly see as he pumped his arms and legs through the mucked mud squelching against every rapid movement.

"You there!" the duke shouted out to one of the marshals. "Follow him! Lest he altogether drown."

Roderick sprinted onward toward Georgia, charging through puddles. Arctic spatters of water rose up time and time again, soaking his trousers and boots more and more. He gnashed his teeth as numbness slowly overtook his body.

The hooves of a horse trembled the ground, following him, as Georgia disappeared around a corner where another mud street crossed.

"Georgia!" Roderick dodged oncoming carts and carriages as people stepped out from beneath the eaves of buildings to watch him dash. He sucked in breath after breath, pumping his legs faster and faster until he turned the corner, momentarily sliding to make the turn.

He spotted her disappearing through a narrow stone archway of a stone wall stretching almost the length of the street. Gigantic green-leafed oak trees flourished on the other side of the old wall that hid a looming, abandoned church beyond.

"Georgia!" he yelled above the rain.

Glancing back toward the lone uniformed man on his horse, which was splashing torrents of mud, Robinson pointed the marshal toward the church and direction he was going, before dashing through the narrow stone archway where Georgia had disappeared.

The rain vanished as a canopy of large branches sheltered him from the downpour. The rushing silence pulsed against his ears as a decrepit, perpendicular-style church towered before him within the small courtyard. He swiped away the water from his face and glanced around, finding only quiet, crooked gravestones and mossy grounds bordered by stone walls. It was as if Georgia had never been.

"Georgia?" He jogged through the old churchyard, scanning the empty courtyard. Occasional drops of rain dripped through the branches of the trees, the eerie silence making him wonder if these grounds had ever been touched by the living.

A small ivy-covered stone crypt, separate from the church, made him pause. The mildewed stone had markings that had faded against time and its black iron gate had been left wide open.

He made his way through the open gate. Small mossy

steps appeared, leading down into what appeared to be a small pool of water hidden deep within. He stepped down and into the shadowed darkness. Cool, stale air pushed up from the bottom, as if the crypt were breathing.

"Georgia?" he called, his voice echoing around him.

"Robinson?" a choked voice echoed back.

Relief frilled his soaked body. Step by step, he made his way down toward her, the moist air growing heavier as rotting wood filled his nostrils. Shafts of gray light from the outside world illuminated the scaly, dark walls covered with dead ivy and moss.

Georgia's shadowed figure kneeled before him at the very last step that disappeared into what appeared to be murky water. She glanced up at him, a soft gray line of light exposing only the right half of her wet face. "I didn't think I'd see you again."

He stepped toward her, tension and frustration knotting his muscles knowing that she thought so little of herself to not only have almost given up on them, but that she would also feel the need to lurk in the shadows of a crypt like some ghost. "I am absolutely *livid,* Georgia, knowing that the moment you realized you were the pauper and I the king, you knelt upon broken glass even as I offered you the means to carry you over it. You will never kneel like that before me or anyone else again, allowing your dignity and all that matters to you to bleed. Do you understand me? *Always* be the woman I know you to be. Be the one who wishes to go west when everyone else is going south. For that is the *only* woman I could ever allow myself to love. Because I need a woman to do more than love me. I need a woman willing to fight for me even when I am unable to fight for myself."

She lowered her gaze and half nodded, but said nothing.

He swallowed, trying to calm himself. "My real name is Viscount Roderick Gideon Tremayne, though I also appear to go by yet another name. Yardley. I wanted you to know that. For maybe now you will have me."

She glanced up.

"In truth," he went on, "I much prefer being Robinson. For he, at least, was a good man. One I relate to." He let out a shaky breath and stepped closer until he was at her side. He crouched alongside her. "What are you doing in here? 'Tis morbid."

She touched a finger to the water at her feet. "I always come here."

He glanced toward her but could barely see the soft, hazy outline of her face. "Why?"

"It's been my sanctuary for years," she admitted, her voice drifting and echoing around them. "When Da was still alive, he told me every time we passed this way, that the water sittin' in this crypt could foretell the future if one had the patience to stare at its reflection long enough. Daft though it may be, I've been starin' at the water since."

Roderick gazed down at the water below their feet, seeing only the blurred, darkened outline of their figures. "Has it ever foretold anything of worth?"

A harsh laugh escaped her. "Yes. It would seem my future is bleak and undefined as the water itself."

Roderick leaned toward her and cupped a hand beneath her warm chin, turning her shadowed face to him with chilled fingertips. She lifted her gaze to his and he felt himself melting away. "Your future is so much brighter than you think." He released her chin and gestured toward the water. "I ask that you tell me what you see."

She paused. "I don't see a thing."

"Yes, you do," he insisted, pointing at the water before her. "No matter how distorted or shadowed the reflection may be, I ask that you look and tell me what you see."

She paused, shifting against the wall of the crypt. "I see the dark outline of my face."

"Exactly." He rose to his feet. "You are your own future, Georgia, which is probably what your father was trying to say. Because no one can foretell it in the way you can. Sometimes, we become victims of misfortune and the mistakes we bring upon ourselves, but even then, we have the right to fight for what *will* be. Why do you think I am standing here before you? Because you willed it and because I willed it. *We* made our future by chasing it when it mattered most."

He continued to watch the fuzzy, darkened outline of her face. "I will admit that whilst I stand here and lecture you, I bear my own burdens I have yet to comprehend and face." He swallowed. "If I were to tell you that in my former life I was a bastard of the worst sort, would you still embrace me for what you now know me to be?"

She stared at him. "Whatever did your father tell you? Or did you…remember it on your own?"

"My father told me and I sense it all to be true. I am unmarried, which is a blessing, to be sure, but it would seem I was romantically involved with my brother's wife. I am no more, but I was."

Georgia rose to her feet and turned toward him. The shaft of gray light from the outside world illuminated the other half he had not earlier seen. "The Robinson I know would have never done such a thing."

His throat tightened. "I know."

She sighed, glancing away. "What fools you and I make. You, who seeks to remember a past that is best forgotten, and I, who seek to create a lofty future that is as ridiculous as I. We ought to both be hanged."

Roderick stepped back, sensing she was already pulling away from him due to what he had so honestly confided. "I would understand if you no longer wish to associate with me."

She was quiet for a moment and met his gaze. "What do you really want for us, Robinson? Be honest."

He stepped toward her. "In ten days, I leave for England. Come with me. I want you to share in everything I have for the rest of our lives whilst we learn to love each other more. That is what I want. Say you will go with me."

She gawked at him. "You want me to go to England?"

"Yes. To London, in particular. That is where my former life appears to be."

"London?" She feigned a laugh. "'Twould be like throwin' a wee Irish pebble out into vast Brit water and watchin' it sink on impact. I'm not exactly what you would call respectable society. Even I know that. Aren't most Brits Protestant? I'm bloody Catholic. Emphasis on the *bloody.*"

"Does it matter? You will learn to become one of us and earn their respect. Just as you learned how to read and write despite barely holding up a quill."

"And what if I disappoint you? What if I can't learn to be anythin' more than what I already am?"

The ache within his chest only seemed to grow with his need for her. "You could never disappoint me, Georgia. Wealth is meaningless if its holder has no integrity. And you have enough integrity to fill not only my heart but an entire kingdom."

She searched his face, her features softening. "Do you mean that?"

"I do, and only hope that my former life doesn't disillusion you or hurt you because I have no idea what awaits us in England. None."

"As long as you continue to be the man standin' before me, I'll stand beside you."

He stared at her in disbelief. "You will come? Regardless of whatever my past holds?"

She nodded. "Yes."

He swallowed. "I… Why?"

"Because I have faith you'll not disappoint me or yourself. I have faith you've already learned how to be a better man but have yet to see it yourself."

He softened his voice, honored to no end that he had

somehow earned the love of such an incredible woman. "I vow that you will never regret having faith in me."

She eyed him and intoned half-seriously, "They'd better have apple trees in London, Robinson. Or you and I are finished. You got that?"

A gruff laugh escaped him. "I will have them shipped in and planted in the front yard the moment we arrive to ensure we last." He held out his hand. "Come. Let us not stand here in the shadows of a crypt."

She hesitated and slid her cool fingers into his own. "Whatever shall I call you? *Roderick?*"

"No. Call me Robinson. For I am he at heart." He tightened his hold on that hand and led her up the small stone steps of the crypt and out past the gate leading them back into the churchyard. "Georgia. There is something else you must know. Something that will complicate our lives."

She glanced toward him, her bundled wet hair hanging adorably lopsided. "What?"

He fingered her small, calloused hand, thankful she would never touch another pail again. "Though I am wealthy, I cannot sever my father's favor, for in doing so, I would be sending us both into poverty. As such, we cannot marry until I am able to prove your worth to my father. Is that something you can accept given that we might not be able to marry for what may be months? Or even…years?"

She enthusiastically shook his hand. "Don't you worry. I'll prove my worth. However long it takes." She poked at him. "But you'll have to teach me how to be a lady, in turn."

"You are a lady."

She rolled her eyes. "Don't you be givin' me that. I know what I am, and if we're goin' to impress your father, we're goin' to have to work piss hard."

He laughed. "I suggest we start by having you use more respectable language. If you think I offend easily, the duke offends worse." He brought her hand up to his lips, kissing her hand. "Now come. My father awaits."

She paused, bringing them both to a halt and gesturing toward her soaked gown and muddied bare feet. "I can't meet him like this."

He scanned her gown, which clung almost indecently to the curves of her small breasts. "I rather like what you're wearing."

She smacked his shoulder. "For all the wrong reasons, you rake."

"Right you are." He grinned, tugging her by the hand toward the entrance where one of the marshals still stood waiting. He called out to the man, "Inform His Grace that I will be escorting Mrs. Milton back to her tenement, so she might properly dress before our departure."

The man inclined his head and disappeared into the rushing rain beyond the wall.

Roderick tugged her forward. "Come. Patience is not a virtue of this man who is apparently my father. Whilst you put on a new dress, I will stall for time and poke about his character to better understand what we are up against."

She drew them both to a halt. "I'll have to do more than pull on a dress. I have to wash my feet and pack."

"Pack?"

"Yes. I have all of my pots, cups, plates, linens and such. I'm also not about to leave my box in the wall for the next person to find. There's a good ninety-eight dollars and ninety-six cents we can make use of. Not to mention all of the gold coins your father gave me. We're goin' to need it."

Roderick drew closer, bringing her cool, callus-roughened hand up to his lips again. He kissed it several times, allowing the warmth of his lips to seep into that skin, and said mockingly, "I am heir to a dukedom, my dear. Do you know what that means? Or do you need me to expound it?"

She scrunched her nose. "It means I don't need to pack. Is that what that means?"

"Exactly. Only pack your clothes, as there won't be time to properly clothe you until we get to London. Leave everything else of worth to Matthew. *Especially* the money. He could use it."

She gasped. "I'm not leavin' that bastard my money."

Roderick leaned toward her. "Georgia. Just imagine what one hundred and ninety-eight dollars and ninety-six cents will buy us, given how much Matthew has done for us for a mere four and forty dollars, what with him running around to banks, letting me grope his step-mother and even giving me clothes?"

She gawked up at him. "He'd bend over for all of England wearin' a smile, is what."

He grinned. "Exactly. And the more friends you and I have supporting our union, the more likely everything will fall into place."

CHAPTER ELEVEN

The only thing that stops God from sending forth
a second Flood is that the first one was useless.
—Nicolas Chamfort,
Caractères et anecdotes (1771)

DRESSED IN HER BEST SUNDAY gown, which she'd stitched herself with great pride, Georgia pushed out a breath and glanced around her tenement one last time, lingering in the small kitchen of what used to be her life. Smoothing her still-damp hair, which she'd assembled into a coif she hoped looked respectable, she wandered over to the small wood table and emptied the contents of her box upon it for Matthew to find.

Leaving the box open, she hurried to the wall and reached up and over the doorless cupboard for her mother's rosary, lifting the wooden beads off the nail. She kissed them, thanking the Lord in heaven for all of her blessings, and let the beads fold down and into a pile at the bottom of the box before pressing the wood lid back into place.

Aside from all of her gowns, which she'd bundled up in a large sack, her father's box and her mother's rosary were the only things she cared to keep of the life she was leaving behind. One day, when her own children were old enough for stories, she would show them the roots of her past and take pride in it for what it was. Tucking the box into the wool sack, she knotted the material into itself to hold it closed.

She slid the brass key off the table, grabbed up her sack and opened the door, stepping outside. After turning the key in the lock, she pulled it out and sighed. No more worrying about counting pennies. Imagine that.

She lingered before the door, touching the well-worn wood panel one last time with the hand holding her key and hoped that the path she had chosen for herself would be everything she had dreamed of and more.

"You're leaving, aren't you?"

She jumped and whirled toward John, who lingered in the open door of his own tenement. His darkened blond hair was matted against his forehead from the rain he had yet to dry from. His shirt and trousers were still as wet as the rest of him.

She drifted over to his side of the door, bringing her sack against her hip, and paused before him. "Who needs the west when I found all four corners of the world in one man?"

He folded his arms over his chest, lowering his gaze. "I'm sorry about yesterday. I swallowed too much whiskey."

She sighed. "I'd rather we not even talk about it. I'm on my way out. I need to drop off this here key to one of the neighbors and leave instructions for Matthew."

John held out his hand. "I'll do it for you."

She rolled her eyes. "I'm not givin' it to you."

"He'll get it."

She pointed at him with the key. "Do you promise to deliver this with the *right* instructions?"

"Aye." He set his hand against his chest. "Upon me mum's grave and soul. That I swear."

Knowing his mother had once meant everything to him, Georgia sighed and held out the key. "Tell Matthew to cancel the room, unless he wants the cheaper lease, and inform him that everythin' I left behind is his to do with as he pleases. He also needs to gather the laundry from the front room, and take it over to the priests over on Barclay, Mott, Sheriff and Ann lest they arrest us all for stealin' their shirts and trousers."

She drew in a breath and let it out. "Tell him that although I'll miss him in a morbid sort of way, that I'll not write, because I'm goin' into respectable society and can't be associatin' with thieves. He knows I've always felt that way, even prior to Robinson, so it shouldn't surprise him."

John hesitated, reached out and slid the key from her hand. "I'll tell him." He shifted closer toward her and lingered, the scent of rain and must clinging to his skin and clothes. "Take care of yourself."

"Oh, I will." She stepped back, cradling her sack up and against her chest. "One last thing. It involves you."

He quirked a blond brow. "What?"

"Remember my good friend Agnes Meehan? The one with the bright blue eyes that always lingered about your mother's door a few years back?"

His grin faded. "What about her?"

"She still isn't married, despite her father's grumblings. I know you once had a hot eye for her before she moved west. Get the address from her cousin and buy yourself a stagecoach ticket."

"I doubt she even remembers me."

"I bet you she does. In the last letter, she asked about whether or not you were still lookin' to marry."

He glanced up, eyeing her. "When was her last letter?"

She bit back a smile. "A month ago." She leaned toward him and poked his chest. "Just stay away from the whiskey and razors thinkin' it'll impress her. Because it won't."

He reached out his other hand and skimmed her arm, his features twisting. "I'm sorry, Georgia. I didn't mean to make a mess of things. I just—" Grabbing her, he yanked her hard against himself, awkwardly squelching the sack between them. He buried his wet head into the curve of her shoulder.

She stiffened but realized the poor man was only looking for comfort. She wrapped an arm around him, adjusting the sack between them, and patted his back with her free hand, her fingers sticking to his wet linen shirt. "There, there. I forgive you. So go on and forgive yourself."

He nodded against her shoulder, tightening his hold.

Footfalls bounded up the stairs and paused on the landing somewhere off to the side.

Sensing it was Robinson, she stepped outside the embrace and pointed at John one last time. "Write Agnes. Don't sit about Orange Street waitin' for somethin' better to come along, because it won't. We Irish have to align our own stars given that everyone else seems to think they own the goddamn sky."

"Right you are in that." He nudged his shaven chin out in the direction beyond her. "I suggest you leave. Your Brit is waiting." John held up the key, assuring her Matthew would get it, and put up a hand in farewell, before quietly disappearing into his tenement. Lowering his gaze, he shut the door.

Georgia lingered, hoping John would someday know happiness. With a sigh, she swiveled toward the direction of the stairs and hurried toward Robinson with her sack. "We can go."

Robinson met her gaze. "You cannot be holding men like that anymore, Georgia."

Her brows rose. She jerked to a halt and thumbed toward John's direction. "I barely kicked that one to the pavement. Don't you be next."

He glanced away, adjusting the wet linen shirt that clung to his wide chest. "This isn't about jealousy. In my circle, from what little I do remember, men and women do not touch each other like that unless they are married. And even when they are married, such things are only done in the confines and privacy of their home. I just don't want my father to judge you."

Her heart sank knowing that most likely his father might *never* accept them. But at least they would be together and in each other's arms every day and every night. "I understand."

"Good." He cleared his throat. "I actually came up here to clarify some etiquette before I formally introduce you to my father. When you and I are alone, you may freely call me Robinson, but in the presence of others, especially my father, you must refer to me as 'my lord' or 'Lord Tremayne.' It is a sign of respect. Will you be able to remember that?"

"Of course. You are 'Robinson' when we are alone and 'my lord' or 'Lord Tremayne' when we are not."

"Very good. Whenever you speak to my father, regardless of whether you and he are alone or in the presence of a thousand, always refer to him as 'Your Grace.'"

She blinked. "As in the *grace* of God?"

"Yes."

"Isn't that a bit sacrilegious?"

He let out a laugh. "I suppose it is. 'Tis something we will both have to swallow. The man is staunch and therefore you'll need to play into his idea of respectability when in his presence."

"You mean you want me to act like this?" Thrusting out her chin, she stiffly held out both hands before her, ensuring her sack didn't fall from her hand, and wobbled about for him from side to side.

He leveled her with a stare. "Are you being serious?"

She laughed, hitting his arm with her free hand. "I was tuggin' your rope. I know exactly what you mean."

He laughed and dabbed her nose with a cold finger. "I want you to spend as much time with my father as possible. That way, he will get to know you for the queen that you are. Make your time with him count. Do you think you can impress him with intelligent conversation devoid of all things crass?"

"Of course I can. I've seen plenty of upper-circle

women converse with upper-circle gentlemen over on Broadway. Watch." Georgia regally set her chin, softened her lips and kept her features calm and poised. Demurely meeting his gaze, she intoned in her best prim and most civilized voice, "I do believe I shall faint from displeasure knowin' this foul weather is goin' to ruin not only my lace parasol but my bonnet."

Robinson boomed with laughter, his features twisting in merriment. He staggered backward, bumping against the wall behind him, before falling forward again. He laughed and laughed and laughed until there were actually tears emerging from the corners of his eyes.

She blinked. By Joseph, she'd never seen him laugh so hard and couldn't help but feel offended knowing that her best attempt at being civilized was being mocked. "Did I do it wrong?"

Still laughing, he waved toward her face with a forefinger as if attempting to rearrange her features and choked out, "That wasn't exactly what I call... intelligent conversation."

"It wasn't *that* bad."

"Oh, yes, it was. Don't ever do that again." Still laughing, he yanked the sack from her arms and held out his other hand. "Come. The marshals guarding the carriage are soaked to the skin and my father is as restless as they are. Even worse, people are gathering out of curiosity."

Grasping his hand, she quickly followed him down the stairs and out into the rain, which had lessened to a soft mist. She nervously gathered her beige cotton skirts, lifting them above her ankle boots to keep them from touching the mud. Clean. She had to stay clean.

Just as she was about to step off the pavement, Robinson grabbed hold of her waist and scooped her up and into his arms, balancing her and the sack all in one sweep.

"Oh!" Her heart skipped as she grabbed on to his soaked coat to steady herself within his muscled arms. She glanced up at his well-stubbled face, which hovered barely above her own. "Whatever are you doin'? I can carry myself, you know."

"I'm ensuring you don't touch the mud."

She grinned. "Where, oh, where have you been all my life? You could have saved many a gown for me."

He grinned, in turn. "I regret not having been able to arrive into your life sooner, madam, but I intend to save every last one of your gowns from here on out." Carrying her toward the open door of the carriage, he leaned her up and toward the landing within the carriage, righting her effortlessly.

The familiar scent of mulled spice and cedar tugged at her senses from the interior. It reminded her of when she'd first met Robinson on the street. It smelled like him.

Catching herself against the doorway, she hurried in and plopped herself onto an incredibly plush, soft seat opposite a stiff, aged man with silvery hair that had been swept back with tonic.

The duke adjusted his well-fitted black coat about himself and leaned back against the upholstered seat as if to better observe her.

Noting those handsome, rather kind brown eyes intently scanning her face and gown, she primly arranged her best Sunday dress about herself, ensuring that it covered her ankles.

She smiled brightly, placing her bare hands on her lap atop each other, as she'd seen wealthy women do whilst riding about in their open carriages, and offered, "Good mornin', Your Grace. I apologize for makin' you wait. 'Tis a pleasure to make your acquaintance and I appreciate your generosity in allowin' me to come." There. That was certainly polite enough without slathering too much honey all over the man.

Holding her gaze, the duke inclined his silvery head toward her, but said nothing.

At least she got the incline of a head and a direct look in the eye. That was far more than she was used to getting when heading into shops with placards in the window saying *No Irish Need Apply.*

The carriage gently swayed as Robinson's tall, muscled frame entered. He bent forward to prevent his head from hitting the velvet-pleated ceiling above them and seated himself beside his father, directly across from her, as the door to the carriage was slammed shut by the footman. Robinson leaned forward and set her sack beside her on the seat, tucking it deep into the corner. Leaning back again, he set his broad shoulders and cleared his throat, holding her gaze as if preparing her for a very long and very separate journey ahead.

She gathered by the way he had opted to sit next to his father, instead of her, that a man was *not* supposed to sit anywhere near a lady whilst in a carriage. She had

a niggling feeling that there were several thousand un-
spoken rules she had yet to learn. And here she thought
wealthy women had it easy.

Georgia paused and glanced around the lavish space
of the carriage. Tut, tut, tut, was it ever fancy. One could
turn it into a harem given that every inch of its walls
and ceiling was fastened with gray velvet.

The carriage rolled ahead, jerking her far forward
and toward them. She squeaked, popping both hands
out, and caught the edge of the seat to keep herself from
spilling forward altogether. She gargled out a laugh
in response to her own squeak and slid farther back
against the cushioned seat, rearranging her skirts. "I
about fell off my seat with that one. You'd think they'd
warn a woman with a bell or somethin'. Unlike you
boys sittin' in flaps and trousers, I got a full set of skirts
that could've damn well left me showin' nothin' but
arse over turkey. And that certainly wouldn't have been
good."

Robinson pressed a rigid hand to his mouth and
glanced away, shifting toward the glass window at his
elbow. He closed his eyes.

Oh, no. She had said *arse,* hadn't she?

She leaned back awkwardly against the upholstered
seat and set her chin, feeling her cheeks growing unbearably warm. She glanced toward the duke, whose
gray brows were still lifted toward his hairline. "Forgive me, Your Grace. My mouth has yet to fully kiss
the true meanin' of bein' civilized."

The duke leaned over toward Robinson, who still sat

with his hand over his mouth. "Oh, London will be impressed with this one."

Robinson dropped his hand heavily into his lap and blew out an exasperated breath. "London be damned. What do they know about good character?"

Georgia pressed her lips together, knowing Robinson was nobly defending her. Drat his father. If the old man thought she couldn't be all boring and civilized like him, he had yet to see Georgia Emily Milton at her finest. She'd put every last woman in London to shame even if it meant biting her tongue until it bled, because she was marrying her Robinson and getting her field and her apple trees.

CHAPTER TWELVE

Even God cannot change the past.
> —Agathon, *Nicomachean Ethics* (Aristotle)
> (as published in 1566)

The Adelphi Hotel

"I LEFT EVERYTHING UNTOUCHED. Everything." The duke gestured toward the large suite beyond the open door. "Mock me for being sentimental, but I was so panicked about your disappearance that I felt if the servants touched even the bed, it would prohibit your return."

Gripping the frame of the doorway, Roderick leaned in and scanned the overly decadent French-inspired room. A sizable four-poster bed had been done up with mounds of sterling white coverlets and goose-down pillows. No more chairs, thank God. A mahogany table was set off to the side, laden with piles of books. A chair beside it had also been laden with books. This explained all of the stories and words in his head. He apparently had a fancy for literature.

Though he tried to envision and match at least one of those items in his head and remember what this room might have meant to him, nothing came. Not a whisper and most certainly not a shout. Just beyond that table, a towering wardrobe and several open trunks revealed far more clothing than any one man really needed. And there was not one, but *three* walnut lacquered sideboards that had been tucked against the palomino walls with a mirror over each. Every sideboard had everything he needed to attend to his appearance as well as many daily comforts and extravagances. From tonic to brandy.

He paused, his gaze falling on several crystal decanters of port and brandy alongside matching glasses all perfectly lining the top of the main sideboard. It appeared he liked to drink.

Roderick glanced back at his father. "How long have we been renting here? And what have we been doing with our time?"

His father's gray brows came together. "You and I have been renting several rooms for about seven months now and spent most of our hours investigating leads and interviewing debauched areas and souls I would rather forget." A breath escaped his father's lips. "Your disappearance was unnerving. I didn't know if it was related to Atwood's circle of people or because something else had happened."

Roderick's brows came together. "Who is this Atwood you keep referring to?"

The duke smiled, his eyes unexpectedly brightening. "Once you have been properly tended to and settled in, we will talk more and get you reacquainted with your life." The man set his aged shaven chin and turned toward Georgia, who lingered quietly in the corridor behind them. "Follow me. There is no need for you to linger about this corridor." The duke paused and flippantly tossed back at him, "I had the footman assign her to room eight and twenty. That will ensure she is within your reach whenever you feel the need to call on her."

Roderick drew in a ragged breath in agitation, feeling both his honor and Georgia's being slapped. And this was just the beginning. "Whilst I appreciate the arrangement, Your Grace, I ask that you not insinuate before her *or* myself that her only purpose is one suited to a bed."

The man pointed at him with a gloved finger. "I am merely laying out your own cards, boy. So don't you be tossing pawns at me. Mrs. Milton? This way, if you please."

Setting both gloved hands behind his back, the duke stalked down the length of the corridor. He disappeared down one of the adjoining corridors.

Georgia, who'd been staring at the duke in what appeared to be genuine fascination, also set her hands behind her back. Swiveling on her heel, she strode after the duke, her skirts rustling about her extended long strides in a flurry as she replicated the man's gait right down to the bloody stagger.

What was she doing? "Georgia?" he called out.

She swung back toward him, those hands still set behind her back. "Yes?"

"I've never seen you walk like that. What the hell are you doing?"

She set both hands on her hips. "Observation is key, my dear Robinson. One must first learn what *not* to do before one can learn what they *ought* to do."

His brows came together. "That makes no sense whatsoever. Adhere to only what you *should* be doing."

"Oh, you're no fun at all." She eyed him and lowered her voice. "Do all men of status walk around like that?"

He blinked. "Walk around like what?"

She thumbed toward the direction the duke had disappeared to and then staunchly set her chin and brow, marching in place with her chest thrust forth. "It's like he's marchin' straight into the pissin' mouth of hell but is damn proud of it."

Oh, God. He was going to have to hire several hundred women to instruct her on how to bite that tongue, or twenty years would pass before his father would ever accept her.

He angled toward her. "I adore you to no end, Georgia, you know I do, but can you please not say *piss, hell* and *damn,* let alone use them all in *one* sentence? 'Tis incredibly important you mind your tongue or the man will never learn to see past it."

She blinked, deflating her overexaggerated stance, and blurted, "I'm sorry. You're right." She nodded and eyed him, playing with the tips of her fingers. "Robinson?"

He smiled, sensing she was unusually anxious. "Aside from taming crass words," he offered, "just be yourself. There is no need for you to panic. I'm not going anywhere."

"It isn't that."

"What, then?"

She hesitated, then lifted her gaze to his and whispered in a tone as if she feared the world would hear, "I

love you. I really do. And I can't believe you're takin'
me with you."

His breath hitched at hearing those words for the first
time. "And I love you. I couldn't imagine leaving you
behind."

They lingered in the silence of the corridor, intently
and heatedly staring each other down. He could feel her
eyes and her stance caressing the length of his body and
soul and inwardly yearned to make that caress real.

Knowing he shouldn't linger, lest he make a dash for
her and make a mess of all that he hoped for her and
them, he cleared his throat and tried to sound indifferent. "After you settle into your room, shall we meet
over a late breakfast?" He playfully lowered his voice.
"I have no doubt the food from here on out will be free."

She giggled, her features brightening. "Free is a price
I can always afford. Late breakfast, it is. I should go.
Lest your father think me rude." Turning, she swept
down the remaining length of the corridor in her beige
stitched gown, her corseted hips swaying with the unexpected grace of a woman in full possession of not only
her body but the world.

He drew in a ragged breath, watching those hips.
Now *that* was a walk he could watch all day.

She paused, as if sensing him watching her. Angling
back toward him, she smiled and offered a sultry glance
over her shoulder, which softened her features and those
bright, mischievous green eyes. "I might as well say
this whilst we're still alone." She lowered her voice.
"My room or yours tonight? And what time? I'm feelin'
rather amorous, if you know what I mean."

His pulse throttled against his ears just thinking about making her gasp beneath the movement of his body and his lust. He edged toward the safety of his room, whose door was still open, knowing they couldn't and they shouldn't and therefore they wouldn't. Damn his insufferable need to make her respectable at the cost of his own sanity. "We can't."

Her brows came together. "Why not?"

Only Georgia would need an explanation. "I…" He hissed out a breath in disbelief as to what he was about to say. She needed her respectability for it was the only form of dignity he was going to be able to bestow upon her. Desire and lust held no place in this. Not at the cost of her worth. "We will reserve all intimacy for when we marry. 'Tis best."

Her eyes widened. "But that may take months."

Fighting his own angst, he nodded. "I know. I simply refuse to turn you into the mistress my father expects you to be. We already know what we want and need of each other. That isn't what this discussion is about."

He cleared his throat, trying to stay focused. "What we did over on Orange Street should have never happened. You deserve more than that and I intend to ensure it doesn't happen again. I want others to respect you in the same way I do."

She fully faced him with her hands on her hips. "You expect us to…*wait* until others approve of us?"

"Yes."

"What if no one ever approves of us? What then?"

"They will."

"No. They won't. Not in the way you want it, at least.

I know what I am, Robinson, and they know what I am, and I'll never be able to change that even if I never bed you again."

"Georgia, please." He stared her down. "A relationship can be founded outside a bed, despite what you've been taught to believe over in the Five Points. We will survive this and I will prove you wrong."

She gasped. "Don't you dare lecture me about the foundations of a relationship! I know what a bed is for and what is shared in it. I also know what happens when *nothin'* is shared in it." She marched back toward him, fiercely holding his gaze as if he had best prepare himself for the worst. "I'm not settlin' for anythin' less than all of you. You hear?"

God save him. She was like a blazing fire and he the log. He shifted closer toward her. "This isn't Orange Street anymore, Georgia. Your world as you know it and all of the rules have changed. Just as you did everything within your means to prevent *me* from getting dirked by pistol-toting bastards, I am now doing everything in my means to prevent *you* from getting dirked from moral-toting bastards."

She glared up at him. "Whilst I agreed to put on a jig and a show for the world to clap along to, I didn't agree to sell my soul to a man who's goin' to lecture me on the sins bestowed unto us by Adam and bloody Eve." She pinned him with a self-righteous stare. "Last night, you asked about the dancin' hole and what it meant to me."

He blinked, half expecting her to say more, but when she didn't, he prompted, "Yes?"

"I'm ready to tell you." She thrust out a reprimanding hip. "Does respectable society allow for intimate conversations? Or is that banned, too?"

Her words stung, and the bewitching devil that she was, she knew it. He shifted toward her. "You can *always* share in an intimate conversation with me. That is far different than us sharing a bed."

"They're actually one of the same, you prude. Only one involves the body and the other involves the soul, linkin' the two together and makin' them one. And regardless of what you and *respectable* society may think," she now shouted, pointing toward herself and then the floor, "I need *both* to call *this* a bloody relationship!"

Gritting his teeth, he snapped a finger to the open door of his room at the insult. "Given that you clearly wish to keep talking well above a rational tone, I demand you step into my room. Because I am not about to let you make a strumpet of yourself like this in public."

Her lips parted. She slowly stepped back, searching his face. "You're not my Robinson. I don't know who you are."

His gut twisted. "I am still the same man, Georgia. What you don't seem to understand, however, is that men of my status do not go about bedding women outside of matrimony. Do I need to tell you what people will whisper about you? Do I?"

She kept on shaking her head from side to side, tears welling her eyes. "'Tis obvious you've got two opposin' voices in your head. One belongin' to my Robinson and the other to this—this…Tremayne. But you can't be both, Robinson. You can't. Because they're not the same men. What *Robinson* wants for me is what *I* want for me. Love with every breath, laughter when everythin' is dire, kindness above all else and never-endin' honesty even when the world has none. As for what this *Tremayne* wants for me? Hell if I know what he wants!"

He threw his head back, praying he had the strength to survive against that fire that always seemed to sear him. "You and I were born unto two different circles, and though we may love each other, if this is going to work, you will have to be the one to bend to the rules of *my* world. Because if I bend, Georgia, it will send us straight into poverty, and I will *not* have that for you or my children. *I will not*. Not after living it." He leveled his head. Glancing down the empty corridor to ensure their privacy, he met her gaze again. "I want and need to know all about the history of the dancing hole and ask that we retire into my room to ensure your privacy."

"You think I care what the world thinks of me? They already passed judgment on me long ago." She crossed her arms over her breasts and shot him a cool, disapproving look. "Once upon a time, there was a girl set to marry a dashin' mason known as Garvin the divine. Every woman in the Five Points wanted to wear her apron, given he made almost four dollars a week. Though she wanted to bed this Garvin well before the weddin', he wouldn't let them, given he was a good Catholic. At the time, it irked her to wait, but she was glad for it, because she most certainly didn't end up with the bastard."

Roderick's lips parted, knowing Georgia was actually talking about herself. Though he wanted to give way to a sweltering fury knowing that she had been involved with yet *another* man outside of her husband and John, he sensed this story was about to toss itself into a dark corner he had yet to understand. "So why didn't you marry this Garvin? Why did you marry Raymond?"

She glanced off to the side and blinked rapidly. "The night before she and Garvin were to marry before a priest, they went out to celebrate and have themselves a bit of mince pie and whiskey over at the dancin' hole. That's when the ever kind, ever serious and ever respectable *Mr. Raymond George Milton,* whom she'd lived with since he'd nobly rescued her out of a coal bin, followed them there. He sat in the corner of that dancin' hole all night, quietly watchin' her and Garvin. He sat there and sat there without movin' until the place was empty of but three and a fiddler."

Roderick couldn't breathe. "What did he do?"

She trailed her gaze up back to his, her features tightening but her face remaining strong. "What I hoped he would. He kneeled before the door and said, 'Georgia, I know you are set to marry, and fool that I am, I waited until the last breath, but to live without you would only make me feel as old as I already am. Say you love me. Say you love me, because I love you.' I was as moved and astounded as I was overjoyed. He'd never once breathed his affection to me, even though I had secretly yearned to be with him since I was fifteen. Raymond was kind, noble and educated and dashin' in a way no man in the Five Points was and always treated me with far more respect than I'd ever given myself. It didn't matter that he was thirty-five years older than me. I was madly in love with his mind and his soul and everythin' he'd given me as a person. He taught me to *always* want more for myself."

She shook her head, lowering her gaze. "And that's when Garvin hit him. Raymond took the blow but never fought back, sayin' he had to say it and I was so glad he did. Because I loved him. I've always loved him, but never once thought he'd want me in that way, given I was nothin' but a rag he'd patched up. So I married Raymond the next morn despite bein' spit at by Garvin's family. You think I cared? 'Twas bliss I'd found, and though I tried lovin' Raymond the best I knew how, he always shied away from all things physical. It wasn't that he didn't lust for me. He did, and he proved it when I forced him to, but he had this—this *voice* in his head that kept tellin' him his age was a vice in our relationship. No matter how hard I tried, I couldn't dig that voice out. He kept thinkin' he was debauchin' a young girl he'd managed to drag into his mess of a life, even though I was willin' and a full eighteen and his wife."

A lone tear trickled down the side of her cheek and a choked sob escaped her lips. "And then Raymond, damn him, died all but seven weeks later, on his own at three and fifty. His heart stopped. I cried over that bastard to no end knowin' that I gave him everythin'—my heart, my body and soul—only to be left with nothin'. And I fear I'm goin' down that path again with you. What if I give up everythin' and only end up with nothin'?

What then, Robinson? *What then?* My heart can only be patched up so many times."

Roderick swallowed, unable to quell the choking angst writhing within him. He reached out a trembling hand and cupped her tear-streaked cheek, utterly and madly in love with everything she was. It didn't matter that he wasn't the first man to touch her or love her. What mattered was that she was giving him a chance to love her. "Georgia," he rasped. "I would force my own damn heart to beat beyond its years to be with you. Everything I am doing, I am doing for you."

She pushed his hand away, swiping away tears. "And there's Robinson again, reachin' out for me in a way I know Tremayne wouldn't." She sniffed and sniffed again, waving her hand about. "I'm done tryin' to figure out who you really are. Just tell Robinson, if he's listenin', that I fear this Tremayne is goin' to break my heart because he and I were born of two different worlds." Her expression stilled and grew serious as she held his gaze. "Just tell me. And be honest. Will you really be able to love me with enough fire to make this last for the rest of our days? Even if your father should turn against us?"

"Georgia." Feeling the temperature of his body warming his still-rain-dampened clothes, he edged back to ensure he didn't grab for her lest he unravel and take her up against another wall. "I *know* this fire and this passion within me will outlast everything and everyone around us. Let there be no doubt in that."

She shook her head, her lips pinching together as if she were trying to fight the last of any emotion she felt.

"The words came out so beautifully, but instead of you steppin' toward me, damn you, you stepped back."

His throat tightened. "Georgia, I—"

"Don't you 'Georgia' me. You asked me to never again kneel on broken glass and yet you're makin' me kneel even though I'm tryin' to get up." Her green eyes were no longer streaked with anguish but with a raging fire that threatened to burn him to ash. "I'm willin' to play whatever role you want me to durin' the day, but I'm not doin' it when the curtain falls and the audience goes home at night. I need more than words to cradle against my heart whilst I sweat like a pig dancin' in silk for you and the world."

Still staring him down, she added, "I'm just not about to settle for a man who is goin' to do the same thing to me that Raymond did. Makin' me feel undesirable because of who and what I am. If I were you, Robinson, I'd be in my room and in my bed at nine tonight or we're done. You hear? We're done." She pointed at him one last time as if *he* were responsible for all of their troubles, then swung away and marched down the length of the corridor where the duke quietly lingered with both of his hands in his coat pockets.

Roderick swiped his face in exasperation only to wince given his hand was still tender and raw.

"Your Grace," Georgia demurely intoned to the duke in a form of artificial passing. "I'm sorry. It needed to be said."

The duke inclined his head. Lifting a gloved hand out of his coat pocket, he gestured toward the corridor beside them. "The footman is ready to settle you into your room."

"Thank you, Your Grace." She glanced back toward Roderick, set her chin and majestically swept out of sight as if she were the duchess and *he* the derelict.

Damn her.

The duke slowly made his way toward him. "Yardley."

And so, yet another battle was set to begin. "Yes, yes. I know, I know. There is a problem." Roderick gestured toward the open door of his room. "Can we take this inside?"

"Yes. I would prefer that." The duke strode past and into the room beyond.

Roderick followed him in. Quickly shutting the door, he swung back, meeting those overly serious brown eyes. "How much of our conversation did you actually overhear?"

"Her voice carried itself down every single last corridor long before I made it back into sight. I heard everything. And I do mean everything." The duke winced and adjusted his black morning coat.

Roderick groaned and bit back his frustration. "I ask that you forgive her. She is incredibly passionate."

The duke reached out and laid a heavy hand on his shoulder, bringing the scent of cigars and port. He leaned in and lowered not only his gaze but his voice. "Yardley. You will never hear me say this again, for it is none of my business who you love, but you would be a bastard of the worst sort to destroy that poor woman by dragging her into your life. It sounds as if she has already endured more than enough. You shouldn't ask her to endure more."

Roderick glanced toward him in heart-pounding astonishment. The man had indeed heard *everything* and apparently had *wanted* to hear everything to have lingered about so damn long.

Violently shoving that large hand away from his shoulder, Roderick stepped back. "Setting aside that you had no right to willfully impose and listen in on what you *knew* to be a private conversation, I am not about to stand here and listen to you prattle on as to how I seek to destroy her. *You* are the one putting *your* name and wealth before what is most important to me—*love*."

The duke pointed at him, shaking his gray head, and edged back. "No. That is where you are wrong. For I wholeheartedly believe in love and would never put anything before it. I was married to your mother, for God's sake, and *that* was a love I dare you and the rest of the world to match!"

The duke dropped his hand heavily to his side and glanced away. Drawing in a ragged breath, he hissed it out, lowering his gaze. "I never knew fire until your mother came along." The duke threw back his head and blinked rapidly as if fighting tears. "The very thought of her still makes me ache despite her being gone all these years. It just so happened that she and I were born of the same world. Such is not the case with you and Mrs. Milton."

The duke leveled his head. "Even if I allowed you to marry this poor girl for love, in the end, it is not you or I who will suffer, but her. Bless her heart, but that woman doesn't breathe like us or think like us. Your desire to make her into the sort of woman London will accept is ludicrous. It takes *years* to create the lady London wants and by then she'll be dead to you. They will only shred her apart and shun her until all of that fire you love in her will turn against you and burn you to cinder like you damn well deserve."

Grabbing hold of both his shoulders, the duke turned him toward himself and shook him gently. "Our wealth and our name are strong. They will survive this if I relent, give or take a gash or two. But *she* won't survive any of it. She sees the tide rising well above her head and is already warning you of it, yet she is still willing to drown for you. By God. *That* is a woman worth loving, and I am asking you to not only love the poor girl, but save her. Your mind isn't what it should be, which is the only reason why I have to tell you any of this. She will have everything except for the one thing that matters most—respect. And that respect will never be earned by handing over our title through marriage. She will only be seen as some wretch you plucked up off the street. Is that what you want for her?"

Shifting his jaw, Roderick glanced away and eased out of his father's grasp. "What are you asking me to do?"

"I am asking you to let her go before she suffers beyond anything your love could save her from. You must not remember what truly awaits her in London, Yardley. Or you wouldn't do this to her. I know you wouldn't. Not if you loved her."

Roderick squeezed his eyes shut in anguish. He was

damned either way. To live with her meant seeing *her* suffer, but to live without her wouldn't be a life worth living at all.

He reopened his eyes. "I cannot let her go. She is the only thing left in my life that feels real. I still know nothing of myself other than I am surrounded by a tainted world that won't even allow me to love the woman *I* want to love. Do you know how goddamn bizarre all of this is to me? I can't breathe knowing that I may be forced to live forever within a mind that isn't even my own. A mind that cannot remember anything!"

The duke was quiet for a long moment. "Though you have yet to know it, you are still the same man. Let me tell you who you are. You are a good man. A man who has always sought to do right by himself and others. You are also a learned man who earned not one but seven Oxford degrees by the time you were nineteen, putting your damned brother and everyone, including myself, to shame. Sadly, despite all that astounding knowledge you acquired, much like the rest of us male idiots roaming the world, you were unable to translate a woman's heart. 'Tis an age-old dilemma no university will resolve. You didn't learn that sometimes a man must set aside his passion before it destroys the woman he claims to love. Such was your story with the marchioness, and sadly, such will be this story."

Roderick glanced toward him, unable to believe a word of it. He had destroyed a woman? With his love? Was this before or after he had involved himself with his brother's wife?

The duke paused and patted him on the shoulder.

"Do what you will, Yardley. I am merely trying to give you sound advice. Something I haven't done much of throughout the years, given all of my damned responsibilities to the estate and life in between. Just know that regardless of what you decide, even if you should choose to make her a wife, I have decided I will stand by it. Because a true father doesn't abandon his son in a time of need, especially when it involves his lifelong happiness."

The duke patted his shoulder one last time. "I am in room one and twenty should you feel the need to further discuss this. We have ten days before we leave to London, which gives you more than enough time to resolve this. Now. I want you to get out of these wet clothes. I've already called for the footmen and the valet. They will be here shortly." The duke hesitated as if wanting to say more, but instead strode back toward the door. Opening it, he glanced toward Roderick one last time and closed the door behind himself.

When would he remember his mess of a life? When would *any* of this make sense? When would he be able to—?

Stalking toward the closed door, Roderick gnashed his teeth and kicked that door with a muddied boot, marking it with sludge. Gritting his teeth, he kicked the door again and again and again, trying to lash out his frustration, wishing that the entire world would just stay the hell out of his head.

He stumbled back, leaving the pristine oak paneled door smudged with booted muddy marks, and tried to level out of his ragged breathing. Dearest God. He was going to have to decide on something that would haunt him and Georgia for the rest of their lives. He didn't know if he had it in him to let her go, even if it meant seeing her suffer at the hands of the London elite.

Removing his muddied boots, he tossed them aside and stripped his soaked stockings, drenched coat, shirt, waistcoat and trousers, flinging them away one by one. Standing in mere undergarments, he stalked toward one of the open trunks and whipped out a dry snowy-white linen shirt, yanking it up and over himself. He tugged it down into place and smoothed it against his chest with a shaky hand, feeling the warmth slowly returning to his still-cool, damp skin. He paused and glanced toward his feet, realizing a strip of crumpled black silk had fallen out of the trunk when he'd swiped up his shirt.

He blinked. He knew what it was. It was a mourning band worn to denote the memory of someone lost. The same one Georgia had insisted he'd worn the day they had met on Broadway. It appeared he had more than one mourning band made. For how else would it have appeared here at the hotel?

He bent and carefully gathered the silk, fingering it. When would he remember the brother and the life he had lost? He glanced up and scanned the countless, useless items cluttering the room. Aside from the mourning band itself, nothing seemed to whisper of who he had once been. It only bespoke of wealth, extravagance and cosmetic comfort that had been blanked by a self-righteous mask of importance. Had he only cared about all things superficial?

He tightened his hold on the black silk, wishing that

its touch could fill this void that continued to linger in his head. Though he didn't remember being the cad his father described, he was already becoming one by forcing Georgia into a life she clearly didn't want to be a part of.

Roderick's gaze paused on the one thing in the room that did whisper of who he might have really been. Those methodically piled old leather-bound books, which had been stacked atop one another on a sizable mahogany table and a chair. Given their frayed white edges, they appeared to be well read and old, and given how perfectly they had been arranged and aligned atop one another, they also appeared to have been well loved and important to him.

He wandered over to the table, his brows coming together as he set the mourning band aside. One of the old books had been left open and set apart from the others. It was as if it was the last thing he had touched before leaving this room and disappearing from his own life.

Leaning toward it, Roderick dragged and angled the open book toward himself and read the first words he saw.

How miserably am I singled out from the enjoyment or company of all mankind. Like a hermit (rather should I say, a lonely anchorite) am I forced from human conversation. I have no creature, no soul to speak to; none to beg assistance from.

Those achingly miserable words penetrated his own breath like a blazing sword being plunged straight through his throat. He *knew* what this was. He'd read it countless times since youth.

Roderick paged through the musty, browning and roughened pages and slapped the book shut. The worn leather binding revealed the fading gold lettering of the words *The Life and Most Surprising Adventures of Robinson Crusoe, of York, Mariner.*

This book had once been his life.

Grabbing it up, he savagely dug his fingertips into that well-worn hard binding, drawing in uneven, ragged breaths. Every last emotion and thought he'd kept in his head, his heart and his soul exploded like thunder, causing his vision to blur against tears as he tried to ease the excessive trembling in his hands in an effort to keep holding that book.

He remembered.

He remembered *everything.*

He winced. Everything, that is, except for a sizable blank that simply wasn't there. Why couldn't he remember getting on a boat or arriving in New York? Why couldn't he remember what he'd done all of these months whilst *in* the city of New York? And why couldn't he remember Atwood or—?

He paused, swallowing hard. Dearest God. He and his father had found Atwood. He was alive.

Smite him, what a mess this was. What a mess. Aside from Atwood, he *still* couldn't remember the one thing he wanted to remember most: meeting Georgia prior to that omni mishap that had rendered his mind blank.

Not that it mattered anymore.

His father was right. His circle would never accept Georgia as his wife, and in time, she would only hate him in the way she already did for trying to change her, and *that* he could never live with. For her sake and for the writhing love he would feel for her given all that she had done for him when he had no one and nothing, not even a thought in his head, he would give her *everything*...by letting her go.

It was time to send good old Robinson Crusoe back into the pages of a book where he belonged.

Gently setting his book atop the stack of other books that had been given to him by his mother long ago, Roderick aligned it with the others with a trembling hand. He simply was never meant to know happiness. Not in this lifetime.

A knock made him glance up.

"Your bath is ready, my lord," a footman called from the other side of the closed door.

He cleared his throat, trying to erase any lingering emotion that still rattled his thoughts. "Thank you. You may enter."

The door veered wide and a procession of footmen in gray livery entered carrying in a large bathing tub and buckets and buckets of steaming hot water.

Once he had soaked, scrubbed and shaved and returned to a state of physical cleanliness he hadn't seen in days, he would go to his father and announce that he was leaving Georgia behind. Not because he didn't love her, but because of a new and far more disturbing

memory. He refused to destroy Georgia in the same way
he had allowed Margaret to destroy him by turning him
into something he was not.

CHAPTER THIRTEEN

Reader, I think proper, before we proceed any farther together, to acquaint thee, that I intend to digress through this whole history...
—Henry Fielding,
The History of Tom Jones (1749)

This is what had actually been, once upon a damn time in a faraway land known as England

ANYONE WHO HAD EVER MET Viscount Roderick Gideon Tremayne, if even for a quarter of an hour, became fully aware that he was unlike any man in London. Or England, for that matter. To some, he was a quintessential genius whom scholars idolized for having earned seven Oxford degrees by the time he was nineteen. To others, Roderick was nothing more than an overeducated prick. In truth, he simply held no patience for those who weren't as devoted to the art of learning as he.

His fondest memory, even as a tot, was tucking himself against the skirts of his governess at the base of her chair, and demanding she read his favorite story, *The Life and Most Surprising Adventures of Robinson Crusoe* by Daniel Defoe. The moment she'd finish, he'd promptly supply, "Again. Only slower." After all, the story should have lasted six days. Not four.

The woman would dutifully page to the beginning and read Robinson's story all over again, drawing out the words in an effort to better please him. The moment she'd finish, he would tug on her skirts and demand, "Again. Please?" The poor woman had no choice but to commence reading it again and again.

Despite him being only four, she eventually insisted to his mother and father, the Duke and Duchess of Wentworth, that he learn how to read, given his most unusual fondness for it. His father thought him far too young for such an ambitious endeavor, but his mother agreed, insisting that he should commence at once, given his unprecedented interest. Her only rule was that he was never allowed to touch or read any books pertaining to the French Revolution.

It was divine intervention. Reading was like discovering how to spin gold out of paper. Although *Robinson Crusoe* was well below his level of intelligence even at four, he'd always identified with being shipwrecked and, in turn, felt that he was the only civilized person left in the world.

His father and brother were certainly proof of that. As Roderick grew older, the duke only insisted he play more, not read more. Whilst his brother, who had been born first and therefore had been graced with the grand title of Marquess of Yardley, only trotted around the house with a blunt-edged sword and hit everything with it…including Roderick. Yardley would insist that he learn to be a man of twelve, like him, by carrying his own blunt-edged sword, so that they could battle Napoleon and his minions together.

Despite being three years younger than his brother, Roderick always felt as if he was the more mature of the two and loathed the idea of playing a Brit going up against the French. Napoleon's confinement to the island of Saint Helena in that year of 1815 by the British had reignited a burst of patriotism across England that had leaked into their father's conversations and straight into Yardley's gullible head. No one seemed to understand that Napoleon had been far more educated than most Englishmen, which was probably why it had been so damn difficult for the British to defeat him. Brain Over Brawn was his motto and, oh, how he wished it was everyone else's, too.

In an effort to avoid playing with his brother, the moment the sun touched the sky, Roderick would slip into the farthest corner of the house with a book he'd stolen from his father's library and disappear. Yardley only saw Roderick's need for privacy as great sport. With that blunt-edged sword held high, Yardley would dash through the vast corridors of their Wentworth home and strategically march from room to room hollering *"Tremaaaaaaaaaaayne!"* like the savage that he was.

No matter how well Roderick hid, that bastard always managed to yank him out of whatever corner, room or wardrobe he was hiding in. In regime-style, Yardley would then point the tip of his sword at Roderick's unevenly buttoned waistcoat and say, "You'd best cooperate or I'll tell Father that you're stealing books out of the library again. You know he doesn't want you reading books that aren't appropriate for your age."

Everything about his brother was so annoying, and him being heir only further overinflated that stupid head. Even worse, no rational form of explanation kept Yardley from seizing one of Roderick's own books and dangling it over the hearth as ransom for play. Yardley knew that the dangling of any book over a flame always riled Roderick into full cooperation. Despite grudgingly relenting to his bullying every time, Roderick insisted on being Napoleon Bonaparte himself instead of a mere British soldier, for at least then he could lay out maps and strategize how to take over the world.

When he'd grown tired of having his best maps ripped in half and being called a *Frenchie* by his brother, which yielded no educational benefits whatsoever, he refused to play with Yardley ever again. It earned him not only several unmerciful blows to the head that made him bleed, but resulted in the charring of his favorite 1734 edition of *The Complete Mineral Laws of Derbyshire* by George Steer.

Roderick did everything he could to keep himself from sobbing like a girl when he finally dragged himself up off the floor. He eventually sniffed himself over to his father and choked through tears about his burned book *and* the fists he'd taken to the head.

Every time, his father would jump to his feet and roar toward the open doors, "*Yardley!* How many times do I have to crop you? How many?"

"Leonard, really," his mother would insist in a stern tone. "Instead of yelling across the house, go directly to him and take care of it. And when you are done, send him my way. I am rather concerned with that boy's aggressive tendencies. I suggest we take away his sword."

Oh, how he loved his mother so! Even the utterance of her name—Augustine Jane Ascott, Her Grace the Duchess of Wentworth—defined her beauty and glittering greatness. She was an astonishing sixteen years younger than his staunch, overly serious father and was therefore youthful and compassionate, but firm when most needed, and above all, always sought to support his love for the written word. She would even sneak various books out from the library for him, always whispering that it was their little secret. It included books that popped his eyes wide open. Like *Le Diable amoureux* by Jacques Cazotte. It made him want to move to France and take a wife at the age of eleven.

In 1818, on his twelfth birthday, his mother, whose belly was large with yet another child, had gifted him with a stack of ten books ranging from the philosophies of Socrates to the *The Arabian Nights' Entertainments*. Inside each book, she had slipped a single uneven strip of parchment imprinted with ink that he was supposed to piece together with all the rest like a puzzle. She insisted that once pieced together the parchments would lead them on the greatest adventure they would ever know, but that she would only share said adventure *after* she'd given birth and *after* he'd read all ten books.

Roderick commenced reading within the hour and hoped to finish all ten books before his next sibling arrived. He also prayed unto whatever Lord there was that his sibling was a girl. He preferred having dolls and gowns thrown at him, as opposed to fists and swords.

Two days and four hours later, his mother died attempting to give birth to what would have been a little girl who hadn't properly turned within his mother's womb. His mother's screams, which had echoed throughout the halls well into the night, though forever silenced, still echoed within his mind and his soul, for he had lost the only person who had truly loved him. He'd never stood second in her eyes. Not once. Not ever.

His father went into an unconventional form of mourning that demanded they pray before her portrait every Sunday after church for the rest of their lives. The man swore never to marry again and never did.

Unlike his brother and father, who solemnly bore their suffering in silence like real men, Roderick sobbed through his prayers like the sop that he was, knowing that his mother was never coming back.

His mother had wanted him to be a great scholar, whilst his father only wanted him to be a mere boy. So in honor of his dear mother, whom he still sought to make proud, Roderick became both. He donned a sword during the day to please his father and brother, and at night, he retired into his covert library in the dressing chamber and read the remaining books his mother had gifted unto him. The moment he finished each book, he anxiously pieced together yet another strip of the uneven parchment hoping to discover what had been left unsaid.

When Roderick had at long last finished reading all ten of his mother's books, and had pieced together all ten of those uneven parchments, he was astonished to discover it was a map of New York City as had been laid out by the commissioners and altered and arranged to the present time. One area, in particular, to the far east of that map had been circled with smeared black ink, similar to how a thief might have marked his next heist.

Though he had asked his father about the map and why his mother had given it to him, the duke became unusually huffy and demanded he put it away lest he burn it. It was a very odd reaction to a mere map, but he most certainly didn't want to upset his father. So Roderick tucked the mysterious map within the pages of his *Robinson Crusoe,* which he always kept at his bedside, hoping that he would eventually come to understand its true meaning.

In the year of 1819, which marked the one-year anniversary of his mother's death, two days before he was set to leave the house and join his brother at Eton, he pulled out all ten strips of the map in her honor and pieced it back together again. He strategically laid everything out across the floor of the library wondering if his mother had actually wanted them to go to the marking shown. And if so, why? What would he find there?

When his father strode into the library unannounced and saw him hovering over the map, the man frantically gathered all of the pieces and insisted he cease meddling with superstitious taradiddles. Though his father tried to burn the pieces, Roderick flung himself before the hearth and begged in the name of his mother that it not be done.

His father grudgingly relented by returning the

pieces back into his hands under the proviso that he never see it again. To ensure its safety from any of Yardley's book-burning rants, Roderick stacked all ten of his mother's books and tucked all the pieces of her map between the pages of his *Robinson Crusoe*. He then snuck up into the garret and buried his mother's books in his covert trunk.

Two days later, he left the house to join his brother at Eton. He forever worried about that map, but was too paranoid to mention it to anyone lest he be robbed of it. Every holiday, when he and Yardley visited their father between academic terms, he would tiptoe into the garret at night to ensure that his trunk and its contents were still there. They always were.

In time, he became far less paranoid and thought of it less and less. Life held far too many of its own adventures and he most certainly was not old enough to travel to New York City on his own. He was simply going to have to be patient and bide his time.

Unlike his brother, Tremayne reveled and thrived at Eton and became rather popular with all the boys because he was always willing to do everyone's work in exchange for books he couldn't afford to buy on the measly pension his father gave him. Roderick soon acquired an extensive and impressive collection of more than three hundred books on divinity, civil history, poetry, anatomy and jurisprudence.

Based on his perfect marks that exceeded even his own expectations, the headmaster transitioned him straight into Oxford University at a mere fourteen. When Roderick had effortlessly passed every examination required of him during his terms and became the youngest Oxford scholar to hold a degree at sixteen, his father said, "By God. That all went rather fast. What now? You don't plan on getting more degrees, do you?"

That only irked Roderick into throwing himself all the more into university life, which had become his greatest passion. By nineteen, he had acquired a total of *seven* degrees, astounding university professors into thinking he was a genius. He wasn't. He merely had the unique ability to remember everything he read.

But his father, damn him, only kept interrupting his studies by nagging Roderick on the hour about his lack of *social* interaction. The man's definition of *social* meant women. Because Roderick was always out and about *socializing* with scholars, professors, students and book collectors. His father's nagging stemmed from quips in all the circles that Roderick was not only a virgin, but a bibliomaniac who preferred a good book over a woman.

Which was, in fact, true. He *did* prefer a good book over a woman and was indeed a virgin. Not because he was a queer who didn't find women attractive, but because the women in his books were far more fascinating than the ones surrounding him. If swiving was about all a *real* woman could offer him outside the pages of a book, he knew he could easily accomplish equal ecstasy from a pornographic novel without the complication of being nagged by yet another person who would *never* understand him. Based on all the grouching of fellow university friends who only complained about their woes regarding sex and women over decanters of port, he simply wasn't interested in joining in on the grouching.

Despite his unconventional view, he acknowledged his father's concerns and, like a good son, tried to render the quips. He sought to keep it respectable, however, by methodically planning out how he was going to land the perfect wife by creating a list of all the qualities he sought in a woman. When he arrived in London during the opening Season of 1828, at the age of two and twenty—and yes, still very much a virgin— Roderick announced to his father that he was ready to wade through the marriageable women London had to offer.

His father astounded him by handing him a cigar, even though Roderick didn't smoke. The man then proceeded to strut around the study like a rooster about to mount his last hen and clucked on and on about all the grandchildren he'd have and how he hoped it was soon, given that Yardley was more interested in bordellos than marriage and duty.

Roderick had at long last found something to make the old man proud. With that newfound pride in his pocket, Roderick donned his finest, ensuring the valet trimmed his hair, which was beginning to hang well past his eyes, and took on the appearance of a true gentleman in honor of the Wentworth name. He vowed to marry the most beautiful, intelligent and respectable woman London had to offer and rode out into the crowds to find her.

Night after night, he endured pointless conversations

about food and wine and danced alongside morbidly silent debutantes.

Yardley only annoyed him throughout his hunt for a wife by swooping in on him at gatherings and mouthing excessive encouragement from behind a hand shortly before Roderick was set to dance. "Always dance with the one with the largest tits, Tremayne. They jiggle more. Same rule should apply to the wife you take. After all, you will be looking at the same goddamn tits for the rest of your life."

Yardley was breathing proof that some men remained children all of their lives.

Needless to say, Roderick was beginning to lose hope that any woman would ever catch his eye. But then it happened…much like a stray arrow piercing his heart on an angle between the fourth and fifth ribs, just as diagrammed in his anatomy book. A certain Lady Margaret, with bright blue eyes and curling blond hair, made her debut and breezed into London's ballrooms, catching not only *his* eye, but every man's who'd ever been born with an ambition to love.

Whilst every man of the *ton,* including Yardley himself, went about quietly admiring her with a reserved reverence that was expected from respectable society, Roderick went about shouting out his admiration at every breathing turn.

His father had to repeatedly tell him to calm down.

Those first few times her pretty gaze had fluttered over to his, endless unwritten words floated between them, stirring far more than his mind. He had at long last discovered the savage need to hold more than a book and finally knew why men subjected themselves to a lifetime of grouching.

Lady Margaret was everything known as divine. She danced with him at every ball whenever he asked her to put his name on her dance card. She always seemed to dance with far more enthusiasm whenever it was with him, *especially* if it involved the ever-daring waltz. Her gloved hand would squeeze his in the oddest of moments during their gliding steps, as if she were openly professing her love. He returned each and every squeeze of that small hand, assuring her that he ardently felt the same.

She laughed so beautifully whenever he expounded upon humor that no one else thought was funny, and listened to everything he had to say, no matter how boring. There was one particular night, however, that he'd never forget.

It was the night when he grabbed her hand and placed it over his heart on his chest, whilst they lingered in the alcove during a gathering at his grandparents' home. Her chaperone had been unusually preoccupied in speaking to his grandmother across the room, so he deviously took advantage of it. Lady Margaret responded by grabbing his own hand and setting it back onto his chest over his heart, whispering, "You must call on me and Mama with an offer. Why do you wait?"

He had waited because he wanted to be sure she felt the same. He had doubted that she had, given all the damned rules of their circle that didn't allow them to convey what it was they truly felt for each other. He knew it was time to propose before someone else did and approached his father about it. His father not only consented to the match, but was so thrilled that he insisted Roderick call on the woman and her mother at once to ensure a June wedding.

So Roderick decided to send over a footman with a note to the marchioness, requesting he be allowed to call upon her. He was worried that his note would get lost amidst the throngs of bouquets, visitors and calling cards from countless other gentlemen, both titled and gentry alike, who littered his Margaret's doorstep on the hour like an infestation of locusts out of the Bible. He panicked upon discovering one of those titled men was none other than his own damn brother.

But he outsmarted them all.

Roderick paid every last one of Lady Morrow's servants to strategically place his note on the marchioness's dressing table as opposed to the parlor. Within a day, a messenger presented him with an invitation from the marchioness to call upon her and her daughter, Lady Margaret. That was when he knew he was going to be a husband. He and his father merrily toasted and drank port in honor of his success.

Nervous as hell, Roderick arrived with his hat in hand, and waited in a pale blue drawing room that had been fragranced with expensive French perfume. It was a strong lilac scent he would forever associate with the frantic beat of his heart and that glorious moment when his Margaret and her staunch widow of a mother, Lady Morrow, sashayed into the room in unison to formally greet him.

Margaret beamed as she and her mother gracefully

seated themselves on the settee across from him and he knew that it was time to toss the dice in the right direction. So he commenced their conversation by stepping away from all things formal and sharing *A Dissertation on the Phaedon of Plato* and its investigation of the nature of the soul. It was cheeky and metaphoric. Margaret stifled a laugh, while the marchioness only tartly stared him down.

Sensing the woman's humor was similar to that of his father's, he casually inquired about nothing in particular. The marchioness looked decidedly more pleased and proceeded to discuss the weather, before pausing to inquire about his father's health and if he was taking care of himself for she was rather worried he wasn't. Ghastly though it was—for his father took very good care of himself—Roderick sensed she wanted to know when his brother would be inheriting.

Barely twenty minutes into his call, the marchioness visibly grew bored and glanced toward the French clock on the mantelpiece, signaling that his visit was over.

He knew it was now or never.

"Lady Morrow," he announced in a formal tone. "Before I depart, I humbly wish to claim the honor of your daughter's hand in matrimony." Roderick drew in a steadying breath. "I love her."

The marchioness paused and leveled him with an alarmed stare. "Whilst I am endlessly humbled, Lord Tremayne, I regret to inform you, especially given your unexpected affection for my daughter, that Lord Yardley has already offered on her hand and I have accepted his offer all but two days ago. I invited you to call on me today, not to entertain an offer, but as a means of getting to know you as family."

Roderick met Margaret's bewildered gaze, which reflected his own, and felt himself unable to breathe. "What?"

Margaret intently held his gaze, fear and angst noticeably freezing those blue eyes and trembling lips. "I…" She lowered her gaze and after a long moment confided, "I was not aware of the offer, my lord."

Roderick shifted forward in his seat, trying to rein in his disbelief. He glanced over at Lady Morrow. "How is it that your own daughter is unaware of this offer, given that two days have passed since it was made? Do you find this sort of backdoor business respectable, madam? To be casting aside your daughter's own happiness without allowing her an opportunity to vie for her own future?"

Lady Morrow rose from her seat, her lavish morning gown cascading into place around her slippered feet. "How dare you insinuate that I seek to invest in my daughter's misery? To insult me is to insult everything we represent. I ask that you depart at once, my lord, lest my footman toss you and your hat out the door."

Roderick narrowed his gaze. "Your footman can go to hell. Your daughter loves me, not Yardley. As such, you will inform Yardley that you are retracting your acceptance of his offer and giving her hand to me."

The marchioness gasped, her face blanching. "Leave."

"No," he bit out. "My brother is unworthy of her. He barely treats me with the sort of respect I deserve.

What sort of respect do you think he will bestow upon her? *None*. He knew I intended to propose to her. I told him."

Gathering her gown from around her feet, the marchioness hastened toward the open parlor doors. *"Harvington?"* she called out, her voice panicked and trembling. "Harvington, remove this man and ensure he never calls upon this house again."

Margaret, whose tears were freely streaming down her anguished face, regally rose from her seat. She set her chin, trying to keep her features stoic. "My lord. I ask that you leave with the dignity you arrived with. My mother knows what is best. Respect that and me."

His eyes widened. "You intend to blindly accept this slap against my honor and yours?"

She closed her eyes. "My mother is all I have."

"Margaret—"

"There is nothing more to be said or done, my lord." She reopened her eyes and stubbornly set her chin. "Please."

"I see." He rose from his upholstered seat, still holding her gaze. It was obvious his Margaret wasn't going to fight for the love he had so stupidly thought was theirs. He refused to degrade himself by loving such a woman. "Given your devotion to your mother and my brother, I formally withdraw my offer. I wish you and Yardley much happiness. Good day." He strode out of the parlor, trying to appear indifferent as the footman yanked open the entrance door.

Days later, rumors had surfaced all across London about how unrefined and conceited he was to think he could have *any* woman he wanted. It was the first time in his life he had ever felt the true impact of being shipwrecked and deserted upon that desolate island known as the Second Son.

His father was anything but pleased and rambled on and on about how stupid he was to have destroyed his own happiness by his lack of patience and tact. The duke insisted that he call on Lady Morrow with an apology and try to get her to agree to breaking off the agreement with Yardley. Roderick refused to degrade what little he was worth and told his own father to go to hell. If Margaret wasn't about to contest the marriage, why should he?

Within days, a wedding was set to take place in June, though it was not his own. Lady Margaret and his brother formally announced their engagement before all of London. Yardley, whose idea of true literature was *The Accomplished Whore,* had at long last sought to abandon whoring to become a married man, claiming *Roderick's* woman for his own.

His father, who knew Yardley's intentions were simply to best his brother, had repeatedly tried to talk Yardley out of it, but Yardley insisted no other woman would do and that it wasn't *his* fault Roderick hadn't been able to impress Lady Morrow.

Barely a day after the engagement had been announced, Roderick was further stunned when Margaret appeared at his door late one night, cloaked from head to toe in her scullery maid's clothing. She had even smudged her face with ash to keep anyone from recognizing her. She begged that he forgive her for submitting to her mother's wishes but that she still loved him.

He told her to leave.

She wouldn't.

So he grabbed her by the arm to lead her straight back to that front door, but Margaret, damn her, grabbed *him* and kissed him with an unnerving passion that ended whatever rational thought he'd placed in his head since he was four. All was lost. From that moment on, he only sought to listen to the beat of his own heart, no matter how erratic or deranged it was.

Whilst they frantically and savagely kissed, they eventually stumbled off into his study to ensure their privacy and closed the doors. They kept kissing and kissing until he lost a cravat and she lost a bonnet. Everything was slowly fumbled off of their bodies one by one, until they were naked.

Though they hesitated every now and then in the silence of his study, knowing they shouldn't, the passion between them was far too great, and to his disbelief and joy, Margaret begged that he ruin her so that they could be together.

He couldn't say no.

Or rather...he *wouldn't* say no.

He ardently penetrated her virginity with his own, branding her and himself for life. When they were virgins no more but well-sated sinners, he cradled her softness against his chest and informed her that he would sell everything of worth so they could leave to Paris within the week. What did it matter if they no longer lived like kings and respectable society turned against them? All that mattered was seeing their love crowned.

Margaret quietly eased out of his arms and eventually whispered, "We cannot publicly shame our families by disappearing to Paris. It would slaughter my mother's name and all would turn against her, blaming her for my sins. She wouldn't survive this."

He grabbed her and yanked her back into his arms. "What will you have us do, then? Live here? It would be hell of the worst sort, no better by any means. London would spit at all that we represent and my father could very well disown me, given that your banns have already been printed and announced in church."

She wouldn't look at him and only half nodded as if in a daze, just now realizing the futility of what she'd done. "'Tis obvious what must be done. I do not wish you disowned or shamed, nor do I wish the same for my mother. I must therefore…marry your brother."

"Marry him?" he seethed out, shaking her in savage restraint. "But you are mine now, Margaret. *Mine,* damn you. Not his."

She still wouldn't look at him. Her hand trembled as she swiped away loose strands of blond hair from her cheek. "What choice have I in this? My mother wills it and your brother and all of London and the church expect it."

And so the inner rot within him truly began.

Oh, how he hated her. How he hated her for not only sacrificing herself in the name of everyone and everything around her, making her own heart and dignity bleed, but he hated her for seizing the last of his own heart and his virginity, which he had sought to gift to his own wife on his wedding night. Now it would appear he had nothing to gift. It had all been taken away.

What a fool he'd been to think he could actually love a woman within his circle without turning it into super-ficial duty and lies. Every last woman of the aristocracy was bred to obey the rules of their elders and their circle by putting duty before their hearts, even when that duty was rotten to its core and undeserving of being honored.

UNWILLING TO FACE HIS BROTHER after what he had done, let alone attend the wedding that should have been his, Roderick wordlessly left London a week before Yard-ley made it to the altar. He went to Paris with a univer-sity friend instead.

Napoleon Bonaparte had wronged his beautiful France by making the world think the worst of it, be-cause Paris, sweet Paris, was the breath of glorious air he'd been gasping for. He extended his stay beyond the mere month he had originally arranged and decided to stay for another five.

Everything about Paris was not only riveting but rav-ishing. Aside from the people, the food, the music, the gardens and the streets, delightful discoveries of incred-ible books like *La citoyenne Roland,* sitting crookedly upon dusty old shelves of quiet bookshops, made him all the more thankful to be part of everything known as France.

He was pleased to discover that the women in Paris, unlike those in London, could be paged through and opened like books without snapping any of their bindings. French women were by far more intelligent and valued the real worth of a man, be he a first son or a second or a third. He loved them all for it, and they, in turn, loved him because he always paid the bill.

Although he generously showered countless women with gifts, no matter the expense or her status or lack thereof, he didn't do it for a fuck like the rest of the men around him. He did it because he enjoyed sharing his money with those that had none. In truth, when it came to *fucking,* he had become so morbidly selective after what Margaret had done to him that he refused to physically get involved with a woman at all.

He eventually decided, however, that he needed to move on. So he created a list in the hopes of yanking himself out of the abyss by unearthing a woman worthy of him. One he could share a corner of his life with without the expectations of his circle or matrimony.

After staring at a blank parchment for half the night, only *one* requirement came to mind: she had to be able to make him laugh before he'd so much as loosen his cravat. Though his requirement seemed stupid and easily attainable, there wasn't a woman in Paris who *could* make him laugh. His soul had become far too warped and dark to find *anything* amusing and he hated Margaret *and* his brother all the more because of it.

But thankfully…that changed.

Whilst attending a social event for local artists looking for patrons, he met a certain Mademoiselle Sophie, a flamboyant actress with brick-red hair and a saucy smile who wasn't at all pretty but was *incredibly* witty and had enough fire to burn down all of Paris. She had a remarkable gift, for she could not only make him laugh about the most foolish things, twisting her words and facial expressions at the most perfect of times, but she could actually make him laugh *so* hard, he'd be close to crying. And God, did he ever need it.

When he eventually decided to invite Sophie up for an evening alone in his flat after weeks and weeks of flirtations spent over champagne, conversation and theater, it was the best decision he'd made. He learned to love sex in a way he never thought possible.

One rainy morning, whilst Sophie lounged naked on his bed, reading aloud the latest in French gossip, which she always lived for, Roderick sipped on his coffee and wandered over to the window of his flat on *rue des Francs-Bourgeois.* As the grid of the streets below laid itself out like a bird's view of a map, he came to remember his mother's map for the first time in years. The one he'd buried long ago against the eaves in the garret of his father's home.

Roderick was appalled, realizing he'd been obsessing over all the wrong things in his life. He knew he had to retrieve that map and do right by it, but he also knew it meant going back to London and facing his brother, whose wedding he'd never attended and whose wife he'd bedded.

Days passed and thoughts of his mother ate away at his ability to breathe and think. After avoiding the reality of the mess he knew he had to return to, Roderick sucked in his pride and returned to London. He toted back not only Sophie, whose friendship he'd grown dependant on, but several trunks filled to the lid with books he'd acquired from Paris. After he settled Sophie and his trunks, he decided to visit his father and announce to the man that he was back from Paris.

As his coach arrived through the vast iron gates leading to the Wentworth home, Tremayne was astounded to glimpse through the narrow glass window a funeral wreath hanging upon his father's door. The door had even been painted black as had been done on the death of his mother those many, many years ago.

CHAPTER FOURTEEN

'Twas dead of the night, when I sat in my dwelling;
One glimmering lamp was expiring and low;
Around, the dark tide of the tempest was swelling.
Along the wild mountains night-ravens were yelling...
—By a Gentleman of the University of Oxford,
St. Irvyne; or, The Rosicrucian, A Romance (1811)

A PULSING KNOT OVERTOOK Roderick's breath. Flinging open the carriage door before it could even roll to a halt, he jumped down, skidding against the gravel beneath his boots, and dashed up the paved stairs leading to the main entrance of his father's home. He pounded and pounded on the door with a gloved fist, his chest and throat tight as he tried to ignore the funeral wreath.

When the butler unlatched and edged open the door, he shoved past the man and stumbled inside. *"Father?"* he shouted, his voice eerily echoing around him as he sprinted toward the direction of the study where he knew the man would be if he were still alive. *"Father!"*

The duke staggered out from the study like an apparition floating out from the shadows into candlelight, making Roderick skid to a halt. The man's gray hair was unusually shaggy, heavily mussed and oily as if he hadn't tended to himself in weeks. His evening attire was as disheveled as the rest of him, lacking not only cleanliness but a coat and cravat. A near-empty decanter of brandy was in his hand.

"Father?" Roderick whispered in disbelief.

Tired and darkly solemn eyes that were under the influence of brandy met his across the length of the corridor. "Typhus took Yardley. It took him. No doctor could…save him. I sent word to you in Paris, but obviously neither he nor…I meant anything to you or you would have come sooner. Don't bother me tonight. We will…talk on the morrow." He lowered his gaze and staggered back into the study.

The corridor swayed and he along with it.

Roderick fell against a wall and slid down its length, unable to withstand the weight of his own limbs. He'd never received anything. Not a letter. Not a word. Not even a whisper of a word.

Oh, God.

He stayed on the marble floor, a gloved fist pressed against his temple, too overwhelmed to do much of anything. When the servants had commenced lighting more lamps and candles to keep him from sitting in darkness, Roderick willed himself to stand on booted feet. A part of him still refused to believe that Yardley was gone.

Removing a lit candle from the nearest sconce, he drifted up the stairs he'd climbed so many times in his youth and turned down the corridor, pausing before Yardley's old bedchamber. The door was ajar and the room softly lit by a lone lamp.

Roderick quietly wandered inside, the lingering smell of leather and shoe polish reminding him of

Yardley. Upon glimpsing the four-poster bed, Roderick paused, the candle almost slipping from his trembling gloved fingers. A faded red ceremonial sash and a blunted sword had both been set upon the bed linens as if Yardley would trot into the room at any moment in the form of a child, snatch them up and don them, challenging Roderick to yet another game of Napoleon against British soldier.

Tears stung his eyes. He should have been a better brother. He should have been a better man. Instead, he had proven to be an even bigger prick than Yardley could have ever been. Roderick swung away and blew out the candle with a puff, flinging it to the floor where it rolled out of sight. Stripping his gloves from his hands, he tossed them.

Roderick wandered about the corridors aimlessly until he paused before the small wood door inlaid behind the top stairwell leading into the garret above. He stared at the latch. It had been many years since he'd last opened that door. How was it he'd so heartlessly lost sight of everything that had once meant the world to him?

Creaking open the door, he slowly made his way up into the narrowing garret, a headache pinching his skull. Though he tried to steady his breathing, the horrid ache he felt within his chest wouldn't go away.

Kneeling before the trunk he'd tucked against the eaves so many years ago, he unbuckled the leather straps and pushed it wide open. Shadows covered its empty bottom. He staggered in disbelief and clung to the edges of the trunk in an effort to balance himself.

Every book his mother had given him, including his cherished 1775 edition of Defoe's *The Life and Most Surprising Adventures of Robinson Crusoe,* which held his mother's map of New York City within its pages, was gone.

It was as if his life had been erased.

After staring at that empty bottom for much too long, he shut its lid and prayed his father had simply placed all of the books into the library. Hefting the leather trunk up into his arms, he made his way down and out of the garret, past Yardley's old bedchamber, and veered down that vast stairwell leading down to the main floor.

Walking in through the open doors, his heavy steps dissonantly echoed against the expanse of the study. Depositing the trunk before his father's desk with a thud, he lingered, unable to voice all of the agonizing emotion buried within him.

His father glanced up, the rim of yet another half-empty brandy decanter hovering before his lips. "What is it?"

After a moment of awkward silence, Roderick choked out, "Do you think so little of me as to believe that neither you nor Yardley meant anything to me? You are the only person left in this world that I can love and that I can trust. As for Yardley...he may not have understood me or respected me in the manner that I deserved, and I may not have understood him or respected him in the manner that *he* deserved, but we were brothers. I never received word of his passing whilst I was in Paris. If I had, I would have come. I simply didn't know."

His father's large hand trembled. He swallowed a

gulp of brandy and set aside the decanter with a *clink*.
Lowering his gaze to his hand, which limply rested on
the desk beside the brandy, the duke finally murmured,
"The damn post is never reliable. Don't blame yourself."

The duke scrubbed his hair and fell back against his
leather chair, eyeing him. "Both Lady Morrow and the
Marchioness of Yardley have been inquiring as to your
whereabouts. I suggest you call on them. Offer whatever comfort they require in the name of your brother."

Roderick's throat tightened. He knew full well why
they were inquiring. He'd heard the rumors well across
into Paris that Margaret's marriage to Yardley had
yielded nothing but misery over its five short months,
and with his brother now gone, only one man remained
heir to the entire Wentworth estate. *Him*. "I refuse to
see either of them."

His father's gray brows rose up to his hairline. "You
don't intend to offer your condolences to your own
brother's wife?"

"No. I don't."

Color bloomed in his father's features. He leaned
forward in his chair. "If you don't call on them at
least once, London will be left to wonder why and I'll
not have whispers floating about my name." His fist
slammed against the desk, causing the brandy within
the glass to slosh. "'Tis indecent enough you weren't
here when Yardley was lowered into the ground. I
expect you to be devoted not only to the memory of
your brother but to the duty you were born to. And now
that you have inherited your brother's title, you will

heed the responsibility that accompanies it. You are no longer merely Tremayne. You are now a Yardley."

Roderick shifted from boot to boot, already feeling himself being fitted into the role his brother had left behind. "I wasn't born into the role of heir and therefore you cannot expect me to play the part of one. I will devote myself to the memory of my brother by wearing a mourning band for the rest of my days, but I have absolutely no desire to see the marchioness *or* her mother and console them over a death I have no doubt they care little about. They used me to get to Yardley and they will use Yardley's death to get to me."

His father glanced toward the entrance of the study and lowered his voice, meeting his gaze. "Yardley seethed on and on about you and the marchioness prior to his death. He claimed you bedded her prior to him taking her to the altar. Is that true? Or was he just being a cad as always?"

Roderick set trembling hands behind his back, the sting of those words biting into the last of what he was. "'Tis true. I had hoped to convince her to run off with me to Paris. Obviously, I did not succeed."

"Dearest God." The duke threw his head back with an exasperated groan. "I would have expected this from your…brother, God rest his soul. He was a man's man and rough around every edge no matter how many times I took a crop to him. But I would have never expected this from you. What became of that boy I loved so much?"

Roderick swallowed against the tears that overwhelmed him. It was the first time his father had openly admitted to not only having had pride in him but to having loved him. Though little good that did him now. He had destroyed that love and that pride, and, in turn, had destroyed himself.

The duke leaned far forward and into the desk and hissed out a breath. He eyed the empty trunk Roderick had toted into the study and gestured sloppily toward it. "What is that?"

Roderick's voice faded, remembering why he'd come to him to begin with. "I found it empty up in the garret and wish to inquire as to what has been done with its contents. They held some of my old books."

"Books?" The duke blinked rapidly. "Ah. Yes. Books." He nodded and shifted in his seat. "A book collector who'd been visiting with your cousin kept pestering me. So I had the servants wade through everything in the house and let him…take everything away."

Roderick stared at him in agonizing disbelief. The man had no idea what those books meant to him. "Those books were given to me by Mother."

His father's gruff tone softened and he seemed to momentarily appear sober. "What?"

"She gifted them to me shortly before she died. I placed them all in a trunk in the garret to prevent anyone from touching them."

His father closed his eyes, rubbing the palm of his hand against his temple. "What the hell were they doing up in the garret? Why didn't you…tell me?"

"I always hid things in the garret with Yardley being prone to burning my books. Something you may or may not remember. Either way, I want those books back. 'Tis all I have of her."

Reopening his eyes, the duke dropped his hand onto his lap. "The man already left England."

"Whatever do you mean he left England?" Roderick echoed. "You handed them off to a foreigner?"

"An American. From New York."

He choked. *"An American from New York?* Dear God. What if he finds the map? What if he thinks it's of worth and never gives it back?"

His father squinted up at him. "Whatever the devil... what map?"

"The map!" Roderick roared, unable to contain his own agony. "The one Mother gave me. The one of New York City! The one you threatened to burn every time I pulled it out. I placed it in one of those books for safe-keeping and you gave it away!"

His father's lips parted. "I didn't know."

Roderick squeezed his eyes shut and forced himself to lull his tone and his stance. "Why did she give it to me? What was it? What did it mean? And why was it so oddly separated into pieces?"

The duke lowered his gaze. "'Twas nothing," he mumbled. "'Twas nothing but a damn...fabrication."

Reopening his eyes, Roderick intently held his father's gaze. "For something that you wished to burn every time you saw it, 'tis clearly more than a mere fabrication. What was it?" His throat burned in a desperate effort to keep his words and himself calm.

The duke half nodded and eventually murmured, "It pertained to her brother."

Roderick's brows rose. "I never knew she had siblings."

"One. 'Twas a sad story, that." His father shifted in his seat, adjusting his coat. "His name was Atwood. He and your mother were incredibly close. He was heir to the…Sumner estate and all but ten years old when he disappeared."

Roderick held his father's gaze. "What happened to him?"

The duke rubbed at his temple. "Your grandfather had whisked them all out of London and into New York back in…oh, I don't know, 1800 or so, as he was negotiating investments. Shortly before they were set to return to London…he disappeared. That was the last they had ever seen of him."

Roderick set a hand against his mouth in disbelief and asked through his hand, "Did they not find anything?"

"No. Not even a body. When they eventually returned to London without him, Atwood's portraits and all of his belongings were stripped from the home. Your mother managed to confiscate a miniature of him from a servant and carried it with her at all times…. The whole thing…haunted me. It still does."

His father shifted his jaw and leaned back against his chair. "Many, many years later, she appeared to me clinging Atwood's portrait whilst I was at breakfast. She…she told me she had a dream about a parchment that had been torn into ten different pieces and that… when she had pieced them all together, it revealed a map of New York City bearing a circled area that showed his location. She claimed that in her dream, she knew without any doubt he was still, in fact, alive. As such, she demanded we purchase every map of New York City we could find that would best match it."

The duke shook his head. "It was...*illogical*. She spent weeks replicating it. Right down to...tearing it into pieces. I kept telling her she was falling into the realm of superstitious hysteria. But it only got worse. She wouldn't sleep, she wouldn't...eat. And all she kept telling me was that she wouldn't know peace until the matter was resolved. She was pregnant at the time with our third and I was worried. So I told her if she promised to eat and to sleep, that once she'd given birth, we would all go to New York and lay it to rest." His father's voice faded. He pressed his fingers against his stubbled chin and lowered his gaze. "Only she never survived the birth, damn her. She never survived. She...left me. She left us."

Silence pulsed between them.

All of his poor mother's pent-up hopes of finding her brother, whom she had yearned to love to the very end, had sat up in that damn garret untouched, unsolved and unloved. It was monstrous. "You knew what it meant to her," he rasped, "and yet you never sought to look into the matter yourself? Even after she died?"

The duke glanced away, struggling to sit up in his chair. "'Twas nonsense I didn't care to break my heart over. I had two boys left to raise on my own."

"'Twas *nonsense?*" he echoed, stepping toward the desk. "How could anything that meant so much to her be considered nonsense?"

Roderick leaned toward him, slamming both hands on the smooth mahogany between them. "We are getting that damn map back, even if we have to buy out this bastard's entire shop and all of New York. When did you dispose of those books?"

His father eyed him. "A few weeks ago."

"Which means they can still be recovered."

"If the man hasn't already sold them all."

"We'll ensure he buys them all back. We'll make it worth his while." Roderick swiped a hand across his face. "Do you have a name? An address? Anything?"

The duke blew out a pained breath. He glanced up, his features tightening in an effort to remember. "Hatchet. He was this—this…stocky, boisterous fellow who owned a shop somewhere in…New York. Though I don't remember much else. Your cousin Edwin would know more."

Roderick pushed himself away from the desk and straightened. With his brother now gone, their family was tragically dwindling into nothingness. It was heartwrenching. What if the map his mother had created did, in fact, lead to something? What if it led to Atwood? A part of their family would be restored and honored. "I'll call on Edwin in the morning. The moment I have an address, I intend to leave on the next ship out and retrieve that map in person. I also intend to investigate whether or not the map is true. There must be clues investigators missed. For all we know that map might reopen the investigation into Atwood's disappearance."

His father jumped to his feet, sending the chair backward with a clatter. He swayed in an effort to stare him down. "Are you mad? Do you actually intend to run off to the other side of the world looking for clues based off of a…dream?"

Despite the flaring of his own nostrils, Roderick still managed to remain calm. "What if you're wrong? What if that map leads us to something? Anything? Even a whisper of anything is more than *nothing*. We won't know unless we put this to rest."

"No. I am not about to—"

"If you go against me in this, Father, I will never forgive you for not loving your wife enough to oversee her last wish."

The duke glanced away, his ragged features twisting. Sniffing hard, he glanced down at the empty decanter. A tear traced its way down his weathered cheek.

Setting his shoulders, his father cleared his throat. "You and Yardley were the only reason I survived her death." The duke leaned heavily into the desk and pointed at him through tears and choked out, "You are all that remains of her. You are the *only* assurance I have that she was even real. You can't be putting yourself in harm's way. Because if anything happens to you…I won't survive it. I will slit my bloody throat and *die*. Do you understand me?"

Reaching out over the desk, Roderick forcefully grabbed ahold of his father's large hand and squeezed it hard, crushing it against his palm. "I understand you more than you think and I am touched to know I mean so much to you. You mean just as much to me." Intently holding his father's gaze, he offered in a choked tone, "But she entrusted that map to me, Father. I intend to uphold her honor as is my right as her son, and I wish to restore what little remains of our family." Roderick leaned in closer and whispered, "I ask that we do this together. She would have wanted us to. Don't you think?"

His father released his hand and turned away, stumbling away from the desk. He swiped a shaky hand across the back of his neck and lingered as if battling between a drunken mind and drunken heart.

Do not disappoint me, and above all, do not disappoint her, Roderick inwardly chanted. *Love her. Love her this one last time.*

The duke eventually swung back, his features tightening. "To hell with London and the…time and the… expense. We go. We go and put your mother's soul to rest."

It would seem Roderick had been blinded into never seeing the greatness of the man standing before him. Drunk though he was. "Do you still have that miniature? We will need a detailed description of what he looked like when he disappeared. We will need his likeness. At least his coloring, provided he will have aged."

The duke lowered his gaze and shook his head. "I tucked it into your mother's hand before she was buried. But I…I've seen it enough times. Black hair. Black brows. And blue eyes. Very striking eyes that were so unusually bright in color, they almost looked like…blue glass."

"We need more than that," Roderick insisted. "We will have to go to Grandpapa and Grandmama with this. They would be able to provide us a better description as well as any other details pertaining to his disappearance."

The duke paused and leveled him with a warning gaze, slowly shaking his head from side to side. "No. No. *No.* I don't want your grandfather involved in this. He must never know. *Never.*"

Roderick blinked and leaned toward him. "I would think he has the right to know. It involves his own son. He could help us."

The duke continued to stare him down. "No." He lowered his voice. "That man was responsible for Atwood's disappearance."

Roderick stared at him, his breath hitching. "*What?* How so?"

His father glanced away and shrugged. "It wasn't anything your mother or I could ever prove, even though we repeatedly tried to involve the crown's investigators throughout the years. They only…brushed it off and were convinced it had been American patriots who had committed the crime. Only it didn't make sense. In my opinion…given what we are about to do… we tell no one. This way, nothing will impede the reopening of our investigation."

Sagging both palms against his father's desk, Roderick hissed out a breath. "God help us if any of this is true."

"I know," his father muttered. "Believe me, I know."

It would seem a map based off of a dream and a rather sorry description of a ten-year-old boy who would no longer be ten—*if he were alive*—was all they had. It already appeared improbable that they were going to find anything. But then again...the boy had been old enough to have known who he had once been. Perhaps that boy was now a man who still remembered what had happened. Regardless, he and his father had money and time on their side.

Not even a day later, Roderick was fitted for a set of mourning bands. He donned one on his arm that day in honor of his brother, swearing it would never leave his arm again, except when he retired at night. With a heavy heart, for he knew it was best, he dismissed his Sophie, who he had dragged all the way over from Paris, and tucked a hundred pounds into her hand, thanking her for being a friend. She assured him he could always find her in Paris should he grow bored. No sooner had he kissed her hand goodbye than he called upon his cousin and had Mr. Hatchet's shop address in hand. He and his father arranged to have everything packed and ready to leave on the next ship out of Liverpool.

The morning before he was to board the ship that would take them to New York, Roderick visited his brother's crypt and ardently prayed before it for hours. Tears blinded not only his eyes but his soul. Nothing would change what had come to pass.

When he eventually returned home that afternoon, after having spent five torturous hours lingering before his brother's crypt, he decided to get drunk along with his father, both of them swearing to each other they would never get drunk again as it solved nothing. But they had a good time doing it. By evening, when Roderick could barely stand, and his father had fallen asleep on a sofa, he called for his carriage and demanded it take him over to Margaret's town house.

Despite it being long past respectable calling hours, he was admitted the moment he'd given his name and was even asked to wait in the study, as opposed to the drawing room. Whilst waiting for Margaret to appear, he staggered toward his brother's desk. Gripping the outside edge, he leaned against it and willed himself to stay focused on why he was there.

"Tremayne?"

He stiffened and swiveled toward the direction of Margaret's choked tone. A slim figure draped in a bombazine gown stood in the shadows, the hallway beyond much too dark to reveal a face. She drifted into the room with determined grace and poise, the golden glow of the candlelight revealing the soft, delicate face of a woman he remembered all too achingly well.

Her thick golden hair had been swept up into a mature top knot as opposed to those debutante curls she used to wear. She turned and slid both paneled doors shut.

She turned back toward him, silently crossing the room, and paused to linger before him. The delicate scent of lilacs bloomed around him, heightening his awareness of her. She reached out a bare hand and touched his arm. "You came."

He pushed away her hand. "Not for the reasons you think."

She flushed, her features growing tight. Taking back the distance he'd put between them, she leaned toward him and awkwardly forced her warm fingers into his hand.

Roderick stiffened as the heat of her soft hand warmed his own. Jerking his hand out of hers, he asked tonelessly, "Did you at least come to love him? Give me peace and assure me you did."

"I wish I could give you peace in that." She leaned toward him and whispered with a vivid angst that penetrated her blue eyes, "Yardley knew about us. I told him days into our marriage. I was so disgusted with myself, and with everything, I was hoping that his anger would cast me out so that I could join you in Paris. Unnervingly, it had the opposite effect. Yardley became so morbidly driven to replace you and refused to let me out of his sight, even for a moment. He commenced dictating when and how my heart should beat, much like my mother did, which only made me hate him all the more. But it was God Himself, in the end, who dictated when and how *his* heart should beat by making it stop altogether."

She set herself against the desk, tears streaming down her face. "I am done submitting myself to others at the cost of my sanity. Please tell me that something remains of your love for me so that I may crawl across whatever broken glass you lay before me in the hopes of reclaiming what had once been."

Roderick glanced toward her, his pulse thundering against his skull. He couldn't breathe knowing that she had chosen *everything* over their love. Everything.

The scent of lilacs and the brandy still warming his veins twisted his common sense as the sparse candlelight within the room blurred. He veered toward her and savagely yanked her up off the desk. "You knowingly destroyed me and for that I will never be able to forgive you. You had your chance to prove yourself to me when it counted most and you failed."

She let out a sob. "Tremayne. My heart never ceased beating for you. Not once. Please. Show me that you still—" Her hands jumped to his face and tried to pull him down toward her lips as she had that night when she had first seduced his naive soul.

Roderick grabbed her hands and violently shoved them away, stumbling back in disbelief. "I ask that if there is any compassion or remorse left within you, that you cease this. Cease loving me, because I have long ceased loving you."

Her anguished sob rippled through the air. "Tremayne—"

"'Tis Lord Yardley now, my lady. Sadly. I have inherited my brother's name and, with it, it would seem, his heart. I am done with you and this. Do you understand me? I am done and ask that you never call upon me or whisper my name again." Swinging away, Roderick staggered out, feeling as if he had *finally* set a part of his condemned soul free.

The following morning, whilst vomiting his excesses and wincing against every noise, he left London with his father to begin his journey to New York. While his father discussed matters of the estate and all that would now be his, Roderick couldn't help but loathe himself to no end knowing at what cost the spare had become the heir.

CHAPTER FIFTEEN

*To save a man's life against his will
is the same as killing him.*
                                    —Horace, *Ars Poetica* (18 BC)

*Adelphi Hotel
The present hour of 12:45 p.m.*

CLASPING THE BLACK MOURNING band against the upper
biceps of his gray morning coat in reminder of all that
had once been, Roderick lingered before his father's
door marked 21. Drawing in a ragged breath, he shifted
toward the closed door and, after hesitating, knocked.

"Yes?" the duke called out from within.

Roderick willed strength into his voice. "'Tis I."

There was a pause. "The door is unlocked."

Pushing down on the latch, Roderick opened the
door leading into his father's suite and eased into the
lavish room, quietly closing it behind him.

The duke glanced up from the unfolded newspaper
he'd been reading in a chair set in the far corner of
the room. Refolding his newspaper, he slapped it onto
the mahogany side table next to him and rose, coming
toward him.

Letting out a low whistle, the duke chided gently, "You clean up rather well."

Roderick stripped his top hat from his still-damp hair the valet had trimmed, and quickly strode over to the man, grabbing hold of his father with one hefting arm. Fiercely holding his father against his chest, as if he were not a man but a boy, he whispered, "Forgive me for not having loved you in the way you deserved."

The duke stiffened, wrapping awkward arms around him. He patted his back. "What honor is this?"

Pulling away, Roderick confessed, "I missed knowing who you were and what you meant to me and ask that you forgive me for treating you with disdain when I last saw you." Roderick placed his top hat back onto his head, angling it in preparation for the long walk he had yet to take, and grabbed those broad shoulders, squaring the duke toward himself so he might better look at his aged face and dark brown eyes. "I remember what had once been."

Astonished gray brows rose. Blinking several times, his father intently searched his face. "You remember me?"

"That I do."

"How? What happened? I don't understand."

Roderick shrugged. "It was like God Himself had touched a finger to my head."

The duke stepped away and pointed at him, issuing the challenge of, "Tell me something that only you would know about me. I want to know this is real. I want to know that your mind is what it should be."

Roderick couldn't help but smirk. "Faith was never

enough for you, was it? All right. What do I know of you, O Father? I remember how you always roared across the house before cropping Yardley. It felt like all you ever did on the hour was roar and crop Yardley on my behalf. Which I did appreciate."

A boisterous laugh rippled through the air. "Now, why is it you would go and remember something like *that* about me? Though I will admit that boy had the devil in him. All of hell, actually."

"That he did," Roderick drawled. "Good old Yardley."

The duke fell quiet, lowering his gaze. "Mischief-laced though he was, he was still my boy. It wasn't right he died so young."

Roderick swallowed, reached out and squeezed his father's shoulder. "No. It wasn't. And my biggest regret is that I didn't make an effort to guide him more. I only judged him."

"Nothing would have ever changed him. He was what he was." Drawing in a huge breath and letting it out, the duke shook his head and eyed him. "Please tell me we are set to leave in ten days, as planned, because I am well and done with this piss of a city. We've done everything we set out to do. My Augustine at long last knows peace. My only regret is that she never had the chance to see him before she…" His voice trailed off.

Roderick let his hand drop away from his father's shoulder, tensing from the reality that he might never remember what had happened since leaving England. "Though I remember quite a bit, I cannot remember getting on that boat or what happened thereafter. What happened? However did we find Atwood? Was it the map? And why isn't he coming home with us? Doesn't he wish to reclaim all that is rightfully his, given he is the sole heir to the Sumner estate?"

The duke swiped his face and swung away. "If he goes back to England, it would mean facing his parents and the past before all of London. You have no idea what that poor boy has been through, Yardley. It would be a damn rag-gossiping frenzy of the worst sort that would drag itself through every last court and torment London's base understanding of humanity."

Roderick's eyes widened. "You mean…?"

The duke nodded grimly. "According to Atwood, your grandfather had wronged an impassioned man he shouldn't have. A man who then sought to avenge himself by taking the one thing that mattered most to him— his son."

Sucking in a breath, he edged back. "Whatever the hell did he do to the man to make him do such a thing?"

The duke swung back toward him. "'Tis a story deserving of its own book. One we will discuss throughout our journey to London, and one that must *never* leave your lips until Atwood is ready to emerge on his own." His father paused and shook his head. "And now you wish to make an even bigger mess of our lives by dragging yet *another* poor soul into it."

Roderick slowly turned away so he didn't have to reveal his own agony. "You needn't worry about Georgia. She will not be accompanying us to London." Closing his eyes, he swallowed and went on, "I intend to end our relationship tonight."

"What?" His father seemed not to understand.

"I love her far more than I could ever love myself. And so I shall let her go." Opening his eyes but still keeping his back to his father, Roderick cleared his throat to push a sense of staid calmness into his quaking voice. "I intend to gift her a lifelong yearly annuity in parting and ask that it be arranged through your estate before we leave New York. I need Georgia to not only live incredibly well, but have servants, as her poor hands are so damn roughened by work they will require years of rest. She wasn't deserving of being dragged into my life. She deserves more than this. She deserves more than me." When only mere silence hummed, Roderick turned to his father.

The duke's features were still morbidly stoic as if he were not involved in their conversation at all.

Roderick stared. "You will go to the bank before we leave New York and arrange an annuity of five thousand a year. Do you understand?"

His father glanced away and half nodded. "I will call on the bank this afternoon if that is what you want."

Roderick threw back his head, almost causing his top hat to fall away, and rapidly blinked back tears he swore he wouldn't cry. In a choked tone, he confided, "It will allow me a measure of peace."

"The entire estate is set to go to your pocket, anyway," the duke muttered. "What do I care how much of it goes where?"

Roderick swallowed, leveling his head again and adjusting his morning coat about his frame. He cleared his throat. "I am set to go for a long walk about the city on my own, and will be gone for most of the day and most likely well into the evening, depending on where my mood takes me. I have to gather my thoughts about how the hell I am going to announce all of this to Georgia without breaking her."

He winced and glanced away. "She expects me at her door at nine tonight, so I have no choice but to be back by then. That said…I wanted you to know that despite all that has come to pass, I never sought to willfully dishonor you or her and will *never* shame our name again by involving myself with another woman, be that woman of our circle or not. I made that decision after Margaret and don't even know what the hell I was thinking when I still had full possession of my wits. Sadly, my circle has too many expectations and I cannot willfully mold Georgia into becoming something she is not and expect the woman I love to survive. She won't. She just won't."

EARLY THAT EVENING, AND ALONE at last from the flurry of the female servants who had bathed her, oiled her, dried her, massaged her, clothed her and tugged and pushed and pulled her freshly washed hair in every direction to assemble it into ringlets and a coif, Georgia spent most of her afternoon wandering about her lavish room. She had purposefully locked herself away to avoid Robinson. She had even supped alone in the room with a tray laden with poached salmon and creamed carrots that almost made her faint in well-pleasured anguish when they touched her lips.

The entire world appeared to be hers, and yet with

Robinson putting her at a distance, it was meaningless. Adjusting the belt on the embroidered rose-colored robe she'd been wrapped in after a divine bath scented with orange blossoms, she padded over to the sideboard that had been arranged with female toiletries the chambermaid had methodically set out for her.

Though she tried to recall what was what—the woman had rattled off all of the cosmetics so fast—she really couldn't remember. Leaning toward the silver tray laden with small glass bottles and tins, she poked at the open tin of rose rouge that for some reason the chambermaid had said was *green* rouge. The woman must have been color-blind.

Either way, good rouge went for a quarter a piece in stores and it was obvious this here was good rouge. Georgia had always wanted to buy a tin and see if it could make her prettier, but thought it vain and a waste of money. But now…it kneeled before her as if she were a queen and whimpered to be of service.

Georgia smiled and excitedly plucked it up along with the small bristled brush set next to it. Perhaps she could make herself pretty enough to make Robinson think twice about saying no to her.

Leaning toward the oval gilded mirror hanging above the sideboard, she held up the tin with the tips of her fingers and dabbed the brush into the powdered substance like she'd seen women do in the shops. Dashing it across each side of her cheekbones, she tilted her head from side to side to observe how it sat.

She leaned closer to the mirror and squinted. It didn't do a thing. Perhaps she hadn't put on enough. Dabbing a more generous amount onto the brush, she swiped it across both cheeks and paused. Reddish rouge skid marks streaked her pale skin.

Her eyes widened. "Oh, dear."

She couldn't have Robinson seeing her like this. Setting aside the brush and the tin back onto the silver tray with a clatter, she frantically swiped at her cheeks. Pinching her lips together, she leaned in closer to the mirror and rubbed both cheeks hard, her calloused fingers burning her skin. She paused and gawked at her reflection and her poor skin, which was a glaring red.

Georgia groaned and dropped her hand away from her face. She looked like a whore who'd been slapped by too many men in one night. She needed to wash it away.

Glancing down at the array of glass bottles, she grabbed up what she read was angel water. 'Twas an infusion of myrtle flowers and water that the chambermaid claimed would freshen her skin. If it could freshen skin, it could damn well clean it.

She carefully uncorked it and tilted the bottle slightly onto its side to allow a small amount of the pungent, sweet-smelling liquid to trickle out. It splashed out of the bottle, slathering and cooling her entire hand, dripping to the wood floor at her feet.

She rolled her eyes in exasperation and huffed out a breath. Was nothing in life easy? Setting aside the bottle, she rubbed her wet and now very heavily scented hand against her cheeks. Fortunately, it came off against her fingers, although her cheeks were still angry from all the rubbing and swiping she'd done.

She brushed her wet hand against her robe and paused, lifting the tips of her fingers to her nose. She sniffed. Lovely. Now she smelled like a walking Garden of Eden.

Swiping her hands against each other one last time, she stepped back. "If you can't handle the makeup, Georgia," she muttered, "how will you handle the man?"

This was just the beginning of transitioning into Robinson's life. She wasn't afraid of any of it, really. She was secure enough to know that with or without makeup or fancy gowns and servants, she'd still be the same girl. What she wasn't quite so sure of was whether or not Robinson would be the same man she had fallen in love with.

Turning away from the sideboard, she edged herself over to the next sideboard set against the wall and paused, noticing a crystal decanter filled with some sort of amber-colored liquid set next to a pair of crystal glasses.

Plucking out the stopper, she leaned over it and sniffed the strong vapory-like scent. Alcohol? Hmm. She sure as hell needed it. Though it didn't look like any alcohol she'd seen. In her parts it was either white or piss-yellow.

Lifting the heavy decanter, she slid the empty glass beneath it and poured the amber liquid up to the rim of the large glass, setting the decanter back onto the sideboard. Daintily placing the stopper back into its place with the tips of her fingers and feeling, oh, so accomplished, she carefully picked up the brimming glass, trying not to spill it.

She took a large sip and paused as a cedarlike, burning smoothness coated her throat as she swallowed. She smacked her lips, trying to decide if she liked it. Then, she took a much larger gulp and let it sit in the well of her mouth before swallowing. "Not bad. It's not whiskey, but it's not bad."

Sipping on the alcohol, she turned and made her way around the room to see what else there was to explore. The large mahogany paneled dresser, which now housed all of the ten gowns she'd brought with her, looked more impressive than the frayed, limp dresses within it.

It was all too symbolic of how she felt. Here she was a frayed gown desperately wanting to be made new. She only hoped Robinson didn't give up on her when he realized she was going to make a hundred thousand mistakes before she got any of this right.

A knock on the door made her turn.

Her heart fluttered. Robinson was almost two hours early from the time she had set. Was that a good thing or a bad thing? She headed toward the closed door and slowly pulled it open, taking another large gulp of her drink to see her through this one. She froze with her glass close to her chin, her mouth still full of alcohol.

It wasn't Robinson at all.

The duke blinked, his gaze falling to her robed appearance and then the drink in her hand. He gestured toward it. "Ah. Good to know you have some. Good to know. My brandy tray is…empty." Snapping his gaze back up to her makeup-marred face, his gray brows came together. He paused. "What happened to your face, Mrs. Milton?" he slurred.

By gad, the man was soused!

Georgia choked on the liquid pooled in her mouth. Unable to swallow, she spit everything back out into the glass with a gush. She coughed several times in an effort to free her burning throat of constriction and choked out, "Rouge. I applied too much…rouge."

He staggered past her and into the room. He fumbled with his cravat and then stripped it, whipping it aside. "Pour me another brandy. I need it."

She awkwardly closed the door and glanced back at him, wondering if she could trust him in his inebriated state. For safety's sake, she decided not to latch the lock. Just in case she needed to run.

Hurrying to the other side of the room, she set aside her own glass and with a trembling hand poured him a brandy into one of the other crystal glasses. "Are you certain you should be drinkin' anymore? You look like you've had more than enough. You're barely standin'."

He trailed his way toward her and lingered. "When I lose consciousness…only then will it be enough. Now hand it up."

"You'll regret it, Your Grace."

"What don't I regret?" He drunkenly wagged his fingers toward her.

She sighed and topped off the glass, setting aside the decanter. Slowly swiveling toward him, she passed him the glass and snatched up her own, trying to pretend like they were old friends. It was awkward. She didn't know him any more than he knew her.

The duke took a long swallow of his brandy before lowering his glass. He eyed her. "Do you love him?" He paused and pointed at her with his glass, causing the liquid to sway. "Because I do. I love that boy. I love him more than any father should."

She fingered her glass, astounded that this drink that he called brandy could reduce him to this. It was obviously stronger than whiskey. "Yes, I love him. I wouldn't be standin' here subjectin' myself to your kind if I didn't. You think a fish likes bein' pulled out of water?"

He momentarily closed his eyes and nodded before reopening them. Taking another swig of brandy, he shook his head. "What a mess this is. Here I am…well respected…have vast estates…titles to match and *all* the money in the goddamn world, but I can't make my own son happy. I just can't, no matter how hard I try. All of this is so damn…*wrong.*"

Her throat tightened. "Why isn't he happy? I know he yearns to be and has the means to be, given his kind, open heart. So what prevents him from havin' it and knowin' it? I don't understand."

He leveled her with a stare. "'Tis called impending dukedom and having everything but having nothing all the same. It weighs heavily upon a man in London society in a way you Americans could never fully… comprehend. Love is but an afterthought. 'Tis duty that is one's life." He drew in a ragged breath before letting it out. "He has always lived his life inside his own head and inside his own heart. By God, you should have seen that boy in his younger years. He used to be so much more. So much more. Society and duty and being betrayed by his own brother is what reduced him to what you now see. He…he clearly loves you. 'Tis obvious he does or he would have settled on merely dragging you into London as his mistress. He…came to me, you know, and told me of his intentions. He still hasn't returned from his walk, and I'm trying not to worry, but…he intends to end things between you and him. I wanted you to know that. That is why I am here. I wanted you to be ready for it."

Georgia almost dropped her glass, her chest tightening. "What? Why?"

"Because I…told him to. I put it in his head. I meant well, I just… If you think life in a slum is difficult, child, you have yet to meet the *ton*. They will ensure your chamber pot sits in the right corner lest they piss in it and make you drink every last drop. Even their own aren't good enough for them. So can you imagine what they would do to you? A damn witch hunt is what it would be and I didn't want that for you or him. Despite my well-meaning intentions, I…I cannot help but feel I have wronged my own son by making him turn against the last of who he is. Yardley…my first boy… *he* would have tossed you in the name of duty. That boy was a master at shuffling women and their hearts as if they were cards in a deck. But my Tremayne…no. No. My Tremayne wouldn't have submitted to this. His heart always came first. Always." The duke winced and took another swig of his brandy. "I'm sorry. I'm sorry I made a mess of things."

She met his gaze in anguish. "All I want is to love him. Is that so wrong?"

The duke's brown eyes softened. "And do you know what I want for him? Above all else? His happiness. Plain and simple. And it appears he has found it in you." He lowered his gaze to his glass and heaved out a breath. "I've been…thinking. I really think you and Yardley should…stay here in New York. London is nothing but a circus and a half, anyway. I would be losing my only son to the union, obviously, but…at least I wouldn't be murdering the last of who he is. I wish there were a way to allow you both to live freely with me in London. I really do." He sniffed. "I want grand-children. I want to feel like there is still some—some… meaning left, even though my dearest Augustine and my first Yardley are gone and my own life is veering to an end." He angled toward her, reached out and slop-pily patted her head. "If I had the means to buy your re-spectability, child, I would. I really, really, really would. Why? Because knowing how much my son adores you makes me adore you. If he deems you worthy, you are."

Georgia blinked rapidly, endlessly touched by his words. She paused and shifted toward him, taking a quick swallow of her own brandy. Wait. Now, there was an idea. It was a crazy Five Points idea laced with Raymond's and Matthew's views of society, propaganda and government politics, but one that would allow her to live freely and openly with Robinson in London so-ciety. Why settle for a measly half acre in the west with him when she could seize all four corners of the world and make everyone happy? "If I gave you the means to *buy* my respectability, Your Grace, would you? Could you?"

He blinked. "I don't quite follow. I'm a bit…muddled."

She gestured toward him with her glass. "With your prestige and wealth and my will and my way, we could, in fact, whisk me into your circle. The question is, would you be up for it?"

He chortled. "And I thought *I* had one too many brandies."

"I'm not drunk, Your Grace. I barely had a few sips. What I'm sayin' is that you could *buy* my respectability in the same way a politician buys public opinion and then its vote."

He cleared his throat and lowered his voice, eyeing the closed door. "One cannot *buy* respectability. It doesn't work that way."

Georgia tossed back the rest of her brandy, letting it warm her throat, and quickly set it back onto the side table. "I disagree. Kings knight peasants and elevate them well above their status within a day if it so pleases them. Why couldn't we do the same for me?"

The duke let out a laugh, reached out and patted her head sloppily again. "Whilst my fortune is vast, it isn't quite *that* vast. And sadly, women can't be knighted."

She smiled. "You don't have to knight me. All I ask is that you make an American heiress out of me. As my dearly departed husband used to say, if one wishes to control society, one merely has to locate its pulse, place a finger on it and then press hard. What we'd be doin' is forgin' a campaign, of sorts, that would allow me to become respectable in the eyes of society whilst allowin' Tremayne and I to marry without mass opposition."

He snorted. "Not to offend, Mrs. Milton…but the moment you show up in all your American glory covered in rouge and holding a brandy, the game is…over. Mass opposition is inevitable."

She held up a finger and stepped toward him, intently holding his gaze. "Ah. But what if I don't show up as Mrs. Milton covered in rouge and holdin' a brandy? What if I show up as someone else? Someone draped in vast wealth, refinement and a lace parasol in hand?"

"I still don't quite follow and I don't think it's the brandy."

"Raymond used to say that governments all over the world are notorious for creatin' and perpetuatin' *factual farces*. And that's exactly what we'd do. We'd be creatin' a factual farce to appease society in the way a politician does." She paused and eyed him. "Do you know what a factual farce is?"

He blinked, leaned over and set aside his own glass onto the side table. "'Tis…propaganda. Yes?"

She clasped her hands together. "Exactly. Upper levels of government use propaganda to bend the public to its will by slippin' whatever farce they want the world to believe into every crack of society until it fills every tongue and mind and becomes fact due to its source. What we'll be doin', Your Grace, is fillin' in *my* cracks and slippin' *me* into your circle. *That* is the political game we'll play and *that* is the political game that will win. Are you in? Or do you need to be more sober to agree to any of this?"

The duke lowered his chin. "Bloody on high. Am I even hearing this?"

"That you are. You have the money and I have the will. We'll pay people to mold me into the sort of woman London would accept, and introduce me as such to society."

The duke set his jaw and rounded her, his gait uneven but determined. Scanning the length of her appearance, he drawled, "It takes a lot to impress London." He scanned her again. *"A lot."*

She rolled her eyes. "I'm not lookin' to be canonized here. I'm as tough as any blade and am fully aware of what is and isn't possible. The real question is, what do you think would be easier for London to swallow? A Five Points widow your son met on the street here in New York? Or an American heiress he met in the drawin' rooms of London and wishes to court and marry?"

The duke swiped his face and glanced toward her, his brows coming together. "An American heiress, no doubt."

"Exactly. So make me one."

He stared. "But you would be turning away from all that you are. He doesn't want that for you. He made that very clear."

A small smile touched her lips. "Sometimes men don't really understand what women want. Sometimes a woman has to tell a man what she wants before he mucks everythin' up. I'm not about to tear your son away from you, nor am I about to turn away from him merely because a bunch of snobs think me incapable of bein' a lady. The only solution is to eliminate the divide without the world knowin'. And only you and your money can do that."

"Me and my money. Huh." Setting his hands behind his back, he lowered his gaze and slowly paced back and forth, back and forth. He paused. "This idea of yours intrigues me. It would depend on…the people we involve. It would also have to be incredibly well done. You and Yardley would have to conduct a public courtship before London for any of it to be mildly be-lievable. The Season is over for the year, but will be opening again in…early April, I believe." He winced. "That would barely give us ten months to orchestrate this. It wouldn't be enough time. We would have to give ourselves the following year of '32."

Her pulse fluttered like a butterfly caught in a capped jar. "I'm not willin' to be apart from him that long. I'm just not. We'll have to make all of this come together in the ten months you speak of."

"Mrs. Milton, I like you, but I don't think—"

"If you and he were to go back to London in ten days' time as planned, and leave me here with a sizable fund to oversee the creation of my identity, I know it *could* be done. Whilst I build my name here, you could assist by building my name in London. What do you think?"

"'Tis a bit…ambitious. Rumors can easily be seeded within the upper circles in as little as a few months. But you…" He gargled out a laugh. "Not to offend, but you are not even a sliver of what my circle would consider to be acceptable. Ten months would barely cover etiquette, let alone the rest of you."

She glared at him. "I'm from the Five Points, Your Grace, and we Five Pointers know how to outplay anyone. I have full faith it can and will be done. I can do this in ten months' time. Just give me a chance and I promise that everyone is not only goin' to sit down for the show but they won't even question what the hell they're seein'. But I can't do it without you. I'm goin' to need money. Lots of it. Because as with any campaign, I'll have to wine and dine my way into every level of society here in New York by feedin' them the same farce London will be feastin' on."

He swiped at his mouth. "But that would only leave us…ten days to…launch this. Tremayne and I leave for London in ten days."

"Ten days is doable if we make it count. You've been here for seven months, Your Grace. I'm certain you've met plenty of men in the upper circles here on Broadway. Haven't you? All we need to do is to find *one* of those upper-crust New Yorkers with a powerful reputation who'd be willin' to play our game and play it well. Someone who'd benefit from what we're tryin' to do, either financially or through other means."

He let out a whistle. "No wonder Yardley's so smitten. You bloody have a mind to match." Rounding her, the duke grabbed the decanter, refilling his almost empty glass. Slowly setting the decanter aside, he paused and turned back toward her. "Mr. Astor. *He* would play along."

Georgia lifted a brow. "And who is that? How well do you know him? Well enough to entrust him with our scheme?"

He leaned against the sideboard, causing it to hit the wall. "I would venture to say yes. His connections are astounding. From street to heaven. *And* he is quite the eccentric." He snorted.

"Good. I want to do this. Can we?"

"Consider it done." The duke smiled, reached out and patted her cheek affectionately as if she were already his daughter-in-law. "I will call on Mr. Astor in the morning when I'm not so…bashed out of my senses. The room is still spinning. Just a bit, but it's spinning."

Georgia flung herself against him, wrapping her arms around his waist and squeezing him tightly against herself. "How I pray you'll feel the same come morning. Oh, how I pray. Will you even remember our conversation?"

"Of course I will." He awkwardly patted her back and kept on patting her as if silently pleading that their embrace end. "And if I don't…all you need to do is tell me that Augustine would spit upon my soul from the heavens if I didn't do this for our son."

She eased back and smiled. "Augustine was your wife?"

"She was my soul." The duke's features twisted as he adjusted the sleeves of his coat and cleared his throat. "Good night, my dear." Wandering over to the door, he pulled it open, and staggered out, slamming it behind himself.

A big rush of air escaped Georgia's lips, leaving her

standing there dazed and in disbelief. She was going to be a lady. A *real* one. That is if the duke could be trusted not to go back on his word. He was about as soused as any man could get.

Gathering her robe from around her feet, she slowly made her way back toward the large four-poster bed and fell into its divine softness. She let out a shaky breath, rolling herself regally onto her back. Robinson loved her. He loved her and it was time to love him back in the way he not only deserved but would never expect.

Spreading her arms and legs as far and wide as she could, she slid them up and down across the smoothness of beautifully clean and perfect powder-blue linens. Nothing was going to come between her and her man. *Nothing.*

CHAPTER SIXTEEN

Et tu, Brute?
>   —William Shakespeare, *Julius Caesar*
>   (as published in 1811)

AN HOUR LATER, A KNOCK ON the door startled Georgia into scrambling out of the bed she'd been lounging in whilst examining all the labels of her makeup. Hurrying over to the door, Georgia paused only long enough to quell the fluttering in her stomach. She unbolted the door and edged it open. She paused and drew in an astonished breath.

Robinson lingered in the candlelit corridor outside, a dove-gray top hat in his black leather-gloved hands. His thick black hair had been brushed back with tonic and that square jaw was shaven and soft looking. A snowy silk cravat bound his throat, that well-muscled frame beautifully held together by an expensive embroidered waistcoat, well-cut morning coat, fine trousers and polished black leather boots.

He was even wearing another mourning band. It was as if he had formally returned to being the man she first met, and her Robinson, as she knew him, was no more.

She swallowed. It was as if he had remembered all that had once been.

"Good evening to you, Georgia." His husky voice was endearingly soft as he heatedly met her gaze. "I missed you."

The man said it as if he hadn't seen her in years.

Fingering the rim of his top hat, his gray eyes traced her hair. He searched her face. "Your hair looks pretty. Very pretty, actually. I like it."

She paused. Patting the pinned curls the chambermaid had earlier arranged for her after her bath, she shyly lowered her gaze. He had never once commented on or noticed her hair before. It appeared as if he had indeed fully reverted to the man she'd met on the street and she honestly didn't know what to make of it. "'Tis fancier than the rest of me, to be sure. I need a better gown to go with it." She shook out the calico skirts she had slipped into.

He half nodded and fell back into silence, his features tightening.

She sighed, sensing he was avoiding the conversation he had come to deliver. "So where have you been all day?"

He cleared his throat and shifted from polished boot to boot. "I, uh, I went for a very long walk from one end of Broadway all the way down toward where it leaves the city and touches field. I never realized how big this city was until I started walking it. I took coffee several times and ate a meal on my own. It was depressing as hell, but I needed time to think about our situation. And no matter how many times I laid out those damn cards, Georgia, they still came up the same. Nothing but small cards and all of them unworthy of you."

She glanced up. She could hear the pain in his tone and could see the anguish in his stance and in those gunmetal eyes. "Everythin' is goin' to be fine, Robinson. I promise."

"Georgia." He leaned in closer, bringing with him a divine scent of mulled spice and cedar. His freshly shaven face lingered above hers, looking boyishly charming as he sought the right words.

His brows came together as he glanced down toward his top hat, whose curved rim he continued to finger. "We must end this. I ask that you forgive me for submitting to this decision. It wasn't an easy one for me to make. I am actually hoping that you and I will be able to write and that I can visit you here in the States as often as you will allow. As friends. Because I wouldn't be able to entirely let you go. Even if you married."

Tears overwhelmed her. He didn't even sound like Robinson anymore, and what was worse, this man was giving up on them without even fighting. "You remember your life. Don't you?"

He wouldn't meet her gaze. "Yes."

Raising herself up onto her stockinged toes, she leaned toward him, closing the space between them, and planted a gentle, pleading kiss on his full lips. "Don't give up on me quite yet. Fight for me, regardless of what you remember. Fight for us. We can do this. We can take on London. I know we can."

He stiffened.

She pulled away and disclosed in a soft tone, "I'm sorry I was bein' stubborn earlier and wasn't willin' to compromise, given your duty to your father and your

title. You have responsibilities to your name and family
and I understand that now. I don't have a family dependin' on me the way you have your father dependin' on
you. Which is why I intend to bend. I don't want the
west. I want you."

ROBINSON'S JAW TIGHTENED AS HE resisted his need to grab
Georgia and demand she not give him any hope when
there was none to be had. A hot, clenching ache arose
deep inside his throat as she blinked up at him, bringing attention to those incredible emerald eyes.

He tossed his hat and gloves to the floor and grabbed
her. Ignoring the pinch of his still-raw palm, he pulled
her roughly into his chest, burying her softness against
his body. He possessively wrapped one arm tightly
around her slim shoulders and pressed his other hand
against her smooth cheek, feeling as if his chest would
explode.

She gazed up at him, those pretty strawberry curls
swaying against the sides of her freckled face.

His body overheated in anguished yearning. He
kicked the door shut with his booted heel, making her
stiffen against the resounding bang of wood hitting the
frame.

Her green eyes widened.

He firmly pressed his hands to the sides of that silken
face. "Georgia," he whispered, holding her gaze. "Even
if I were to change my mind, you would only be mold-
ing yourself into something you are not. You deserve
so much more."

Tears traced down her cheeks. "All that matters is that I'm your wife."

He swallowed. "God, Georgia, don't…don't do this to me. I'm not about to let you destroy the last of you by making you kneel before others. I'd have to kill everyone to ensure they didn't look at you as if you were some—some…rag. I wouldn't be able to function."

"I can put up my own two fists, Robinson," she whispered.

"I know that, and though I love that about you, you've been putting them up for much too long and I…" Unable to stay away anymore, he lowered his mouth to hers. Forcing her mouth open, he urgently sought that hot satin tongue and buried his own tongue within the softness of her mouth. He ground his tense body against hers and devoured that mouth all the more, refusing to think about this being their final kiss.

Blindly exploring the soft outline of her smooth face through their kisses, he gently trailed his fingers alongside its soft surface. How he wanted to forever melt into that skin.

Slowly, he dragged his fingers away from her face and up into that thick, silky hair, enveloping himself with the beautiful sensation of touching her. As he sank deeper and deeper into the storming waves of a passion he knew he had never felt for *any* woman. He pressed himself harder against her, pushing her breasts and every inch of her body toward him with the hopes of remembering her without stripping her bare.

Her hands pushed at his chest, breaking their kiss.

She scrambled outside of his embrace. "Don't be kissin' me like that unless you plan on keepin' me."

He reopened his eyes. He had to be stronger than this. For her. "I'm sorry. I shouldn't have done that."

She smoothed her hair away from the sides of her face. "I'm willin' to fight for you. I'm willin' to become everythin' you want and need me to be. All you need to do is say you want me and it's done."

A shaky breath escaped his lips. "I won't let you crawl in my name. I love you too much. We will simply have to accept that you will never be anything more than my dearest Georgia from Orange Street."

She stared at him as if she had just been slapped despite his proclamation of love.

Narrowing her gaze, she bit out, "You barely got your mind back and you're already feckin' it all up. In case you didn't know, Robinson, Orange Street is just that. A street. I have two feet to take me to any place I want to call my own. And I plan on doin' exactly that. You told me you needed a woman to more than love you. You told me you needed a woman willin' to fight for you even when you're unable to fight for yourself. And seein' you've stopped fightin', I'm about to prove my love to you in a way you have yet to prove yours."

Turning, she hurried over to the wardrobe and flung the doors open with a bang. Yanking all of her dresses off the hangers, she stuffed them into her wool sack. Shoving her feet into her boots, she yanked up the sack into her arms and turned toward him. "I'm headin' over to Orange Street one last time and havin' myself some whiskey with the boys. I'll be back in the mornin' to settle some business with your father, but just so you know, this'll be goodbye until we see each other again next spring. I'll see you at the opening of the Season. That's when you and I will make our relationship public."

Heat flooded his face. "What?"

"I'll be visitin' you in London, *Lord Yardley*. And I'm announcin' here and now that I'm goin' to make you *crawl* in a way you never crawled for *any* woman before. I hope you're ready for it."

He glanced toward her, capturing her gaze. "I'm trying to protect you and love you in the best way I know how. Why won't you let me?"

Her features twisted as she rounded him, tugging her sack tighter against her chest. "Because I love you *and* myself too much to settle for anythin' less than a life together. I'll see you next year, Brit. And mind you, look both ways before crossin' any street. I need you in one piece." She hurried past and headed toward the door, pulling it open.

He turned to follow her, his chest tightening. "Georgia, I don't want you doing this. Not for me."

"This isn't just for you. It's also for me. See you in April, Robinson. And don't worry. I'll make sure I make you look good." With that, she tugged her sack of clothes up toward herself and hurried out and into the corridor, disappearing from sight.

Winded, Roderick trailed over to the bed she hadn't even had the chance to sleep in and sat heavily on its edge, staring at the floor. Dearest God. How he prayed she didn't come to London. How he prayed. For her sake. Not his.

Part 3

CHAPTER SEVENTEEN

Nobility has its own obligations.
— Duc de Lévis, *Maximes et réflexions* (1808)

Evening on a long, dark road
just off Manhattan Square

"LADY BURTON AWAITS." Mischievous, hook-nosed and beady-eyed Mr. Astor grinned cheekily within the waving shadows of the carriage lanterns that barely sliced through the darkness. With a gloved hand, he reached out and enthusiastically patted Georgia's cheek through her black veil, as if she were a horse he was about to race with his last dollar. "You will find my friend to be most *dedicated*. Most."

"Thank you, Mr. Astor. I appreciate all that you've already done for me."

Holding up a hand, Mr. Astor marched back toward the carriage and climbed into it with a dignified grunt. He disappeared inside without looking back as his footman refolded the stairs and shut the door before hurrying up onto his own seat in the back of the carriage.

And so she was merrily tossed toward an imposing house whose large, narrow windows were illuminated by the glow of light. Rain drizzled down upon her veil in a mist as Georgia gathered her satin skirts from around her slippered feet. She strategically avoided puddles on the narrow stretch of pavement, heading toward the lone farmhouse that sat ominously upon a night-cloaked field, surrounded by a vast, starless sky above. She hurriedly bounded up the wide, shadowed stairs leading to the main entrance and paused.

Letting out a shaky breath, she glanced back at Mr. Astor's unmarked carriage one last time. The driver rounded all four horses through the thick mud, the lit glass lanterns attached to his box swaying against the shadows. Picking up its pace, the carriage eventually disappeared down the long stretch of road, trudging back toward the main city that was two miles out east.

Georgia scanned the glaring darkness beyond the porch she lingered on. There didn't appear to be a single house in sight and she didn't know if that was a good thing or a bad thing. She swiveled back to the door and tugged on the bellpull beside it, chiming the calling bell within.

The farmhouse itself belonged to a certain Lady Burton, who had endured some sort of scandal in London that Mr. Astor and the duke had refused to go into. It appeared the path of becoming a gilded lady was to commence on a very dark night in the middle of God knows where with a woman who had done God knows what.

The soft breeze of the cool summer night rolling in from the surrounding fields rustled her skirts as the entrance door was dragged open by an old man in livery. He blinked out at her, tufts of his bushy gray brows rising as he graciously gestured for her to enter with a white-gloved hand.

She hurried in out of the night.

The moment the door closed and she was no longer in public view, she stripped her bonnet and veil, releasing the breath she'd been holding. She had made it without anyone seeing her. She paused within a large foyer decorated with potted orange blossoms. An oak staircase swept up to the floor above, giving an air of simple but impressive grandeur. Sea-green and white-flowered wallpaper covered all of the walls in sight, lending to a soft, cozy elegance.

The elderly butler took her veil and bonnet, placing them upon a side table. Setting a hand to the brass buttons on the waistcoat of his livery, as if he were a general about to march with orders, he guided her toward the right. His gloved hand eventually stretched toward a candlelit room beyond, indicating where she was to enter.

Georgia hurried into the room and paused to find it empty. Where was Lady Burton? She turned back. "Isn't Lady Burton—?"

She blinked.

The butler had already disappeared.

Georgia awkwardly turned back to the room and lingered in the pale malachite drawing room, noting all of the paintings on the walls depicting lush, exotic landscapes of places she knew nothing of. Marble statuettes and a variety of gilded clocks scattered the mantelpiece of a most impressive marble hearth that dominated the large room.

So *this* was where she'd be locked away from the world until she was ready to be presented into New York society. It was purgatory at its finest.

Wandering across the wooden inlaid floors, Georgia carefully angled past several upholstered chairs and gleaming marble-topped pedestal tables, ensuring her verdant gown didn't brush up against anything it shouldn't.

She glanced around, rather liking the place. Vibrant white lace curtains shrouded the night-blackened windows beyond, whilst pretty etched glass lamps alongside the expanse of the walls had all been lit, giving the room a warm glow that made her feel welcome and at home.

The clicking of heels echoed from down the corridor, drifting toward her through the open doors. Turning, Georgia set both hands behind her back and stared at the shadowed entryway, waiting for whatever was about to walk into her life.

A voluptuous, petite woman appeared in the doorway, her embroidered powder-blue evening gown rustling to a halt. Pinned sable curls streaked with silver swayed against the arresting movement, settling around sharp but pleasant features that whispered of a refined age of at least thirty. She wasn't particularly pretty but something about her was stunning. Velvet azure ribbons were intricately woven and braided into her hair, holding all of her gathered curls into place with a single visible knot that had been fashioned into a flower. The woman's full lips parted, as black, hauntingly sad eyes met Georgia's expectantly.

Georgia curtsied, sensing the woman was waiting for *her* to say something. "Thank you for havin' me, Lady Burton. I'm ever so grateful knowin' that you're willin' to—"

"Having, knowing and *willing,"* Lady Burton said in a smooth British accent, drawing out each word. "You must learn to pronounce your *g*'s."

Georgia blinked, sensing she had just been reprimanded.

Those haunting eyes met hers again as the woman stepped forward and into the room, allowing the butler to wordlessly slide the doors closed behind her and leave them in private.

The woman quietly observed her. "A pleasure to meet you, Mrs. Milton. I look forward to educating you about London society and ask that you refrain from blurting words. Instead, allow them to leave your lips slowly to ensure control. Now say the following. 'I am ever so grateful *knowing* that you are here.'"

Oh, this woman was good. Georgia wet her lips and focused. Drawing out her words in a slow and steady manner, she repeated, "I'm ever so grateful…*knowing* that you're here."

"That was passable but passable will not see you wed. Elongate each word. Say 'I am,' instead of shortening who and what you are with a mere 'I'm,' and say 'you are' instead of insulting me with 'you're.' Now say it again and remember to pronounce your *g*'s."

"Yes, my lady." Georgia drew out her words slowly, controlling every sound as best she could. "I…*am*… ever so grateful…*knowing*…that you…*are*…here."

Lady Burton sighed, her dark brows coming together. "We will focus on procuring a more natural, sophisticated tone." She paused, scanning her length. "Given your ambitious plan to launch yourself into London society by April, our schedule will entail a grueling eight hours a day, allowing you rest only on Sundays, which will be spent in silent prayer. During daily hours of lecture, I hope never to hear the words 'I am exhausted' or 'I cannot.' Do you understand?"

It was like being in the military. "Yes, my lady."

"Lovely. Now before I introduce you to your nightly routine, which you will carry to the grave, I would like to briefly test your basic understanding of protocol so I may better coordinate tomorrow's lesson plan. Is that acceptable to you?"

"By all means. Have at it."

Lady Burton's brows lifted. "Women do not ever 'have at it,' my dear. Men 'have at it.' And we most certainly do not care what men do, let alone what they think. We women will not be mentioning men at all unless it involves a lesson on how to make them better service us. Do you understand?"

Damn. Who had dirked this woman? "Yes, my lady. I'll not mention men again."

"I *will* not mention men again."

"I...*will* not mention men again."

"Very good. Now pay attention." The woman gracefully held up a small ivory card between slim fingers, as if she'd been holding it all along between the folds of her gown. Presenting it at eye level, Lady Burton breezed closer, her full skirts rustling against poised, elegant movements. "Do you know what this is, Mrs. Milton?"

Georgia blinked. "A…card?"

Lady Burton paused before her and held the card tauntingly closer. "Yes, but what *sort* of card? Do you know?"

Georgia blinked again, not understanding her point. She glanced nervously toward the card, observing its characteristics. "'Tis a very expensive, crisp white one? With gold embossed letterin'?" Georgia paused and added, "And as pretty as it is, it's probably also perfumed or powdered."

Lady Burton pursed her lips. Still holding Georgia's gaze, she daintily ripped the card in half and, with the flick of her wrists, sent both halves fluttering to the floor. "It *was* a calling card, my dear. Until I ripped it in half in an effort to contain my disappointment in how hard you are going to make us both work. A lady *never* perfumes or powders her calling card. Why? Because it insinuates that she needs more than a name to carry her through respectable society." She sighed. "'Tis obvious we will be working ten hours a day, not eight."

Georgia cringed, sensing the woman was already agitated with her. "You mean a lady goes about handin' out cards to everyone? What for?"

"Handing," Lady Burton chided, rounding her and scanning her again as if she were a smashed yam on a cart. "And no, a lady does not go about *handing* her card to just anyone. Would you flip up your skirts and place your leg into *everyone's* hand as a means of introducing yourself?"

Georgia pressed her lips together and shook her head.

"No. Of course not. Because that would be as crass as *handing* out your card to everyone. So as to better explain this, Mrs. Milton, a calling card is an incredibly important extension of your identity. It announces *who* you are, it announces *where* you live and, above all, it announces whether you are worth anyone's time." She lowered her chin. "And as of right now, my dear, you are not even worth mine."

Georgia's lips parted. And she thought *she* had a tongue on her. "Is it necessary for you to toss off to me in such a condescendin' tone?"

"The tone I am using is the same condescending tone you will hear from the lips of every waxed apple who dares call herself an aristocrat. Seeing you willfully intend to marry into my circle, I suggest you learn to not only cradle everything known as condescending, but that you kiss its little forehead until those lips of yours bleed."

Satan clearly had a wife. "Might I ask, why are you helpin' me, aside from being Mr. Astor's friend? With you bein' a rich aristo and all, you certainly don't need money. Or do you?"

Lady Burton lifted an arched dark brow. "There are some things in life, Mrs. Milton, that cannot be bought. A woman's way of life is difficult as it is without society weighing in on it. And in truth, the idea of twisting an invisible blade into the gut of London society is the only reason I am doing this. Those self-righteous bastards, who dare act like gods thinking their blood is pure, deserve to have their blood tainted."

Georgia swallowed, wondering what happened to this woman to turn her into *this*. London had to be a hell and a half to be breeding women like her.

Settling primly before Georgia, Lady Burton gestured casually toward her attire. "Where did you get this atrocity?"

Georgia awkwardly brushed the sides of her satin skirts, which she actually thought pretty. "I rather like this gown. Mr. Astor's wife gave it to me during my stay with them and her lady's maid was kind enough to cinch it to better fit me."

Lady Burton tsked. "We will have to change what you like, my dear, because poor Mrs. Astor, along with half of New York, has no taste whatsoever. I could pay them all to go out and buy taste and they still would only disappoint me." She paused, glancing toward Georgia's own breasts. "Of course, you are terribly underweight. You need larger breasts if we are going to make you a success with men."

Georgia's hands jumped to cover both of her small breasts buried within her satin bodice. She glanced down at them. "I didn't realize I could make them bigger." She jiggled what little she had and glanced up. "How do we do that?"

Lady Burton daintily tapped her hand away from each breast. "The secret is *food*, my dear. Something you clearly haven't had enough of. Once you gain a far more desirable weight, only then will we invest in an extensive wardrobe. The Duke of Wentworth insisted that I build your name here in New York whilst he builds London. Therefore, once you are able to properly fill a gown, we will do our part by bringing in the most talented French seamstresses Broadway has to offer. That way, when our hired gaggle of French seamstresses are done, they will bustle off and share their succulent little tales of servicing an unknown wealthy lady just outside of New York. People in every circle will squirm to learn more about you and, in time, we will give them more."

Lady Burton held up a manicured finger. "Now. Whenever in the presence of others outside myself, you will always abide by the golden rule of silence. That means whenever anyone enters this home or whenever you leave this home, you are not to speak. You have yet to learn how to articulate your words like a woman of quality and we do not want the wrong sort of *oui-dire* floating about New York, lest it take a boat and find itself in London. Do you understand?"

This was like a ten-dollar circus she had stupidly paid for. "That I do."

"Good." Lady Burton casually waved a hand about, a diamond ring glinting. "Over these next few weeks and throughout all the many months ahead, various men and women will be wading through these doors, tutoring you in the arts of dance, the pianoforte, riding and much more. The same rule will apply to them as to our lip-flapping seamstresses. You are *never* to speak, not even to say 'yes' or 'no.' You will only *do* as you are told. There will be no exceptions. Even if a candle should overturn and the house should catch fire, you will evacuate the premises in complete and utter silence."

Gorgia gawked at her. "Even durin' a fire? What if people die?"

Lady Burton gave her a withered look. "Let everyone and everything burn. Lesson one—never pity those who would merrily see you burn, in turn. These men and women servicing you are not your friends. They are but pawns we are using to win a game."

"But won't they suspect we're up to somethin'? Given that I'm learnin' all of these things and not sayin' a word?"

"No." Lady Burton smirked. "They will all be informed to believe the following, which I myself so brilliantly scripted. Mr. Astor kindly brought you into his care after the death of your stern mother, who had locked you away in a monastery in Ireland, which shall forever remain nameless due to the heartache it always brings you upon its mention. Tragically, you were born frail. Illness has kept you in a bed all these years. It is merely by the grace of God Himself, who touched His hand to your blessed head, that you are finally well enough to learn all of the things that had been denied due to your poor health. This does not mean, however, that you will ever fully recover, as you are prone to fainting spells. Given Mr. Astor's overly compassionate nature, his sole aspiration in life is to see you wed to a respectable man willing to look after your health, whilst he also tends to your impressive fortune of—" Mrs. Burton paused before announcing in an elegant, theatrical tone "—thirty thousand a year."

Georgia choked. "Thirty thousand *a year?* Isn't that a bit much?"

"We could have easily made it more, given Mr. Astor is a millionaire in investments alone, but the duke and I decided it was best to settle on a more respectable amount that was impressive without being vulgar."

Georgia slowly shook her head from side to side, realizing this was all turning into a thousand and one pawns piled onto the smallest board she'd ever seen. "I know this is all my idea, but it's still quite a bit to lie about. It feels wrong slaughterin' so many people with so many fibs. Can't we ease off on some of the drama?"

Lady Burton leaned in and pinched her cheek, teasingly cooing, "Weep not for the aristocracy. They deserve it."

Georgia huffed out an exasperated breath, already feeling overwhelmed. They hadn't even started. "Do ladies of quality ever have fun?"

"No. If you are having fun, the aristocracy considers you to be a whore."

Bursting into laughter, Georgia leaned toward her. "Surely, you jest! You mean women don't *ever* dance or play cards or drink whiskey?"

Lady Burton smirked. "Do not make me laugh. While women dance and play cards in respectable moderation, whiskey is out of the question. As a lady of quality, you will only be allowed to drink tea, milk, hot chocolate, soda water, juice, champagne and wine. Nothing more."

Georgia groaned. "But I like whiskey."

"It doesn't matter what you like. Whiskey will never touch your lips again. Not even in the privacy of your own home."

Georgia's eyes widened. "I would think I have every right to drink whatever I want in the privacy of my home. It's my home, after all."

"Ah, now, that is the American in you grouching, my dear. You Americans do love to flaunt your freedom, but remember, it always comes at the price of others. In London, one's home is the altar of a church you had best respect, for although you may think the world is not watching, all of your servants are. Oh, yes. Those naughty, naughty servants who dutifully bow to you left and right and say, 'Yes, my lady' and 'No, my lady,' are always looking to squeal to the rest of society. 'Tis the only power they have over their masters and the *ton* will use them to judge you and dunk your head into the Thames."

"What good is bein' rich if you can't do anythin'? In my opinion, you Brits are missin' the whole point. Even God had to take a piss on Sunday." Georgia set her hands on her hips. "Are all Brits this morbidly up-tight?"

"Yes. Why do you think I left?" Lady Burton reached out and grabbed Georgia by the hands, forcefully removing them from her hips and yanking them down hard to her sides. "You must learn poise."

Lady Burton paused, her dark brows coming together as she brought Georgia's hands up between them. Turning them upward and exposing her palms, she drew in an astonished breath, glancing up. "What have you been doing to your hands?"

Georgia slid her hands out of Lady Burton's grasp. "There isn't a thing I haven't done with them."

Lady Burton's features softened. There appeared to be a genuine charity buried within her, after all. "We will make them new again. A pumice stone and a daily soak in almond milk will ensure they soften. Now. Let me look at your pretty face." Reaching up, Lady Burton grasped Georgia's chin firmly, tilting her face toward her before nudging it from side to side. "Tragic though it is, freckles are not at all popular. We will have to fade them by using benzoin and cover them with powder whenever you are in public."

Lady Burton stepped back, tapping the tip of her finger thoughtfully against her full lips. "I have decided on the name we will use. *Miss Georgiana Colette Tormey. Georgiana* will be easier for you to assimilate as it is but an extension of your real name, *Colette* gives you a dash of French class the British love and *Tormey* is of the Irish Gaelic that means Thunder Spirit. What do you think? Is it enough to seduce the masses?"

Georgia smiled. "I like it."

"So do I." Lady Burton eyed her. "Oh, how I dread the thought of watching you pick up a fork at breakfast tomorrow morning. I have a feeling you will be cracking the same egg for hours. That said, *Miss Tormey,* let us go upstairs. We shall begin your regimented nightly routine. Be forewarned, it involves knotting your hair with paper curls for the rest of your life."

Georgia cringed. She had knowingly condemned herself to almost a full year of *this?* Was any man worth all of this? She paused. Yes. Yes, Robinson certainly was. Damn him.

CHAPTER EIGHTEEN

You are not worth the dust
which the rude wind blows in your face.
                    —William Shakespeare, *King Lear*
                              (as published in 1770)

9th of April, 1831
The opening of the Season in London—Rotten Row

BY JOSEPH, SHE FELT LIKE A horse being led by a horse.

Georgia thought it so odd that the path she and her well-groomed horse were on would be called Rotten by the aristocracy given it was *their* bloody row.

Directing her horse at a slow pace alongside Lady Burton, whose gaze was primly fixed on the path leading through the park, Georgia tightened her gloved hands on the leather reins and prayed she didn't fall off the saddle.

"On the path before us, if I am to believe the color of his gloves, is the infamous Lord Seton," Lady Burton announced in a casual tone, tilting her chin toward her. "He has a twin. The two wear different-colored gloves to allow the public to differentiate them. Lord Seton wears white and his brother, Lord Danford, wears black. The two play at switching gloves all the time, but we are about to beat them at their own game. Do you see him? He is the only gentleman on the path before us and is heading our way."

Georgia scanned the dirt path before them, noting the only man visible through a crowd of carriage-riding mothers and their daughters just beyond Rotten Row itself. A young, dark-haired gentleman in a black horse-hair top hat, garbed in a well-fitted riding coat and gray trousers, steadily veered toward them. His black leather boots gleamed in the sunlight with each trot of his black stallion.

Georgia glanced toward Lady Burton. "I see him. Yes."

"The purpose of this ride is to formally introduce you to London society and ensure everyone clamors to further know you." Lady Burton smiled and stared out before them, guiding her horse toward him. "Follow me. From what I know, after poking about for good targets, Lord Seton is not only a flirt, but happens to be within the circle of your Yardley. Producing a flurry of male interest that will rile your Yardley into full cooperation is exactly what you want. So I suggest you make this Lord Seton notice you. And now is your chance."

"You want me to entertain him? Here on the road?" Georgia wrinkled her nose. "Wouldn't that be considered crass?"

"No. Rotten Row is designed to showcase a woman's potential. I am not asking you to flip up your skirts. I am asking you to smile. Do you want to marry or not?"

Georgia sighed and guided her horse to fall into a trot beside the woman. "I'm ready to be showcased."

"Good." Lady Burton glanced toward her with un-usually bright and eager dark eyes. "Now keep up. The moment he passes, hold his gaze as if he were Yardley himself and you wanted him naked. Then we pass and you are done."

"No words?"

"No words. Respectable society excites very easily, my dear. Here in London, you are dealing with a very different breed of men. They are well-trained dogs, so to speak. But dogs all the same. Now here he comes. Silence and poise."

Georgia set her chin and kept her gaze trained on the young gentleman whose horse was about to pass their own. He casually glanced toward them, his dark eyes scanning Lady Burton before jumping to Georgia. His straight brows rose a small fraction as if he were genu-inely intrigued.

In the name of every Five Pointer who would never see the glory of this day, Georgia heatedly met his gaze for a very long and very sultry moment and hoped to God it was sultry enough. Still holding his gaze, she lavishly smiled.

He slowly grinned, his shaven cheek dimpling rather adorably. A gloved hand came up to touch the rim of his hat as he passed.

Georgia inclined her head, in turn, before altogether ignoring him and sweeping her gaze back to the dirt path before her. She trotted on with her horse in silence until he disappeared off the path.

Lady Burton slowed their pace. "Well done. And now the gossipmongers cometh. Remember. They can smell discomfort well over a mile and these two hags are no different."

An open black polished barouche with two elderly women well adorned in oversize bonnets and daffodil-yellow and teal-patterned gowns extravagantly embroidered with lace steered out of their path to round them. They slowed their horses and leaned toward each other, exchanging quiet words whilst glancing toward her.

Ah, yes. The gossipmongers.

In unison, they set their aged chins and veered closer, slowing their barouche. The eldest of the two, with thick white sausage curls, smiled and regally called out, "My dear Lady Burton. Was New York truly that devoid of entertainment?"

That sounded like an insult. Which meant it probably was.

Lady Burton feigned a gracious smile and slowed her horse so as to better engage them. "I rather adored New York, but my American friend, the ever-charming Miss Tormey—" Lady Burton sweepingly gestured toward Georgia "—insisted that I join her and Mrs. Astor for the Season."

Both of the women's eyes widened. They stared up at Georgia in unison, almost bringing their barouche to a complete halt.

One of them eagerly leaned forward, searching Georgia's face. "Miss Tormey. I have heard so much about you. I am Lady Chartwell and this is my sister, Lady Hudson. We welcome you to Town."

Hudson. Like the river that never stopped piddling. Georgia counterfeited a smile and tugged on the reins of her horse. Using her right boot against the side of the horse, she came to a halt. She focused on her words and her stance, knowing every breath counted. "I thank you for the warm welcome and confess I am rather smitten with London. The gentleman are so civilized and the women so well dressed. You must recommend who oversees your wardrobe. 'Tis divine."

The two women beamed.

The one with the sausage curls smugly offered, "The Nightingale over on Regent Street is where every lady ought to be outfitted whilst in London. They only hire seamstresses out of France and never replicate any of their patterns." She perused Georgia's riding outfit and paused. "I don't believe I have seen a riding habit so well put together. Was it assembled here in Town?"

Georgia tried not to smirk. She thought she'd never hear rich society compliment *her* outfit. "So lovely of you to notice, Lady Chartwell, but no. It was assembled on Broadway in New York. Their seamstresses are all French, too. Though I will admit, I am rather bored with my current wardrobe. I will have to visit this Nightingale's in the hopes of entertaining myself."

"You will not be disappointed," the woman chimed in return. "I do hope you will be able to find some time during the Season to call upon me and my sister over on Park Lane with Mrs. Astor. We have yet to meet her. I hear she will be acting as your chaperone? Is that true?"

"Yes," Georgia offered.

Noting that Lady Burton was bringing her horse to a trot and was silently signaling that it was time for them to go, Georgia did the same. "It was a pleasure. I hope to see you both soon. Good day."

"Yes. Good day." The two prodded their barouche onward, glancing toward each other in exasperation as if they had just witnessed a woman sprinting naked across Rotten Row.

Superficial bitches.

When they were well out of sight, Lady Burton tossed out, "You did well."

Georgia sighed. "Do I actually have to call on them now?"

"You said you would, so yes. You have to."

Georgia groaned. "I hate London."

"This is probably where I should remind you that you have come to town to wed and stay in it."

"Oh, yes. That." Georgia bit back a smile. "I wonder what Robinson will think of me when he sees me."

"He will most likely faint." Lady Burton paused, her dark arched brows suddenly rising. "Well, well, well. It appears the row is more rotten than usual today. I love it. For the sake of your reputation, my dear, ignore these two men approaching on horseback. Heaven only knows who they are and what they want."

Georgia darted her gaze over to the two who were riding on black stallions in worn black coats, worn leather boots and no hats. One had black disheveled shoulder-length hair and the other had sunlit chestnut hair and a worn leather patch over his...eye?

Her eyes widened as she tightened her hold on the reins. It was Matthew! Matthew and...*Coleman?* What the bloody hell were they doing in London? Had they followed her?

Oh, this wasn't good. She couldn't let them see her lest they engage her in public and ruin everything.

She quickly yanked the rim of her hat as far down as it would go until she couldn't even see the road before her and only the reins in her hands. She also yanked the long trailing veil of her riding habit up and over her face, burying herself in it.

"The veil *never* goes over your face," Lady Burton chided. "'Tis meant for decorative purposes only."

"Not today it isn't." Georgia lowered her voice. "I know those two. They're from New York. And of all things, they're from my part of town."

"Are they?" Lady Burton sounded not only intrigued but smitten. She was quiet for a moment, then casually inquired, "Might I ask who the man with the patch is? He looks rough enough to be fun."

Georgia glanced over at the woman in complete disbelief and though she couldn't see her because of her drawn hat and veil, she hoped to God she could convey that any interest in Matthew was a very, very bad idea. "He's the last person you want to ever involve yourself with. He's a thief."

Lady Burton let out a laugh. "All men are. Now quiet. Here they come."

Georgia prayed and brought her horse to a full trot in the hopes of passing faster.

A low whistle escaped who she knew to be Matthew. "Apparently, I've been living in the wrong city all my life," he drawled. "Ladies."

She cringed as their horses trotted past one another. Georgia even sped up her horse in an effort to fling off the words Matthew had just unknowingly tossed at her.

Lady Burton called out for her to slow. "Miss Tormey."

Georgia hissed out a breath. Flopping back her veil, she readjusted her hat and choked out, "That was disgusting. I felt like I was being groped by my own brother."

Lady Burton aligned her horse beside hers and slowly grinned. "Speak for yourself. I rather enjoyed that."

CHAPTER NINETEEN

*Then be not coy, but use your time, And while ye
may, go marry:*
*For having lost but once your prime, you may
forever tarry.*

—Robert Herrick, *Hesperides* (1648)

15th of April, 1831
The Wentworth home on Park Lane

"SPEAKING OF GRANDEUR...I was rather astonished His
Grace had invited *Miss Tormey* into our circle. The
moment she was announced, His Grace greeted her
quite warmly, as if he was genuinely charmed. Curious,
that. She must be of *some* notable worth. Lady Chartwell, I hear, was rather taken by her, as well."

"You mean to say that *Miss Tormey* is here?" There
was a tsk-tsk-tsk and the fluttering of a fan. "Whatever is the Season coming to? We only seem to acquire crawlers these days." The conspirator lowered her
voice. "Though I will admit I *have* been most curious to
glimpse her. Is she really as beautiful as some claim?"

There was a tittering, dismissive laugh. "'Tis but
her coffers that make her breathtaking in the eyes of
London, I assure you."

Roderick felt like gouging his ears out so he wouldn't have to listen to any more. At least his father had shown him some mercy and hadn't insisted that he stand by the main entrance to greet all of the incoming guests.

Swiping a flute of champagne off a silver tray, Roderick rounded yet another group of fan-fluttering, eye-darting women. Taking a long swallow of the tart-zinging coolness, he strode toward the farthest section of the candlelit ballroom.

Seeing his grandparents quietly lingering with a large group of men and women, he tightened his jaw and averted his gaze, hurrying past to avoid them. 'Tis all he seemed to be doing these days. Avoiding people.

He veered toward the farthest corner and paused, finding Lord Seton and Lord Danford leaning against the paneled candlelit wall, occupying his usual space.

Though everyone in London usually steered clear of the two men, given that they were twins notorious for placing monstrous bets on *anything* and almost always emptied the pockets of every man in a breath, Roderick rather liked Danford and Seton. They were good men who always donated whatever they won to local charities. They were two of the few gambling men in London who actually made the church proud.

As Roderick approached, he noted that their dark heads were still bent toward each other, their foreheads creased in what appeared to be a most serious discussion. Though the two brothers were impossible to distinguish by eye, they assisted the public by wearing different-colored gloves.

Roderick's brows came together as he veered in.

"Danford? Seton? Is everything all right? You two look a bit frazzled."

Both men paused from their conversation and glanced at him.

Danford pushed away from the wall, his coal-black eyes taking on that devious sparkle they were known for. "Frazzled? More like *dazzled*. Always good to see you, Yardley. Even if it isn't all that often anymore, given this damned romance you're having with the university. What is this business with you being a professor, anyway? You're making the rest of us look stupid and lazy, as always."

Roderick bit back a laugh. "I just needed something to occupy my time. It keeps me out of trouble." *And distracts me from thinking about Georgia.*

Danford paused and waved Roderick over with the wag of his black-gloved fingers. "Speaking of trouble…"

Roderick drew closer. "What?"

Seton, who was closest to Roderick, yanked him closer, almost spilling the champagne out onto his white gloves. "Not *what,* my friend. But *who.*" Seton leaned toward him, his shaven face bearing new mischief. "Have you had a chance to meet Miss Tormey yet? By God, I did. Saw her over on Rotten Row a few days ago. I had to bloody send that woman flowers. She gave me this—this…*look* that I'm still trying to recover from. Hmm. Hmm. Hmm."

There was that name again. "No. I haven't met her yet. Who is she?"

A low, long whistle escaped Danford's teeth. "*That* about says it all."

Roderick eyed them both. "*That* was only a whistle, and not a very good one at that."

Seton lowered his voice, leaning toward him. "Allow me to put this into words, Yardley. If this heavenly creature were surrounded by fire-spiked walls, I would climb said walls more than once to be with her."

Roderick smirked and hit the man's arm with the back of his gloved hand. "More than once? Sounds like matrimony to me, you poor bastard. Have you formally introduced yourself?"

Seton glared at him. "Mother would have a fit."

"Mine, too," Danford added. "Given that we have the same mother. Ha."

Roderick eyed him. "How old are you two bastards, anyway? Halfway to thirty? Since when do you need your mother's approval to marry? Set off to Gretna Green. Men do it all the time."

"Speaking of Gretna Green…there she is now." Danford and Seton angled themselves in unison to get a better look, resembling identical hounds pointing out the same hare to its master.

Seton reached out to Roderick, gesturing toward his champagne. "Hand it up. It's not like you're drinking it."

Roderick rolled his eyes and shoved the glass into his hand. "Don't choke."

"I only ever swallow." Seford smirked and held up the glass in a half toast. "To Miss Tormey and Gretna Green. It would break Mother's heart." He tossed the rest of the champagne down his throat and went back to staring. "The more I look, the more I want."

Roderick glanced over to the woman in question, but couldn't see past the small group of men lingering around her and her chaperone. Adjusting his black evening coat, Roderick looked back toward Seton and Danford. "Whilst you two can afford to gawk, I have a class to teach in the morning. I should probably retire." He pointed at each of them. "Stay out of trouble. It's hard, I know, but we have to do the best we can."

Seton grabbed his shoulder with a white-gloved hand, blocking him with his own body to keep him from going anywhere. "We should all go over and put ourselves on her dance card. Come with me. I'm not doing this alone."

Roderick shoved Seton's heavy hand from his shoulder, growing annoyed. "Unlike you two, I actually earn my wages and haven't the time for women *or* dance cards." Roderick tried to round him.

Seton jumped back in front of him and leaned in, poking his chest. "Fifty pounds says the moment you lay eyes on her, class will teach itself. I'm telling you, Yardley, this woman will lift more than your brows. *Fifty* pounds says she is the most attractive woman you've ever seen. Fifty. Are you in?"

Easier money he'd never made. No woman could ever be more attractive than Georgia. "Fifty, it is. Where the hell is she? I'll point out every last flaw down to the nose."

Seton grabbed his shoulders and jerked him toward the direction he needed to look, better squaring him toward where she stood. "*There.* She just came into view again. I dare you to find any fault with *that.*"

Roderick blinked.

A regal-looking beauty with thick, pinned strawberry curls that had been piled to softly frame her oval face made him suck in an astonished breath. By God. The woman reminded him of…Georgia.

He hissed out a breath knowing there wasn't an hour that passed when Georgia and her haunting words of finding him in London didn't come to mind. He'd been waiting for her ever since.

Edging back, he paused and skimmed the woman's length, which had just come into full view, trying to make sense of what he was seeing. Despite what appeared to be a most striking resemblance, it couldn't be based on that figure alone.

This redhead was quite elegant, draped in a chartreuse off-the-shoulder full evening gown, trimmed with snowy lace that rounded an incredibly low-cut neckline boasting a set of impressive breasts. Large teardrop diamonds hung from her ears and throat, gleaming and shimmering against the vast candlelight.

As that curvaceous redhead daintily wrote several names onto her poised dance card with the pencil hanging from her gloved wrist, she glanced up and scanned the room. Her intent gaze rounded its way before settling on him.

She paused.

Stunning bright green eyes he knew all too well captured his gaze. Roderick's breath hitched as an inner shiver of awareness rippled throughout the entire length of his body.

Georgia.

A taunting whisper of a smile touched her full lips at seeing him openly stare. It was as if she were silently announcing, *You are damned for the rest of your days, Robinson. Start crawling.*

His throat tightened. His palms actually grew moist beneath the tightness of his white evening gloves knowing it *was* Georgia. His conniving son of a bitch of a father. *That* was why the man had insisted on his presence tonight and wouldn't desist until he came. He knew Georgia was coming.

Casually breaking their gaze, she gracefully set her chin as any other lady of the *ton* would do and returned her attention to the group of men gathered around her.

A gentleman leaned in toward the elderly woman who lingered beside Georgia.

Who the hell was that?

The elderly woman swept a gloved hand toward Georgia, who graciously inclined her head, briefly offering her hand to the gentleman before bringing up the dance card dangling from her gloved wrist. Four other gentlemen lingered, all patiently waiting to add themselves to her card, as well.

Roderick almost staggered. This couldn't be happening. He was *not* actually watching men of *his* circle gather around *his* woman from Orange Street.

Leaning in, Seton eyed him. "And?"

Still staring at Georgia, lest she disappear from sight, Roderick blindly reached out and seized Seton by the back of his neck, crushing it beneath rigid fingers. Yanking Seton close, he pointed to Georgia. "What do you know about her?" he rasped, trying to remain calm. "And *what* are people actually saying about her?"

Seton shifted toward him. "After I glimpsed her over on Rotten Row riding with Lady Burton, I started digging around to find out more about her and it was well worth the dig. That there is Miss Georgiana Colette Tormey. She is the distant cousin of Mr. Astor, the richest self-made American millionaire who deals in furs across the world. Miss Tormey came for the opening of the Season just last week with Mrs. Astor acting as her chaperone. Mr. Astor insisted Miss Tormey have her Season here in London as opposed to New York. Do you know that conniving American bastard is hoping to have her married to one of our own? Boasting that nothing would best crown her wealth of thirty bloody thousand a year? Can you imagine running your fingers through all that money *and* that woman? Apoplexy take us all."

Georgiana? From *New York City?*

Roderick dropped his hand heavily from the man's neck. Shit. So *this* was what she'd been up to all this time when she'd disappeared from his life without so much as an explanation, leaving him to fester in his own anguish and damn mind.

Roderick lowered his chin against his silk cravat, still staring her down. By God. She looked nothing like herself. If not for those emerald eyes he knew so well, he never would have recognized her. Hell, even her breasts had undergone a transformation, overfilling her embroidered bodice in the most tantalizing way.

Georgia primly turned toward a newly arrived set of gentlemen seeking introductions. She graciously extended an elegant gloved hand to each and smiled.

He had *never* thought her capable of accomplishing *this*. Or rather, he hadn't let himself hope. Edging closer, he purposefully angled himself to better see her past those gathered around her.

He intently watched her as she glanced and spoke in every direction but his. He swiped at his mouth, still in disbelief, and almost dug his teeth into his hand to keep himself from dashing for her and making an idiot out of himself. Whilst he was beyond flabbergasted and more than impressed, a part of him didn't know if he liked what he was seeing, because it simply wasn't her. It was an elegant and refined, overly gussied-up version of Georgia Emily Milton. Where was that fire he loved so much? Was it still in there somewhere?

He paused and glanced over at Seton and Danford, who were leaning toward each other.

"I've never been with a redhead before," Seton casually intoned, lowering his voice. "Do you think she has freckles everywhere?"

Roderick narrowed his gaze and snapped his fingers at them. *"Seton. Danford."*

They both glanced toward him.

"I have an announcement to make." Roderick pointed at each of their heads in warning and said in a tone that he hoped dripped with enough blood to make his point, "If either of you so much as look at her again, let alone make any more inappropriate and vulgar comments about her, I will take my father's ceremonial sword that hangs on the wall in the next room and gut you both with the same tip, impaling you together onto the doors of St. Paul. Because that there woman, who calls herself *Miss Tormey,* is going to be my wife by the end of this Season. So be sure to inform every last bastard in London of my intentions, lest they all *die* right along with you. Are we plain?"

Seton blinked.

Danford gargled out a laugh and popped out a hand. "Fifty pounds. I'll let poor Seton recover from his loss." Danford glanced over at Seton, adding, "A hundred says she will move on to a better offer within the week, given that *his* interest will mobilize other men to do the same. 'Tis fair game for you now, Seton. Fair game. All you have to do is tell Mother that the Duke of Wentworth's own son is making a run for it. You know the way she coos over the duke. Your success is assured."

Roderick shifted his jaw, dug into the inner pocket of his coat and yanked out whatever folded banknotes he had, not even bothering to count them. He slapped them all into Danford's hand. "I will not only see your bet, Danford, but I'll raise it to *ten thousand pounds.*"

"Ten thousand?" Seton and Danford echoed in unison, shifting toward him.

"That's right, boys. *Ten thousand.*" Roderick smoothed his cravat against his throat. "Now if you will excuse me, I intend to formally introduce myself to Miss Tormey. I'm not getting any younger."

CHAPTER TWENTY

Do not alarm yourself: I am not a thief, unless that title be attached to those who take from thieves.
—*The Arabian Nights' Entertainments*
(as published in 1792)

MRS. ASTOR PURSED HER THIN lips and glanced toward Georgia's dance card. "To be considered a success, Miss Tormey, every last dance must be spoken for. Especially the waltz. That is as much true in the States as it is here. Why must you insist on keeping it unaccounted for?"

Georgia tried to remain indifferent, even though she felt unbearably hot and unnerved in the stuffy heat of the room.

Everyone's breaths seemed to press against one another and all of the walls. Even worse, the gown draping her body weighed more than six pails of water.

The inquisitive gaze of every man and woman in the room scraped across her skin and soul. Some of those glances were laced with genuine admiration. Some with indifference. Some were laced with a mocking haughtiness insinuating she wasn't worthy of breathing. Indeed, they were not only looking at her, but coming to their own conclusions as to what they thought of her. They were vultures—every last one of them—and they were circling and circling, waiting for signs of weakness.

Though her limbs felt heavy, she managed to offer Mrs. Astor a genteel reply, focusing on her diction. "I do beg forgiveness, Mrs. Astor, but I wish to save the waltz for a gentleman worthy of it." She glanced toward where she'd last seen Robinson, only to find that he had long disappeared. Surely, he had recognized her. She was sure of it given the way he had stared and stared.

Mrs. Astor shook her head, her gray-and-white coif swaying against the movement. "I promised Mr. Astor you would be a success, and success isn't found by tossing opportunities. I will assign your waltz to the next worthy prospect who approaches."

Drat it all. Here she was, putting on a show in the name of love that would make Shakespeare stand up to applaud, and in the end, she was going to have to give it all away to the next flat, hair-parted fop who dared call himself a man.

"Mrs. Astor?" a husky male voice casually inquired from behind her. "Might I formally seek an introduction from the lady standing beside you?"

Georgia's heart skittered, her eyes widening. By all that was blue. It was *Robinson*. She bit back a gushing smile. He couldn't stay away.

Though she wanted to promptly turn and acknowledge him in her full glory, she decided to make him work for it as she had warned him she would, and remained indifferent even as a long drop of sweat trickled down the length of her back beneath her chemise and corset. She didn't even look at him.

Mrs. Astor glided toward Yardley with a more than enthusiastic smile. "'Tis an honor, indeed, my lord." She swept a lace-gloved hand to Georgia. "This is Miss Georgiana Colette Tormey. She is the distinguished distant cousin to my dear, dear husband, Mr. Astor, who regrets having to stay abroad due to business. Miss Tormey?" Mrs. Astor gestured toward Yardley. "This is the Marquess of Yardley, the son of our host, His Grace, the Duke of Wentworth."

Georgia casually turned to Robinson and regally outstretched her gloved hand toward him. Although it was difficult, she tried to appear bored. "My lord."

Those seductive gray eyes intently clung to her face with a sensual determination to seize her every last breath. He grasped her hand, the warmth of his large gloved hand tightening with an urgency that pinched. He lifted her gloved hand to his lips and fiercely kissed her knuckles, covertly and quickly nipping her glove and the skin with his bottom teeth. He met her gaze again and grinned, saying in a most provocative and suggestive tone, "I am without breath."

"You flatter me," she drawled, withdrawing her hand.

His grin faded as his gaze dropped to her throat and then her breasts before returning to her face. "Is the waltz available, Miss Tormey?"

The heat of the room and having him so close overwhelmed her and frayed the last of her vision. Until that moment, she never realized a man really *could* make a woman swoon.

RODERICK JUMPED FORWARD and grabbed hold of Georgia as she limply spilled toward him. His heart pounded as he frantically adjusted his hold on her arm and waist, trying to keep her from cascading to the floor. Was it the heat? It had to be, given that he himself was sweltering.

He gathered her into his arms in one smooth motion.

Mrs. Astor gasped as others paused to stare. Unfolding the fan dangling from her wrist, she hurried toward him and frantically waved her fan over Georgia's flushed face. "'Tis dreadfully hot in here. I don't blame her."

"She needs cooler air." Roderick's fingers dug into Georgia's limp softness, a pulsing knot overtaking his ability to breathe. He whipped toward the entrance hall, stalking as fast as he could through the crowd. Though the music and dancing continued, the rumbling of voices and whispers around him lifted to a crescendo that pierced his ability to think or breathe. He glanced down frantically at Georgia as he hurried across the floor, her face still tucked and buried against his heaving chest.

He tightened his arms around her and moved faster and faster, weaving through others.

Several men, including Seton, who had made a sprint from the back, hurried toward him.

"Is there anything we can do, my lord?" someone insisted.

Roderick rounded them. "Hunt down my father."

Two of the men darted off, disappearing into the crowd.

Seton anxiously trotted alongside him, trying to keep up and glancing repeatedly toward Georgia. He quickly leaned in and tried forcefully wrenching Georgia out of his arms. "Allow me to carry her for you."

Gritting his teeth, Roderick shoved Seton back with the weight of his shoulder. "I will see to her myself," he growled out, shoving his way past all of them.

Despite the crowd pressing in on them to catch a glimpse of Georgia, Roderick barreled onward, shouldering his way through and forcing men to hop-foot out of his path.

Heading into the cool stillness of the vast corridor, he bounded up the length of the sweeping marble stairs, tightening his hold on Georgia, and hurried toward the guest chamber.

A *tap-tap-tap* on his shoulder made him jerk to a halt and glance down.

Georgia's weary but sharp-looking green eyes searched his face. "Sorry about that."

His throat tightened as he trained his eyes before him and resumed his pace. "You are done for the night. And needless to say, I am not at all pleased with the way you disappeared. Regardless of your reasons."

Angling Georgia sideways, Roderick hurried into the bedchamber and closed the door behind them. He strode over to the four-poster bed and draped her across the feathered mattress, ensuring her legs were pulled straight and that her skirts covered her. Leaning over her, he quickly arranged all of the pillows behind her head, tucking her into them, and drew up the linens to cover her.

"We might as well settle this here and now." Georgia grabbed his coat by the lapels and yanked him down toward herself with surprising force. He gasped as his body fell into hers, crushing her softness beneath his tense muscles.

He tried to shift away, but she fiercely held on to him, weighing him down toward her. "Georgia—"

"I have infiltrated your circle, Lord Yardley," she tossed up at him. "Now the real fun is set to begin." She primly settled herself back against the pillows, nestling herself against them, and arranged her skirts with a more than smug smile. "What do you think of Miss Tormey? Impressive, isn't she? You should see this woman trot a horse. Every man was craning his neck on Rotten Row. Every man. Some even whistled. Though I'll never tell you who."

He heaved out a breath, not knowing how he was to even begin apologizing, given all he put her through. "I'm sorry, Georgia. I'm sorry I didn't have more faith in you."

"Do you know that Lord Seton almost fell off his stallion when he first saw me? Do you also know that in three short days, he not only found my address but sent me four dozen flowers in one basket along with a request to call? All because I looked at him and smiled. You aristos are so easy to bed. Though I do plan on letting him call. I rather like that adorable dimple that appears on his cheek when he smiles."

Roderick gave her a long, black layered look, not in the least bit amused. "You won. I lost. Are you quite finished?"

She paused. "Far from it. I told you I would make you crawl, and crawl you shall." Erasing all emotion from her pretty powdered features, she breathed out a delicate, albeit dramatic, breath and regally settled herself back against the pillows. Draping the back of her gloved hand gracefully against her forehead, she fluttered her eyes shut. "Lord Seton is all things divine. As is his brother. I imagine it would be like getting two men for the price of one."

His lips parted. By all that was twisted. She had not only learned the ways of a lady, but the ways of a seasoned actress! He leaned in and grabbed her nose, twisting it hard enough to ensure it hurt.

"Ow!" She winced and swatted at his hands, shoving them away from her nose. "That hurt."

"I'm glad for it. *That* is for blatantly trying to make me jealous when I am clearly repentant." He shook his head, scanning the pompous amount of shimmering large diamonds covering her throat. Those diamonds rested atop plump, cock-twitching breasts that pushed tauntingly against a very tight bodice. "My, my, my. What have you done to yourself? I have yet to decide what I think of it."

She casually redraped a hand across her forehead, feigning boredom. "I intend to tote this with pride and make you squirm all Season long, which will give you plenty of time to decide what you think of it."

His eyes clung to hers, daring her to make him squirm and crawl. "I don't need time. And you will be kissing me and telling me that you love me in less than a minute, Georgia. So get to it. We're done playing games."

"You clearly don't know Georgiana."

"Oh, I think that I do."

"Let us forget what you *think*. Let us talk about my breasts instead. You want to touch and fondle them, don't you? Admit it. You do."

She really was something. He waved his forefinger toward them. "In truth, I think they are overdone. I preferred them the way they were. Small. Less men notice small breasts. As such, I ask that you get rid of them."

She feigned a laugh. "Sadly, they're nonreturnable, because I'm not giving up my painted éclairs. I'd sooner remain a spinster than give up the few joys a lady *is* permitted without being considered a slut. Unless, of course, you think sucking on a painted éclair is the equivalent of sucking on your cock."

He lowered his chin. Beneath all that finery, she was still his Georgia. Thank bloody God. "Enough. You have made your point."

Georgia haughtily adjusted her draped hand against her brow and tossed up at him, "I don't think I have."

He swiped a hand across his face, glancing off to the side before shifting back toward her. "Jesus Christ, Georgia. Do you really intend to draw this out? I have suffered more than enough all these months without hearing a word from you and dreading you were going to show up at my door naked just to give the *ton* something to talk about. And the sad thing of it? I wanted you to do it. I wanted you to show up naked."

She paused, peering up at him past her limp hand

draped against her forehead. "That would have actually been a good idea. But I have bigger plans. Something that involves a lot more…*suffering*."

Shifting against the bed, he leaned down closer toward her draped figure and growled down at her, "I dare you to draw this out."

"Dare taken."

Stripping his gloves, he whipped them onto the bed.

He then skimmed his hand across her throat and leaned down and kissed the smooth, powdered skin just above the upper round of her left breast. "I'm sorry." The tantalizing scent of lemon blossomed from her heated skin as he dragged his lips across its softness. "Take me back, Georgia. For God's sake, take me back. Take this idiot back so that he may spend the rest of his life making it up to you."

She snorted. "You are going to have to do better than that, *Yardley*."

He kissed the well of her throat, firmly pressing his lips against that throbbing pulse, and then licked its entire length, causing her to suck in a breath. "If you haven't noticed, your Robinson depends on you for everything. It would be nothing short of cruel to deny him of you."

"I'm not taking you back."

He lifted his head from the heat of her throat and glared at her. "Georgia, Christ. Are you serious? I've barely been in your presence for forty minutes and I'm already exhausted."

"Yes, well, I'm the one who is really exhausted after almost a year of 'don't do this' and 'don't do that' lest you be called a whore. Do you have *any* idea how hard it is being a lady?"

He lifted a brow. "Do you have any idea how hard it is being a lord? Especially after having met you?"

She sighed. "Now I do. 'Tis piss hard, is what. These bastards expect the world from us yet give us nothing, in turn, but superficial airs laced with misery."

He bit back a smile, rather impressed she had already learned their role in society. "Whatever you want, you shall have from here on out. You have more than earned it, madam, and I look forward to crawling for the rest of my life."

He grabbed up her hands, stripping her gloves, and kissed their softness repeatedly. He paused and held up one of her hands, fingering its smoothness. His gaze snapped to hers in disbelief. "Your hands."

"I know. It took a lot of scrubbing and daily soaks. They're still not what they should be, but in time, they will be."

His heart squeezed as he glanced back down at those hands that seemed so small in comparison to his own. "Oh, Georgia." He kissed the tips of her fingers and then those knuckles. "A part of me is so sad to know that I have forced you to change yourself and your life merely to be with me." He kissed her hands again. "I will miss my Georgia. I will miss her so damn much and only pray she won't entirely disappear."

She slowly smiled, watching him kiss her hands. Releasing her hands, he dragged his own down the length of her body and back up again, reveling in the feel of her softness and the smoothness of her silk embroidered gown.

His chest tightened, along with every muscle in his body, realizing that *this* and *she* were real. She was here in London. With him. "God, did I ever miss you," he whispered. "I waited and I waited for you to come. It was torture of the worst sort. I cannot believe you did all of this for me. I am beyond honored."

She raked her hands and nails through his hair. "I can't believe it, either. You owe me."

"I know I do." He leaned in, angling his mouth toward hers. "Be forewarned, this is about to get rough."

"Now, now, keep it all buttoned up." She sat up on the bed, daintily scooting out of his reach and away. She scrambled out of bed, hopping down to the floor with a soft thud and rounded the bed with the *click-click-click* of slippered heels as she sashayed her way to the closed door.

He paused and then swung toward her direction, the linens dragging up and shifting beneath his movement. "Wait. What are you doing? Where are you going?"

"This isn't Orange Street, you know. I have a reputation to uphold and I don't trust you any more than I trust myself." Opening the door, she pushed it wide with the graceful thrust of a gloved hand. "*That* will ensure we don't get into trouble."

She paused, glancing toward the empty corridor beyond the open door, and then turned toward him, dragging up one side of her gown. Gathering the vast amount of material, she exposed the shapely length of a leg draped in a white silk stocking that was held in place above her knee with a tied bright red garter. "Do you like my stockings? I just bought them. They're silk. *After* we marry, you may take them off. If you're deserving of it, that is." She primly dropped her skirt with a rustle and rearranged her gown.

He slid off the bed, his muscles roaring in lust. Only Georgia could ever make him crawl and make him love every moment of it. Striding toward her, he purposefully towered before her.

She snapped her gaze up to his face.

He grinned. "How about we close the door and tell London to go to hell?"

She stepped toward him and poked him hard in the chest. "Go get Robinson before I dirk you, Yardley."

He tsked and grabbed her by the waist, and holding her firmly against himself, he grazed the tip of his finger across her powdered cheek. "It appears I'm not the only one going by more than one name, *Miss Georgiana Colette Tormey.*"

Georgia smacked his shoulder and lowered her voice all the more. "Georgia is no more until *after* we marry. Do you understand? There is to be no touching or kissing until I *legally* become Lady Yardley. You hear?"

"I hear," he murmured, searching her face. "Will you at least please pass on one last message from me to Georgia, Miss Tormey? Given that I won't be seeing her again until my wedding night?"

A smile touched her lips. "What is your message, my lord?"

Glancing toward the door and the still-empty corridor, Roderick leaned down, grabbed her face and kissed her, aggressively parting those soft, warm lips with his own. Closing his eyes and giving in to an ecstasy he never thought he'd know again, he kissed his Georgia passionately and lovingly and erotically, tracing her teeth and her tongue and her lips before releasing her.

He stepped back, opening his eyes, and hissed out a breath, wishing it didn't have to end. "Tell her that I love her."

Georgia lingered before him with her eyes still closed, and her chin tilted upward, those full moist lips parted as if half expecting his return. She eventually opened her eyes and whispered, "I'll be sure Georgia knows."

Quick footfalls echoed from down the corridor heading their way. *"Yardley?"* the duke yelled out, those steps now breaking into a run. *"Yardley!"*

Her eyes widened. She gathered her skirts and dashed back to the bed, her slippers skidding across the wood floor. Scrambling up and onto the mattress, she frantically arranged herself and her skirts around her, before draping herself calmly and demurely onto the bed.

Roderick dragged in a much-needed breath. He doubted any woman had ever gone *this* far for a man in the name of love. "I ardently hope you feel better soon, Miss Tormey. I would hate for you to have come all this way only to never see past a bed. Though I have a feeling illness may overtake me soon, as well, and we will both be confined to the same bed. What will London say?"

"Shh!" Her head jerked up to give him a reprimanding glare before settling herself back against the pillows.

He grinned.

"Yardley!" The duke skidded into view and stumbled into the doorway, his face panicked and flushed. "How is Georgia?"

"Quite well, Your Grace," she called out, a hand darting up into the air before it dropped back down onto the mattress. "No need to panic."

The duke huffed out a breath. "Good. One less thing to worry about. This night is about to turn into a mess."

Roderick's grin faded as he swung fully toward his father, his pulse roaring. "Does someone already know about Georgia?"

"No." The duke jumped toward him and seized him by the lapels of his coat, shaking him. "Atwood arrived into town. He's *downstairs*. He approached his father just this morning, demanding he fess up to what had led to his disappearance, but the man is denying everything, along with his legitimacy, and there appears to be no goddamn proof of his likeness anywhere. I haven't told Atwood yet, but I mean to help him. I mean to help him in the name of your mother. So, God save me, I am about to not only publicly turn against your mother's family, but I am about to dig up that portrait that was buried with her thirteen years ago to prove his likeness and who he is. Are you with me in this? Will you see me through this, knowing Atwood is all we have left of your mother?"

Bloody hell. All of London's mightiest bridges were about to come falling down. Roderick swallowed against the tightness overtaking his throat and half nodded in a daze, knowing he had *no* idea what he was getting himself into. "Yes. I am with you."

"Good. Good. I want you to go to him. Go! He is in the study and I have to tend to my guests lest this turns into a circus. I'll join you as soon as I am able. Keep him in the study, and for God's sake, don't let anyone see him. The man will only scare people. I told him he really needs to do something about his appearance. Now go. Go to him. I'll be there in about a half hour." His father turned and jogged back out.

Glancing back at Georgia, who had sat up, Roderick pointed at her. "Stay where you are. Keep playing the game. I'll be back."

He dashed out of the room and sprinted down the corridor after his father, knowing full well he was going to finally see the face of a man he had yet to remember. The face of what had started this all.

Pounding down the stairs and weaving past guests that were lingering outside the ballroom, he jogged toward the closed doors of the study. He slid both doors open and quickly stepped in, sliding them closed behind himself.

The solid broad back of a tall man, whose shoulder-length, disheveled black hair bore whispers of silver, lingered before the portrait of his mother, the Duchess of Wentworth. The one he, his father and Yardley used to pray before every Sunday after church. It appeared Atwood was praying, too, the way he stood in silence. The black boot-length riding coat he wore was heavily frayed to gray and even bore a rip at the curve of his shoulder. It was as if he had crawled out of the Five Points itself.

By God, he was about to meet and face yet another blank he had never regained. It was eerie. The floorboards creaked beneath Roderick's boots as he slowly made his way toward Atwood. He paused several feet behind him.

The man continued to blankly stare up at his mother's pale face and those soft gray eyes as if in a trance.

"No portrait did her justice." Roderick's voice echoed in the room, sounding a bit more nervous than he intended.

Atwood turned and fully faced him. The yellowing glow of the study's candles illuminated a shaven, lean face framed against disheveled, shoulder-length black hair. Cool ice-blue eyes that bespoke of a hard life held Roderick's gaze. His large gloved hand gripped the hilt of a dagger that was sheathed and attached to the leather belt resting on his hip.

"I'm your nephew," Roderick offered to reassure the man that the blade was unnecessary. "Yardley."

"I know who you are," Atwood replied in a low but casual tone that was laced with an accent that appeared to be an odd combination of American and British. "We met. Back in New York."

Roderick swallowed. "Forgive me for not being able to remember. I had an incident that—"

"I know. You needn't worry. I'm not all that memorable, anyway." Atwood eyed him. "Allow me to get to the point of my visit tonight, nephew of mine. One I have

yet to convey to your father. After a less than construc-
tive meeting with my father this morning, who refused
to let my mother see me, I have decided to kill him.
Tonight, actually. After he leaves this house and heads
into his carriage. And I intend to have all of London
witness it. Why am I telling you this? Because when
you are brought before the jury, I don't want there to
be any doubt as to what my motives were. Tell them it
wasn't revenge but a savage need for peace."

Roderick stared, not knowing what astonished him
more. Those words or how casually he had said them.
"Don't do this. Killing him will only see you hanged."

"Exactly. Peace."

Oh, no. No, no, no. The man was not about to do this
and drag him and his father into another nightmare. He
edged toward him. "Killing him and then getting yourself hanged will change *nothing*."

Atwood flexed his leather-gloved hands. "I know."

Hell, the man was serious. Not to mention absolutely
insane. "Uncle. If you do this, you will not only destroy
yourself, but you will ruin my father, and me, as well.
You'll also be destroying the wife I hope to take and the
children I hope to have. All we would ever know and
hear and see would be the blood you rashly spilled and
the mess you left for us to mop up."

His uncle pointed a gloved finger to his own head.
"I am *not* going to live inside this head a breath more."

It was as if he were meeting a deranged version of
himself prior to regaining his memory. "No one understands you more than I. Believe me. Living within
a head you would rather step out of is a curse of the

worst sort, but there are ways to allay the misery. But not like this. You will find it through the support and love of your family."

Atwood's face darkened. "The Sumners are not my family."

"Right you are in that. The Sumners are not. But we are. I am. My father is. My father loves you given all that you represent. He loves you enough to unearth his own wife's remains, which I know will kill him considering what she meant to him. Despite that, you mean to dirk him? You mean to dirk the last person who remains standing in your corner in order to entertain some morbid urge for revenge?"

Atwood searched his face. "He means to disturb my sister's grave? I won't have it."

"'Tis the only means we have of proving your legitimacy. My father told me about my grandfather denying your legitimacy, but *this* would prove it. 'Tis the only known portrait of you in existence with a label of your name and it lies buried with my mother."

Atwood momentarily closed his eyes. "She was buried with my portrait?"

"That she was. She carried you upon her lips and within her heart until her last breath was taken and spent her entire life wanting to find you. If you don't mean to honor the living, Uncle, I ask that you at least honor the dead. My mother deserved as much."

Atwood's features twisted as he swung away. After a long moment of silence, he turned back and wordlessly unfastened the leather belt from around his hips.

He folded the belt around the sheath of his dagger and held it out. "Take it before I use it."

Roderick grabbed hold of the belt and dagger, a breath escaping his lips. He tightened his hold on the worn leather and slowly shook his head. "You need to find peace."

Atwood set his shoulders and slowly rounded him. "I hear death is a nice long sleep. Sounds peaceful enough to me."

Roderick drew in a ragged breath and let it out. "Take back the life that was so maliciously taken from you and create something worthier. Surround yourself with people who will love you and support you whilst taking your place back in our circle where you belong. That is how you will find and know peace. Give yourself a chance to know it. Consider starting a family and commencing anew."

A gargled laugh escaped his uncle. "Taking an aristo for a wife, who'd never understand the chaos within me, would only beget children whose bedtime stories would involve my nightmares. I don't think so."

Turning toward him, Roderick offered in a sympathetic tone, "You underestimate a woman's worth and her ability to redefine a man. A woman can give you hope in a world that has none. She can fight for you when you have ceased fighting for yourself and everything you believe in."

Atwood glanced toward him. "Smitten, are you?"

"Beyond. You should be so lucky."

Atwood smirked. "Distract me. What's her name?"

Roderick bit back a smile. "Her real one? Or the one

she is parading under? For I will confess I am about to marry two women for the price of one. She is divine intervention. I have never known anyone or anything so exquisite."

"I could use a little divine intervention." His uncle strode back toward him and leaned in. The smell of leather penetrated the air. "Would you be willing to share her with your uncle from time to time? When I'm feeling particularly lonely? Or are you the territorial sort?"

Roderick tossed aside the leather belt and blade with a resounding clatter, lest he use it himself, and stared his uncle down, fury streaking through his body and his mind. "Do I look amused?"

Atwood snorted and patted his cheek, the cool leather grazing his skin. "Now, now, you aristos are so easily ruffled. I was joking."

"Were you?" Roderick reached out and purposefully gripped the man's muscled shoulder hard, digging the tips of his fingers into the flesh beneath. "Don't cross the only family you have left, Atwood. Don't even *joke* about it."

His uncle's ice-blue eyes seemed to be taunting him. "You needn't worry, nephew. I only cross those that cross me. And you haven't crossed me...*yet*." Flinging Roderick's hand away, he started backward toward the doors of the study, still holding his gaze. "I think I'm going to like London. There are just so many civilized people crawling around my boots looking to lick them clean. Now if you'll excuse me...I intend to find myself a dance partner and scare the shite out of people."

Swinging away, he slid open the doors with a single sweep of his long arms and disappeared with the billowing movement of his long riding coat.

Roderick winced, knowing he was supposed to keep Atwood in the study, but had a feeling all of London was fecked either way. So he let him walk, thankful to no end that he had Georgia to see him through whatever mess lay ahead.

EPILOGUE

Òmnia vincit amor; et nos cedamus amori.
Love conquers all things: let us, too, surrender
to Love.
　　　　　　—Virgil, *Eclogues:* Book X (70 BC–19 BC)

Seven years later, evening
The Tremayne household in London

THE DOOR TO THEIR BEDCHAMBER creaked open inch…by inch…by inch…by inch.

Georgia sat up against the pillows, setting aside her needlework, and tapped at Roderick's open book. "'Tis set to begin."

Roderick slapped his book shut and tossed it with the flick of his wrist onto the linen before them, shifting toward the door. Adjusting his robe, he called out toward the now-open door, "The answer is still no. So I suggest you go back to the nursery and mope about it to your brothers, who have yet to care about anything beyond milk."

Their daughter, Ballad Jane, padded into the room, twirling her dark braids, and eventually paused beside their bed, her large green eyes darting from Georgia to

Roderick. "Uncle Atwood wouldn't say no to me. Nor would Uncle Milton."

Georgia glanced over at Roderick and drawled, "Now, how can you argue with that?"

Roderick threw back his dark head and huffed up at the ceiling, "The answer is still *no*."

"But, *Papa*—" Ballad fell against the edge of the bed in exasperation, leaning toward him. Reaching up, she patted both hands against the mattress she barely reached, each pat emphasizing every word she insisted on saying. "I really, really want an elephant. Preferably a girl elephant. No, not preferably. Definitely. Definitely a girl elephant. It can sleep with me. I don't mind. Really. *Please?* I only want one."

Georgia burst into laughter. "That child is yours, Robinson. Not mine. You were the one to read her all of those stories about India. Now handle it."

He sighed. "Come here, love." His dark brows came together as he leaned toward the edge of the bed, reached down and yanked their daughter up and onto his lap.

Settling her into place and yanking her white nightdress down over her small stockinged feet, he lowered his head to hers, intently holding her gaze. "Where on earth are we going to keep an elephant in the middle of London? Animals of such size are only meant for the wilderness. Even Hyde Park would make the poor thing feel unwelcome. How about we get you a dog instead? The biggest one we can find? Or a pony? Would you prefer a pony?"

Ballad puckered her lips as if *he* were being ridiculous. "I don't want a dog and I don't want a pony. Everyone has dogs and ponies in London and I don't want what everyone else has. I want an elephant. No one has any of those."

A laugh rumbled out from Roderick's lips. "There is a reason for it."

"Papa, *pleeeeeease*." Ballad clasped her six-year-old hands together and shook them up at him pleadingly. "I will never, ever, *ever* ask for anything again."

He sighed. "The answer is still no and you are old enough to understand why I am saying no. Are we done?"

Ballad dropped her clasped hands into her lap. She glanced up at him and swept a finger out toward Georgia. "Mama said that if we take up Grandpapa's offer of living at his estate in Surrey, there would be more than enough room for an elephant, given all the acreage he has. Can't we call on Grandpapa and tell him we are moving in? That way, I get to see him every day *and* I get an elephant."

Roderick turned to Georgia, glaring at her. "You didn't actually promise her an elephant if we moved in with my father, did you?"

Georgia grinned and leaned toward him. "You wanted a *big* family, Robinson. It doesn't get any bigger than that." She jabbed his shoulder. "*But*…if the elephant is a bit much, and I'll agree that it is, I suggest we take the child to India for a few months instead, lest we never know peace. I've always wanted to go. Wouldn't it be fun?"

"*Fun?*" Roderick eyed them both, even as his daughter's eyes had lit up at Georgia's suggestion. "Crawling into the mouth of a crouching tiger in the middle of a sweltering jungle is not what I call fun. How about we go to France?"

Ballad crossed her arms and huffed out a breath, grouching, "I never get anything. Not the pistol that I wanted. Not the sword that I wanted. Not even the monkey. And now this. What good is having money if we never use it for anything?"

Roderick elbowed Georgia hard. "We know where that tongue comes from." He paused, shaking his head, and eventually blew out a breath. "Fine. We go to India. That at least would be educational and money well spent. Only, we're leaving *all* of the elephants *there*. Is that understood?" He gently tapped at Ballad's forehead. "I also don't want any more of this talk about how I never give you anything. Money is a privilege, Ballad, not a right."

"Yes, Papa."

Ballad let out a joyful screech, throwing up both hands. She scrambled out of his lap and off the bed, landing on the floor with an echoing thud. *"India!"* Dashing out the door, with hands still waving, she disappeared into the corridor shouting, "I have the best Mama *ever!*"

Roderick paused and jerked toward Georgia. "That little brat forgot to thank the one person who is paying the goddamn bill."

Georgia grabbed hold of his robe, dragging him down toward her onto the mattress. "All that really matters, Robinson, is that *I* know who is paying the bill.

It could be worse. She could be wanting a cougar. Can you imagine?"

Roderick let out a growl, replicating one himself, and shoved his warm hand beneath her nightdress, causing her to squeak. "And what do *you* want, Lady Yardley?"

"Move your hand a little lower and to the left. And when we're done, I want you to go fetch us some whiskey."

"Yes and yes, madam. Anything else?"

"Yes. Close the door."

* * * * *

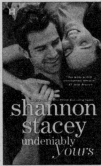

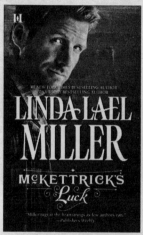

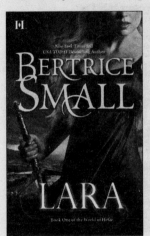